for Kaity

C000301082

The Firelighters:
Book One
A Spark Of Fire

Enjoy the magic!

JENNIFER L ROTHWELL

For Dean
who saw the magic first.

FIRST EDITION

All characters and events in this publication, other than those clearly in the public domain, are fictitious and any resemblance to real persons, living or dead, is purely coincidental.

GREEN CAT BOOKS

www.green-cat.co/books

"Those who don't believe in magic
will never find it."

Roald Dahl

1

A Nose For Trouble

The first taste Felix Spark ever had of magic was the copper penny tang of blood.

Her own blood, of course, not the blood of some sacrificial magician, the notion of which is hilarious really when you consider how selfish magicians are. Not that they would ever describe themselves as selfish. Righteous, perhaps. Noble? Oh, definitely. But not one magician in all of the Magistry of London would admit that they were self-interested, self-involved, self-glorifying bastards. Only the commoners knew that truth, none more so than Felix Spark, who, at the tender age of nine annums, was slapped so violently by a magician that her nose broke, causing the blood to gush down her throat until she gagged.

Had she deserved it? Probably. She always did have a nose for trouble, even then.

'Don't dare open your mouth young lady or I swear on St Nick I'll knock you so far into next week you'll be able to read my future,' Nanny Maude had hissed when Felix, along with the other orphans, were lined up for inspection.

Nanny Maude had been especially annoying that day, bustling around Felix and the other strays, spitting on hankies and wiping imaginary dirt off their noses, clouting them if they stood on their tippy-toes to see.

Felix rolled her eyes because why on earth would she say anything to Linus Godspell? He was just a spoiled rich kid, son of the Rt Honourable Corbin Godspell and probably a ferocious bore and it was just con-dee-send-ing (a word she had discovered in a book and rather liked) for a nine or ten or whatever annum old snob to come and *inspect* the Commoner's Quarter, like it belonged to him or something.

Which it did, of course.

Linus Godspell, a black-haired weed of a boy, paraded up and down the square of the Quarter like a runted raven. His gloves were red, a stark contrast to the inky shades of his waistcoat, trousers and tails and they stood out a mile away as they were meant to; they were, after all, the mark of a magician.

When he'd stopped near the orphans, he'd smiled a watery smile, one that was perhaps meant to look pitying but instead just looked like his was constipated and Felix had snorted. She'd thought she'd hidden it well, but, in keeping with having a nose for trouble, Linus Godspell had heard her and had one of his supervising COPPs pull her out of line. They'd stared at each other, Felix and Linus, for a single moment. Felix was a whole head taller than Linus and maybe he resented having to look up to *her,* because the next thing she knew, she was on the cobblestones, vomiting up the blood that she'd swallowed and wincing at the searing pain of her broken, trouble finding nose.

She couldn't remember the whack of a gloved hand on her face nor could she remember seeing the frenzy of a fist flying towards her. No. This had been magic, and as she watched Linus Godspell walk away from the Commoner's Quarter, Felix Spark, aged nine annums, learned how to hate the magicians like all good commoners ought to.

Seven annums later and Felix was not so different to that bloody-nosed little girl knocked down to her knees. Her nose had grown slightly crooked but she had remained on the ground, knocked down by magicians all her life, at least metaphorically speaking. She was a commoner, an orphan and a nobody. Even in the Commoner's Quarter, where she belonged, she felt at a distinct disadvantage to everybody else. She had a boy's name and a surname that immediately announced her lack of parentage; the only one in fact, in the whole orphanage, who had absolutely no knowledge of her origins. She was a 'Spark', the Magistry term for a mystery, a person missing their heritage and it meant she received even more disdain from the few magicians she ever encountered and worse, it invited pity from the commoners themselves. Pity, even, from Nanny Maude whose cruel and imaginative punishments meant that Felix was isolated from her peers, educated privately by the StoryKeeper and, frequently, locked away in Nanny Maude's office 'for safekeeping', like some pathetic version of a storybook princess.

Only she wasn't a princess. And this wasn't a story.

Her only solace, rather shamefully, was a fantasy.

Some dreamt of battling sewer pirates, of storming the Citadel or of taming the mountain dragons and training them to burn the magicians alive.

Felix dreamt of her parents, or more specifically, she dreamt of finding them.

Perhaps this was not unique to Felix. She often wondered as she looked at the faces of the orphans around her, if behind their dim eyes and grimy skin there was a gleaming pearl of the very same wish, the same longing that burned so fiercely that it kept them warm in the freezing rooms of the orphanage. She would never know for she never asked and in turn, nobody asked her. But each night, she would chant, as though it was her own little spell: when I get out of here, I'm going to find my parents.

And on the morning of her sixteenth birthday, the morning she was released from the care of the state, that's exactly what Felix Spark did.

After a fashion.

2

A Birthday Surprise

It was a warm day in August and the pea green whiff of the quarter was infecting everything. It crept from the Mire, past the Borderlock, all the way through the streets to the orphanage and it chased Felix to the door of Nanny Maude's office.

'I'm all ready to go now, Nanny Maude,' Felix said, knocking on the door.

'Come in, Felix.'

She pushed open the door and stood, waiting for instruction. It was the nicest room in the orphanage. Every time she'd come in here, Felix had always been distracted by the cosiness of the fire, the ornaments and treasures cluttering up the shelves and especially by the books that sat gathering dust in piles at the far side of the room. To the left of the door, a round mirror hung on the wall, cracked and dirty but a blessed mirror still. Felix glanced into it covertly each time she entered, checking to see if she had changed much since the last time she'd seen her face. Her dark hair was always unruly and uneven, its length a hindrance though Nanny Maude would never cut off more than an inch on chop days. Blue eyes were framed by dark eyebrows and her slightly crooked nose held a dusting of freckles. She had not changed much over the annums; though perhaps her eyes were colder, meeting her own gaze more easily as she grew taller.

Felix looked away from her reflection and instead turned her attention to Nanny Maude, sitting at her desk, guarding the treasures around her like Cerberus guards the doors of hell.

Of course she owned pretty, delicate and interesting things. She was, after all, the owner of the orphanage, but still it irritated Felix whenever she came into the room for punishment or some other such inconvenience, that Nanny Maude got to have nice things. Felix didn't own a single solitary thing. Even the jeans on her legs and the shirt on her back belonged to the state.

Nanny Maude was old, though, and she remembered a time before the magicians had come to power. Further than that - a time before anybody even knew about magicians at all. Felix couldn't picture it. Besides, it was forbidden to talk about the Common Time, but every now and then, information dripped through and Felix had eventually built up a little puddle of knowledge.

She remembered Mr Gelding, her teacher when she was ten annums, who had disappeared one day. It happened the morning after she'd asked him if Corbin Godspell had assassinated the Queen of England and Michael Browning, the Prime Ministry (or something like that) in order to seize power. Mr Gelding had confirmed, through tight lips and disgust, that it was true; Godspell, the Rt Honourable, had had them 'done in'.

The rumour was all over the school like wildfire the next day, fuelled by the fact that Mr Gelding and his whole entire family had just vanished overnight, no explanation. Nobody needed one. Everyone knew the COPPs had come for them, probably for treachery. Mr Gelding had known the law and it was understood, obviously, that the magicians had word traces and ears everywhere. Felix hadn't known that. She did now.

After that, Felix wasn't allowed to go to school anymore.

She tried to imagine what it must be like for Nanny Maude and for the others who could remember life before the magicians but she couldn't. She'd been a commoner all her life and would be until she died. So really, she couldn't begrudge Nanny Maude wanting her own cosy, comfortable room with all her little knick-knacks around her. They were all she had left of her life before.

'Sit down, Felix,' Nanny Maude said from behind her desk. There was a brown envelope and a wodge of other documents on it that she had her chubby arms folded across.

'Happy birthday,' the old woman said, but there was little cheer in her inflection. Birthdays were rarely marked at the orphanage and sixteenth birthdays were less of a celebration and more of a dismissal. Felix nodded her thanks and slumped down into the armchair opposite the desk.

'All packed?'

Felix nodded. She had a patched-up rucksack with the clothes that weren't really hers stuffed into it at her side.

'Any advice?' Felix asked taking a shaky breath. Nanny Maude nodded and started leafing through the paperwork in front of her.

'I sent word to Calvin Taylor at his lodgin' house in the quarter. He's expectin' you this afternoon, said he'd put you up fer a couple days whilst you get yerself fixed for work. I also got you booked in at the DCC tomorrow to 'elp you find a job. Gave you a good recommendation fer what it's worth.'

She pushed over a piece of paper with her wonky handwriting on it that stated Felix was bright, reliable and a quick learner.Felix raised her eyebrows.

'Err, thanks,' she said.

'I try to do right by my kids.' Nanny Maude gave a rare smile, and through the wrinkles and the dark bags under her eyes, Felix thought she saw the pretty woman that Nanny Maude had probably been.

A tugging sensation suddenly lurched in Felix's stomach and she glanced down at her knotted hands. Nanny Maude followed her gaze and her face fell. She seemed to be struggling with something.

'I guess I'll, err, be seeing you, then,' Felix mumbled, standing up a little clumsily and knocking her bag against the desk. She thought there was something in her eye and she had to blink quite a few times to stop her eyes from leaking.

'Felix,' Nanny Maude said in a very quiet voice.

There was something in her tone that caught Felix's attention immediately. She turned and looked at the woman, who was stroking the brown envelope with care. Felix was suddenly very curious about what was in it.

'I...I'm not sure if...' Nanny Maude trailed off.

Felix slid back into the chair, her pulse suddenly beating loudly in her ears.

'You're not sure if what?' Her voice was shaking.

Nanny Maude looked at Felix carefully, an emotion in her eyes that Felix didn't recognise.

'I'm not sure if you know... ' Nanny Maude halted and shook her head in exasperation.

Felix was silent. All she could hear was the loud ticking of the clock on the wall. She didn't know quite what to say.

'You were such a tiny thing when I found you,' Nanny Maude began to whisper and when she looked up at Felix, her eyes were glassy.

Felix was horrified. She had never, ever seen Nanny Maude cry. She had thought her tear ducts were dried up actually. Felix froze awkwardly, not sure if she ought to pat her hand or something. Did Nanny Maude cry when every orphan left? Was this just a cruel and imaginative prank?

'Only a few hours old, you were. Swaddled up, crying bloody murder. Didn't know what to do, did I? Things were so different then. But I took you in, o'course. You were the first one.'

The tears fell down the old woman's chubby cheeks. Felix was holding her breath and she let it go. This really didn't feel like a prank.

'The first what?' she asked.

'Orphan. My first girl.'

'I don't understand.'

'The rest of the kids came after you, and a lot was older. Parents left 'em, else they was killed. See, I was a Nanny before I took you in. I was paid to look after children, some of them were even magician's children. This was back when... when things were ok. This was my home, mine an' Bill's. He were me husband, an' we had youngun's too.'

Nanny Maude opened a drawer in her desk and pulled out a photograph. Felix knew what one was of course, but nobody could take photographs any more. She looked down at a young Nanny Maude, plump and pretty, standing next to a tall man with thinning hair and glasses. At their feet was a young boy, clinging onto his father's leg to hold him up on his chubby little legs, and in Maude's arms was a little baby girl with sticky out ears and a wide laughing mouth.

'My Lily and George,' Nanny Maude said thickly.

'What happened to them?' Felix whispered, not entirely sure she wanted to know.

'Dead. Bill, he was political minded an' all that. Didn't like it when them magicians started takin' over. He used to go on these marches and riots. I didn't like it, but he was set in 'is ways. One day, he took little George and Lily to the playground. It ain't there no more, but it was George's favourite place to go. I was here. I remember it like it were only yesterday. I was makin' dinner for when they got home but by the time it were ready, they hadn't got back yet. I thought, Bill's lost track of the time, y'know? Or George was playin' up and askin' to stay longer. I turned on the telly...you know what one o'them is?'

Felix nodded. They had an old one at school, but it didn't work anymore; there were no broadcasts or aerial signals now anyway.

'News were on. There'd been an attack. The magicians had started their first wave of bombin's, though I'm not sure you can call 'em that when they weren't usin' bombs. Don't need to when they've got magic. I were upset, naturally, but then I saw the playground, or what were left of it. The news lady said there were no survivors. I thought, maybe they're on their way home. Maybe they escaped. I waited all night, but I knew. They weren't never comin' home.' Nanny Maude sniffed loudly and blew her nose on her dirty handkerchief.

Felix was dumbstruck, her mouth open in a small 'o'. She closed it and swallowed but her mouth was dry.

'I found out after that Bill had tried fightin' the magicians, tried to save a few people but then the magicians chased after him to the playground where he'd left George and Lily. He was a ruddy idiot. Nobody stands a chance against magicians. Things went to pot soon after. Riots and marches, they weren't doin' anythin'. There was so many got killed. Magicians didn't even take em' prisoner, just killed anyone standin' up to them. I couldn't believe it. I'd known magicians, worked for 'em. I didn't understand how things could change so much, so quickly. But it wasn't them; not really. They was just actin' on orders from *him*.'

'Corbin Godspell?' Felix asked. Nanny Maude nodded.

'It were all him. At first, I thought that the magicians would stand up to him. We'd been gettin' on, workin' together y'know? But they're bloody cowards, the lot of 'em. I think they liked the power they had over us, and then they just got used to it and didn't do nothin' to stop what *he* was doin' to us. My Bill, George, Lily... they was killed and it was him that killed 'em, when he took over.

'I found you the next mornin'. Right after they was killed. There were a knock on me' door and I thought, it's them, they've made it home. But when I opened the door, it were just this tiny little bundle, all wrapped in newspaper and a blanket.'

Nanny Maude unlocked a drawer at her desk and pulled out a square piece of material. It was beautiful, soft and shimmering, with glittering black spirals embroidered on a dusky rose cloth. Nanny Maude passed it to Felix.

'Oh,' Felix said, taking the baby blanket. It felt pure and clean...and expensive.

'This were with you,' Nanny Maude said, pushing the envelope towards her.

Felix picked it up numbly. Her mind was dazed and the loud thudding in her ears had moved up to her head. She rubbed at her forehead and tried to stop her fingers from trembling as she opened the envelope. Inside was a small card, no longer than her thumb and it was yellow and curling around the edges. As she held it between her thumb and forefinger, she saw that there was a gold pressed font embossed onto the centre of the card that said, in a swirling script "The London Library".

Felix scrunched her face up in confusion and she turned the card over to see that it was a library card.

A library card?

'I don't understand,' she said, tossing her hair over her shoulder.

Nanny Maude looked down at the card in her hand and shrugged.

'Am I meant to go there?' Felix asked, flipping the card over in her hands as though it might reveal something, *anything* else, but if it had secrets to share, it would not confide in Felix. On its reverse was a small chart, empty, save for her name, hand written in a beautiful script in sepia ink followed by her date of birth.

Whatever this library was, it looked like she was a member and had been since the day she was born

Maybe it was the sheer disappointment of being given a library card when she had expected a letter or a birth certificate or something that could tell her who her parents were…or who they had been. She'd have been happy with just their names. Or maybe it was the fact that it was her birthday and she was leaving, and the reality of her miserable, murky future was sinking in.

Whatever the case, Felix began to cry.

Nanny Maude passed over a handkerchief, one of the tatty stained ones that she always used to wipe the children's faces with, the way she had once wiped hers. For the first time, Felix saw a lily embroidered into it and it brought on a fresh wave of tears.

'Felix,' Nanny Maude interrupted softly, far more softly than she had ever spoken to Felix in the sixteen years she'd looked after her.

Felix lifted her eyes to her in acknowledgement.

'The London Library…it's in the Magistry,' she said, and the words waited on the air, ready to be understood.

The Magistry was the City of London claimed by the magicians. It *belonged* to them.

Felix looked down at the library card…a card that had come from a magician's library…a card that had her name on it.

'What the…?' she trailed off. She didn't know what to say and she dared not think what her name on that card might mean.

'I know you ain't goin' to see Calvin Taylor this afternoon,' Nanny Maude said gently. Felix traced her thumb over the shimmering gold letters on the card but said nothing. 'I know you well enough by now. You're goin' to go to the London Library. I can't stop you. I wish I could…but you've never paid heed to me.'

To Felix's surprise, Nanny Maude smiled as though remembering a happy memory.

'You need to be careful gettin' into the city,' she continued. 'You'll need a permit...'

Nanny Maude went into her drawer again and pulled out a red tag. On it was the stamp of the Magistry and Felix's name and age. It said she was a scurry girl at the London Library.

'Fake,' explained Nanny Maude. 'It won't stand up to proper inspection, but it'll give you a bit of time to find the Library without bein' stopped every ten paces. I had it made for you.'

Nanny Maude stood, waddled around the desk and looped the tag's string around one of Felix's coat buttons. It stood out like a red scar. Felix blinked quickly.

'Thank you,' she said hoarsely. Nanny Maude shook her head and smiled sadly at Felix, holding her upper arms tightly.

'Y'know, you an' my Lily was nearly the same age? If she'd have lived, I reckon she would've turned out a bit like you.'

Felix gritted her teeth and kept her eyes wide, not trusting herself to blink or speak. Instead, she nodded and threw her arms around Nanny Maude and breathed in her smell of cooking grease but now, she could detect a hint of sweet magnolia behind it. Why had she never noticed that before?

Then, before she could change her mind, Felix grabbed her rucksack and took three strides out of the door and left the orphanage.

Behind her, Nanny Maude sat in her empty office and wept.

3
Lost In London

To get into the Magistry of London, Felix had to gain passage on a locomotron, a steam fuelled carriage that ran from the Commoner's Quarter, under the Mire and into the Magistry. Several lines ran through old sewer pipes, taking travellers to their various destinations around the city. If for one moment you thought that this granted the commoners a modicum of freedom, you would be very wrong. The locomotrons were heavily guarded by the COPPs and were in use only to ferry commoners who had Magistry permits, stating their place of work and the hours that they were granted access. Should a commoner be found without a permit or within the Magistry limits past his access times, well it was the Tower for him.

As it was, Felix had never been on the locomotron nor had she been past the gates of Borderlock, though she had stared at the mudbrick red of the wall around the quarter all of her life. A magician would argue (of course they would) that the wall was for the commoner's protection from the Mire, the great wasteland outside the Magistry of London. It had once been suburban dwellings; apartment blocks, family housing, schools and care homes just like in any other city of the world. Now, the Mire was a barren land of dust, concrete and ashes. A foul stench rose from the far reaches of the Mire where the magicians' waste and excrement had grown into a huge mound that the commoners, not so affectionately, named Mount Mudslop (only the adults didn't say 'mud' and instead said something much more alliteratively witty). Upon Mount Mudslop feasted unknown yet fearsome creatures that the magicians had brought with them when Godspell took power, creatures that were unwelcome in the Magistry but encouraged to run free in the Mire.

If you were cynical, you could say that they were guards to keep the commoners away from the Mire and the Magistry beyond it.

If you were cynical, you'd be right.

This reek from Mount Mudslop pervaded the Commoner's Quarter, bringing with it a green mist of effluvium that bathed the commoners every single day. When magicians screwed up their noses whenever a commoner passed them and mumbled behind their gloved hands that they stank, it was true; the stink of the quarter was fetid, like manure and had earned the commoners their epithet for they were, much to the magicians' glee, "common as muck".

Felix had grown used to the smell and so she did not wrinkle her nose or wince her eyes as she walked towards the gates.

The Borderlock came into view. It was a large red brick building with two tall towers on either side of an arched metal gate. Behind it, the tracks of the locomotrons were visible before they were swallowed by the wide-open mouths of the sewer tunnels. COPPs patrolled the gates and walls that stretched like open arms the quarter. Felix took a deep breath and adjusted the red tag that Nanny Maude had fastened to her coat. She joined the band of commoners that were waiting to be waved through the gates as they made their way into the city for their menial jobs. The COPPs suffered them to pokes and jibes, laughing cruelly at the elderly and shoving them to the ground, hitting anyone who helped them up.

There was little order. Like cattle being herded, the drift of red tags trampled through the gates, each of them holding their red tag up towards the COPPs positioned on the watchtowers.

'Don't they check for fakes?' Felix whispered to herself. She'd been quietly terrified of this possibility, hoping she'd be able to slip through the gates in the middle of a thick crowd, exactly as she was doing now.

'No point,' replied a stooped old man wearing a grey cap next to Felix. His face was very wrinkled, and dirt clung to the lines making him look even older than he actually was.

'Once you get into the city, you're surrounded by them.' Felix knew he meant the magicians by the disdain in his voice.

'You'll have your permit checked at work, or you'll be stopped by a COPP in the street and if you've got a fake then it's the Tower for you.' Felix's eyed widened and she clutched at her permit with sweaty hands. The man smiled kindly down at her.

'First day at work?' he asked, and Felix nodded, flushing a little at the lie. She always tried to be extremely honest.

'Where you off to?' the man probed as the COPPs began to wave them through the gates. Felix began to shuffle next to the man.

'Err, scurry girl at the London Library,' she mumbled quickly. The old man nodded, raising his eyebrows.

'You've been lucky. Didn't know them libraries took on commoners, what with them being so exclusive.'

Felix frowned a little. If the library was so exclusive, she'd have trouble getting in, even with a permit. She remembered another problem she had been thinking about too, and glanced at the old man. Perhaps he could help.

'Yeah, they don't take on too many commoners, but they have to have scurry girls to keep all the books dusted and stuff,' she lied a little too easily for her liking. 'But, I've got a problem. See, I don't know where the London Library is. They took me on based on my reference. The DCC recommended me highly.'

The old man looked at Felix curiously and Felix tried to hold his gaze. She smiled as innocently as she could.

'Well, that's unusual,' the man said gruffly. 'But then times are changing. Suppose they don't need to be as strict as they used to.'

He looked up unconvincingly at the COPPs who were kicking at a teenage boy not much older than Felix. Their black boots were shiny with his blood. Felix swallowed and looked away.

'London Library is in St James's Square. Bit of a way. You'll have to walk quickly, once you get in,' the man continued, looking down at Felix. She nodded and smiled in thanks.

They were through the gates now and the crowd dispersed. Felix found herself staring at the desolate landscape and felt herself quietly wishing Nanny Maude was with her. She didn't have a long time to look, though, as she was funnelled down an embankment towards a makeshift platform.

In a panic, she craned her neck to see where the platform would take her and like a brick in her stomach, it hit her; she had no idea which locomotron to take.

Westminster? Islington? Wandsworth? Southwark? And a dozen more. She was being pushed and shoved by the commoners who made their way to their tunnels, grumbling at her to move out of the way and Felix knew she was causing a hold up. She dared not ask where to go; drawing any attention to herself would be unwise and she knew it.

'What's going on over there?' shouted an angry voice and Felix saw the red top hat of a COPP knifing his way through the crowd, beating people out of the way with his shining crimson baton.

The COPPs wore a distinctive uniform consisting of a double-breasted coat, the colour of a fresh wound, hanging down to their black boots which accompanied their batons and top hats but what made them even more distinctive was their red skin. It was rumoured they stained it scarlet with the blood of the commoners. Felix didn't really believe that but she didn't want to get close enough to find out. Yet now the COPP was getting closer and closer to her and the knot of people pushing and shoving behind her as she blocked the way. She was breathing fast, her eyes darting over the entrances to the tunnels.

Which way? Which way?! She panicked.

'Psst! Girl!'

Felix whipped her head around and saw the old man she'd been talking to at the entrance to a tunnel marked Lewisham.

'You want Westminster!' he said in as hushed a voice as he could, pointing towards a tunnel to Felix's right.

She nodded quickly, mouthed a thank you and then she fell into line behind the other workers that were entering the Westminster Tunnel.

Inside it was dimly lit by lanterns hanging from the top of the pipe so that many of the workers had to stoop below them. The smell was foul, which was saying something after growing up in the Quarter, and Felix fought the urge to gag. Her feet quickly became wet as the sludge at the bottom of the pipe leaked through her old trainers.

Ahead, the faint black shadow of the locomotron she was to ride in lurked in the dull light. She could hear the hissing of the engine and the grinding of the pistons as it prepared to leave the dock. As she got closer, Felix felt her mouth drop open, though she quickly closed it when the rank taste of the air touched her tongue. She'd never seen a train, only pictures in books and whilst this wasn't exactly a train, it was the closest thing to one that she'd ever seen. It was a steel and wooden contraption, with carriages that held about twenty people. Leaning back to stare down the tracks, she saw carriage after carriage after carriage until the shadow consumed them. She squinted, hoping to see some evidence of the engine that was starting to squawk but she felt a firm nudge on her shoulder.

'Get a blinkin' move on, will you?' snapped a tired looking woman standing directly behind Felix.

'Sorry,' she muttered, gripping a sweating rail and pulling herself up into one of the carriages. Inside, it was lit with three hanging lanterns. There were no windows, or seats, but there were strange leather and rope loops hanging down from the overhead of the carriage that people were gripping. Felix reached up for one and just in time as the carriage jerked abruptly, sending people swaying and bumping against each other.

She wasn't sure how long she was stood inside the crowded carriage for; long enough for her to begin to feel nauseous as the carriage swayed and rocked and the people began to sweat out the Mudslop fetor they lived in. It seemed to Felix that the carriage became smaller and narrower and she imagined that she could feel the weight of the Mire above her head, waiting to come down on her.

To distract herself from her claustrophobic thoughts, Felix remembered what Nanny Maude had said and questions sprang to her mind like water from the ground. What did the library card mean? Were her parents there, waiting for her? What if, as was more likely, this was all a trick, a prank designed to humiliate and break her?

More than once, Felix thought she should turn back to the quarter. Maybe she still had time to see Calvin Taylor about lodgings for tonight and then she could make her appointment at the DCC tomorrow. Surely that was the sensible thing to do? But Felix couldn't have turned back even if she'd really wanted to. The tunnel was a one-way system and there were no stops for her to switch routes. She had no choice but to keep going forward, though she had no idea what she'd find when the tunnel ended.

Eventually the engine growled as it stammered to a halt and once again the commoners were thrust against each other. Someone, probably a COPP, opened the door from the outside and Felix blanched, wondering if they'd been locked in the carriage the whole time. She stepped out onto a dock, hoping there'd be some fresh air to breathe but instead she was hit by a gush of humidity and another darkened tunnel. She followed the crowd and finally the tunnel began to widen, and the workers poured into an entrance foyer. Felix felt herself hustled along with the crowd and stumbled up some stairs, vaguely aware of COPPs glaring at them, lined up as they were along the stairs. When she reached the top, Felix had to cover her eyes with her arm to shade her face from the blinding light.

The air smelled of heat and the light felt like fireglow on her skin as the undeniable essence of magic hung in the air.

Had she been born blind, she would have been able to sense the magic. It crackled and breathed, like the air before a thunderstorm, announcing itself subtly but definitely. The hairs on her arms stood to attention yet she was not cold; rather she was warm, blissfully, reassuringly warm and a feeling of serenity filled her bones and she realised she had never truly felt the contented sensation of cosiness that she felt now. It was as though she had been cold all of her life and had never known it. A strange comfort stirred in Felix's stomach, replacing the nerves and fear she had felt throughout her journey but at the recognition of such a feeling, the edges of her mouth turned down into a bitter frown. Magic was her enemy as were those who could wield it and yet here it was, embracing her as though she was an old friend.

Slowly, Felix's eyes adjusted to the light and she looked around her, unable to stop the gasp of air her lungs demanded at such a sight.

What she had taken to be sunlight was actually a balmy glow from shining orbs that floated ten or eleven feet in the air, casting bright beams down to the streets below. The buildings were so tall that as Felix looked up at them, she felt disorientated and dizzy, but she noticed that they were squashed together and seemed to be leaning against each other, higgledy piggledy. Natural sunlight was all but blotted out by these buildings and by the steam that billowed above them, blocking out the light and making a night time in the day.

'A city in clouds,' Felix muttered, her eyes fighting to focus as they were drawn this way and that. The undeniable heat brought sweat to the back of her neck and she absently twisted her long hair and tied it back into a haphazard bun. She noticed, now, the network of wires stretching from one tilting building to another, some of them looped around iron bridges and as the cloud of steam cleared for a moment, she realised that magicians were walking on the bridges, using them as gangways between buildings.

It was like the magicians has used up all the spaces in their Magistry and then simply built upwards using iron and steel bridges instead of roads.

'Incredible,' Felix whispered, because it was. This dark city, lit by firelight and steeped in steam was the stuff of daydreams.

Felix felt an annoyed poke from behind her where the tired looking woman was eyeing her in exasperation.

'Sorry again,' she mumbled, realising that once again, she was in the way and she stepped aside, her head tipped back as she stared at the city around her.

Felix had never expected the Magistry of London to be so fascinating. She was a canary, newly freed from the cage she had been kept in all of her life and had suddenly been let loose to realise that there was a whole house to explore.

As if of their own volition, her feet began to walk, not really paying attention to where they were taking her. The roads were cobblestoned with no potholes or crumbled stones and they led to doorways of shops with amber light glistening through windows. Signposts hung at odd angles from these shops with hand painted names upon them. "Helebor's Herbals", "Grinnion's Finest Alchemical Equipment", "Penhaligon's Wordsmiths." Felix read them all with delight and peered with hungry eyes into the windows. There were jars filled with strange flowers and coloured smoke that danced in front of her face. Another window was lit by little flames that flickered mid-air and illuminated piles of leather-bound books with gold hinges, sticky with dust. Crystals made up the window frames of one store, flowing water at another. Music played everywhere; tinny harpsichord melodies, heartbreaking opera, mournful jazz and peaceful guitar tunes. If she listened too closely, she would find herself drawn into the harmony and follow it to the doors of a storefront as if it was a siren's call.

And the scent. Felix had never in all of her life smelled such delicious aromas. The caramel gold smell of cinder toffee piqued her appetite at every turn, a treat often longed for and rarely given in the orphanage, for it was a magician's delicacy and here a bag of it cost only a vim. She could have made a killing trading it in the quarter. A spicy sweet fragrance tickled at the back of her throat and for one moment she could taste it, hot and tingly and trickling down her throat as she read a café sign advertising cinnamon tea with a side of tindersweet, something Felix had never heard of but longed to try.

Through it all was the hypnotising sensation of comfort, of contentedness, like every breath she took bewitched her.

A little shiver of betrayal ran through her, for it would not do for her to *like* this place. But it was so hard not to prefer it when compared to the dirty, rotting streets of the commoner's quarter, with its green fog and putrid stench.

She closed her eyes and rubbed at the dull but constant thud in her head that had been annoying her all morning, and so she did not see the building until it was right in front of her, but as soon as her eyes found it, Felix stopped dead in her tracks. Facing her was a tall glass building that reached into the sky like a sword. Continuing to rub at her forehead, Felix looked at it for it seemed out of place amongst all of the older quainter buildings around it. The dizzying height of it made her feel queasy but as she looked away, her eyes caught a flickering image in the glass. She stepped towards it slowly, hardly aware of the people milling around her. There, in the crystal-clear glass was the face of a man, the length of a full storey. He was smirking, his hooded eyes proud and fierce and his dark hair severely slicked to the side with oil. Felix swallowed and felt her breath catch in her throat as the image disappeared replaced by glittering words that seemed to shout without sound:

Godspell's London: You owe him your allegiance.

Felix felt ice overtake the warm welcome. He wasn't really there of course, it was just an illusion but as the face of Corbin Godspell shimmered into view again Felix had to look away, sickened at the message that was being delivered to the magicians who hurried past it. In fact, it struck Felix that even the magicians seemed to pale when they saw it and they picked up their pace to escape those cruel, glowing eyes of their leader.

She looked at them now, the magicians in their bizarre clothing. They wore puzzling outfits, for they looked like they'd stepped out of the forbidden history books that the StoryKeeper had shown her, only they had been altered by the materials they chose. Leather and oilskin were popular, but she saw one woman in an iron corset and several magicians with iron braces over their clothes. The men wore smart, stiff suits, some with tails and bow ties, others with leather waistcoats and long ruffled frock coats. They wore ankle boots that buttoned at the sides and they all seemed to wear hats; bowler hats, top hats, caps that rested askew in a dandy sort of way on their heads. Many of these men had strange glasses and goggles perches on the hats but they had several different coloured lenses; not like real glasses at all and Felix wondered what on earth they were for. But what was even stranger were the colours. Not merely black and navy and grey, but magenta, puce, aquamarine, jade and colours that Felix couldn't even name.

The women too were dressed brightly but they wore long skirts that swished breezily around their feet and coats that dragged along the floor, fastened with corseted belts. She even saw one woman with feathers in her hair. Felix couldn't help but smile at how silly some of them looked and she was glad that the commoners had the good taste to stick to normal clothes. Still, she felt very out of place in her jeans ripped at the knees and her black coat with buttons missing and her red fake work permit dangling down.

Adjusting her rucksack, Felix began to meander down the cobbled streets, feeling lost in a labyrinth as alleyways and roads forked off from the street she was on. Once or twice, she saw another commoner, marked by their plain clothing and their flapping red permits tagged onto them in some way. They were weaving quickly between the magicians, clearly on errands for their masters and Felix soon began to feel conspicuous. She began to spot the sneering glances flashed in her direction from a passing magician and knot of doubt that had been hidden behind her fascination reared its head again.

She hadn't a clue where she was going.

Fairly soon, she would run into a COPP who would undoubtedly demand to see her permit, so it was imperative that she get to the London Library as soon as she could. Yet she had no idea where St James's Square was, if that was indeed where the library was supposed to be, but then the worker who'd told her that hadn't looked to be a liar...but then neither did she and yet she had lied so easily when questioned.

Stopping outside the storefront of a snooty looking shop (though, really, they all looked snooty), Felix thought she should probably ask for directions.

'Excuse me,' she said loudly, stepping in front of a man with a pince-nez on his nose and a pork pie hat. He quickly looked down and pushed past her forcefully, almost knocking Felix to the ground. Straightening up, she tried to stop a lady who had an elaborately wrapped parcel floating behind her.

'Hmph,' the lady snorted, turning her head away in disgust when Felix spoke to her. Shoulders slumping, Felix leaned against the doorframe of the shop but immediately crashed to the floor as the door opened.

'Oh, his first pair of gloves,' squealed a squeaky female voice that was followed by a heavyset woman bustling out of the door.

'Mumsy's so proud of her little Tristan!' She leaned down and planted a wet, lipsticky kiss on the end of a little boy's nose. Felix, laying on her back and rubbing her backside in the gutter, couldn't help but giggle even though her bottom hurt quite a lot, and unfortunately she caught the attention of Mumsy who drew back in shock rather melodramatically when she saw Felix piled haphazardly on the kerb.

'Well,' she said loudly, thrusting her nose up snobbishly. 'We shan't shop here anymore if they'll let *commoners* loiter in their doorways.'

And with that, Mumsy yanked little Tristan's gloved hand and pulled him away, though he looked back to stare at Felix curiously.

Felix felt her face flushing and she stood quickly, bumping into a man who had heard the commotion from inside the shop. He was bald and had a large handlebar moustache. She at once thought of a walrus.

'Away with you!' the man said, shooing her away with a handkerchief that had a large G sewn onto it. Felix stumbled back onto the cobblestoned road, looking up at the shop sign that read, "Grieves and Hawkins: Fine Glovemakers".

'Go on, get away!' the walrus man shouted again, pointing at her with his own gloved hand. Felix felt herself pushed backwards even though he hadn't touched her, and she landed on the other side of the road, banging her head on the kerb. She cried out and scrambled to her feet, flashing a furious look at the man. Longing to fight back but thinking better of it, she turned and ran. She felt ashamed and humiliated, and her head was pounding with pain so that her vision was beginning to twist everything. Anger simmered in every pore but she choked it down, the way she choked down her tears at what was turning out to be a very unhappy birthday.

She raced past magicians and pushed through them, seeing nothing but gloves and feeling all too fiercely the open air on her naked hands.

Felix slowed only when she reached the end of the road and she slipped into a narrow alleyway, trying to catch her breath and resting her hands on her knees.

'What am I going to do?' she asked aloud, clamping her eyes shut to try and stop the black spots swimming in front of her eyes. She was completely lost and it felt like an impossible task to find the London Library without anyone to help her. She doubted whether or not she could find her way back to the locomotron station and she cursed herself for not paying better attention to where she was going. She was lost; lost in London.

Eventually, her breathing returned to normal and the pain in her head subsided a little. She felt angry; furiously, viciously angry. She hated the magicians, *hated* them. Why on earth was she here?

Regretfully, she thought of Nanny Maude and her DCC recommendations and the lodgings she'd arranged for Felix. If only she hadn't been so impetuous, she'd be in a comfortable if dingy bed waiting for a meagre but free meal. But then... if she had stayed, she would always be wondering *'what if...?'* wouldn't she?

Felix sighed and rested her head against the wet bricks behind her. She was half hidden in shadows and she peered out onto the main street where magicians sauntered past, but a large, shaggy grey dog caught her attention on the far side of the street. He seemed to be staring at her and he looked rather curious with his head cocked to one side and his tongue hanging out of his mouth. Felix looked away, tucking herself further into the shadows but, when she looked back at the street, she saw the dog trotting over towards her alleyway.

'Just what I need,' Felix groaned. There were thousands of strays in the quarter, as many as there were orphans and she saw them only as competition for food... and affection.

The dog came to a halt in front of her and sat back on its hind legs. It really was abnormally large, with a long pointed snout that looked almost like he was smiling.

'Scram,' Felix said in irritation, waving him away. The dog cocked his head at her again.

'Bugger off, you daft dog! I haven't got any food so go bother someone else,' Felix stepped around him and glanced down the street, wondering which direction to take.

'Dog? I think not.'

Felix spun around facing the narrow alley. It was dark with shadow and wisps of steam floated by like ghosts.

'Who said that?' She asked, her voice not nearly as strong as she wished.

'Look down.'

Felix obeyed and saw nothing but the dog. He licked his snout.

'Err...' Felix murmured, looking back up and down the alleyway again, but there was nobody there.

'It's just a dog,' she said, more to herself than to the voice that had spoken.

'I'm not a dog,' the voice said evenly. Felix jumped and looked down again.

'Dogs don't talk,' she mumbled, thinking she must have hit her head harder than she'd thought.

'No, dogs can't talk. But dire wolves can.'

Felix had been looking at the dog that time and she was certain that he hadn't moved his lips. She let out a nervous laugh and began to back away slowly, but the dog began to move after her, his head tilted to one side again.

'Err... ok I'm going now. Can you please call your dog off?' Felix shouted down the alley in panic. Perhaps she was standing in a private alleyway of some awful magician who would think nothing of setting a ginormous dog on a commoner...

'I told you. I'm not a dog. I'm a *dire wolf!*'

Felix stared open mouthed at the dog. She thought she'd seen him shake his head and there was a look of annoyance in his eyes. But she was being stupid. Animals couldn't talk. Could they? The dog nodded his head.

'Woah!' Felix jumped back, gripping onto the bricks of the alleyway with her nails. A dog was *talking* to her. With his *mind.*

'I've officially gone round the twist,' she whispered to herself. Again the dog shook his head.

'Nope, you've not. You're quite sane,' the dog blinked.

'So you're a talking dog,' Felix squeaked.

'Dire wolf!' he growled in reply.

'A dire wolf,' she repeated, looking down at him blankly. 'Sorry, but what exactly is a dire wolf?'

The creature glared at her in a way that suggested he thought she might be stupid. When he replied, his voice was much slower as though talking to a small child.

'Well, basically, I'm a wolf, *not* a dog and I can talk with my mind. I can also read thoughts, if the thoughts are there to be read, and, now this is where I come in really useful, I have an excellent sense of direction.' He puffed out his chest proudly.

'So?' Felix asked raising an eyebrow. The dire wolf deflated and shook his head in frustration.

'Your thoughts are little bit more perceptive than what comes out of your mouth,' he sneered, rolling his eyes. Felix blinked.

'I can help you get to where you want to go,' he explained.

'Oh. *Oh!*' Felix straightened and chewed on her lip, thinking about what this meant.

'So, you can get me to the London Library then?'

The dire wolf dipped his head once.

'Won't it look pretty weird for me to be following a do- err, a dire wolf?'

The dire wolf glared at her and then shook his head very slowly.

'No,' he replied with condescension, as though she should know this.

'Ok. If you're sure,' Felix mumbled uncertainly. 'Do you want, err paying or something? I don't have very much. A few vims and a couple of tans? I've only got one pyre though and I need that for -' She stopped rooting through her bag for her coin bag when she heard a deep growl coming from the dire wolf. She had thought people only gulped in books but it turned out, people did actually gulp when they were scared. She could now attest to it.

'No payment,' his gruff voice said inside her head. Felix grappled with her rucksack and shuffled it back onto her shoulders, shaking a little.

'Alright then.'

She stepped forward but hesitated for a moment as she saw the dire wolf's sharp teeth, his tongue flopping over them at the side of his mouth. Felix shook her head, hardly believing this was happening. A talking dog, or dire wolf or whatever he was. She felt like she was in a completely different world and she frowned, unsure if she could really trust this animal.

'You can't be sure,' the dire wolf said, lips unmoving. 'But really, what other choice do you have?'

He turned around and trotted out of the alleyway and back onto the main street. Felix gritted her teeth and took a deep breath before jogging after him.

4
The Dire Wolf and the Catchoo

They walked some way without speaking, but a question was plaguing Felix and as she passed more and more magicians, the more the question burned, but she was still caught up in the absolute insanity of talking to an animal that could actually reply. The dire wolf clearly noticed her curiosity because he sighed in an irritated manner and lifted his head to face her.

'Go on, ask me,' he said.

'Ask you what?'

'The question that you're so obviously dwelling on. You're guarding it, so I can't read what you want to ask, but I know you want to know something.'

Felix flinched, unnerved that he could see what was in her head.

'It's just,' she faltered. 'The gloves. Why do magicians wear gloves? I know it's like their trademark or something, but I don't get why.'

Felix wiped her forehead with the sleeve of her coat because the warmth that had started out as inviting was now beginning to feel muggy. It wasn't helping her headache at all.

Dire wolf narrowed his eyes and flicked over her coat, seeing the red work permit hanging from one of the only buttons remaining.

'You're a commoner?' he asked finally. Now it was Felix's turn to look at him as though he was stupid and she nodded.

'Hmm,' dire wolf frowned, his bushy eyebrows bunching together. 'Well, they wear them to wield magic, so as not to burn their hands.'

Dire wolf walked on at a slower pace and Felix caught up to travel beside him, interested against her will at the mention of magic.

'So magic is hot or something?' she asked.

'Err, I don't really know,' dire wolf admitted with a faint shrug of his shoulders. 'How I would explain magic and how a magician would explain it is very different.'

'Why?'

'Well, a magician sees magic and uses it. I can't use magic, because I'm made up of the stuff.'

'Oh, right,' Felix said, feeling confused.

Dire wolf rolled his eyes at her.

'There are different levels of magic, some more dangerous than others and the same goes for magical creatures like me. I'm a level one creature, according to the Magical Creature Charter. I'm apparently not very dangerous.'

Felix looked again at the dire wolf's teeth and thought differently.

'You don't sound very happy about that Charter,' she said. She'd never heard of such a thing.

'It's not just commoners that Godspell likes to control, you know?' dire wolf barked. Felix stumbled back away from him, eyes wide.

'I'm... I'm sorry. I didn't know. It's my first day here. I don't know anything about all this.'

Dire wolf relaxed and nodded.

'Of course. I know that. I didn't mean to bark. It's just that, I was once wild and free to roam. I had a family and answered to no-one.'

'What happened?' Felix asked softly.

'Godspell,' dire wolf sighed and Felix understood. That name meant woe and pain for everyone...even dire wolves.

'So now... you're a guide?'

'Yes. On the... where I used to live, I sensed lost souls and helped them find peace, guiding them to their afterlife. Here, I just wait around until I sense someone has lost their way and then it's my *duty* to help them.'

'Is it your job or something?' The dire wolf snorted, his pink nostrils flaring.

'No, it's my life. I either 'contribute to the Magistry' or I'm sent to the Tower.'

'You too?' Felix muttered. 'What happens to the lost souls?'

The dire wolf's ears flattened against his head, his thick tail falling between his legs. When he spoke, his voice was low.

'They drift, and I can always feel them.'

Felix's face puckered in sympathy but her hatred for Godspell simmered under her skin. Control was so important to him that he'd let lost souls drift aimlessly for eternity? Did he rule his people even after their deaths? She shuddered and tentatively reached her hand down to stroke the soft hair of the dire wolf's back. He flinched as she touched him, but the tension left him as Felix ruffled his fur gently.

'Come on,' he said, kindness breaking the ice that had been in his voice. 'Let's get you to the library.'

***

Before long and to her own surprise, Felix began to feel comfortable with the dire wolf. His presence was strangely calming and completely at odds to his sharp demeanour and even sharper teeth. She realised that she had to let the weirdness of her situation drift over her, otherwise she thought she might scream, or laugh, or simply go a bit mad (and she wasn't entirely sure she hadn't already.)

Dire wolf navigated the busy streets with ease and once again Felix began to observe the city around her. It was overwhelmingly huge and felt like a maze. Each street led to several more and the shops became even more tightly packed, stacked higher until she couldn't see the tops through the ever-present steam ceiling. But one thing struck Felix as being very strange. Along the brick walls there seemed to be a superfluous amount of doors. They were planted in between shop fronts and to her surprise she saw an entire side street lined with doors, but there were no windows to suggest that there were homes or shops or offices behind them. And even stranger, magicians opened these doors freely, without the aid of a key and stepped inside the darkness behind each door. This unnerved Felix and she squirmed, feeling an unshakable feeling of déjà vu, for all these doors reminded her rather too much of the dreams she'd had for as long as she could remember, though really, if she was being honest, they were nightmares.

'What's with the doors?' she mumbled quietly, knowing the dire wolf could hear her.

'Oh they're just hatches,' he answered indifferently.

Felix shrugged. That meant nothing to her.

'Oh yes. Commoners don't have them,' dire wolf continued. 'They're the way the magicians get around. The doors lead to the hatchway, the travel network. The magicians just open the door and say where they want to get to. As long as there's a door for them on the other side, they open it up and arrive at their destination. Not every door is a hatch though; they have to be registered destinations.'

'Amazing,' Felix said with wide eyes as she saw a teenage magician in a green leather waistcoat opening a large oak door and walking through into nothingness before it shut behind him. Dire wolf smiled in amusement.

'You've never heard the phrase 'down the hatch'?'

'Yes, but I had no idea...' she trailed off.

'Where did you think it came from?' Dire wolf shrugged. 'Now, you need to stick close to me. We're heading into Piccadilly Circus.'

'What's so dangerous about a circus?' Felix snorted, still distracted by the doors, but she understood as soon as they turned the corner.

In front of them were large, domed tents collected together at a circular crossroads. The road was wider, much more worn and far less immaculate than the rest of the city. Litter cluttered the roads and scrolls of dirty paper scurried around as though the breeze was chasing them.

There were four tents that Felix could see, the thick canvas fabric shifting a little in the air. They were all in varying shades of red and patched in places so that the overall impression was one of rust and fading opulence.

'Woah,' Felix said loudly. She'd read about circuses, but had gathered that they were small affairs with people called 'clowns' and 'acrobats', but seeing one up close made her dismiss these ideas.

She had a feeling this wasn't a normal circus.

Her stomach began to flutter nervously for the roads leading the Circus were half empty and there was an air of tension about the place that made the hairs on the back of her neck prickle. Even the dire wolf had his ears flattened and seemed wary as he crept closer to the flapping entrance of the main tent.

'Where is everyone?' Felix swallowed, feeling foolish at her inexplicable fear.

'Most people avoid coming this way. That's why there are so many hatches nearby, so magicians can travel without having to come through here. But you're a commoner, so...' He shrugged his shoulders and nodded towards the tents.

'Why do they avoid it?' Felix asked, unsure if she wanted to know the answer, unable to take her eyes off the flickering light coming from the entrance. As they stepped closer, a curious sort of music became audible and Felix felt herself beginning to sway along to its disjointed rhythm.

'You can lose yourself in the Circus,' dire wolf whispered. 'Hold on to my fur and stay focused.'

Felix nodded quickly and grabbed a large tuft of the dire wolf's hair.

Entering the tent, Felix clenched his hair tighter, making him yelp a little and she instinctively let go when he jumped, but before she could reach for him again, her attention was split between a hundred different mesmerising things.

Caravans were strewn around the edges of the tent, their doors open revealing their wares. Ladies in headscarves and long elbow length gloves beckoned towards Felix, thrusting twinkling jewellery in her face.

'Pretty girl,' one lady cooed. 'A pretty amulet to protect that pretty neck. Only two tans for you.'

'A charm to charm your sweetheart,' sang another, actually trying to drape a jangling necklace over her head. Felix shook her head and ducked away but the women followed her. Others lurched out, grabbing her hands and mobbing her, separating her from the dire wolf.

'Let me read your palm, my love. I can tell you when you'll die.'

'A scarf for you, a beautiful scarf! It will strangle your enemies. Six tans and a smile.'

'No, no thank you!' stammered Felix, scrambling away from their outstretched arms and bloodshot, desperate eyes, but turning around she found a man with most of his teeth missing and a crazed expression was pressed against her.

'You like books, my lovely. I can tell. I have books and they'll read for you, oh yes they will. Just for you.'

Felix stopped trying to escape and looked towards his green caravan with thick scented smoke curling out of the door. She coughed, unable to get the cloying smell out of her nose which was making her dizzy. But inside the caravan there were indeed books. They filled the caravan in teetering piles and she could hear the soft gushing of words that overlapped creating a maelstrom of whispers.

'The books read themselves?' Felix gasped, her words strangely slurred and she stepped towards the caravan. The man nodded vigorously, revealing his toothless smile and a tongue that was tinged with black. Felix felt revulsion but she couldn't pull away.

'For you, my lovely girl. All for you,' he was saying, his gloved arm snaking around her neck. Felix began to climb up the steps into the caravan, the whispering books summoning her inside and she couldn't quite find it within herself to turn away.

A vicious growl broke into her thoughts and the man recoiled from Felix. Shaking her head to dispel the nauseating smoke, she stepped away quickly, spinning to see the dire wolf baring his teeth and lowering onto his front paws threateningly. The sellers backed away, their whimpers of fear sounding more like cries of pain. Felix dashed quickly to the dire wolf and seized hold of his fur again, looking back in alarm at the caravan she had nearly stepped into, but she no longer saw the entrancing mounds of books. In their place were sheaves of parchment and curling old scrolls that seemed to be newspapers. She glared angrily at the toothless man who cackled at her and began to dance around in circles, hopping from foot to foot and waving his hands around madly.

'They're all crazy,' Felix breathed.

The dire wolf nodded sombrely.

'Addicts,' he said in a low voice. 'Driven mad by poppyblood.'

Seeing Felix's confusion, he explained that it was a sweet tasting sherbet that blackened the tongue and loosened the mind, driving one irrevocably into madness.

'They burn it, too. It fogs your perception, luring customers into their caravans where they're usually mugged and then dumped out in the streets with no memory of what happened. They're Houdinis; tricksters, unable to perform real magic anymore because of the poppyblood. Everything they do is illusion. They're not to be trusted.'

Felix swallowed, blood throbbing loudly in her head. The ache there was becoming unbearable.

They walked on gingerly and Felix tried to keep her mind straight, but it was so difficult in the close, smoky atmosphere of the tents that all seemed to merge together. The light was dim, too, making her feel sleepy, but the dire wolf pulled her along so that she kept tripping over the rugs beneath her feet. Yet, even the rugs seemed to taunt her, with swirling patterns that appeared to move and embroidered eyes that watched her. They reminded her of the blanket Nanny Maude had given her, the blanket she'd been found it, now tucked away in her rucksack.

There were other magicians there, stumbling with glazed eyes towards the Houdini's and Felix watched helplessly as they emptied their pockets of their coins for crystals and rings that promised to protect the wearer from curses, and clay poppets that ensured their enemies would feel whatever pain was inflicted upon the little doll.

Barely dressed girls poured black powder down their customers' necks and shrieks and cackles of laugher broke out from the gauzy tents and tatty curtains that reeked of honeymead and ashwater.

The whole place was terrifying. Felix had seen the hollow-eyed girls of the Bawdy House in the quarter and had witnessed the smashed glass screams of drunken men and women, but compared to the intoxication of the Circus, the quarter's idle drunken behaviour seemed like child's play.

'Nearly there,' dire wolf murmured wearily as they left one tent and entered another. Felix breathed heavily in relief, half choking on the poppyblood smoke. This tent was less crowded but it was mistier and the music was louder. Felix disliked it; the music seemed to dig its hooks into her brain, making her mind sway against her will. She rubbed her head and closed her dry, itchy eyes.

'Stop!' boomed a voice that made the dire wolf yelp and leap backwards. Felix cried out and tripped over the dire wolf's hind legs so that they both landed in a heap on the floor. The dire wolf barked loudly, his teeth sharp and shining.

'Who's there?' shouted Felix, twisting around and seeing nothing except the swirling smoke that was getting thicker and thicker.

'I am the daughter of Echidna and Typhon,' proclaimed the voice. 'I am at the bow of Athena's helmet. I have guarded the city of Thebes and been bested only by Oedipus. I am the Sphinx.'

The dire wolf chuckled, surprising Felix who thought this was not the time to be laughing. She thought perhaps the smoke was getting to him.

'What do you want?' Felix demanded, her voice trembling to her annoyance.

'An answer in payment for your time at the Circus.'

A figure loomed in the shadow and it spread high up against the tent. Felix couldn't actually see the sphinx, she didn't really want to, picturing a monstrous mutation of a winged lion with the face of a man, but the shadow somehow conjured up her dreams once again and the familiar fear crept through her veins so that she began to shake.

'What answer?' she asked.

'Feed me and I live. Give me drink and I die. What am I?' the sphinx asked smoothly.

Felix groaned. She hated riddles. Straightening herself, she looked to the dire wolf who actually had one eyebrow raised to see what she would say. Felix decided he had definitely breathed in too many poppyblood fumes. She could feel them inside her own head, muddling her thoughts.

'What happens if I get it wrong? Or if I refuse to answer?' she demanded to know.

'Then your life is forfeit to the Circus!' exploded the voice, making Felix start. The shadow before her in the smoke swayed.

'Or you can pay the toll. Two tans each,' said the voice quite steadily. Felix looked again at the dire wolf who was rolling his eyes at her.

'Con,' he said, and Felix could tell only she could hear him. Felix nodded, beginning to realise that this, like everything else in the Circus, was just a trick. She decided to play along.

'Oh great sphinx,' she said dramatically. 'Truly you are wise! Allow me a moment to think.'

The dire wolf covered his snout with his paw to stop from laughing. Felix stood slowly and began to pace back and forth, trying to make it look as though she was considering her answer, which she actually was, despite no longer feeling that she needed to rely on it to be correct.

'Hmm, what is killed by water?' she mused, stepping further towards the shadow, which grew smaller as she did so. In fact, she thought she could see something very near to the exit, behind all of the smoke. Felix felt the dire wolf treading slowly next to her and she paced towards the exit on tiptoes.

She knew exactly what she was seeing now, and it certainly wasn't a sphinx.

'I know!' Felix shouted, excitement in her voice as she figured out the riddle. 'You're fire!'

As she answered, she leaned down and picked up a long, flicking tail.

There was an almighty yowl followed by a fit of hissing and Felix heard the dire wolf laughing loudly, little amused growls slipping from his throat. Felix began to giggle as she held up a very sorry looking tabby cat by her tail.

'Put me down!' she mewled, her claws lashing out at Felix aimlessly.

'You'll let us pass?' Felix asked, biting her lip to stop from smiling. The cat nodded sullenly so Felix placed her gently on the ground where the cat began to lick her rear end immediately.

'Charming,' dire wolf sniggered. The cat turned to face him and stuck out her little pink tongue.

'Bog off,' she spat at him.

'Shut it, fleabag,' dire wolf snarled. 'Let's go.'

He turned and began to pad over to the exit. Felix giggled again at the cat and began to follow him, but the cat began to weave her way between Felix's ankles.

'Don't you want to know your future?' she purred, tail raised and head nuzzling Felix's leg.

'No she doesn't,' muttered dire wolf.

'I don't believe I was talking to you. Go fetch something,' the cat said turning her rear towards him. She pounced up onto Felix's shoulder and waved her tail in Felix's face so that she spluttered on the bushy fur.

'I have a fortune for you,' the cat hummed.

'For a price,' dire wolf grumbled. 'Ignore her. She's just another tricksy Catchoo.'

'A what?' Felix asked, wincing as the cat dug her claws into her shoulder as though she was playing a piano.

'A Catchoo,' dire wolf said with disgust. 'She's a Houdini pet trying to con you and catch you out. She just wants money. She can't tell the future if her life depended on it. And it might if she doesn't leave us alone.' dire wolf growled impressively, revealing his teeth. The Catchoo hissed at him, her shackles raised.

'I can too tell the future, and I'll give you a fortune for free just to prove *him* wrong,' she meowed at Felix, glaring at the dire wolf as though he was a particularly unpleasant insect.

'The riddle I gave you is appropriate. Feed the flame and it will grow; the same goes for you.'

She jumped down from Felix's shoulder and sauntered past the dire wolf, fluffing her tail in his eyes.

'Sorry, but what's that supposed to mean?' Felix asked, bewildered. The dire wolf shook his head in aggravation and glowered at the Catchoo, who smiled smugly. She sat in front of the exit and licked her paw before answering.

'I see a future filled with many trials,' she said slowly. 'The biggest test will be your own blood. You are filled with a fire; a fire that will consume you if you can't control it. Already, you are on your way to your destiny, but there are things waiting for you that you will wish you had not found. You must ask yourself this: will the good things you find outweigh the bad?'

The question hung in the air and silence filled the tent. Felix stared into the large green eyes of the Catchoo.

'Ignore her. She's a fraud,' dire wolf said, licking his nose and stretching his front legs. But something about the Catchoo's eyes made Felix doubt what he was saying. Her words lingered in Felix's mind, making her feel hazy again.

'Bye then,' purred the Catchoo, looking knowingly at Felix as she walked lazily back into the thick mist of the tent. Felix watched her disappear and gazed back at the dire wolf who was striding out of the tent. She followed him, pleased to breathe the steamy air again after the smoky Circus but the words of the Catchoo resonated in her ears.

'Let it go,' dire wolf said a little impatiently. 'Pay no attention to the fleabag. She's just got her nose out of joint because you didn't fall for her sphinx trick.' He began to chortle and Felix rubbed a finger between her brows trying to sooth the ache.

'Sphinx,' dire wolf laughed gently to himself, though Felix could hear him. 'Everyone knows that sphinxes don't exist.'

***

Felix's tummy was beginning to rumble. She didn't know what time it was, and the sun was no measure for her because she could hardly see behind the cluttered buildings and patches of steam clouds, but she knew it must be well after midday. It felt she'd been walking for hours and the memory of her meagre breakfast at the orphanage seemed annums ago.

'I'm hungry,' Felix groaned. Dire wolf turned to her.

'I know you are. You haven't stopped thinking that since we left the Circus.'

Felix smiled sheepishly.

'You have to stop doing that. It's freaky,' she muttered and dire wolf chuckled.

'You can eat when you get the library,' he said. 'Why are you going there anyway?'

Felix stopped in her tracks. The dire wolf trotted on for a few more paces before he realised she was no longer behind him and came back for her.

'What's up?' he asked. Her face was pale and there was a small crease between her brows.

'You don't know?' Felix asked a little harshly, tapping the side of her head. Dire wolf raised an eyebrow.

'No. I told you, I can only read the thoughts that aren't guarded.'

Felix began to chew on her lip, her shoulders slumping.

'I don't know what I'm doing here,' she mumbled to herself, kicking at a cobblestone before looking back at the dire wolf.

'All I know is that the London Library is where I need to go...to find answers.'

The dire wolf nodded slowly and he heard the whisper of a thought coming from the strange girl in front of him.

'You shouldn't let what the Catchoo said get to you, you know?' Dire wolf said softly.

He nudged her with his nose and Felix tickled the fur on his head.

'I can't tell what you're thinking exactly, but I know you're doubting yourself.'

Felix nodded slowly, thinking again of the Catchoo's fortune. Something about her biggest challenge being herself? And something about not liking what she would find. Well, what if that was true? What if she didn't like what she found? Felix reached down to the commoner's work permit and stared at it, answering her own question: she'd go back to the commoner's quarter. Really, what other options did she have?

A grumble from her tummy distracted her and she rubbed at it soothingly.

'What I wouldn't give for a spam sandwich right now,' she said, beginning to trudge along again.

The dire wolf grimaced, his tongue spat out between his teeth. 'Spam? Eugh. Give me cinder toffee any day, and a big bowl of macaroni cheese.' He licked his lips, flicking little droplets of drool on the floor and Felix laughed because the idea of this huge vicious-looking wolf daydreaming of macaroni cheese was just too funny.

They walked in an amiable silence and just as Felix was thinking that they'd never, ever get there, the dire wolf led her around a corner into a large square of tall townhouses which surrounded a patch of garden in the middle.

'I give you, the London Library,' the dire wolf said, bowing a little down on to one front leg.

Felix's eyes drifted over the square. It felt airy and fresh and far less crowded than the surrounding city. In fact, the sun was breaking though so that rays of afternoon sunshine lit the square in a warm, summer glow. The houses were tall, reaching to three storeys, some even higher, and they had clean iron fences and gates. Many of the houses even had fluted columns in front of the doors. The flagstones outside the houses and the cobbled road around the green practically sparkled, and the grass of the square garden at the centre was neatly trimmed. Felix unconsciously tried to neaten her hair a little in its bun (though she knew it was pointless; in the heat of the Magistry it was probably a wild, frizzy mess).

'Bit posh, isn't it?' she said down to the dire wolf. He shrugged indifferently and strolled after her as Felix stepped into the green. It was almost like a small park, with trees and bushes arching overhead so that the sunlight there was mottled on the gravel pathway. They passed a statue at the very middle of the green and Felix looked up at a beautifully carved man riding a horse.

The whole square had a sense of quietness and solitude about it that Felix liked. She had to remind herself that just around the corner, the labyrinth city curled around her.

'Over there,' dire wolf shouted over to Felix, motioning to a tall, squashed looking townhouse at the north west of the square. Felix glanced over and walked slowly towards it.

'That's the London Library?' she asked, and the dire wolf nodded.

She reached inside her jeans pocket and pulled out the library card. It felt warm, like it knew it was nearly home and was flush with anticipation.

Felix took a deep breath. It was a narrow, sand coloured building with a red wooden door surrounded by arched brickwork. There were three storeys and a triangular roof with dozens of little square windows below, all with a glowing amber light peeping through them, so that they looked like eyes staring down at her. It didn't look at all like a library, but as she stared at the door, she saw a little golden plaque stating that it was indeed the London Library.

'It's not that small inside,' dire wolf said having read Felix's thoughts.

Felix exhaled loudly and widened her eyes to try and ease some of the pressure behind them.

'Well, I suppose this is goodbye then?' She declared to the dire wolf, looking down at him ruefully.

He nodded and sat back on his hind legs, tongue hanging out of his mouth again. Felix grinned and he cocked his head, spreading his toothy smile across his face.

'It's been a pleasure aiding you in your dire need, miss,' he said dramatically bowing his head to her again. Felix chuckled and tickled him behind his ears.

'Felix,' she said, suddenly realising that she hadn't introduced herself to him. Dire wolf looked up at her with his golden eyes.

'Felix,' he repeated, nodding slowly, and she knew he'd probably already known her name from her thoughts.

'See you around then,' she said. 'And thank you.'

Dire wolf dipped his head once and watched her climb slowly up the stone steps to the front door. She looked back and gave him a nervous smile, before pushing the door open and disappearing into the flickering candlelight of the library.

Dire wolf whimpered but then loped off into the shadows of the green. He heard the echoing thoughts of those who were lost in the city around him and he felt their pull, but he turned back to stare up at the library. He licked his nose and shook his whole body, trying to rid himself of the girl's thoughts, but he could still hear her, still feel her fear.

There was something about her. He'd smelled it on her the first time he'd seen her, frightened and timid in that alleyway. Her heart seemed to call out for help though she was clearly unconscious of this; she didn't seem to know herself at all.

Those who cannot find their true selves will always be lost, he thought to himself and he whimpered again, torn between her and the calls from the city that only he could hear. Then, he made a decision. He circled on the grass several times before slumping down next to the bushes, where he poked his snout through the leafy shrubs so that he could just about see the library.

'Felix,' he whispered to himself.

He waited.

5
The Magician Named Alchemus J. Fiddle

The magician named Alchemus J. Fiddle sat in his favourite armchair tucked away in the Reading Room of the London Library. Above him, the windows were grimy with dust and seemed to catch the sunlight and keep it trapped making the room dim. It was lit only with flickering candles and the orange glow of a dying fire, for the room was tall and wide, and did not allow for much warmth, no matter what season of annum it was.

The fire was performing its final dance at the centre of the cavernous fireplace, so that it looked like the flames were being swallowed by the dark mouth of the chimney.

Alchemus J. Fiddle stared at the greying coals but it would have been clear to any observer that he was not seeing the embers. His face was stern and there were lines on his forehead that appeared to be from overuse rather than age, though nobody could say that he was a young man. Beneath his prominent chin and neatly trimmed grey beard that fell into a single curl onto his chest, the magician pressed his fingers together to create a steeple and he was still; as still as the books around him. They stood on their shelves with many coloured spines and the fragrance of yellowing paper and old leather filled the air, as it always did in the Reading Room.

The only sound was silence; that heavy, ringing sort of silence that is waiting to be broken, and only occasionally was there a creak from the resting iron galley that ran around the walls of the shelves, leading downwards into a rusty spiralling staircase. Even the clock on the wall, a brass and copper contraption that had several cogs turning within the face, did not make a sound as six different hands moved in concentric circles at differing speeds.

Alchemus J. Fiddle inhaled deeply, as though he had been forgetting to breathe. He turned his head very slightly but his eyes remained on the coals. Then, his eyes darted down to the small round table next to him. Upon it rested a decanter of honey coloured liquid and a crystal tumbler, about a quarter full but next to these items lay a sheaf of papers. With a speed that was surprising for a man who had been so still, the magician swiftly gathered the papers and looked at them one by one.

The first was a long scroll and whilst it looked yellowed and creased, it was evident that this was an artificial aesthetic. In swirling sepia ink, the title was revealed as "The Monacle" and with narrowed blue eyes, Alchemus. J. Fiddle read the headline and the article below it, his creased forehead bunching slowly as he read.

Grand Vizier Secures Citadel: Godspell praised for the banishment of commoners

It was revealed yesterday that our most beloved leader, Grand Vizier and the Right Hon. Corbin Godspell, has taken much needed steps to secure our political seat from attack only a day before the inauguration of his sixteenth annum in power.

The Citadel, seen by many as the architectural gem of London, is home to the Magistry, protectors of magicians and commoners alike, and provides jobs for hundreds of hard working magicians.

Yet it has been discovered that a resistance of commoners have been planning to attack the Citadel using home-made explosives that would undoubtedly kill and wound many of those who live and work in and around the Citadel. These barbaric devices, relics of the commoners' misguided past, have yet to be found but ParisLovelock, the master of the Guild for Commoner Care has ordered a search of every commoner home in the borderlocked Commoner's Quarter.

In a statement released yesterday evening, Mr Lovelock said:

"This is a last resort. We do not want to raid the commoners' homes but they bring this upon themselves in their act of hatred towards us. They must understand that the safety of our city and the Citadel is vital, not only for us magicians, but for the commoners as well. Where would they be without us?"

It is a well-known fact the Magistry, under the guidance and rule of Grand Vizier and Right. Hon Corbin Godspell, has protected the commoners after he came to power sixteen annums ago and he has spoken of them graciously.

In previous statements, the Grand Vizier has said: "they are a simple people and they must be guided to our own enlightened state of being.

They have proved, through their own destruction of natural resources that they are unworthy of the power that they have grasped for centuries. But they must be handled carefully, for they have violence and hatred in their hearts."

Mr Lovelock, after meeting with the Grand Vizier, who resides in the west wing of the Citadel with his son, Linus, said in his statement: "A decision has been made by our most esteemed Grand Vizier, to henceforth remove all commoner workers from the Citadel and banish them forthwith from the surrounding areas. Our loyal Commoners' Order Police Patrol shall be doubled and all worker permits will be checked upon entry to Borderlock and to the city from tomorrow. Grand Vizier Godspell wishes to express the pain in which this decision has been made and that the commoners facing redundancy will be compensated and will receive references to enable them to find work elsewhere."

Reported by G. Simpkin

The magician named Alchemus J. Fiddle scrunched up the scroll angrily and threw it with good aim into the fireplace, where the embers began to char the paper until it burned in a great rush of crackling fire.

He stared down at the next document, another newspaper, this one called The Town Cryer. This newspaper was printed in cerulean ink on crisp white paper but the magician simply rolled his eyes as he read the heading and the opening paragraph.

GRAND VIZIER CUTS COMMONERS FROM CITADEL
'ATTACK IMMINENT' SAYS GODSPELL

BY TABITHA BLOYD

Commoners are to be exiled from the Citadel after an 'imminent' bomb attack from the disgraced commoners was exposed, it was revealed yesterday. Grand Vizier, The Right Honourable Corbin Godspell has quashed growing fears with this assured and much needed action. It is hoped that the expulsion of the commoners from the Citadel will mean less crime on the streets and will help keep the surrounding neighbourhoods clean.

Alchemus J. Fiddle leaned over towards the fireplace and using the flames curling around the balled up copy of The Monacle, he set The Town Cryer ablaze with an almost bored expression on his face, as though he burned it frequently. As he leaned over, the final text fell onto the threadbare rug at his feet. The expression changed on the magician's face immediately and he threw himself to the floor to pick it up gently, then stood whilst holding it like he was clutching a sacred text.

It was a grubby, pathetic little newspaper. There were leaves of pages held together by a piece of greasy string looped through the top left hand corners and it looked as though it had been folded several times and shoved into many different pockets. Fingerprints were visible in dirt or grease or ink and each page had been written on in different coloured inks, in different handwritings. Lifting the first page gingerly, Alchemus J. Fiddle smiled as he saw additional handwritten articles sewn onto other pages, or stuck onto the sides with a slightly foul smelling adhesive.

He sat down, the old leather groaning under his weight as he shuffled into a comfortable position. The title of this newspaper was faded and in a very plain font. In fact, it wouldn't have stood out at all if somebody had not drawn a very realistic match and flame next to the title as an illustration.

The Touch Papers

The Magician's eyes glittered as he read the tagline underneath.

Pass It On

He had spent all day tracking down this newspaper, visiting a number of shady back alley shops to speak to his contacts and he finally had his hands on it.

The Touch Papers. The commoners' secret newspaper.

It was a precious acquisition, not least because each copy was different depending on who had risked adding to it and how many people had followed its command to 'pass it on'.

Of course the commoners weren't allowed their own newspapers; they were fed the daily drivel from The Monacle or worse, The Town Cryer and the appalling Daily Moon.

But that didn't stop the commoners.

Alchemus J. Fiddle smiled at the thought and for a moment, the age slipped away from his face, revealing skin less wrinkled and weather worn, wider eyes and dark brown hair with salt and pepper flecks of grey that curled about his face, stripped now of the mask he had to wear. He stretched his neck from side to side, closing his eyes and breathing deeply and calmly.

'I am Alchemus. J. Fiddle,' he whispered to himself in a tremulous voice. 'I am still here.'

Opening his eyes, the wrinkles magically folded into his skin, his hair and beard faded to a shimmering grey and his blue eyes twinkled as they narrowed under the loose skin.

The magician looked desperately sad.

Sighing, he began to read the headline article on the front page of the commoner's newspaper. The headline was very different to the others and as he read, the small smile began to tickle his lips.

Godspell's Paranoia Grows

Workers sacked from Citadel

Pretender to power, Corbin Godspell has allowed rumours of 'commoner' attack to fester inside his mind and has succumbed to the paranoia by sacking magically indifferent workers from the Citadel, lair of the Magistry.

Hundreds of workers now face extreme poverty and here at Touch, we ask you, our faithful readers to dig deep and help out our neighbours in need.

Godspell, the 'right honourable' has released a statement through his minion Paris Lovelock, that workers will "be compensated".

This reporter would like to respectfully say in response to this blatant, downright, dirty, great, fat lie that Corbin Godspell and his cronies can go and take a long walk off a short cliff.

Jack Dickinson, 38, a pipe-scraper at the Citadel said yesterday evening: "Didn't like that scummy job anyway. For all their airs and graces, them magicians go to the bog just like the rest of us. Believe me, I've seen and smelled the evidence!"

Daisy McCrawley, 22, worked as a dust watcher in the basement archives. "It was the most mind numbingly dull work I've ever known. I'd rather watch paint dry. No really, I'd rather be a paint-blower than a dust-watcher!"

Rumours of attack have been circulating for several weeks and speculation grows amidst our community as to who is part of this rebellion against Godspell. Whilst there are those of us, (i.e me) who fully support all assertions of a resistance and an attack, it is incumbent upon me and the rest of the contributors to Touch, to advise you that should you be part of such a rebellion, you must cease this futile mission and accept our poor, dust-watching fates.

Only kidding. Blow him to smithereens!

By Derek Robbins

The magician named Alchemus J. Fiddle chuckled and flipped through the tatty pages. It was full of joyless news. Rations cut, evictions, homelessness at an all-time high, missing commoners. And yet, there was a sense of hope written in the articles as though the mere act of reporting news was rebellion enough against Godspell. He stroked the paper and with deftness and agility that was surprising for a stooped old man, he strode the length of the Reading Room and climbed the complaining iron staircase, before pulling out an insignificant, rather beaten looking book entitled "The Lost Art of Crochet".

The old tome fell open to reveal a small collection of The Touch Papers, to which he added the latest copy, but just as he did so a loud jangling noise rang in his ears and he dropped the book in surprise, scattering The Touch Papers along the galley. Frantically, he began to gather together the pages, sprawled on the galley floor, as the jangling sounded again.

'Nigel!' he shouted, shoving copies of the newspaper into the pages of the book. Once again, he grimaced as the bells rang, as though an alarm was jingling urgently right next to his head.

'NIGEL!' He shouted again but the ringing continued. 'Damn that boy!'

He pulled himself to his feet and let the book go, but this time it floated midair. With a flick of his wrist, Alchemus J. Fiddle motioned the book back into its unassuming slot on the shelf. Racing down the stairs, which seemed dangerously close to collapsing under the effort, he began to mumble incoherently, an angry frown scarring his face. As he arrived at the Reading Room door, he paused and straightened his long, midnight blue frock coat and pulled up his worn emerald green gloves. He lowered himself into a stoop and opened the door with deliberate care, before stepping through it with a slight limp that made him look as though he ought to be using a walking stick. The jarring bell made him grit his teeth.

'Will you stop ringing that godforsaken summoning bell!' he roared, as he turned to the foyer where the checkout box was empty of staff but had a lone girl standing stiffly next to the incriminating gold bell.

She looked at him, eyes wide but winsome, face pale, with a mess of dark hair in a tangled pile on her crown. The magician froze as he perceived her state of dress; ripped and baggy denim jeans swamping her small frame, muddy trainers of a style from a bygone era and a black mackintosh with too many patches and not enough buttons. A commoner, clear enough, though as confirmation he saw the red work permit swinging down from one of the only buttons her coat had left.

'Sorry,' the girl whispered, though she had to clear her throat several times before the word was audible.

The magician glared at her with cold eyes and his shoulders slumped, but he was no longer stooping for effect.

'Are you the owner of this establishment?' the girl asked, squaring her shoulders and thrusting her chin out determinedly, though her voice betrayed her nerves.

The magician named Alchemus J. Fiddle closed his eyes and breathed deeply and steadily, as though he was breathing in the words. When they opened, his blue eyes were softer, but sadness had replaced coldness.

'Has it really been sixteen years?' he asked quietly, searching her face.

He took a slow step towards the girl but as he did so, she stepped away, clutching onto the straps of her rucksack. He sighed and backed off.

'Follow me,' he ordered, turning towards the Reading Room before looking back at her. 'And Felix? Don't dawdle.'

6
The London Library

So he knew her name. Ok. That was freaky, she had to admit, but judging by his gloves and the rest of his mad clothes, he was a magician and after the dire wolf she was becoming accustomed to having people know things like her private thoughts...and her name.

He hobbled with old age and the walk brought on a mild coughing fit. Felix felt she ought to ask him if he needed help, but somehow she thought he'd take great offence to such an offer. The magician led her into a large, wide room with oak bookshelves reaching the ceiling, separated by a black iron walkway running around the middle of the shelves so it seemed like a narrow platform. It was chilly, despite the small fire in the enormous fireplace and it was badly lit, with only a few stuttering candles in glass lamps. Felix turned slowly, staring at the sheer volume of books that surrounded her like a pantheon of knowledge. She'd never seen so many books in one place. The school Book Room only had a hundred or so texts for her to read and she'd devoured all of them at some time or another throughout her limited annums at school. She swallowed, envious suddenly.

'Impressive, isn't it?' the old magician said, folding his arms and twiddling the tip of his curling grey beard. Felix shrugged, but could not stop her eyes wandering over the spines of the books. She longed to touch them and hold the pages to her nose to breathe in that delicious musty smell of old paper. But first, she had more important matters at hand.

'Who are you?' she blurted.

The magician turned towards her, a vague look of surprise on his face which he corrected quickly.

'Currently, I am Archibald Friebel,' he said.

'Currently?'

'Mm, yes. Though I suspect I may soon be someone else again.'

Felix eyed him like he might be a crazy person.

'What?' she asked carefully.

'My real name, dear girl, is Alchemus J. Fiddle, though it has been many annums since I have been able to use that name.'

Felix opened her mouth to ask another question, but he halted her quickly by holding up a finger and shaking it dramatically. The question went unasked.

'Please, sit,' Fiddle motioned to a high backed, red leather armchair with gold studs on the arm rests.

Felix nodded but spent a moment longer admiring the books, as though making him wait would show him that she was not someone he could order around. She removed her rucksack with a grateful sigh and let it fall with a heavy thud to the floor, before dropping herself into the armchair. Only when she was comfortable did the old man sink gracefully into his own chair.

'Can I get you anything? Something to eat or drink?' he asked politely.

Felix's stomach grumbled in answer, but she shook her head, though it hurt her to be unfriendly to this man who was being so kind. Fiddle smiled.

'I'll tell you what, I'll get you some lemonade and a bowl of summer broth and you can help yourself, how does that sound?'

Felix shrugged again, though her mouth had started salivating at the mention of broth.

'Nigel!' Fiddle shouted so loudly that Felix jumped. He had a very booming voice for someone who looked so old.

'My assistant,' Fiddle said by way of explanation.

Felix looked at him blankly, but the sound of books being knocked over and the thunderous thumps of footsteps tripping down stairs made her look towards the door, which was flung open by a tall, gangling boy with oversized square glasses and curly auburn hair. He looked flushed and exasperated.

'*What?*' he yelled at Fiddle, and Felix immediately felt angry at the boy.

'I'm up in the Alchemical *Equation* Room of all places, categorising texts just like *you* told me to do, and all I here is you screaming after me all day! So what is it? What could you possible wa- oh!'

He stopped abruptly as he saw Felix, who had leaned around the back of the armchair and was looking at him as though he had brought a very nasty smell with him.

'We have a visitor,' said Fiddle smoothly, an eyebrow arched in a way that looked far more menacing than a sneer. 'Felix, this is my assistant and would-be apprentice, Nigel True.'

The boy bowed his head quickly; his cheeks flushing a brighter shade of red, making his freckles fade over his prominent nose.

'I'm sorry Miss- wait. Did you say Felix?'

He looked towards Fiddle and then back at Felix, his eyes scanning over her face as though she was a rare kind of bird. Felix shuffled uncomfortably, glaring at Nigel and thinking he was the rudest boy she'd ever met, ruder even that that awful magician boy who'd slapped her when she was little.

'I did,' Fiddle said archly. 'Now, if it's not *too* much trouble, pupil-mine, would you *kindly* arrange for some lemonade and a large bowl of the summer broth to be brought up for our guest? I believe she is rather hungry.' Nigel nodded absently, still looking at Felix who was getting angrier and angrier by his obtrusiveness.

'Yes, of course,' he murmured, turning to leave reluctantly. 'I'll be right back.'

'By all means, take your time,' Fiddle mumbled, rolling his eyes and leaning his head on his knuckles. Nigel left the room and Felix looked at Fiddle.

'He's a relatively new assistant,' he confessed.

Felix shifted in her chair, conscious of Fiddle observing her. Questions that she'd wanted to ask seemed to have abandoned her brain and she felt the old ache in her head returning.

'You are in London for work?' Fiddle asked, nodding down at her work permit. She considered him for a moment, but decided that he was a magician after all and that she couldn't exactly tell him her permit was a fake. He may report her. Even so, she really hated lying.

'Yes,' she nodded, feeling her face redden. 'I start work as a scurry girl at the Citadel tomorrow.' Fiddle raised his eyebrows which were a shade darker than his hair and beard.

'Really?' he said, looking down at the charred mess in the fireplace. 'How interesting.' Something in his tone made Felix feel that he knew she was lying and she shuffled awkwardly.

The door swung open and Nigel backed into the room carrying a tray laden with a jug of cloudy lemonade, an empty glass goblet and a large bowl of steaming broth with two thick slices of crusty bread slathered with butter. It smelled delicious.

'Here you go, Miss Felix,' Nigel said, placing the tray on a small table that he dragged next to her chair.

Felix didn't have the will to feign indifference to the meal and she attacked the bread, tearing it into chunks and dipping them into the thick broth, before cramming them into her mouth. She couldn't believe how good it tasted. It had been years since she'd had real butter and the bread she usually ate was either stale or over salted to keep it preserved.

As she filled her stomach, she became aware of Nigel's curious eyes watching her in fascination and she began to feel self-conscious. She wiped her mouth with the back of her hand sloppily and tried to eat more slowly.

'So you're a commoner?' Nigel said, and whilst he didn't say it with malice, Felix immediately stopped chewing and slumped back against the chair, shame burning behind her eyes.

Fiddle, who had been politely ignoring Felix's animalistic eating habits by examining his fingernails, looked up sternly at his assistant.

'Nigel, the Alchemical Equation Room will not categorise itself,' he snapped. Nigel rolled his eyes and skulked out of the room, throwing an intrigued glance at Felix.

'I apologise,' Fiddle said gently. 'Please, continue with your meal.'

'I don't want it,' Felix mumbled, pushing the tray away with her fingertips. It was true; she felt sick, partly because she'd eaten too quickly and partly because she felt ashamed that

Nigel had chosen to comment on her upbringing simply by observing her eat.

'Then have some lemonade. Nigel makes it, but it really is very good. Here, try some,' Fiddle poured the cloudy liquid into the glass goblet where it sparkled in the candlelight.

Felix looked at it reluctantly, but she was thirsty. She took a sip and felt like she was drinking pure sunlight.

'Oh, it's nice!' she said in surprise and gulped down the rest.

'Yes,' Fiddle nodded, refilling the glass for her. 'He has a talent for mixing ingredients. One of his more redeeming features.' Felix couldn't help but smile a little and Fiddle smiled back at her, but his lips were thin.

'To business then, I think,' he exclaimed, leaning back into his armchair and crossing his legs.

'What can I do for you, Felix?'

'Who are you?' Felix blurted. 'How do you know who I am?' she asked, narrowing her eyes at him.

'Simple deduction,' Fiddle said in a bored voice. 'You are the only girl of your...background, who would have reason to come to this great place of learning.'

Felix blushed and absently ran her hands over her jeans as though trying to neaten them.

'You said you were currently Archibald Friebel?' she asked.

The man nodded.

'But that you're really called Alchemus J. Fiddle?'

He nodded once more.

'Why did you change your name?' Felix asked, who was growing more confused.

'Because the name Alchemus J. Fiddle is not safe.'

'Why?'

Fiddle sighed and regarded Felix with his shining blue eyes.

'Is that really the most pertinent question you have?' he asked, resting his chin on his fist.

Felix looked away and focused on her hands where she began to occupy herself by cleaning the dirt from underneath her fingernails. Fiddle waited patiently for her to speak, but Felix was very aware that he was watching her and she wished she had not come to the London Library because she really had only one question she wanted to ask and she was afraid of the answer. In the corner of her vision, she saw her baby blanket poking out of her rucksack like a stowaway and she took a deep breath.

'You took me to the orphanage,' she said quietly.

'I did.'

'You left the library card so that I'd come here.'

'Yes.'

'You knew my parents.'

Fiddle was silent for a moment but Felix could not bring herself to look at him.

'Yes,' he said finally.

'Are they dead?'

The question wound itself tightly around Felix. She found herself holding her breath and she felt the blood pulsing in her temples.

'I think you already know the answer to that, Felix,' Fiddle said softly.

Felix kept her eyes on her hands but they started to blur. She nodded quickly, trying to dispel the painful lump in her throat. She felt very tired suddenly.

'What happened?' she asked after a long silence that Fiddle had politely respected.

Alchemus J. Fiddle took a long, deep breath as though bracing himself for a hard battle.

'It's a long and complicated story, Felix. I have been waiting to tell it for sixteen years and yet...yet now I feel unprepared.' He cleared his throat and made a steeple with his fingers under his chin again.

Felix watched him, a strange ticking coming from the odd clock on the fireplace. It seemed to tick hurriedly, measuring something other than time. She waited for him to continue.

'There is more to this story than you think and I need your patience. You can ask questions later, but for now, you listen.'

Felix gritted her teeth but she nodded to show her understanding. Then, Fiddle began to explain.

'I should begin with the most important information, though it is often the most difficult to understand. But for this tale, I am first going to tell you about magic. You have been raised as a commoner and you have no understanding of magic... yet, but trust me, you will.' Fiddle paused, silencing Felix as she began to ask a question.

'Magic is an energy,' he continued slowly, 'a force that is part of all matter, mixed within the very particles of an object. Commoners cannot see this energy, cannot use it; a magician can. A magician can feel the magic in something as though it is part of their very flesh, so they can wield the magic and use it. It takes years to learn how to do this and it takes a great deal of training to understand where magic comes from, for a magician cannot use magic without first learning of its origins.

'In the most simple of terms, the magic in all things comes from a Flame, a fire, neither hot nor cold, that exists on a Plane that commoners and most magicians cannot see. This Flame keeps all magic in balance. Without it, all magic would cease to exist, destroying everything and everyone, yes even the commoners, for even the commoners have magic within them though they cannot see it.

'Now, you must try your best to understand this, Felix. I know you think it has nothing to do with you but it has everything to do with you, and your family.

There is more than one world. In fact, there are three. We magicians call them Planes. The First Plane is the one that we are on now; it is visible to all and it is the world as we know it. Commoners have always lived on this Plane, writing their history upon its pages. The Second Plane is a world beyond this one; the home of the magicians and it is from the Second Plane that the magicians came into this world.

Oh, it is not something the commoners are aware of though there are those who sense it. I believe you call them psychics. The Second Plane is visible to magicians when they wish to see it, though some need special lenses to cross into it, but to commoners it is invisible.

Questions later, Felix,' Fiddle chastised gently as Felix leaned forward, a question on her lips. Setting her jaw on edge in frustration, she sank back into her chair and motioned for him to continue.

'The Third Plane is...difficult to explain if one has never seen it. Again, it is another world beyond this one and beyond the Second Plane. You must imagine it all as...as a rather delicious trifle.'

'A trifle?' Felix asked skeptically, arching an eyebrow.

'Why, yes,' nodded Fiddle with a grin, delighted with his analogy. 'Your world consists of the tangible; the cream and chocolate of the trifle – delicious and satisfying in its own way, though, if you'll forgive me, rather light and frothy. The Second Plane is the transient, yet substantial, jelly underneath. Finally, beneath the jelly, is the custard and sponge; dense, and dizzying with a dash of sherry that intoxicates you if you have too much.'

Fiddle smiled happily, loosening his knit fingers and resting them on the arms of his chair. Felix clicked her tongue. She wasn't sure if she was curious or hungry for trifle. She'd never had a trifle in her life but she thought it wasn't the time to share this fact.

'So...the Third Plane is...custard and sponge?'

Fiddle's smile faded and he cleared his throat before leaning forward again.

'Ah...no. It is the most dangerous Plane. It is a mysterious place that cannot be seen without help. Even the most powerful of magicians need more than special lenses to see it, and it is forbidden for any to enter it without authority and training. It ensnares you for magic is at its most potent on the Third Plane.

'The Flame of Magic originates there, its power radiating through the Planes like an echo resounding in a cave. It is kept safe by a magician who is powerful enough to safeguard it and protect it. This magician is known as the Firelighter, and he is the ruler of the magicians. He makes sure that the Flame is never jeopardised and he keeps it a secret from the commoners. They must never know about it. You see, it is hard for those who have no magical powers to understand the Flame. They cannot understand that magic is as much a part of them and their world as it is ours, even though they cannot see it.'

Felix thought hard, processing this information. She realised she was frowning and she tried to straighten her face.

'So, you're saying there are two other worlds beyond this one.'

Fiddle nodded. 'Yes.'

'And they're layered on top of each other.'

'Precisely.'

'And they're all made up of varying degrees of magic, the strongest of which exists on the Third Plane because of this Flame, which is protected by a magician you call the Firelighter.'

'That's correct.'

'So, because of that Flame, everything has magic within it...like particles?'

'Exactly, Felix. Spot on.'

'Woah,' Felix whispered. She stroked the stem of the glass goblet that held the lemonade with awe as though she was trying to touch the particles of magic themselves.

'Yes, it is rather fascinating. The study of Venephysics. That is, the study of magic within objects. There is an excellent book on it somewhere...'

Fiddle trailed off and pushed himself up out of the chair before walking alongside the book stacks, his head tilted whilst reading the spines and mumbling to himself.

Felix's head was spinning. She couldn't sort through the muddle of questions in her mind. She rubbed her forehead, starting at the static shock of her hand against her face. She felt a thud in her temple and closed her eyes.

'Mr Fiddle?' She mumbled.

'One moment, dear,' he replied, still perusing the books. Felix tentatively touched her forehead again. It felt sore and tender, like she had been sunburnt. She traced a finger down her cheekbone, trembling at the pain it brought.

'Nigel!' Fiddle called out. 'Nigel where is that blasted Venephysics guide? Nigel!'

Nigel was heard before he was seen. He pushed the doors open with a stiff arm, his fists clenched and his teeth on edge.

'You called, Master?' he practically growled.

'"Venephysics. A Very Vague Guide." Where is it?'

'Next to "Science and Sorcery" by Archimedes Bohr,' Nigel said, trying to control his patience.

'Well why is it there? It should be under V.'

'Because you told me to categorise by subject not letter.'

'Well that's a marvellous idea,' Fiddle exclaimed, pulling out a battered and mildewed book from the shelf just behind Nigel.

'Here we go, Felix... Oh my.'

Fiddle stopped dead in front of Felix, the book dropping from his hand and falling to the floor, stopping to float just before it hit the ground. Nigel rolled his eyes and marched over to pick it up but he, too, stopped in his tracks when he saw Felix.

'My dear, are you quite well?' Fiddle asked stepping closer to Felix and crouching over her.

'Not likely,' snorted Nigel. 'Look at her!'

Fiddle fired a firm glance in his direction and Nigel pursed his lips together.

'Mr Fiddle,' Felix murmured, her eyes squinting. The library felt so bright and hot. Her whole world was spinning around, upside down and inside out. Whilst she was never the cleverest girl at the orphanage, she wasn't stupid either. 'Bright,' Nanny Maude had said. Her head lurched.

She knew what all this meant. She knew why he was telling her all of this.

Unbidden, the memory of the taste of blood spread over her tongue until it was no longer a memory; she could taste the sickly metal bite of it, though she knew that if she put her fingers to her mouth there would be no blood.

It was magic. And Felix was a magician.

She asked the question, through shaky lips, her voice not quite working. But Fiddle heard her.

He knelt down in front of Felix and reached for her hand. Felix noted the green leather gloves he wore were shaped so tightly around his fingers that they almost seemed like a second skin. She briefly wondered if he ever took them off. The leather felt soft and warm on her hand.

'I should have thought the answer was obvious, Felix,' Fiddle said imploringly. Felix shook her head, stopping quickly when it blurred her vision.

'She doesn't know, Archibald,' Nigel whispered.

'Alchemus from now on, Nigel,' Fiddle said offhandedly.

He pulled on Felix's hand, lifting her from her armchair. Felix wobbled.

'What's wrong with me?' she asked fearfully. 'What did you do?'

'Nothing is wrong with you, Felix,' Fiddle said gently, leading her to stand in front of the fireplace. 'You're perfect.'

He looked at her meaningfully, his eyes drifting from hers to stare at her forehead and cheekbone.

'Look.'

Fiddle nodded his head towards the mirror above the fireplace. Felix turned her head slowly, meeting her reflection in the mirror. She saw the same large blue eyes as she always did, staring back at her, framed by bushy dark eyebrows. Her face was paler than usual and she looked pained. But her eyes widened as she looked at herself, first in confusion and then, as what she was seeing sank in, in horror. Beginning at her right temple, an inky black spiral twisted its way over her forehead and curled down, over her cheekbone. It continued to spiral, slowly but very certainly, as though it was creeping ivy. She reached her fingers up to stroke her skin and felt the same painful burning sensation she had experienced before. Her mouth fell open. The markings were part of her skin, growing *in* her skin.

'What have you done to me?' she choked.

'Nothing, Felix,' Fiddle said, his voice low and soft. 'These markings are part of you. You inherited them from your mother.'

'Alchemus, she doesn't know what it means,' Nigel said, concern etched onto his face as he looked at Felix in the mirror.

'Yes, she does,' Fiddle said simply.

'I'm a magician,' Felix whispered. She tore her eyes away from her reflection and looked at Fiddle who held her gaze in the mirror. He nodded.

'And so much more than that,' he smiled, tracing his eyes along the spirals.

Felix struggled to breathe. Her chest felt constricted, like a cold hand was closing around her lungs. Her vision began to blur as her pulse banged behind her eyes.

'Alchemus, help her!' she heard Nigel call out, though his voice sounded far away. Felix felt herself falling but she didn't hit the floor.

Magician.

The word echoed in her head tasting of blood and hate and spite.

Her face burned, scalding with anger.

She tried to focus her eyes on something, the spines of the books, jumbling together until they were just spears of colour.

Then nothing.

7
The Room of Ways Out

She was in a room full of doors. She didn't know where any of them led and the doors gave her no clues. They were all wooden, painted different colours; one red, one blue, another was varnished oak, one was a glossy white, scuffed along the hinges. The handles were polished brass and some had funny looking door knockers, like the one that was a pig with a hoop through its nose. The more she turned, the more doors seemed to appear until she felt dizzy. Familiar panic bubbled in her stomach, but she calmed herself.

Just a dream, the same one she'd always had.

Soon she'd wake up, and she'd be wrapped up in her blanket, safe in her bed, tucked away in the orphanage.

But no...that didn't feel right. She'd left the orphanage, hadn't she? The orphanage was gone.

Gone, gone gone.

Like her parents.

She didn't like this dream. She knew, without even trying, that the doors didn't open. They never did, they just kept her locked inside the dark, circular room with a stone floor and no visible ceiling. No real source of light either, yet she could always see.

'Haven't you ever heard of the phrase 'down the hatch'?' The dire wolf said, somewhere, deep in her head, lost in a memory that she couldn't cling to.

The smell of cinder toffee was everywhere.

They're hatches, she realised, and she spun around and around. The doors were hatches. One would take her home.

But which one?

More and more and more doors. A room of ways out that would never let her leave.

She saw a door with spirals, slithering like snakes across the wood. The spirals were black, like the ones on her face. Felix reached up and felt her cheek and forehead. Soft, smooth skin. Burning.

She stepped towards the spiral door and as she got closer, she found that it wasn't a door at all, but a mirror. Her reflection looked at her but it was not truly a reflection. Something marked it as different. Felix couldn't put her finger on why. The malice in the eyes, perhaps? The fierce defiance in the set of her jawline. Her, but not her. Ugly. Evil.

The door opened just a crack.

Felix tried to step towards it but her feet were stuck in a wet, grey green sludge. The pea green stench of the quarter invaded the room.

Wake up, she willed. *Wake up*! She shut her eyes, closing out the malicious reflection taunting her on an open door. It was torture, this place. Torture to be trapped, to be caged this way, always seeing the ways out and never reaching them.

Wait it out, she willed herself. *Soon you will wake.*

Please wake.

She opened her eyes again when she heard a knock against one of the doors.

She looked curiously at each one, unsure which one the noise had come from.

This was unusual. This had never happened before.

There it was again, a little louder this time.

Turning around, she focused on a large, oak door with rusty hinges and a round tarnished handle. The wood was splintered and rotted in places. She'd never seen this door before. She tried lifting her legs and found, to her relief that she could move again.

'Hello?' Her voice echoed several times. Whatever was behind the door stopped knocking. The only noise was her breath, heavy and fast.

BOOM! The door rattled, dust shaking from the beams. The handle began to twist violently and she felt, with a certainty that she couldn't explain, that whatever was behind the door was not friendly.

A crashing, splintering, gnawing sound made her cry out and she stared, eyes wide and horrified as a figure loomed out of the dust and dirt of the shattered door.

She found herself shouting out.

No, screaming to be perfectly frank.

8
Nevermore

The man walked with long, confident strides. Night's shadow cloaked him but every now and then the flickering light from the floating orbs caught the strands of his oiled, dark hair.

Ahead of him, the Tower of London loomed like a leviathan, black and forbidding on its hill crest, overlooking the inky river Thames.

He looked to his right, glared at his hooded eyed reflection in the window of an old abandoned building and smiled lazily, his thin lips revealing perfectly straight, white teeth. He breathed in the salty, slightly acrid tang of the river. No chance of him being followed here. Nobody would venture to this part of London willingly and he let the pride of this achievement envelop him.

Overhead, a raven cawed. The man let his eyes roll towards it and he snarled suddenly. Reaching out a gloved hand, he shaped his fingers as though he was holding the bird's neck. He clenched his fingers into a fist. The raven froze, let out a choked squawk and tumbled down to the tarmac, hitting it with a dead thud in front of the man's polished boot. He stepped forward, nudged the corpse with his heel and then violently kicked it away.

'Nevermore,' he smiled viciously, his voice a silky purr as he straightened his tie, pulling it tight underneath his slim, shaven throat before continuing on his way.

He stopped outside a red bricked building on the corner of an unused junction. The roads and pavements here had not yet been removed and the man sneered with distaste at the remnants of the Common Time. He waited, reading the blackened plaque that hung on the red bricks of the building. The Hung, Drawn and Quartered pub was also a leftover inconvenience from the Common Time, but the man rather liked the name of it, even if it did evoke the unpleasantness of torture techniques used by the commoners in their pitiful history. They were so unsophisticated and-

'So *untidy*,' he murmured, pursing his lips as though tasting something nasty. He hoped he would not be kept waiting long. Corbin Godspell hated to be kept waiting.

'Apologies, Sir,' came a heavily accented voice from the shadows a few minutes later. Godspell flinched but then relaxed, recognising the Slavic voice of his friend.

'Dr Nyxon,' he said smoothly.

'I hope I have not kept you waiting, Sir,' Dr Nyxon replied, stepping across the junction. He was a bent, greying man, thin and haggard with a salt and pepper moustache and tired eyes that lacked warmth.

'Only a little,' Godspell replied icily. 'But genius thinks nothing of time, does it?'

'No, Sir. Thank you, Sir,' muttered Dr Nyxon, stooping lower into a bow.

'Have there been improvements?' Godspell asked, his voice becoming suddenly sharp and business-like.

'Few, Sir. But these things do take time.'

'Yes, of course. But it is...discouraging to see time taking so long, especially with these inconvenient uprisings. A solution is needed, Doctor.' Godspell glared down at his companion. He liked Dr Nyxon and respected him greatly. But perhaps...

'You are working to best of your ability, I trust?' he asked.

Dr Nyxon froze and looked at Godspell fearfully. When he answered, his voice was tremulous.

'Of...of course, Sir! I work day and night, taking little rest and hardly any meals. I've read every venephysical journal I can find and I keep testing...but the answer is not yet forthcoming.'

Godspell cracked his knuckles inside his gloves and picked an invisible speck of dust from the lapel of his immaculate suit. Dr Nyxon swallowed.

'You have trusted me, Sir. I ask that you keep doing so. I will not fail you.'

'I do trust you, Doctor,' Godspell said lightly. He looked towards the brass letters of the pub. 'Tell me...what do you think of the old commoner punishments?'

'Sir?'

'Well, to be hung, drawn and quartered for example. Linguistically incorrect; it should be hanged, drawn and quartered but then, the commoners cared little for detail. But their punishments were certainly imaginative.'

Dr Nyxon shuffled his feet nervously.

'I've never given it much thought, Sir.'

'Oh, then do! Imagine...to be strangled until the point of death and then freed, choking and gasping for air even as your oesophagus collapsed inside your throat. And then worse; cut open, your innards pulled from you whilst you scream for death. So many died at that point...but a few... oh, a few survived and they were most unfortunate. The quartering is really the best part. Your limbs cut away from you, burned in front of your dying eyes until at last you were freed by the executioner's blade as you were decapitated.'

Dr Nyxon's breathing was ragged and loud.

'Yes. Quite imaginative, Sir.'

'And *untidy.* Don't you agree?'

'Untidy, Sir. Yes, Sir.'

'I do hate it when things are untidy. It is so...messy. And yet, sometimes one must make a mess in order to clean it up afterwards.'

'Sir...I...' began Dr Nyxon.

'Find an answer, Doctor,' purred Godspell. 'Otherwise I shall have to dismiss you of your services...and clean up your mess.'

Dr Nyxon's face was white, even in the shadow and faint orbed light.

'Yes, Sir. I will, Sir.'

'Good man,' smiled Godspell, coldly. 'You may go.'

Dr Nyxon let out a relieved breath of air and fell to his knee before Godspell.

'I owe you my allegiance, Sir,' he said earnestly.

He lowered his head to Godspell's boot. In the darkness, the doctor saw a dark, shining liquid on his master's boot, a bunch of soft black feathers sticking to it.

Godspell cleared his throat impatiently.

Closing his eyes tightly, Dr Nyxon pressed his lips to the boot of his master.

'Good night then, Doctor,' Godspell said silkily before turning on his heel. 'Until next time.'

9
The Riddles of Fiddle

Felix jolted awake but did not open her eyes. The scream of her nightmare rang in her ears and burned in her throat, though she knew she'd not really made a sound. Beneath her, the leather of the armchair complained slightly and she stilled, alarmed at the sound. She could smell burning firewood along with an old, musty smell of paper and something she vaguely recognised; something sweet and faintly spicy.

She lifted her head, a dead weight on her neck. Slowly, her eyelids fluttered open and through blurred eyes she saw the dim, firelit surroundings of the Reading Room. She became aware that her legs were outstretched and resting on an ancient and distinctly overused pouffe and her blanket was laid over body, her fingers gripping the hem of it tightly.

Trying not to make a sound, Felix scanned the room. Her eyes hurt as they moved in their sockets. Across from her, on the other side of the threadbare Aubusson rug, the old magician sat in his armchair, legs crossed and one gloved hand clutching a mug of something that steamed in the orange glow of the fire and candlelight.

Fiddle was absorbed in a book and he turned the pages absently, his blue, twinkling eyes drifting across the words. Felix watched him, taking this chance to really see him for the first time.

His long, grey beard rested on the top of his stomach. Though nobody would have said he was a large man, Fiddle seemed to exude a sense of size and authority as he read, as though the fragility of his age was a pretence that he cast aside in unguarded moments.

Beneath an ankle length deep blue coat, he wore a brown, tweed waistcoat with matching trousers and whilst both were pressed and clean, there was evidence of previous tears and rips that had been badly darned. A pocket watch chain ran from a buttonhole on his waistcoat and the clock face peeped from a pocket, polished and undoubtedly expensive. Through the obscurity of his beard, Felix saw a red tie over an emerald green shirt and a tiepin glittered in the light. She could not make it out clearly, but she thought it was a letter; perhaps a C or a G.

Felix studied him as carefully as she could, through half-closed eyes. There seemed to be an air of faded wealth about the man, with his straight, aquiline nose and high regal brow, and yet his charcoal hair was choppy and skimming his collar in uneven clumps, badly in need of a proper cut. His face had the familiar etch of poverty that Felix had seen too frequently in the Commoner's Quarter; it was a tired, drawn expression with a layer of grime that seemed to be hidden behind the skin so that the magician looked somewhat unhealthy.

She remembered his clipped and eloquent voice, his rigid politeness and thought that Fiddle was a man come from money and riches; wealth, it seemed, long past.

Felix creased her brow in confusion and a small yelp of pain escaped her throat at the skin across her forehead wrinkled. In a stab of remembrance, she thought of her reflection in the mirror above the fireplace and saw, in her mind's eye, the tendrils of black growing within her skin. Ice flooded her veins.

'Ah,' Fiddle said softly as she yelped. He closed the book in his lap and glanced over at Felix. 'The dreamer awakes.'

Felix swallowed and sat up, pulling her stiff legs away from the pouffe. She reached to touch her cheek but stopped an inch away from her skin, startled by the heat that emanated from her face.

'I suggest you don't touch your face for a day or two. It may be quite uncomfortable for you,' Fiddle said sympathetically.

Felix nodded and adjusted her position as best she could without moving her head too quickly. It felt thick and heavy, sending waves of nausea through her stomach. She peeled away her blanket and noticed for the first time that her rucksack was open, her few belongings removed and laid on the table next to her. She jerked angrily, wincing at the sudden movement.

'You went through my stuff?'

Fiddle nodded guiltily. 'Yes. I'm rather afraid I did.'

'You can't go through my stuff!' She began to root through her belongings, checking that nothing was missing. Her book. Her only book was gone. She stared accusingly at Fiddle who held up the book from his lap.

'Forgive me. It has been some time since I read a book written by a commoner and this one was an old favourite.'

Felix stood shakily and snatched the book from his hand, looking down at it to inspect it for damage.

'I'm sorry Felix,' Fiddle murmured. 'But I had to check you hadn't told me any more lies.'

'Lies?!' Felix said loudly, ignoring the pain as her eyebrows creased in anger.

'Starting work as a scurry girl tomorrow?' Fiddle accused, though his eyes glinted with amusement.

'I- I...' Felix flushed but as the blood rushed to her face, her new markings began to burn. She flinched and held her hand over her face.

'Hush, dear,' Fiddle soothed her, standing and beckoning her to sit. 'Don't get over-excited. I went through your belongings only out of necessity. I understand why you would lie though I assure you there is no need. I will not be reporting your fake permit, your illegal entry into the Magistry of anything else you may have done to get here. Plus, I saw that you had your baby blanket and I thought it would comfort you to have it over you as you slept.'

Felix rested on the edge of her chair and watched as Fiddle poured hot, amber liquid from a tarnished silver teapot into a mug on the table next to his chair. The spicy sweet aroma once again filled the air.

'Cinnamon tea,' Fiddle explained, passing her the mug. 'It will make you feel better. Drink.'

Felix took a sip. It tasted delicious and warmed her instantly. It was like drinking firelight. She wondered if every drink made by magicians tasted like some kind of light. Immediately, the heaviness in her head began to subside.

'Baby blanket?'

'Hmm?' Fiddle gazed at her.

'You knew it was my baby blanket.'

'Ah. Yes. Well, I recognised it.'

'From when you took me to the orphanage?'

Fiddle twitched uncomfortably.

'Yes, that's right.' He coughed and drank from his mug.

'I believe you may have some questions for me at this point,' he said hesitantly.

Felix nodded slowly but to her surprise, her mind was utterly blank. The events of the last twenty-four hours had not yet been processed and she didn't know where to start. Fiddle seemed to recognise her struggle and intervened.

'I'll explain and if you have a question, stop me. Yes?'

Again, Felix nodded.

'Before you were born, I was a friend of your parents. They chose me to be your Magister; a teacher, primarily, and a guardian should anything ever happen to them.' At this, Fiddle looked down into the liquid of his mug. He coughed lightly.

'After their death, I was...unable to protect you. I had no choice but to leave you in the charge of an old friend.'

'Nanny Maude?' Felix asked in surprise. Fiddle nodded, an affectionate smile drifting over his face.

'How is Maudie?'

Felix raised an eyebrow, unable to connect the rotund, harsh woman she knew with the girlish name Fiddle used.

'Tired. Bitter. Poor. Same as all the commoners,' Felix said bluntly. Nanny Maude had said nothing of this man but somehow he knew her. Had Nanny Maude known all along who Felix was?

She thought back to her childhood. Nanny Maude hovering over her, fussing about rules and safety, removing her from school after the incident with Mr Gelding, locking her away. 'For safekeeping,' Nanny Maude would always say.

Of course she had known.

Fiddle was contemplative. He looked depressed, like the thought of Nanny Maude had upset him. She wondered briefly if he had loved her, but she had the rather distinct impression that Nanny Maude wasn't quite Fiddle's type. Maybe he just felt sorry for her.

'What happened to my parents?' Felix asked, her voice nearly inaudible. Fiddle raised his eyes slowly, his face void of expression. It took him a long time to answer. Felix waited patiently, her blood pumping in her ears, almost blotting out the sound of the clock which was ticking frantically.

'They were murdered,' he said finally, his voice rough and slightly choked. Felix waited for the shock, the grief, the pain; anything at all. But nothing came. She was numb.

'Why?' she asked simply.

Fiddle shook his head and rested his head in his hands. His beard nearly touched the floor as his crouched over his knees.

'I need to apologise once again, Felix. I don't know how to talk about this. Not yet. I promise you, I will tell you everything but...' His voice trailed off.

'They were magicians,' Felix said softly. Fiddle nodded, still holding his head in his hands.

'I'm a magician.'

'Yes,' Fiddle whispered. Felix waited.

She felt as though she was floating above herself, observing the conversation rather than being part of it. Somewhere, deep inside her, she recognised that her whole life had been a lie, that she was part of the very race that she had grown to fear and despise. This information seemed to be stored away in her brain until she recovered enough feeling and sense to deal with it. A breath of air left her mouth loudly and Fiddle quickly looked at her. His eyes seemed leaden and full of sadness. Felix vaguely wondered what he had to feel sad about. This wasn't happening to him. It was happening to *her*.

'Yes, you are a magician. You can wield magic.'

'No I can't,' Felix said firmly. 'I have never used magic in my life.'

'No, you won't have done. Today is your sixteenth birthday. You have come of age today.'

Again, the realisation that Fiddle had known it was her birthday was stored away to be examined later.

'I don't understand,' Felix swallowed. She had seen magician children. She remembered that awful Godspell boy who had slapped her, Tristan being dragged away from her outside Grieves and Hawkins Fine Glovemakers.

'You are more than a magician, Felix. Those spirals on your face are the markings of a Drow.'

'A Drow,' she repeated. The word held no meaning for her. Fiddle sat back into his chair and seemed to have gathered some composure.

'The Drow are a powerful race of elves.'

'Elves? As in pointy ears and treehouses?' Felix couldn't help the disbelief in her voice. A smile even played on her lips. How utterly ridiculous.

'Of course not,' winced Fiddle in distaste. 'This isn't a fairy tale. The Drow are the same as any magician only their ability to use magic comes from their emotions rather than a learned trait. Your mother was a Drow and so you are half Drow.'

'Wait, so you're saying I'm half Drow, half magician,' Felix closed her eyes. Her head felt full of wool, like it couldn't store anything else.

'Yes. A very powerful mix indeed,' Fiddle admitted. 'The Drow are an all-female race, Felix. Their power comes to them when they reach their sixteenth year, which is why you have not shown any evidence of magical ability until now. A blessing, all things considered. The Drow are now all but extinct. Godspell fears anyone or anything that is not a magician. When he came to power, the Drow were slaughtered. You may be the last.'

'Godspell,' she muttered. His face was conjured in her mind's eye. She swallowed nervously. 'What has Godspell got to do with any of this?'

Fiddle locked his eyes on hers. 'Everything.'

'You're confusing me, Mr Fiddle...Friebel...whatever you call yourself. Why is your name unsafe? Why were you unable to protect me? Why was I put in an orphanage for commoners if I'm a magician, a Drow or whatever it is that you claim I am? And who are you, really? What do you know?!' The questions poured out of Felix's mouth, her voice becoming louder and angrier. Fiddle raised his hands up to quieten her and he frowned at the tirade.

'Alright, Felix. Alright,' he answered. 'Please, sit. I'll try to explain. There's so much...It's difficult to know what to tell you, where to begin. I'll try.'

Felix sat down again, a little alarmed at her anger.

'Your father, Everard and I were good friends. I met him when I was fresh out of The Academy and working as a tutor. He was my apprentice and it was my job to train him to use magic, to access the Second Plane. It's a rite of passage for all young magicians, to learn how to see and move into the Second Plane, for it is our birth right as magicians to enter into the Plane from whence we came. He was a studious teenager; very committed. He made excellent progress and was able to access the Second Plane without aid by the time he was thirteen. It was there that he met your mother, Calantha. The Drow have always stayed on the Second Plane. Their markings on their face made them conspicuous on this Plane and, at that point, commoners were not aware of magicians, let alone the Drow.

Calantha was beautiful and powerful. She was three annums your father's senior. Her face was half-covered with shimmering blue spirals that glowed when she used her magic. She was a fierce thing to behold when she was in a temper...something I suspect you may have in common with her. And yet she was as good-hearted a woman as any I have ever met, her fiery nature softened by the stoic calmness of your father.

'Your father fell in love with Calantha when he was under my tutelage. But the divide between them was painful. Everard could not give up his life on this Plane to join her on the Second Plane, nor could she enter this world without living in hiding. Their dream of a life together looked dim until the magicians revealed themselves to the commoners.'

Fiddle paused. He regarded Felix carefully and seemed to be on the edge of a confession. He blinked quickly and returned to his tale. Felix felt certain that there was something he had not revealed.

'At the Great Revelation, when the magicians made known their existence to the commoners, the Drow were free to enter into this Plane and so your mother and father were united at last. I attended their wedding. It was a beautiful day.'

Felix took a sharp breath. She felt her mouth beginning to dry and she drank more of the cinnamon tea. It was growing cold.

'I was, at that time, the Minister for Education. I worked with both commoners and magicians to unite our children in integrated education. I planned for a new curriculum designed to teach the histories of commoner and magician equally. Commoners would not be kept ignorant of magic either. They would learn all about it in their science classes...though I must confess we were not prepared to reveal the source of magic to them. The Flame is too precious for it to be jeopardised. There were talks of revealing this knowledge later, when we were certain that commoner and magician integration had worked successfully on both sides.

'But that was never to be.'

'Godspell?' Felix asked. Fiddle nodded, a flit of hatred dancing across his eyes.

'He was a ruthlessly ambitious young politician. He had always been against integration stating that the magicians were the superior race. Godspell said that magicians were like gods, able to see the fabric that made up our existence and shape it, change it...destroy it. He became purist; condemning any living thing that wasn't a magician, even the Drow. He claimed that they were no better than magical creatures. Their power was frightening to him because it didn't stem from venephysics. It was too unpredictable, too tangled with the emotions of the women who controlled the power. We tried to squash him down. His ideas were drastic and irrational, yes, but he was young and we felt he posed no threat to the integration. How wrong we were.'

'Mr Fiddle-'

'Please, call me Alchemus. It has remained unused for too long and I do think it is such a grand name.'

'Alright. Alchemus, is Corbin Godspell the Firelighter?' Felix watched as Fiddle's eyes fluttered closed resignedly.

When he answered, the very words in his mouth seemed to disgust him.

'Yes, he guards the sacred Flame as the Firelighter. And he's the Grand Vizier, the Commandant of the COPPs, the 'Right Honourable' Corbin blasted Godspell.'

Felix's heart pounded at Fiddle's anger. He was a magician and Godspell was his leader. She had not expected to see such rage against Godspell coming from a magician. She thought such hatred was a trait of the commoners alone. She swallowed more cold tea and waited for Fiddle to calm himself. He ran his fingers deftly through his hair and in the light, Felix could have sworn it looked browner than grey but when she squinted, she saw it was the same charcoal colour as before.

'My history teacher told me he killed the Queen and a man called the Prime Minister. Is that true?' she asked after a moment.

Fiddle didn't try to hide his shock.

'Your history teacher is very brave to have told you that.'

'He was,' Felix nodded. Fiddle held her gaze until he too nodded in understanding.

'Yes,' he sighed. 'It's true. Though Godspell didn't murder them himself. He had them assassinated. He doesn't like to get his hands dirty.' Fiddle practically spat out the words.

'It happened over the course of one night,' he continued. 'The night you were born. In one, single evening, every world was changed.'

'The night I was born?' Felix whispered. Fiddle nodded slowly. Felix began to see a solution to the riddles of information Fiddle was presenting to her.

'Alchemus, did Godspell murder my parents?'

The question froze the moment. Even the strange tick-tocking of the clock stopped and the only sound was that of the crackling fire, swirling in interest as the only witness to the scene.

Fiddle stared at Felix. Her gaze upon him was intense and seemed to bore into him. Almost imperceptibly, he nodded.

'Why?' breathed Felix. The word seemed caught behind a lump that was quickly forming inside her throat. She struggled to swallow it down.

'Felix...your father was the Firelighter. The leader of the magicians and the guardian of the sacred Flame.'

Neither of them spoke.

Fiddle watched the young girl in front of him carefully. Her face, striking in its resemblance both to her mother and her father and rather frightening in the glow of the fire, lighting up her newly acquired Drow markings, underwent a series of emotional transformations. First, her eyes widened, shock freezing their blueness before turning them into burning rage of anger.

The clock began to tick, slowly to begin with, then gradually building in rhythm, matching a heartbeat before whirring into a chaotic thrum of noise. Fiddle looked at it nervously then glanced back at Felix.

'Be calm,' he whispered, holding out his hand as though trying to convince a lion not to attack.

'Calm?' Felix mumbled, her eyes puckering as though she could not understand his request. 'You expect me to be calm?' Felix lurched forward, the half empty cup of cinnamon tea crashing to the floor, smashing and spilling its contents. The girl stood over Fiddle, her face a fury of tears and bitterness.

'How can you tell me this and expect me to be calm? My whole life has been a lie, do you understand that? My whole life has just...disintegrated! Before I came here, to you, I still had a mum and dad; they were alive even if it was just inside my head. And now they're dead but not just that; they've been murdered. By a man I'm now expected to follow as my leader?! How can I be calm?!'

Felix's breath was fast and hard. Her face was burning, like lava was scorching through the spirals on her face instead of blood. A wail began in her stomach, bubbling up into an inhuman moan. When the tears washed over the spirals on her cheek, she could hear the hissing as the liquid steamed. She wanted to break something. She wanted to hurt something. She wanted to cause terror, destruction, ruination. Looking down at her hands she felt how inadequate they were to cause the devastation that she wanted to inflict. The moan turned into a scream and it terrified her. She couldn't believe such a sound was coming from her; it sounded like growling, like a wolf stalking its prey.

'Felix!' Fiddle cried at her. He was stood in arms reach of her and was stepping slowly towards her, but it looked like he was shielding her. She followed his gaze and saw that the growling was not coming from her. She saw the fearsome gleam of teeth, bared and menacing as black lips parted and a vicious growl came out of them. Felix stumbled backwards, tripping over the smashed mug and nearly falling into the fire but Fiddle grabbed her and held her fiercely.

'Get behind me,' he ordered, and Felix saw his whole demeanour change. Gone was the stooped old man with a limp. In front of her stood a man of fifty, hair brown and glossy and eyes ferocious as he stared at the creature threatening them.

Felix felt the influx of pain and anger leave her, like a tidal wave crashing back into a serene ocean. As Fiddle reached out his arm, suddenly much more muscular than they had been, and reached out his gloved hand to perform some sort of magic, Felix stepped in front of him.

'Stop, stop!' she shouted. Her throat was hoarse. She stood between Fiddle and the wolf. Fiddle looked at her like she was insane. 'Stop, Alchemus, he's my friend!'

Fiddle looked doubtingly at the wolf and gripped at Felix's hand to pull her back as she stepped towards the animal.

'It's D.W,' she said as though this was an explanation. 'The dire wolf.'

The creature was still growling menacingly at Fiddle but as Felix crept closer towards him and began to stroke the shaggy fur of his hackles, the dire wolf softened, though he still kept a wary eye on the magician.

'You came back,' Felix smiled but the dire wolf noted relief and pain in her voice. He pricked his ears, listening to the maelstrom inside her mind.

'You were in trouble,' the dire wolf replied in his voiceless manner.

'She was not in trouble until you arrived here,' Fiddle said smartly. Felix glanced at them both in surprise. *He can hear you too?* she thought, and she saw the dire wolf nod.

'I'm fine, honestly. I just had some bad news.'

The dire wolf tilted his head and whimpered a little in sympathy, resting his paw on her hand.

'Alchemus, this is D.W. He led me here to you. He's a dire wolf. Not a dog,' she grinned weakly.

'Yes, I know what dire wolves are, Felix,' Fiddle said in an exasperated way.

'D.W?' the wolf inquired, an eyebrow raised.

'Yes. Do you mind?'

The dire wolf shook his head.

'No. I've never had a name before.' His tail wagged happily. 'You're sure you're ok?'

'Yes, Felix,' interrupted Fiddle. 'Are you?'

'I think so,' Felix answered weakly. 'I don't know what happened. It just all got too much. I'm sorry.'

'You should sit,' D.W nudged her with his nose.

'I agree,' Fiddle said, looking down at the wolf in irritation.

'So what happened?' D.W asked as he trotted alongside Felix, nudging her into the armchair that Fiddle had been sitting in. She let herself fall into it. Fiddle tutted under his breath and glared in annoyance at D.W whilst he smiled back smugly.

'Oh, the usual stuff, you know; found out I was a magician and that my parents murdered by the leader of the Magistry.'

'Yeah, I knew you were a magician,' D.W said.

'What? How did *you* know? Does everybody know more about me than I do?!'

'Only magicians can see dire wolves, Felix,' Fiddle said softly. 'They're made up of magic. Commoners can't see magic.'

'And you didn't think it would be useful to tell me I was a magician?' Felix folded her arms and glared at D.W moodily.

'Hey, you were just a job! It wasn't my place.'

'If I was just a job, why are you here?'

'You still felt...lost.'

Felix continued to glare at the dire wolf and he held her gaze confidently. Eventually, Felix relaxed and looked away, admitting defeat. Fiddle chuckled.

'I think you ought to go to bed, Felix. It's late. I'll make up a bed,' he said, pushing himself up from the chair. Felix noticed that he was back to normal now, complete with grey hair, wrinkles and a limp.

'Oh no you don't. I still have questions for you,' Felix demanded, ignoring the yawn that tried to escape her mouth.

'And I have answers for you. But not now. In the morning. You've had a very long, tiring day. You must rest.'

Felix had no energy to argue with him. She felt drained and empty and oddly thirsty.

'Well now, dire wolf. Thank you for your services. You may leave,' Fiddle said to D.W.

'No chance,' the animal replied, sitting down firmly on his hind legs in front of Fiddle. His head was the same height at Fiddle's pocket watch. Felix shook her head in amazement. 'I'm not leaving her.'

'But-' Fiddle began indignantly.

'Come stay with me, then,' Felix interrupted before Fiddle could answer. She picked up her baby blanket and folded it under her arm tenderly 'That's ok, isn't it Alchemus?'

Fiddle clenched his fists. He rather disliked animals.

'It's fine,' he said through gritted teeth. 'I'll show you to your room.'

Before he closed the double mahogany doors of the Reading Room, Fiddle scanned his blue eyes around the room. With a flick of his wrist, the smashed mug on the floor mended itself and flew up to rest on the table. The cinnamon tea stain dried instantly, though the smell lingered. Finally, Fiddle motioned towards the fire and the flames disappeared as though suddenly having entered a vacuum. With one last look around, Fiddle closed the doors.

The Reading Room sighed and as the books fell asleep, the ticking of the clock fell silent.

10
A True Friend

Doors again. Doors everywhere. Hatches. That's what they were. She knew that now. All she had to do was open one of the doors and she could go anywhere she wanted to. But she was afraid.

'You're on your way to your destiny,' said the Catchoo, tail wagging. 'Just open a door.'

Felix turned around.

'Which door?'

'The right one,' replied the Catchoo. Her purring was too loud. It was distracting.

'Which is the right one?' Felix asked. Panic. More doors. *Wake up!*

The Catchoo shrugged her bony shoulders and purred louder. Felix ran from one door to the next. Red doors. Blue doors. Polished knockers, brass handles. The spiral door was there too, its pattern dancing on the wood. No mirror this time.

Too many, too many, too many!

Boom!

Wake up. Please wake up.

BOOM!

The noise came from the oak door with the old hinges. Dust fell from the wood. The handle rattled as though someone was trying to open it.

'No!' Felix cried out. 'Stay away!'

The door crashed open.

Wake up!

'Felix! Wake up!'

She opened her eyes, gasping for breath. Sweat was trickling down her forehead and it was stinging on her cheek where her skin was burning. She pushed away at the blankets that tangled around her legs.

'Shhh, Felix,' came a voice from inside her head. 'It's ok. You're safe.'

'Dire wolf,' Felix murmured hoarsely. 'D.W?'

'Yes, that's right. I'm here.'

Felix closed and reopened her eyes, allowing them to adjust to the darkness. She felt a heavy weight settle on the bed next to her and she reached out and touched the warm fur of the wolf.

'You were dreaming. I could see,' he said in his secret voice. He nuzzled his wet snout into Felix's hand.

'There were doors,' Felix whispered. She was shivering even though she was still damp with sweat. She felt the dire wolf nod.

'Why is it so dark in here?' she asked. She could barely see anything, just the faint outlines and dark shapes of shelves and a teetering pile of books next to her bed. D.W shifted and jumped to the floor. Felix saw his dark silhouette spring up to the door and heard the scratch of his paws on the handle of the door as he opened it.

Light flooded the room, pouring in from the window above the staircase just in front of her room. Felix squinted, gently touching the tender skin on her face.

She was in a tiny, old study room that had been converted into a makeshift bedroom. The bed was a creaky old camp bed with lumpy pillows and moth-eaten blankets and there was no window. The walls were panelled with wood and a huge, sun-bleached bookshelf took up most of the wall space, with every nook and cranny of it stuffed with books and parchments and scrolls.

'Thank you,' Felix smiled at D.W. He turned to look at her, tilting his head in concern.

'It's just a dream I have sometimes,' she said trying to reassure him, though she couldn't stop herself from trembling. The dream had been so lucid. She swore she could still hear the purring of the Catchoo.

'If I ever see that little fleabag again, I'll wring her scrawny neck,' D.W growled. Felix laughed softly but once again she heard the Catchoo's strange prophesy ringing in her ears.

'I told you to ignore her,' chastised D.W. He trotted over and rested his head on the edge of the bed, looking at her with his doleful, golden eyes.

'Yeah, I know,' Felix nodded. Absently, she pulled her baby blanket towards her and studied the familiar spirals sewn into the fabric. She stopped suddenly, reached down to her rucksack and rummaged through it. D.W watched her for a moment and then, catching onto her train of thought, he too began to study the blanket carefully.

Felix emerged from her bag holding a cracked pocket mirror. She gazed into it, looking hard at the new markings on her face then looking down at the blanket again.

'They're the same spirals,' she breathed. D.W stared at her face and nodded resignedly.

'I guess it's all true then,' Felix sighed. She had half believed this was all some kind of practical joke, or a hoax. It was all just too unreal to believe. But she had to believe it. The evidence was literally staring her in the face. It was *her* reflection, *her* face looking back her, emblazoned with black spirals that snaked their way elegantly down from her forehead; the same spirals that had been so beautifully crafted on her baby blanket.

She fell back against the lumpy pillow with a flump. Was it really only yesterday that she had been lying in her bed in the orphanage, dreaming of who her parents might have been? Never in her wildest imaginings could she have dreamt up the truth; that her parents were powerful magicians and that her own father had been the magicians' Firelighter.

'You need some breakfast,' D.W said interrupting her thoughts.

'Mmm,' Felix nodded in agreement. She wasn't especially hungry but her mouth was parched.

She climbed out of bed and began searching for her jeans; she'd slept in a baggy old t-shirt that she'd brought with her from the orphanage but didn't feel it was appropriate breakfast wear with a magician. D.W turned around respectfully and Felix smiled, thinking that she'd really love some of Nigel's lemonade.

Just as she had thought of his name, Nigel walked through the door. D.W barked at him angrily and Felix, who had her jeans pulled half way up, jumped in surprise and fell over onto her bed.

'Oh! Felix! I'm so sorry!' stuttered Nigel. His face flushed scarlet. 'I didn't think you'd be awake. I'm sorry. I should have knocked-'

'Turn around!' Felix interrupted him, trying to cover herself with her blanket. Nigel spun around quickly, accidentally punching D.W's snout with his fist.

When Alchemus J. Fiddle walked into the room, Felix was scrambling around with her too small baby blanket wrapped around her waist, trying to hold a snarling dire wolf back from Nigel, who was cringing against the bookshelf with a face that could only be described as puce.

'Good morning, all,' Fiddle sang happily. 'How nice it is to have young people around. Fighting already I see?'

A cacophony of explanations and growls arose and Fiddle silenced them all by raising his hand.

'How lovely,' he said serenely. 'Felix, that blanket is simply charming on you, though I think you've rather outgrown it. If the gentleman and...gentlewolf would kindly leave your quarters, you may change into something more suitable.'

Fiddle handed Felix a pile of neatly folded clothes. Before she had a chance to thank him, Fiddle had left her room, followed by a blushing and muttering Nigel who was being menacingly stalked by D.W.

Felix giggled and shut the door a little, allowing her some privacy and a little light. She made a mental note to ask about a lamp. She couldn't see any plug sockets and guessed she'd have to use a candle though she felt rather nervous about that as she observed the precarious piles of books and parchments.

Unfolding the clothes, Felix felt a grin spreading across her face. Fiddle had brought her a beautiful dark blue skirt with black ruffles descending from the waistband. There was a deep purple blouse to match, with fiddly buttons on the collar. But what made her gasp was the beautiful pair of blue silk gloves carefully folded and separated by delicate red tissue paper. She held them tentatively, smiling a little as she saw the label on the inside of the gloves: "Grieves and Hawkins. Fine Glovemakers."

Dressing quickly and feeling awkward in so many layers of fabric, Felix glared at the gloves, leaving them until last. Only when she had finished buttoning her collar and brushing her wild hair, did she pull them over her hands. She moved her fingers inside them. Her hands felt hot and clammy and constricted by the soft material. They were beautiful but she wasn't sure she liked them.

Betrayal rinsed through her as she picked up her tatty jeans and her faded t-shirt. Fiddle hadn't brought her any shoes so she slipped on her old trainers, feeling a strange relief that she didn't have to abandon everything from her old life. She let the skirt drop over them and found that the trainers were not visible beneath the ruffles. Felix smiled, flexed her hands and went to find a bathroom to brush her teeth.

When she opened the door to the Reading Room, Felix found it empty. It was strangely eerie in the grey light and though the room was tall and vast, Felix felt claustrophobic. The fire wasn't lit and it didn't feel as comfortable as it had done the night before.

Walking to the book stacks, Felix traced her fingers over the spines of the books. Even through the gloves, she felt them shiver as she touched them and her fingertips tingled.

So many books, she thought to herself, casting her eyes around the room. She pulled out a particularly old book, intrigued by the cracked, brown leather binding.

'Helebor's Herbals,' she whispered, reading the peeling gold leaf inscription. Smiling at the name, she flicked through the yellowing pages, catching glimpses of detailed illustrations of oddly named ingredients. She placed it back on the shelf and picked up another, this one titled "Astral Astronomy". She read a few lines and felt her head getting fuzzy with the long words and the swirling script.

Putting it back, Felix thought that she would never be able to understand all there was to know about magic. She wasn't even sure that she'd be able to do magic the way the magicians did. She had no training and had barely managed to get her head around the three Planes.

'Hey.'

Felix turned quickly, feeling as though she had just been caught doing something she wasn't supposed to. It was Nigel, standing with his hands in the pockets of his dusty trousers, looking awkward.

'Hey,' Felix replied. 'I was just looking around. I didn't mean to snoop.'

'It's a library. You're allowed to look at the books,' Nigel smiled. Felix shuffled nervously.

'You want some breakfast? I can show you where the kitchen is.'

Felix nodded half-heartedly, though she wasn't really hungry. In fact, she'd lost her appetite entirely. She cast her eyes around the room again and found that she wanted to stay and look at the books.

'I can take you on a tour,' Nigel said, sensing her hesitation. 'If you like?'

Felix smiled. 'Yeah. That'd be great.'

Nigel grinned and stepped towards the stacks.

'These are the reference books. They're mostly old magical texts that gather dust but they're pretty useful if you find yourself trying to do a tricky bit of magic. Archibald... sorry, Alchemus, keeps some general interest reference books on the upper galley. Mostly commoner interests from before the Great Revelation that magicians still enjoy. I can show you –'

'Why did he change his name?'

'Huh?'

'Alchemus. He said he was now Archibald Friebel. What's that about?'

Nigel rubbed the back of his neck and studied a book called "Amulets and Talismans Volume Eight."

'Uh, it wasn't safe for him to use that name after he...'

'After he took me to the orphanage?' Felix finished.

Nigel nodded. 'Yeah.' He finally looked up at Felix. 'Look, he told me what he told you. It must be pretty hard hearing all that. I think he always hoped that you'd know deep down that you were a magician, so he wouldn't have to be the one the tell you.'

'So, you knew about me, too?'

'Of course. Alchemus told me about you annums ago. He trusts me. I think he'd had a bit too much ashwater when he told me, but...'

'You talk like you've known him for a long time. I thought you were his new apprentice?'

'I am. But I've been coming here most of my life. My parents died when I was four, you see, and my great aunt took me in, but she was old and didn't really know who I was. She's a bit batty to be honest. Couldn't do magic properly and was always going into the wrong hatches and getting stuck in between doors.

I started coming here as soon as I could use the hatches to get across the city. My dad was a library member when he was alive and he was always talking about this old eccentric StoryKeeper, 'Archibald Friebel'. When I arrived here that first day, Archi- Alchemus took one look at me and said, "you're Erik's boy". He gave me my dad's old membership and put me to work in the Younger's Room and told me to sort out the good books from the bad.

When I turned seventeen last month, he took me on as his apprentice, which is a good thing really because my great aunt is one egg short of a basket. You know she set fire to her curtains last week because she said they sneezed at her? Batty.'

Felix laughed softly. 'So Alchemus... he's ok? I can trust him?'

'Definitely,' Nigel nodded. 'But then...I am a magician. You can't trust magicians, can you?' He grinned playfully at Felix and she nudged him with her shoulder.

'Well, I guess I'm a magician now, so I'll have to learn to trust you.'

Nigel grinned lopsidedly and rubbed at the auburn curls at the back of his neck.

'Uh..you look pretty by the way,' he mumbled motioning his hand in brown suede gloves up and down her outfit. Felix smiled at the compliment and reached for a stray strand of her hair and began twisting it.

'Thanks. You too,' she replied and immediately felt stupid. Nigel laughed, brushing down his faded cotton shirt and burgundy corduroy trousers.

'I try,' he smiled.

They wandered out of the Reading Room into a hallway where a staircase circled in front of them. There were rooms to the left and right next to a sticky, rusted elevator that was clearly out of use.

'This is the Story Room,' Nigel said excitedly. 'It's one of my favourite rooms.'

He pulled at Felix's elbow and she followed him through the door on the right. It was a small but friendly looking room, with a large polished table at the centre. The walls were shelved with books and the smell of age and well-read pages were even stronger in here than in the Reading Room.

'Listen,' Nigel whispered, closing his eyes. Felix strained her ears and at first, she heard nothing, but then...

'The books!' she said in surprise. 'They're talking!'

'Mmm hmm,' Nigel sighed contentedly. 'They like you. They only talk when they're in good company.'

'What are they saying?' Felix leaned her ear to one of the shelves to try to hear better.

'They're telling stories, of course. All books tell stories, even when nobody is reading them. It's magic...but a completely different kind of magic. Magic that even commoners can do.'

He lifted out a purple paperback book with a picture of a surprised looking young boy on the cover. It looked like it had been read thousands of times.

'One of my favourites,' Nigel admitted. 'It's a book all about magic and adventures, written by a commoner before commoners even knew about us magicians. Godspell banned it, but Alchemus kept this one for me.

So many commoners wrote such wonderful stories; they transport you to another world. And they do it just with words. That's real magic to me.'

Felix smiled and ran her hand over the book just as a soft chug-chugging of a steam train drifted from its pages. She shook her head in disbelief and passed it back to Nigel who stroked it affectionately.

They left the reading room and climbed up the staircase where several storeys of rooms revealed themselves. Felix was bewitched. She had never known so many books could exist under one roof.

'In the quarter,' she said, casting her eyes up at the shelves that reached the ceiling, 'books are really rare. Most of them are burned by the COPPs in raids. I don't even know why; maybe they do it just because they can.'

Nigel cautiously reached for her hand and squeezed it softly.

'Sorry,' he said and there was conviction in his voice. 'I had no idea.'

Felix believed him. His green eyes were honest behind his glasses and she began to wonder if the magicians were ignorant to the hell the commoners lived in.

He showed her the book stacks of the music rooms where the parchments and scrolls of music played their melodies soothingly as she picked up each one. In the Poetry Room, Felix listened to the rhythm and rhymes of words written hundreds of years ago and felt her drifting into a cloud of verse. She left feeling sleepy and relaxed. There was the Art Room, the Atlas Room, the Cookery Room, which had a mouth-watering smell of bacon, though Nigel said all he could smell was vanilla. So many rooms, each of them a wonder to Felix and a million miles away from the tiny book room she had known in the quarter.

Finally, Nigel led her into the History Room and for the first time, Felix was disappointed. It was a sad room, half empty and seeming lonely somehow; as though it had once contained secrets that were now forgotten. Felix looked at Nigel questioningly.

'Godspell,' Nigel mumbled, and he needed to say no more than that. But still, Felix loved the room, with the murals on the wall of ancient battle scenes and tapestries of kings and queens. Nigel explained that the room was rarely used so Alchemus was able to include a little commoner history in there, though it was dangerous to do so.

'He thinks that everyone should be able to access all the knowledge they want. If they're willing to learn, then they should have the opportunity.'

Felix looked around the room sadly, wondering what histories the room had once held. There was so much she wanted to know and she was beginning to worry that she would never discover the answers to her questions.

'Nigel?' she said softly. 'Why wasn't it safe for him?'

Nigel turned and looked at Felix. She was fiddling with a ruffle on her skirt and there was a crease between her brow that seemed to make the spirals on her face even darker; darker, even, than her long, wild hair.

'Godspell knew your parents had appointed him Magister. Alchemus was their friend. If anyone was going to try and get revenge for their death, it would be him.'

'Why didn't he? Get revenge?'

Nigel heard the hurt in Felix's voice and winced.

'You should talk to Alchemus, Felix.'

She nodded but there was something in her eyes that made Nigel feel he had disappointed her. Hesitating only a little, he wrapped his arm around her shoulders.

'Come on,' he said. 'You can help me in the Alchemical Equation Room.'

Felix groaned and Nigel giggled.

'Breakfast, then?' he asked.

'Breakfast,' Felix smiled.

11
The Secret History

The kitchen was a large, rectangular room tucked away in the serpentine basement. Felix felt sure that she would never be able to navigate her way around the winding corridors, especially in the orange light of the floating orbs that illuminated the corridors. Compared to the upper levels, the basement felt oddly industrial. It looked like it had been turned into a sort of underground bunker. There were small, square rooms opening from the narrow corridors, revealing storage boxes and filing cabinets filled with books (of course.) Other rooms looked like pantries, with row after row of shelves with containing tinned food and bottles of water.

By the time, Nigel had led her into the kitchen, Felix was pretty certain that the basement had been prepared as a hideaway for a small number of people and she was curious.

D.W was in the kitchen, lying against a cupboard and licking his snout happily, a large empty bowl at his side.

'Macaroni cheese,' he said contentedly as he sighed.

'I see everything fits you,' Fiddle said, turning around from the long sideboard where he was preparing something which smelled delicious. Felix nodded and thanked him, and he smiled in return.

'Nigel, you let the milk go off,' he said sternly, moving his eyes to Felix's companion. Nigel rolled his eyes.

'I'll go get some more,' he said as his shoulders slumped. He pulled a face behind Fiddle's back and Felix stifled a giggle.

'Wait, maybe I could go with you?' Felix asked excitedly. She was desperate to see more of the city and now that she was a magician, she didn't have to fear the COPPs. Nigel glanced over at Fiddle, who turned and looked at him; both had a wary expression on their faces. D.W's ears pricked up and he sat up on his hind legs, looking at them back and forth in interest.

'What?' Felix asked uneasily.

'My dear, I'm afraid you can't go with him,' Fiddle said tentatively. He turned away from the counter and leaned against it, folding his arms across his beard. Felix noticed he was wearing different gloves today; mustard- coloured ones with a lace frill at the wrist.

'Oh, ok,' Felix deflated. She sat down at the scrubbed table at the centre of the kitchen and began to fiddle absently with a lone fork. 'Why?'

Felix once again noticed Fiddle and Nigel exchange glances.

'I'm off,' Nigel said quickly, making a swift exit. D.W looked at him and the expression on his face suggested that he was thinking about going with him, but instead, he rested his front legs on the floor and placed his head between them.

'You're not going to like this,' he said only to Felix.

'Felix, you can't leave the library,' Fiddle said holding her gaze.

'Today?'

'No. Not just today. You can't leave here for a while. It's not safe for you.'

Felix leaned back in her chair and looked down at D.W for confirmation. He nodded slightly and his eyes were wary, as though she was a time bomb about to explode.

'Oh.'

Felix waited for Fiddle to explain but he was hesitant. She tensed her jaw, frustrated at his silence. After a few moments, Fiddle turned around to the counter and then presented a plate of steaming bacon, eggs and toast to Felix, who glared down at it, refusing to acknowledge how good it looked.

Her stomach gave a low grumble, betraying her.

'Eat,' Fiddle said, setting down a knife to go with the fork that Felix continued to play with. She swallowed, her mouth-watering at the smell of bacon, but she shook her head.

'I'll eat when you talk. You have a lot of explaining to do.'

'Oh? What do I have left to tell you?' Fiddle raised his eyebrows and sat down opposite her. Felix rolled her eyes. She was quickly catching onto Fiddle's skilful methods of distraction and digression.

'Well, for starters, you can tell me why I can't leave the library. Then you can tell me why you had to change your name, and why you suddenly seemed about twenty years younger last night. Then there's always the reason why my parents were murdered, why I was sent to a commoner orphanage and finally, you can explain what happened to me last night when I lost my temper! I think that's rather a lot of explaining, don't you? I'm not an idiot, Alchemus. I know there are things you've neglected to tell me.'

Fiddle began to examine the lace on his glove and pursed his lips in thought. When he looked up at Felix, his fists were clenched. D.W sat up again and trotted towards him. Felix watched and thought that D.W was saying something only Fiddle could hear. The magician nodded and leaned forward.

'You can't leave the library because you have Drow markings and you would be instantly recognised. As I told you last night, Godspell slaughtered the Drow and would not hesitate to do the same to you.

'Jumping to your last question, when you lost your temper you gave a rather magnificent display of Drow magic, though I suspect you have a lot more to give. Drow magic is ruled by emotions, remember? You were quite angry and upset last night. Therefore it is natural for some of that emotion to leak out in the form of magic.'

Felix nodded her understanding with wide eyes. Drow magic was something she would have to learn to control quickly. She motioned to Fiddle to continue.

'I had to change my name because Godspell would have killed me had he found me, simply because I was your parents' ally and I know the truth of their death. As for my appearance, I am not quite as old as I appear.'

'How old are you?' Felix asked. Fiddle chuckled.

'Old enough, though that's beside the point. I changed my appearance so that I am not recognised. I was a wanted man, Felix. Godspell ensured that the public would blame me for your parents' murder.'

'What do you mean?' Felix asked. D.W shuffled on his feet and let out a quiet whine. Felix did not take this to be a good sign.

Fiddle sighed. 'Godspell said that I murdered your parents.'

Felix felt her heart dip into her stomach and for a moment, she thought she would be sick. She pushed away the plate of food, untouched and chewed on her lip, trying to breathe deeply to dispel the nausea. The thought that she was sitting next to the man who had been blamed for her parents' murder was terrifying. What if he was lying?

'He's not lying, Felix,' D.W said to her, his voice firm and comforting. 'I can see that he's telling the truth.'

'Go on,' she said hoarsely to Fiddle. He considered her for a moment and then continued.

'The public had no reason to disbelieve Godspell. He had...convincing reasons in his favour to suggest that I had committed the murders. You must understand that he wasn't feared like he is now. He was simply a young man, highly ranked in the political world. He appeared to be the very picture of grief and revenge at the loss of Everard and Calantha. How easy it was for him to frame me; to say that I was jealous of the Everard's success and envious of his marriage...to say that I murdered them to gain the title of Firelighter. It was bad enough that he did that, but he also accused me of murdering the Queen and the Michael Browning, the Commoner Prime Minister. I didn't of course. That was Godspell, or one of his henchmen. Godspell doesn't like to get his hands dirty.

'He said that I had tried to kill him, too. He appeared on the commoner televisions the next day, and gave interviews in the Magicians' newspapers to say that I had attacked him as he tried to defend Everard and Calantha...all lies.

'And so, you can see why it wasn't safe for you to stay with me. I changed my name, my age, my appearance; I gave up my home, left my family; I did everything I could to keep myself safe.'

'You ran away? He killed your best friends and you just ran away?' Felix spat out at him in disgust. 'How could you do that? I'd have fought him with every bit of strength I had!'

'That's easy to say, Felix, but I had you to think of. You were my first priority. I had to make sure you were safe. You see, there's more to this than you think.

'Godspell knew Calatha was pregnant. The whole nation knew it and the magicians especially were waiting in anticipation for the birth. On the night of the attacks, Calantha gave birth to you, quite unexpectedly as it happens. You were a week early and we have fate to thank for that. Within minutes of your birth, Calantha and Everard were warned of Godspell's attack. The Queen and Michael Browning were already dead.

'Godspell is a ruthless and evil man, Felix. Never, ever underestimate that. He killed your parents in front of you and then gave orders for you to be killed too. He always was a coward; such a helpless, vulnerable baby, screaming in his arms and he couldn't kill you.'

'You say that like it's a bad thing,' whispered Felix.

'It's not,' Fiddle said softly. 'It was a mercy and another little helping hand from mistress fate. He gave orders for your death to a man who was loyal to Godspell, but who was more loyal to Calantha. Your mother's kindness, endlessly given to a man whom others considered to be a sniveling coward saved you from death and made a weak man brave. The man ordered to kill you could not repay your mother for her friendship by taking the life of her child. The loyalty and admiration he felt for Calantha was stronger than any pledge he had made to Godspell and he risked his life to bring you to me. I've never known bravery like it.'

'What happened to him? The man who saved me?'

Fiddle smiled. 'He's safe and still honouring the memory of your mother by working as an 'inside man' at the Citadel.'

'You mean he still works for Godspell?'

'Oh yes,' Fiddle nodded. 'He is one of our greatest assets.'

Felix inhaled deeply and closed her eyes. She saw the events that Fiddle had shared with her like a puzzle in front of her, but there were still pieces missing. She couldn't see the bigger picture.

'I still don't understand,' she said, opening her eyes. 'Why would Godspell want to kill *me*?'

'For one very simple reason, Felix. Godspell wanted to be the Firelighter and you were an obstacle stopping him from achieving his ambition.'

'How?'

Fiddle looked meaningfully at Felix as though urging her to think. She creased her brow, distracted for a moment by the discomfort of the markings on her face but then, she understood. The realisation of what this meant made the blood drain from her cheeks and the sickness returned.

'Me?' she breathed. 'I was the next in line?'

Fiddle nodded.

'Yes, Felix. You are the real Firelighter.'

D.W and Fiddle looked at Felix as she absorbed all of this information. The wolf kept his ears pricked for thoughts that only he could hear but all he heard was white noise. Felix wasn't thinking; she was feeling and dire wolves couldn't read feelings.

'Are you alright?' he asked her, irritated that he was failing to hear her thoughts.

'I'm not sure,' Felix admitted. She stroked the fur on the back of his neck. 'It's a lot to handle, you know?'

Fiddle leaned over the table and reached for her hand.

'We're only given what we can take, Felix. You're strong. Remember that.'

'I think...I think I'd like to be alone for a little while,' she muttered. She felt dangerously close to crying and it was taking all of her strength to keep her tears at bay. She wasn't as strong as Fiddle thought she was. He was wrong.

'Of course. I'll leave you to your thoughts. Take all the time you need, but please do eat.' Fiddle squeezed her hand before pushing the plate of food in front of her. He said nothing more and left the kitchen. Felix heard his footsteps echoing down the long corridor.

D.W studied Felix carefully, rubbed his head against her skirt affectionately and left, throwing one last look of concern in Felix's direction.

Only when the soft padding of his paws had died away did Felix hurl the fork across the room.

12
The Second Plane

What was a magician without magic? Felix stared down at her gloved hands and flexed her fingers, dwelling on the question and trying to ignore the buzzing sensation in her fingertips, which was not dissimilar to pins and needles if she thought about it.

The silk of the gloves was damp from the sweat on her palms and she desperately wanted to tear them off, but both Nigel and Fiddle had warned her not to. Magic was too hot to wield with bare hands, they said. Yet Felix felt it was unnatural to have her hands hampered by gloves.

'Again,' Fiddle said gently, interrupting her thoughts. Felix rolled her eyes and slumped her shoulders. Around her, books scattered the floor of the Reading Room, remnants of her failed attempts.

'I can't do it,' she muttered petulantly.

It was past midnight. The clock above the fireplace was ticking boredly as though it too was exhausted. Firelight illuminated the room and the heat was almost unbearable. Felix wanted to open a window but they were clamped shut; a breeze was no good for books, apparently.

'Yes, you can,' Fiddle said simply. He was sat in his armchair, his chin resting on his steepled fingers. Nigel sat on the rug in front of the fire, running his fingers through D.W's fur. He looked as tired as Felix felt.

Frustrated, Felix stretched out her hands once again, reaching for a book on the shelf which stood a metre away from her. She stared at the book, an indifferent brown, leather-bound text with a faded title. Squinting her eyes, Felix tried to *be* the book, tried to put her energy inside it and lift it from the shelf.

So far, she had managed to make several edge towards her, teetering on the lip of the shelf before falling with a loud bang onto the floor. A couple of times, she'd gotten so frustrated and angry that several books had flown off the shelf and thrown themselves down as Felix had stamped her feet in rage. It was enough to make Felix nervous about getting angry, especially after a rather heavy book had landed unceremoniously on D.W's head, making him yelp and lope off towards Nigel sulkily.

The brown book wriggled a little on the shelf, shuffling itself free of the books on either side of it. Felix concentrated hard, imagining that she could feel the book in her hands and pulling at it. Nothing happened.

'I *can't* do this!' Felix shouted, throwing her hands up in the air and pulling at her hair in irritation. Nigel groaned impatiently and leaned back against the empty armchair.

'It's not my fault!' Felix yelled at him. 'I don't know what I'm supposed to be doing!'

'Now, now, Felix,' Fiddle said soothingly, though Felix could see a slight twitch in his chin to suggest that he wasn't feeling quite as patient as he seemed. He was clearing his throat too much, like he had an angry spout of words stuck in his chest.

'Sit and have some tea,' he motioned towards the armchair and poured her a cup of cinnamon tea.

'It's too hot for tea,' she mumbled, collapsing into the armchair and folding her arms.

'Heat is good,' Fiddle explained. 'Heat amplifies the magic. Remember that magic is fire, only a different kind of fire. There are particles of fire in every single object in this room. As a magician, you have an affinity with fire, you are drawn to it, you can feel it and therefore you can control it.'

'I can't control anything,' Felix grumbled, ignoring the tea that Fiddle set down on the table next to her.

'You can if you believe you can,' D.W said, and Nigel nodded in agreement.

'That's true. You really have to believe you're a magician, Felix, if you're going to work magic.'

'I know I'm a magician, ok? Magician, Drow, Firelighter, all rolled into one. Message received, thank you very much.'

Nigel held up his hands in submission and moved away from Felix gingerly,

'Look, that doesn't help, alright?' Felix burst out. 'You can't keep edging around me like I'm about to explode. I get that I'm dangerous and that I need to control my power; I understand that. Do you think I like feeling like this? Like I'm unpredictable and unstable? Nobody wants to control this power more than me but... but..'

'But you're angry,' finished Fiddle. Felix sighed, long and deep and then nodded.

'Yes,' she admitted. 'I'm furious. I hated Godspell enough when I thought I was a commoner. But now I despise him. He took away my family, my freedom and my future and I don't know you can expect me to just...ignore that.'

'We don't want you to ignore it, Felix,' Fiddle said, leaning forwards and looking at her earnestly. 'But right now, you need to store that anger away until you are strong enough to use it.'

Felix deflated and closed her eyes. They didn't understand; how could they? She had no idea who she was or who she was supposed to be. She had once been so certain of her future, poor as it seemed, yet now her life didn't seem to belong to her anymore. What was she supposed to do now? Learn magic, get a job and serve Godspell, the man who had murdered her parents? She couldn't go back to the Commoner's quarter, not looking like she did. They'd cast her out as a traitor. She felt as though she didn't belong anywhere.

'You belong here,' D.W said, only to her.

Then why do I feel lost? She asked him in her mind.

'Because you don't trust your guides,' he answered.

Felix looked down at him. His golden eyes showed no sign of hurt, but it lingered in his words. She said a mental apology, but realised he was right. She was still clinging to the distrust she had of magicians and that was pointless now. She had to trust Fiddle. After all, her parents had trusted him and he had sacrificed everything for her safety.

'Show me the Second Plane,' she said.

'What?' Fiddle asked. Her demand had ruffled him, and the shock was evident in his face. Nigel looked at his master in interest.

'The Second Plane. Show it to me. I need to see it to know what I'm supposed to be looking for. I don't know what magic looks like *inside* something. I can't see it. You said the Second Plane was more transient, that magic is more visible there, right? Well maybe if I can see it there, I'll know what to look for here.'

'As a Magister, I wouldn't normally show an apprentice the Second Plane until they could see magic on the First,' Fiddle said slowly. He looked mildly pained and rested his hand on his chest.

'Why?'

Fiddle hesitated and looked from Felix to Nigel in quick succession.

'Not all apprentices respond well to so much magic so quickly. It requires a lot of faith and trust between the Magister and the apprentice...you could be overwhelmed.'

Felix considered this and she got the feeling that he was afraid to take her to the Second Plane though she couldn't guess why.

'I trust you,' she said. Fiddle regarded her closely. He seemed to be thinking deeply but when Felix looked to the dire wolf, he shrugged his shoulders.

'It could work,' Nigel said, trying to coax Fiddle, but the old magician kept his focus on Felix. She held his gaze, internally willing him to agree. Finally, after what felt like several minutes, he nodded slowly.

'Alright,' he said, 'but I warn you, Felix, you must do everything I tell you.'

'I will,' agreed Felix.

Fiddle stood carefully, looking, for the first time, as though his aged pretence was real. He moved towards the back shelf of the room and looked for a book on the top shelf which was only just in his grasp. When he returned to Felix, he was holding a copy called "Traditional Garden Gnomes" He opened it and Felix saw that the pages had been hollowed out and contained an odd pair of spectacles.

'Sometimes things are best hidden when they're in plain sight,' he winked as he took out the spectacles. They were wire framed with round, purple lenses, but there appeared to be several other lenses layered over each other, all in different colours.

'Spectoccules,' Fiddle called them. 'These will help you to see the Second Plane.'

'Why are they hidden?' Felix asked.

'I don't have a licence to own them,' he admitted with a wry smile. 'Back in your father's day, magicians didn't need a licence to own Spectoccules. A magician could use them to see the Second Plane if and whenever they wanted to. Godspell, however, has a licence list for all magicians that need Spectoccules to see the Second Plane.'

'Not all magicians need them,' Nigel explained to Felix, who looked confused. 'Godspell thinks that anybody needing Spectoccules is a weak magician and he likes to keep an eye on the weak ones.'

Fiddle handed them to Felix. They were surprisingly heavy.

'Err... so is there a trick to this at all?' she asked, manoeuvring the lenses so that some were lifted up and some were down over the purple lenses.

'It depends on the magician,' Nigel said. 'Some magicians will need to use all lenses to see the Second Plane, and others will need a combination of lenses on one side but another combination on the other side. It's trial and error.'

'Alright,' Felix nodded, understanding. 'And what will I see?'

'When you've got the lenses adjusted in the right way for you, this world will seem blurry around the edges, like it's made of liquid and can ripple to reveal another world beneath it.'

Felix took a deep breath and placed the spectoccules over her eyes, fitting the fine frame behind her ears. They rested heavily on the bridge of her nose. Looking through the purple lenses, the room around her looked foggy and dark.

'I'll be coming with you Felix,' Fiddle said, resting his hand on her shoulder. 'You won't be alone. Just stay focused on my voice.'

'Don't you need spectoccules?' she asked, and Fiddle smiled and shook his head.

'After a while, many magicians can see the Second Plane without the aid of lenses.'

Felix began to flip the lenses down over the purple glass and a strange sensation occurred. It felt as though her eyes were tingling as they strained to see through so many filters of colour. It wasn't altogether unpleasant. She lifted one of the green lenses up and twisted a yellow lens down and looked at the room around her. Everything was bathed in sepia and reminded Felix of an old picture she had seen in a picture book at the bookroom in school.

'You'll start to see this Plane as a veil thinly covering a world beneath it. Allow yourself to melt through the veil. Almost as though you are looking through it,' Fiddle said to her. His voice seemed strangely far away.

'Did you ever see illusion pictures? A picture of patterns that you have to stare hard at to see the picture hidden inside it? Seeing the Second Plane is like that. Stop seeing the world in front of you...see through it.'

Felix lowered the other yellow lens and the room shimmered in front of her. Nigel was right, the world around her seemed like liquid, like she was looking through a lake to see the rocks beneath it. The Reading Room seemed like an image reflected on the clear water of a lake. Concentrating hard, she tried to look past it.

'Once you feel that the Plane around you is no longer solid, try and ground yourself in the Second.'

Ground myself, thought Felix, remembering what Fiddle had told her earlier, before she had failed when attempting to lift and float the books. She closed her eyes for a moment and imagined her feet were like the roots of trees, firmly planted on the ground and holding her steady. Felix felt a calmness as she did this and something within her shifted. It was almost like a jolt, like a feeling of falling in a dream, only to waken safe in your bed. She became aware of a cool, fresh wind whipping at her hair. A faint smell of sulphur and carbon filled the air and momentarily it made her cough, like she had breathed in too much hot air too quickly.

Opening her eyes, Felix couldn't hide her amazement. The Reading Room had disappeared. Although she had made no movements, she was no longer in the same place. Around her, tall grass tickled the hem of her skirt and whispered in the wind. Fields spread themselves towards the horizon, peppered with trees that stretched demandingly towards the skies. Felix removed the specoccules shakily, worried that if she took them off too quickly, she would be dropped back onto the First Plane, but as she removed them slowly, she remained where she was. Above, the skies were a clear periwinkle blue, with rolling white clouds floating through like ducks on a millpond. In all her life, Felix had never seen a place so beautiful. She felt her blood singing, the spirals on her face dancing within her skin.

'Wow,' she whispered.

'Yes, it is a wonderful place,' came Fiddle's hushed voice from behind her. Felix started a little and turned to him. He smiled, his arms fastened behind his back and he sucked in the hot hair and coughed a little the way Felix had.

'Where are we?' she asked him. 'I mean, I know we're on the Second Plane, but are we near a city or a town or something?'

'Why yes, actually. We're in the Southern Realm, close to the Ardere Academy.'

Felix nodded, remembering Fiddle mentioning an Academy before.

'This is all hidden behind London,' Felix whispered, more to herself than to Fiddle, and she shook her head in wonder.

'Not just London,' Fiddle said, bending and running his hand through the rippling grass. 'The Second Plane is a world as large as the one you know. It's just different. The Geography of the Second Plane is similar to the First Plane with some small exceptions, but as you can see, it's not the same. Here, cities are smaller, life is simpler. But it is more magical. On this Plane, magic is used by everyone who remains here.'

'Magicians still live here?' Felix asked in surprise. She had assumed that all magicians had made their home on the First Plane.

Fiddle nodded. 'Some – there are those who have never entered onto the First Plane for various reasons, though most did come to the First Plane after the Great Revelation. Magicians have lived on the First Plane for hundreds of years, living in secret until we were known, but the Second Plane has always been our original home. It's sparsely populated now, home only to the few magicians who stayed, or to those magicians who are selected from applicants to the Academy. And magical creatures of course.'

'And the Drow?' she inquired, looking at him curiously. Fiddle looked at her sadly.

'As I said, Felix, the Drow were wiped out by Godspell. You're the first Drow I've seen since I last looked upon your mother.'

Felix contemplated this and stroked the skin on her cheek carefully. It was less tender now but the spirals were still steeped in mystery for her. She wished she could speak to another Drow, ask the myriad of questions that flitted through her mind like hummingbirds.

'And so to the lesson in hand,' Fiddle said, drawing himself up from the grass. Felix turned to him apprehensively and noticed that his age had once again melted away, leaving him brown haired and taller. She tilted her head to one side and listened to him carefully.

'This Plane is your true home and so its power runs through your veins like a stream flowing into the ocean. You just have to let it in. Can you feel it, Felix? Feel the magic of this place?' Fiddle closed his eyes and took a long restorative breath. Felix did the same. He was right; Felix could not deny the sense of peace that filled her on this Plane. The scent of the grass and earth and sky, all tinged with a faint tang of sulphur, engulfed her and made her spiral markings and fingers tingle. Again she wanted to remove the gloves but grudgingly kept them on.

'Yes, I feel it,' she murmured.

'As a magician, you have the power to see what you feel right now. Envision the sensation in your hands in your mind's eye. Picture the tingle as though fireflies are fluttering against your fingertips.'

Felix did so, smiling as she imagined.

'When you're ready, open your eyes...and just keep seeing.'

Felix could feel the tension in Fiddle's voice and the air seemed electric, like a storm was coming. It was easy to feel the magic inside her. She could feel it whooshing through her body in such excitement that she thought it would lift her off the ground. She wondered briefly if it could, but pulled her thoughts back to the fireflies she pictured around her hands.

'Believe it, Felix,' Fiddle whispered. 'You have to believe it.'

But believing it was so difficult when she had been lied to all of her life.

Felix frowned, chasing away the thought. Her cheek hurt, her hands were burning, like she had held them in front of a warm fire after they had been cold for a long time. She was standing in a beautiful meadow that was hidden on a Plane behind the London Library. She *had* to believe it. She had seen what magic could do. She *knew* what magic could do. Now, she just had to believe that she could command it.

Slowly, as though opening her eyes from a long, dark sleep to a bright light, Felix let her eyelids flutter so that she was seeing the world around her through the shade of her lashes. The grass was shimmering. She opened her eyes properly and gasped.

A long time ago, Felix had found an art book in the Story Room at school. It was mildewed and crumbling but still Felix had carefully flipped through the pictures, drinking in the colours that seemed to have gone missing in the Commoner's Quarter. She had seen one painting of a beautiful field of wildflowers, with a cornflower blue sky and a dappled image of a lady in white enjoying the view. The artist's name was Monet, though the StoryKeeper had said it was pronounced 'Mo-nay'. Felix couldn't remember the name of the painting, but she had never forgotten what it looked like and the way the picture seemed to be made of tiny little dots of colour that, up close, looked senseless and wild, but from far away made a daydream image.

That is what Felix thought of as she looked around the meadow on the Second Plane. Every blade of grass, every dancing leaf on every swaying branch on every rooted tree was made of pinpricks of colour and yet, the pinpricks were not made of paint; they were made of fire.

She hardly dared move her eyes to look at the tall grass she was standing in but as she did, she saw the tiny flames burn as they clustered together to create something solid. Felix drifted her hand through the grass and to her delight and awe, particles of fire clung to her hand and flickered around her fingers, just like the fireflies Fiddle had told her to imagine.

'I see it,' she whispered. 'Alchemus…'

'What you see here can be seen on the First Plane, too, Felix. Maybe not quite as vividly as this,' he motioned around him serenely. 'Yet it is still there to see and to be commanded.'

'It's like the fire is waiting for me to tell it what to do,' Felix breathed, watching the particles of fire roll around her fingers playfully.

'It is,' Fiddle said simply. 'Tell it what to be.'

Felix looked at the fire, at the faint orange glow that now seemed to surround her hand but before she even knew what she wanted to fire to become, she saw it change into blue, then purple and then a butterfly formed from the colours and fluttered delicately on the end of her gloved forefinger. Felix gasped and the butterfly flew away into the grass.

'I made a butterfly,' Felix said, her voice hoarse with disbelief.

Fiddle chuckled. 'You made an illusion of a butterfly.'

Felix watched the butterfly curiously, as it latched onto the stem of a long blade of grass and slowly, it faded and the fire within it merged with the grass.

'Oh!' Felix was surprised. 'Where did it go?'

'Back to its true form,' Fiddle explained. 'Magic cannot create life, Felix. And it cannot permanently be made into something it did not come from.'

'I don't understand,' Felix frowned, running her hands through the grass again and suppressing a giggle as the magical flames pranced between her fingers.

'Magic can make a young-ish man appear old,' Fiddle smiled. 'But that man will not *be* old. You can command the magic within a book to fly, though that book cannot fly on its own. Magic has limits.'

Felix nodded. 'It's all illusion.'

'Yes. To some degree.'

Felix glanced around the meadow and up towards the sky with the rolling clouds stretching over the horizon, all shimmering with the flames of magic that she could now see. She began to walk through the grass, her expression pensive. Fiddle walked beside her, his hands behind his back.

'Why would the magicians ever leave this place?' she asked. 'It's so beautiful.'

'Hmm,' Fiddle agreed. Felix looked to him as saw an emotion she did not recognise on his face. It made her feel uneasy.

'So?' she asked again. 'Why did the magicians leave?'

Fiddle stopped walking so suddenly that Felix nearly tripped over her skirt as she paused with him.

'What?' she asked.

'It's a secret,' Fiddle sighed.

'A secret?' Felix repeated, folding her arms.

'Yes.'

'But you know?'

'Naturally.'

'Why do you know?'

Fiddle looked long and hard at Felix and then continued to walk through the grass.

'Fiddle!' Felix called after him in exasperation. 'You can't pick and choose what you tell me.'

'Only the Firelighter and the Privy Council know how magicians entered into the First Plane and why,' Fiddle admitted.

'Well, if I'm the Firelighter-'

'No, Felix!' Fiddle said sharply, turning to her abruptly with a fearsome look on his face. Felix swallowed and took a step back, stumbling over the hem of her skirt. Fiddle softened.

'There are some things...' he said softly, his blue eyes boring into hers. 'Some things that it is best not to know. You have trusted me this far, Felix. Please trust me now.'

Felix blinked at him and bit down on her tongue. She could see how earnestly Fiddle was pleading with her and yet she wanted to know the answer to her question and his refusal to answer only made her more curious. Yet, she did trust Fiddle. She had to trust him now.

'Ok,' she conceded. She was surprised to see Fiddle's shoulders relax and she realised how strongly he must feel about this piece of information he was keeping from her.

'Come,' he said gently. 'I think you've seen enough for one day. Let's get back and have some of Nigel's lemonade. Magic is thirsty work.'

Felix nodded, and her mouth watered as she thought of the refreshing, zingy taste of what was quickly becoming her favourite drink. But as she took one last look around the sparkling meadow of magic, she felt an odd stirring of fire in her belly; Felix was curious. She wanted to know more.

13
Midnight Meetings

The Citadel, residence to the Grand Vizier and workplace of the Magistry, was situated in the east of central London, standing to the rear of the old Tower of London in the place where the Bank of England, Royal Exchange and the Guildhall had once stood. Its ominously tall glass tower, which reached into the heavens, was the tallest point in London and could be seen from all the other compass points in the city. Inside its finely decorated rooms were pieces of art, most of which were plucked from the National Gallery and hung for the amusement of the Grand Vizier. Red brick buildings, the most recent additions to the intimidating spire, stood at either side of the glass tower overlooking well-tended green lawns and immaculate gardens, making it one of the most beautiful landmarks of London and the magicians' pride. In fact, the magicians often referred to it as The Magician's Shield, a name that demonstrated their faith in the building and all it stood for.

In the west wing of the Citadel, Corbin Godspell was pacing up and down in his chamber. The glass orbs that hovered around him, casting a soft and calming light in the darkness of the night, swerved out of the way as he walked this way and that. His normally slicked back black hair was dishevelled and falling into one hooded eye. He clasped his hands tightly behind his back and his red silk dressing gown appeared to be torn and muddy. He walked towards his divan and sat down, reaching for the crystal decanter of ashwater at the side table. Shakily, he poured some into a glass and took a sip. Suddenly, Godspell frowned deeply and flung the glass against the wall in a rage. He stood up and growled loudly just as there was a knock on the red wood door.

'Enter,' he barked. A bald man with a large belly entered the room and bowed low.

'Sire,' the man said in a deep, quivering voice, 'the intruders have been caught and are awaiting your punishment in the Tower.' He moved towards Godspell nervously. He looked very uncomfortable being in the same room as the Grand Vizier and Firelighter.

'Very good, Larkin,' Godspell said, stepping towards the smashed glass that had landed on the edge of the Persian rug. He pursed his lips distastefully at the mess. 'They are commoners then? Another uprising?'

The man called Larkin shook his head and clasped his hands together, tensely.

The chief advisor to the Grand Vizier's job was not an easy one and today Larkin found himself feeling very ill at ease. Today, the Grand Vizier had nearly been assassinated in his own home. How close they had come, gagging and binding his master and dragging him from his bed into the rain sodden flowerbeds outside his window. It was extraordinary luck, no, more like foresight that Godspell had decided to step up the security only days earlier, arranging for an alarm barrier to be placed around every inch of the Citadel that would go off the minute Godspell left the building unwillingly. And of course, it was now local news that his master had removed all commoners from the Citadel, though Larkin had spent more hours than he would ever dare admit to his master dealing with protests and hate mail directed at Godspell. But this attempt on his master's life was a huge jump from poison pen letters.

Now, the traitors had been captured and taken up to the Tower of London where they would be held in confines that Larkin didn't like to think about, awaiting the wrath or mercy of the Grand Vizier.

'Speak up, man' Godspell snapped irritably.

'Sire,' Larkin snivelled, 'I regret to inform you that your attackers were magicians. Members of your own Magistry.'

'Magicians? Again?' Godspell's face twisted. He spoke slowly, his words full of spite. 'So after all my selflessness, all my hard work guarding the Flame and leading this country; after all I have done to raise the magicians higher than the common scum, this is how they repay me?' Larkin shuffled, the leather of his shoes squeaking. Godspell held Larkin's gaze, his penetrating eyes making beads of sweat appear on Larkin's top lip.

Without removing his eyes, Godspell flicked his hand over the broken glass and the shards raised slowly, floating around his fingers as he held them in mid-air.

'What are their reasons?' Godspell asked, stepping closer to Larkin.

'They are sympathisers, Sire,' the man replied, his eyes flickering nervously to the sharp glass that floated closer towards him. 'They fight for the commoner's plight.'

Godspell took a step closer and smirked.

'Their *plight*?' he repeated, rippling his fingers so that the glass turned in the air, the sharpest points only inches away from Larkin's throat. Godspell's chief advisor froze and swallowed loudly.

'Forgive me, most noble Sire,' he simpered. 'I spoke hastily. I simply meant that the attackers, the dirty rebels, have turned their back on you, the Grand Vizier and holy protector of the Flame, to pursue equality for the scum, as you so rightfully call them, when they are not deserving of equality.' Larkin bowed again, as much as he was able with the shards of glass aimed at him.

Godspell considered these words for a moment and nodded in agreement. He spun around on his heel and the glass turned with him, reforming into a beautiful crystal glass which Godspell placed gently on the table. Larkin relaxed.

'Members of my Magistry, you say?' Godspell asked quietly, his voice menacing. Larkin nodded. 'Well then, they will be punished. Keep them in the Tower. Send the COPPs out to find their families and then all of them shall be subjected to Doctor Nyxon's work.'

Larkin flinched. He hesitated for a moment.

'But Sir, Nyxon's work has not yet seen successful experiments done on commoners. To reverse the work onto magicians will surely result in their death. Are you sure-'

'Do not question me, Larkin,' Godspell spat, he pale face flushing with anger. 'They were sure of what they were doing when they attacked me and now they must face the consequences. Make it known that anyone who is against Corbin Godspell will be punished and if that is not enough to persuade them to come to my way of thinking, then their families will be punished! Do you understand?'

'Of course, Sire. A marvellous idea, ingenious,' grovelled Larkin, backing away from Godspell towards the door.

He jumped slightly at a knock behind him. The door opened without invitation and a scrawny looking teenage boy with sleepy eyes and pale skin entered.

'You sent for me, Father?' the boy asked sleepily, pushing past Larkin who lingered in the doorway.

'Ah, Linus my boy,' Godspell said, his voice suddenly smooth and charming. 'Come and sit with me. We have not had chance to speak this last few days. I have been so busy, you understand. But it is time to give you your birthday present. And I bet you thought I had forgotten.'

Linus shrugged but a small, gleeful smile toyed on his lips. He went and sat beside his father, his eyes catching the mud on his father's dressing gown. He said nothing; his father disliked questions. Godspell reached inside his dressing gown pocket and pulled out a small, leather box. He handed it to Linus, who looked earnestly at his father for permission to open it. Godspell nodded, smiling an oily smile. Inside was a pair of gold rimmed glasses with three different lenses that folded down into the frame.

'Spectoccules!' Linus said breathlessly. Godspell smiled darkly.

'Yes, my boy. You're old enough now, it is time to show you the other Planes. It is time for you to see something very important.'

14
A Visitor

The library continued to amaze Felix for a grand total of three days before she began to feel bored. Even for someone who loved reading as much as Felix, being trapped in a maze of books began to take its toll on her and she longed to be let out of the library, even if only for a few minutes. Fiddle stood his ground, however. He absolutely refused to let Felix out of the building for one moment, not even to walk around St James's Square.

This resulted in two rather nasty outbursts from Felix. The first came when Nigel was trying to teach her a card game named Quest. The aim of the game was simple in premise; each player had to collect cards with different magical creatures on them and play them against opposing cards from other players. The losing opponent lost their card to the winner. It was a great way to learn about magical creatures but it was also a way for Felix to practice her magic for this game required the player to create the magical creature on any given card out of an inoffensive steel dice, a little larger than a marble.

It was a particularly hot and restless afternoon and Felix was losing. She was already in a bad mood and to make it worse, the hand she had been dealt was poor. The best card she had was a wendigo, but as Felix looked at the illustration of the creature on the card and the information underneath, she knew she'd have a hard time trying to create the creature out of the small metal cube she'd been given.

The wendigo looked a little like a wolf, but a completely emaciated one that walked on two legs. It had a snout with viciously sharp fangs and short, patchy fur covered its arms, hind quarters and tail but it also had antlers, like a stag. The antlers were pointed, as were its teeth and looked like they would be used to skewer its prey. All in all, it looked like a terrifying creature and Felix couldn't believe that such a thing really existed. She read the information under the illustration.

"The wendigo's origins are mysterious though it has been described in the legends of the Algonquian magicians and so it is believed that the first wendigo crossed the Planes near the Atlantic Coasts, suggesting that the wendigo may have originated in the Western Realms of the Second Plane. The name 'wendigo' is a Cree Indian word that means 'evil that devours.' The wendigo is a sentient being and is mainly nocturnal, though its hunger can and will drive it out into the day time if necessary. The prey of the wendigo is meat, preferably of the human variety. Additionally, the bite of a wendigo will certainly lead to infection within the victim. Symptoms begin with the growth of soft, downy hair on the skin, followed by a hunger for raw human flesh and blood which, if unsatisfied, will drive the victim to madness. However, once the victim succumbs to temptation and eats the flesh or drinks the blood of a human victim, the transformation into a wendigo is complete.

Wendigo's are found in damp climates, usually in rural areas and can live for an indefinite amount of time. The best way to kill a wendigo is with fire and extreme heat, though like werewolves, they can be injured with silver weapons.

Class: Level 5 of 6 (very dangerous)."

Felix raised her eyebrow uncertainly, hoping that she would never, ever have to witness a real wendigo. In fact, there was a whole menagerie of creatures that she hoped she'd never meet. Chimeras, wraiths, shades, anansis, vampires, hellhounds, actual, real dragons, goblinoid imps called snotterlings and –

'The lamia,' Nigel said smugly, laying down his card and rolling his dice. Felix watched as the cube disintegrated into tiny dots of fire and reformed to create a cloaked woman, standing about three inches high on the wooden table in the kitchen. Felix looked at it in confusion and couldn't understand why Nigel looked so smug. The lamia was a pretty young woman, with red hair peeping out underneath her black hooded cloak which fell to the floor and covered the rest of her slight frame. From under the black hood, large, winsome eyes peeped up at Felix. She felt almost guilty about setting a wendigo on this creature. She'd easily win.

'Alright,' Felix said, smothering a smile. 'Your lamia against my wendigo.'

Felix rolled her dice and willed the fire within it to reshape into the image on her card. Before her eyes, a savage wendigo formed and stalked towards the cloaked woman. Felix had to concentrate hard to keep the form of the wendigo and it took even more concentration to make it battle, so she was glad that the lamia didn't seem to be putting up much of a fight. Felix willed the miniature wendigo to bare its teeth, which it did with ferocious vigour. Felix shuddered and for a moment, the wendigo shimmered like it would dissolve, and Felix had to clamp her hands into fists to keep up her mental strength.

Nigel seemed unfazed by the wendigo and allowed it to step closer and closer to his lamia. He showed no signs of tiredness or difficulty in maintaining his lamia and it annoyed Felix. But then, he had been playing this game since he was three.

The wendigo was standing right in front of the lamia and Felix made him roar murderously in the lamia's face. Only once the wendigo quietened did Nigel command his lamia to move. She removed her hood, revealing the torso of a woman but instead of hips, the woman's body turned into the bottom end of a rattle snake. Felix gasped and her wendigo faltered. Nigel took his chance and the lamia's eyes turned red and glowing as she slithered closer to the wendigo and opened her mouth wide. Felix watched in horror as the lamia sucked the life from the wendigo, leaving nothing but the shiny little metal dice. Felix picked it up and threw it down again sulkily but as she did so, it ricocheted off the table and around the room with a dreadful force. Plates were smashed, wooden chairs were splintered, and Nigel would have been hit if it had not been for D.W, who knocked him down before the dice whizzed straight through the air where Nigel's head had been only a split second before.

Felix had panicked, unsure how to stop the dice but the panic only seemed to make it move faster and more violently.

She fell down to her knees and joined Nigel and D.W under the table, biting her lip fearfully as she heard the clattering and breaking of utensils as the dice wreaked havoc.

But then it stopped and fell to the floor with a little 'ping' when it hit the stone tiles. Felix couldn't say how she had made it stop and it scared her to know how unpredictable her new power was. They climbed out from under the table and Nigel gulped at her and rubbed at the back of his neck awkwardly when he saw the damage that Felix has unconsciously inflicted.

'Uh...' he began. 'I'll help you clean up.'

Felix nodded, eyes wide and face pale. She passed over the wendigo card to Nigel but he shook his head.

'I have one of those already. You keep it. Here,' he said, holding out the lamia card. 'You can have this, too. I have three.'

Felix was about to argue but thought better of it and took the card from Nigel's outstretched hand. She noticed he hadn't stepped closer to her. She glanced down at the card and saw that the lamia was rated the most dangerous class level: class 6 – extremely dangerous. It didn't kill its victims; it sucked their memories out of them, leaving the victim empty unless it sucked out the memory of their birth...and then. Well. Then they didn't exist anymore. Only the howl of a dire wolf could kill them. Felix looked down at D.W.

'Yeah,' the wolf nodded. 'I can kill lamias.' D.W looked proud and Felix smiled a little and began to clean up, but she could have sworn that she heard him mumble, 'but I don't think they're the most dangerous creatures anymore.'

The second incident came when Felix was browsing through the pile of books that Fiddle had instructed her to read. She had a test on the three Planes later in the evening and Felix was determined to do well on it. She'd always done well in her studies and had revised hard but the books that Fiddle had picked for her were really dull. She'd just about worked her way through "Venephysics: A Very Vague Guide' and 'Science and Sorcery" but there were several chapters that had seemed like utter waffle to her. Now, lying on her stomach on her camp bed, she was reading Dante Leadbeater's "In Plane Sight:

Everything You Ever Wanted To Know About The Three Planes."

"The Third Plane is by far the most challenging and dangerous of all Planes. Unlike the Second Plane, which is a world based on similar laws and physics of the First Plane, the Third is wholly unpredictable. Venephysicists believe this is because of the dense magical energy that forms the Third Plane as this, as all Magicians know, is the home of the Sacred Flame of Magic – Flamma Magica and all such variants of its name.

If one was to ask what the Third Plane looked like, the answers you would receive would be different depending on which magician you were to ask. For each magician, the Third varies in its presentation. Some have described it as a black space-like void with firelight instead of starlight. Others describe magical mists or a blurry expanse of blue, as though one is looking up at the sky from under water. Some simply see a hatch which they must walk through. This question of the Third's appearance, however, is redundant since the Licensing Act of 1999 wherein the Rt Hon. C. Godspell, Grand Vizier and Firelighter, sealed the Third Plane and made it inaccessible for all magicians but for a small number within the Magistry who are granted licenses to access the Third. Whilst this was not a popular motion, Godspell explained that it was a necessary one in order to protect the Sacred Flame from the interference of Rebel Magicians and Commoner Sympathisers who, after the Commoner Control Bill of 1999, rallied around the magically indifferent in order to elevate their status after they were expelled from the City in the Commoner Care Act of ..."

Felix stopped reading because the different acts and laws and bills and dates were starting to blur together in her mind and she couldn't concentrate properly. She pinched the flesh between her eyebrows and was about to re-read the section when the library's summoning bell rang loudly, jarring her and making her vision wonky for a moment. Fiddle had ensured that she could now hear the summoning bell too, so that she could remove herself from view when a customer came into the library. Such a thing rarely happened though. In fact, Felix was utterly shocked that so few people visited the library. She'd always expected magicians to be greedy for knowledge and had pictured them poring over books and studying by candlelight until the small hours of the morning but, in reality, the library saw a small handful of about ten or fifteen magicians a day.

So that is why Felix was so surprised to hear the summoning bell at 5 minutes to closing time and she'd been curious. She shuffled off the bed, accidentally kicking D.W, who was curled up on the tiny strip of floor between the bed and the door – no mean feat considering his size.

'Oof!' he moaned as Felix's foot landed on his belly. 'Where are you going?'

'A customer is here. Nobody is answering the summoning bell,' Felix said quickly, creeping out onto the landing and looking down the grand staircase.

'Nigel or Alchemus will get it,' D.W said, stretching out his front paws and yawning. 'You know you're not supposed to be seen. You could be caught.'

Felix rolled her eyes and looked back at him.

'I just want to see,' she whispered and tiptoed down the corridor to the top of the staircase. D.W followed her, demanding that she stop and growling as she ignored him. Besides, the summoning bell was still ringing in her head and she couldn't really hear him, or so she told herself.

But then, half way down the staircase, the ringing did stop. The silence seemed too loud after the bell and she was vaguely disappointed that Nigel or Fiddle had gotten to the customer before she had. She settled down on a stair and peeked through the railings of the banister, pushing her hair out of the way to look down at the service desk. She had to crane her neck rather a lot and it was an awkward angle, but she could just about make out the wild, frizzy red hair of a lady magician who was talking animatedly to Fiddle. Felix strained to hear. The lady looked a little odd – she was wearing a lime green blouse – and Felix was interested in what this magician would want to read. In fact, it had become something of a game to guess what the visiting magicians would be interested in. This lady looked like she'd be interested in something musical or artistic.

'Who are you to say when she's ready?' the lady spat at Fiddle and Felix froze. She thought that perhaps she was mishearing but as she looked at D.W, she saw his normally smiling snout was snapped shut and his eyes were tight and cold.

'What's she saying?' she mouthed at D.W but he shook his head firmly.

'Upstairs,' he snarled. 'Now.'

Felix glared at him for a moment but then she thought the lady said her name. Her head whipped back around and again she tried to listen but all she caught were a few words that captured attention immediately

'The attack failed. We need to.... action now....five more....to the Tower.......if Felix had been with us....'

Felix stared down at the woman. Whoever she was, she knew about Felix and knew she was at the library. Fiddle was motioning to her to be quiet and was pulling her towards the Reading Room. Who *was* this woman?

'Felix, no!' D.W growled as he read her mind, but Felix was already skulking down the stairs as quietly as she could.

'Felix, I'll tell Alchemus!' D.W threatened, pulling at the hem of Felix's skirt with his teeth.

'Don't you dare!' Felix said to him in her head and flashed him a particularly nasty look that made D.W remember the incident with the dice. He cowered back, his tail beneath his legs but then followed her, mumbling sulkily.

At the bottom of the staircase, Felix leaned against the doorpost of the Reading Room and listened. Nothing. No voices. She brushed her hair behind her ears and looked around the doorpost into the Reading Room but nobody was there. She looked at D.W expectantly.

'They're in the Record Room,' he said rolling his eyes. Felix paced as quickly as she could through the Reading Room and through the double doors on the opposite side of the room.

The Record Room was a huge old hall filled with rows and rows of parchments and newspapers that had been organised into different sections. It was a dismally dull room and Felix never spent any time in there, but now she slipped into the room and huddled in the nearest aisle she could – the Housing History aisle – and listened closely.

'The security has been heightened again, of course. It will make it more difficult if we attack again,' the woman was saying. She had a lilting Irish accent that sounded deeply lyrical to Felix.

'What about our inside man? Has he any more information?' Fiddle asked. Felix peered through the pile of papers and tried to see him but he was obscured by a column. Felix stepped soundlessly round into the next aisle – Genealogy and Heraldry. Now she could see better.

The woman was tall and thin; Felix thought she could be described as willowy. She had little purpled ribbons tied into her mess of auburn hair. The colours clashed horribly. Her billowing lime green blouse was tucked into a pair of fuchsia trousers that flared out widely at the bottom so that they appeared, at first glance, to be a skirt and her gloves were electric blue with yellow stars for buttons.

'No. It's getting harder for him to communicate with us,' the woman was saying. 'There isn't time to wait, Archibald! We need to reveal her.'

'I swore to protect her!' Fiddle hissed in response and Felix was startled by his anger. Fiddle was never rude. The woman did not seem at all fazed and looked him squarely in the face. 'And you might as well get used to calling me Alchemus,' Fiddle said apologetically. Felix thought she saw the woman smile fondly.

'It's been out of use for far too long,' she nodded.

Felix looked down at D.W who was listening intently too, though he wasn't just listening to the words they were saying.

'Who is that woman?' Felix asked him with her mind. The thought that she might be Fiddle's wife or girlfriend flitted across her mind and D.W buried a snort of laughter.

'Her name is Aubrey... but that's all I can get. They're both guarding their minds pretty well,' he communicated to her silently.

'I can't let her out until she's ready,' Fiddle continued in a quiet voice. 'If anything happened to her, I don't know what I'd...what I'd...'

Aubrey rested her hand on Fiddle's shoulder comfortingly and there was a familiarity between the two of them that Felix could not fail to see. These two were friends and had been for a long time.

'I know, Alchemus,' Aubrey replied gently. 'But this is what she is here for. Felix needs to be given the chance to reclaim what is hers.'

Felix was suddenly very aware of how loudly she was breathing. They were talking about her claim to the Sacred Flame, they had to be. She was the rightful Firelighter. So did that mean...?

'She's our secret weapon,' Aubrey said. 'She always has been. You knew that the moment you put her on the doorstep of that orphanage. Godspell doesn't know she even exists. You did well to keep her so well hidden all these years. But didn't you keep her hidden for precisely this reason? She must be taught to fight – Felix is the best chance we've got of killing the bastard now.'

D.W looked at Felix as she took a deep breath. For a moment, the wolf thought that she would accidentally cause the papers around her to set fire or something similar, but Felix seemed to be controlling herself; she was learning. But her eyes were darkly powerful and the spirals on her face were shimmering dangerously. Again the dire wolf tried to pull her back to her room but the girl swiped him away and continued to listen.

'How is she?' Aubrey asked Fiddle, who looked very tired and haggard suddenly and he coughed lightly in the dusty room.

'She's coming along well,' he sighed, recovering himself, curling his beard around his finger. 'She shows more power every day but she's struggling to control it. Her Drow power is overwhelming her and I have limited experience in such magic. Her mother had her sister Drow to train her and I can't offer her the same training.'

'Have you thought about taking her to the Glade?'

Fiddle shook his head. 'It's too dangerous. Besides, no sisterly welcome awaits a Drow at the Glade anymore. The place is a ruin. What good would it do her? The girl has barely had time to process who she really is. And she hasn't truly grieved her parents and what happened to them. Aubrey, I understand what you're saying, but she needs to heal and to learn. What use is she to us if her spirit is broken?'

Felix realised she was shaking. She clamped her hands into fists but it was uncomfortable in the gloves. Shivers ran through her but she did not feel cold. In fact she felt burning hot.

'Take her to the Monument then. She could say goodbye to them,' Aubrey suggested.

'No, I can't take her there,' Fiddle said, shaking his head again. 'Monument is too close to the Citadel. Besides, what hope can it give her to visit her parents' ashes? There's nothing for her there.'

The air left Felix in a huff and she felt like she had been punched in her gut. She slumped against the shelf of papers in front of her and some fell to the floor.

'What was that?' Aubrey asked, spinning around. 'Are you sure we're alone?'

D.W looked up at Felix anxiously and pushed against her with his muzzle.

'Leave!' he whispered to her. 'Go on. I'll cover for you.'

Felix rushed past him and ran out of the hall, through the Reading Room and up the grand staircase and back into her room. Once there, she stood looking down at the pile of books on her bed.

Ashes. My parents' ashes. They have a grave.

A surge of anger rose up from her feet. It flooded through her body like adrenalin and she felt the swell of power rising from her in a way that did not feel unpleasant. It prickled in her skin, behind her eyes and on her tongue. Her fingers seemed to be vibrating with power. Felix could not quell it. She did not want to.

Fiddle had known. All along, he had known that her parents had a grave and he had denied her the chance to see it. He had kept her here, like a prisoner because he thought she was dangerous, because she was the secret weapon. He wanted to her to kill Godspell; they all did. They were using her.

Sparks flitted at Felix's fingertips and she watched in detachment as the sparks of fire waited to be commanded. Fury washed through her followed by betrayal and hurt. Without thinking, she directed the sparks at the books Fiddle had told her to study. Instantly, they set alight and began to burn with a force that seemed to match the scalding feelings that rushed through Felix. But the fire spread to the mattress and then to the shelves on the wall until Felix was standing in an inferno of blazing fire that, curiously, did not seem to be burning her. Instead, it licked around her playfully.

'Felix! Get out of there now!' Nigel's voice screamed into the room and Felix turned to see him stood in the burning doorway, reaching for her. She tilted her head in confusion just as part of the ceiling collapsed in front of her. Felix fell to the floor, the flames backing away from her and leaving her unharmed, but the jolt of the fall was enough to bring Felix to her senses.

She felt the heat of the fire on her skin, smelled the thick stench of smoke in the air and climbed to her feet quickly, sprinting out of the room as fast as she could. As she escaped the room, the flames on her body disappeared but the blaze in her room continued.

'I – I'm sorry!' she cried, sinking against the landing banister. Nigel stretched out his hands and tried to suppress the seeking flames that raged out of the doorway and threatened to spread into the hallway, but the fire did not obey him.

'Felix!' he yelled. 'Make it stop!'

'I can't!' Felix wailed, burying her face into her hands.

She heard Fiddle and D.W bounding up the stairs calling her name and Felix glimpsed through her hands. The woman named Aubrey was with them, looking at the fire and then at Felix in horror and awe.

'It's furyfire,' Fiddle shouted over the roar of the flames. 'It won't stop until she wills it.'

D.W was pulling at Felix's skirt again, trying to drag her away from the fire but she wouldn't move.

'Felix!' called Aubrey. 'You have to calm down. Control your emotions. That's the only way to stop the fire!'

Felix began to sob, though tears were trapped behind her eyes. Everything that had happened in the last few days weighed down on her and it felt impossible to control the chaos inside her. She wanted everything to burn. This was the destruction she craved. Maybe...maybe she was evil, like the reflection in the mirror of her dreams. The thought made her sob harder.

'Please Felix!' yelped D.W. His glossy grey fur was blackening with soot and as Felix looked up at his pleading yellow eyes, she felt a fierce urge to protect him. He was her friend. And so was Nigel. They couldn't be hurt by this. Not them. Felix clambered to her feet though she was amazed at the effort it took her to stand. She stepped closer to the fire and reached out her hand. Through bleary, smoke-filled eyes, she saw the fire bend around her and she fought to control it.

'Breathe,' she heard Fiddle command her. 'Let it all wash over you like a river washes over a pebble.'

Felix tried to swallow but her mouth was dry. It was as though she was as dry as the fire she was trying to rule. Closing her eyes, she tried to ground herself, to picture roots planting her into the earth. It soothed her and she felt the tingle of the fire around her beginning to dissipate. With a scorching blast of air, the flames disappeared. Felix opened her eyes and staggered as the heat of the fire withdrew into her but Nigel gripped her under her arms and held her up.

Amazingly, aside from a very strong scent of burning wood and a palpable, oppressive warmth, there was no evidence of any fire. Nothing was burnt or blackened; everything looked entirely normal. Felix opened her mouth to speak but her throat was parched and she had no energy to speak.

'Come,' Fiddle spoke regretfully. 'I think we should talk.'

He led her into a room just a little further down the hallway. It was a small but comfortable room with a bed that sank deeply as Nigel set her down on it.

'I'll go get something for you to drink,' he said to her and left the room which Felix realised was Fiddle's room; it was surprisingly sparse save for a small pile of books on his bedside table, which contained nothing else other than a small brown bottle of what Felix took to be ashwater. There was a faintly medicinal scent to the room which she didn't like and it was meticulously clean. It was unexpected. A single piece of artwork hung on the wall; a painting of a double fronted house, surrounded by flowers and ivy climbing up around the windows, peeping inside. Above a green wooden front door, a sign read 'Fenton House'. Other than the lone picture, the walls were blank and grey with age.

The dire wolf came and sat in front of her, resting his snout on her knee. Felix stroked his nose half-heartedly and glanced up at Fiddle who was looking down at her with stern and concerned eyes. Aubrey was stood in the doorway, her hard stare annoying Felix more and more. She didn't like Aubrey at all.

Nigel returned with a jug of lemonade and Felix didn't even wait for him to pour it into a glass, she just gulped it straight from the spout of the jug. Instantly, she felt lighter and she smiled gratefully at Nigel.

'Sorry,' she mumbled, flicking her eyes up at Fiddle. 'I didn't mean to start the...what did you call it?'

'Furyfire,' he replied. 'It's Drow magic. Basically, it's the physical manifestation of your anger. It's not a danger to you or other Drow but to magicians, it's as dangerous as any fire. Perhaps even more so.'

Felix nodded and swallowed more lemonade. Her eyes found Aubrey's across the room. She had not stopped staring at Felix.

'What?' Felix asked her, an embarrassed flush reaching her cheeks.

'What made you angry?' Aubrey asked her. She folded her arms and regarded Felix with an unreadable expression that made her seem like a strict school teacher. Felix looked down at D.W and shuffled awkwardly, making the bed moan.

Fiddle caught the look between the girl and the wolf and guessed.

'You overheard us talking,' he said blankly. Felix glanced at him and nodded. The magician sighed and looked at Aubrey.

'This is Aubrey Dovepeace,' he motioned to her. Aubrey dipped her head once in greeting. 'She's an old friend and has been gathering together a group of magicians who are tiring of Godspell's reign.'

'A rebellion?' Felix asked. Aubrey smiled a little.

'More like a protest group,' she clarified.

'Uh, does someone want to tell me what's going on?' Nigel said, his eyes shifting from Felix to Fiddle to Aubrey.

'Fiddle's been keeping secrets,' Felix said bitingly. Nigel pushed his glasses up his nose and looked at his master questioningly.

'That's not fair, Felix,' Fiddle said softly.

'No,' Felix spat. 'What's not fair is that you've known all this time that my parents have a grave and you've not had the decency to even tell me about it. What's not fair is that you have a secret agenda that involves me, and I have no say in what happens to me!'

Felix began to cry though she didn't want to. She rubbed her eyes and looked away from everyone. It felt childish to be crying like this but it seemed now that she had started, she couldn't stop.

'Ok,' Aubrey said, interrupting the silence. 'Yes, we have an agenda. Alchemus should have told you, but if you were really listening to what we said then you will know that he only held information from you because he cares about you. I shall be a little more forthright with you. We need you to fight, Felix. I am not a leader though many magicians look to me. The people are scared of Godspell and they do not trust him. There is nothing so dangerous as mistrust. Now is the best time to act, to overthrow him.'

'To kill him?' Felix glared at Aubrey with tear-filled eyes. The woman looked at the girl for a moment and then nodded slowly.

'And you want me to do it,' Felix said, her voice barely audible.

'Only you can,' Aubrey shrugged. 'And only you should. He's the Firelighter, even if it's not his right. That makes him powerful. As you're the true Firelighter, only you can challenge him and beat him. And if what I've seen of you today is anything to go by, I'm more certain than ever that you have the power to kill him.'

I can't, thought Felix. *I'm not a killer.*

'But you are a leader,' D.W said to her. Felix shook her head at him.

'Yes, you are,' he nudged her with his nose. 'I would follow you.' Felix smiled at him a little and stroked him behind the ears.

'What do you want to do, Felix?' Fiddle asked her gently. When she looked at him, he seemed lost. She wondered what D.W could hear of his thoughts.

'I want to go to the Monument to visit my parent's ashes,' Felix said firmly. She looked Fiddle in the eyes and saw his disapproval but she didn't care. 'And I want to go alone.'

15
Monument, Mortimer and Murphy

'It's out of the question,' Fiddle said determinedly and Aubrey nodded her agreement. Felix scowled at her. Hadn't she been the one saying she should go to Monument only minutes earlier?

'You think you can stop me?' she replied fiercely.

'Actually, yes,' Fiddle's tone was humourless. 'Don't push me on this, Felix. It's too dangerous for you to leave the Library.'

'Understand, Felix,' Aubrey mediated. 'You're a threat to Godspell and you're very conspicuous with those remarkable spirals on your face. Nobody has seen a Drow for annums. The COPPs would arrest you on sight. We're just trying to keep you safe.'

'I could take her,' Nigel suggested, his eyes filled with sympathy as he looked down at Felix.

'No!' Fiddle growled as he squared his shoulders. 'The Monument is too close to the Citadel and the Tower of London. I will not risk your capture! I forbid you to go Felix. I forbid it!'

They all stared at Fiddle, but his eyes stayed firmly on Felix and his expression softened.

'Please,' he pleaded. 'Those we love never die. They live in our hearts, Felix. There is nothing for you at the Monument. Don't dwell on death.'

Felix sulked. In the days that followed, she stayed in her room, refusing to do any of the work that Fiddle had told her to do. She only came down for meals and they were stilted affairs. Fiddle, it seemed, was just as angry at Felix as she was at him. Nigel tried to ease the tension between them by cracking jokes and asking questions to try and open up a conversation, but they were as equally stubborn as each other. Besides, Felix was annoyed at Nigel for taking Fiddle and Aubrey's side. She still spoke to him but she felt as though their growing friendship had been tainted. It was as if nobody understood how alone she felt, surrounded by secrets in a world that was beginning to lose its charm very quickly.

Only the dire wolf seemed to care about her isolation. Hearing many of her thoughts, he knew how hurt and betrayed she felt and he tried to comfort her as best as he could. He had taken to sleeping in Felix's room with her but he often woke her in the night, whimpering in his dreams. When Felix shook him awake, he seemed wary and could not get back to sleep but wouldn't tell Felix what he was dreaming about.

As for Felix's dreams, they were filled with the old doors that she could never walk through, though now she knew that behind one of the doors, her parents waited for her. She could hear them shouting for her to find them, but all Felix could do was spin around, looking at hatch after hatch after hatch, begging the Catchoo to tell her which one to open yet receiving nothing but her unwavering feline gaze.

A week had passed since Aubrey had visited. She had not returned. The library felt lonelier than it had ever felt and seemed to be sighing with Felix every time she thought of her parents. The old chant from the Orphanage had become more prominent though it had taken on a new meaning: *when I get out of here, I'm going to find my parents*. Now, instead of waiting to leave, Felix felt as though she was being imprisoned. She knew that Fiddle did not mean for her to feel this way and in the back of her mind, she felt sorry for thinking so badly of him. But he could not understand that she *needed* to go to the Monument. She had to see it for herself, talk to her parents and...and say goodbye, even though she had never known them. It was her right to do that, surely. Hers was the only right. Fiddle was wrong to keep her from them and the conviction of this thought solidified her anger at him.

***

Rain whipped at the library on another uneventful evening as Felix was flicking through the book she had brought with her from the orphanage, hardly believing that she was missing Nanny Maude and the crumbling dormitory with the comforting snores of the other children. It was past midnight and she had conjured a little orb of firelight to illuminate the pages and out of the corner of her eye, she noticed D.W twitching in his sleep. His lips pulled back into a snarl and a growl left his throat. Felix had to admit that he looked really quite terrifying like that and hesitated to wake him but within moments, he was yelping as though in pain so Felix stroked him gently, wondering what it was that troubled him so much.

'Shhh,' she soothed as the dire wolf jumped awake at her touch. 'It's ok. I'm here.' The wolf glared at her and in the golden light of the orb, he seemed menacing. Felix backed away a little.

'What is it?' she asked nervously. D.W shook himself all over and sat on his hind legs, looking at her deeply. Felix became very conscious that he was reading her thoughts and tried to keep him out.

'Don't bother,' he mumbled. 'I already know what you're planning.'

'Planning?' Felix asked in surprise. 'What do you mean?'

D.W narrowed his eyes at her and Felix tried to hold his gaze but failed. She swallowed hard and began to twirl a piece of her dark hair between her fingers.

'It's not really a plan,' she said weakly, 'just an idea.' The wolf continued to stare at her.

'Do you know what I see in my dreams, Felix?' he asked her. Felix shook her head and lowered herself onto the floor next to him.

'I see your nightmares.'

Felix balked. She looked the wolf squarely in his eyes but had to look away. She bit her lip, searching for something to say and finding nothing.

'I see your darkest fears, I feel your longing and your pain. But above all, I feel how lost you are.'

'Sorry,' Felix whispered sheepishly. She felt very vulnerable, as though the wolf was using spectoccules to look straight inside her.

'I'll help you.'

Felix's breath hitched in her throat. 'What?'

'I'll take you to Monument.'

'But...why?'

D.W was quiet for a moment and listened to the girl's thoughts. Then, as if agreeing with himself, he nodded his head.

'Because you're not reckless. You don't want to leave the library to punish Fiddle or to prove a point. You need to see Monument and say goodbye to your parents properly. Without that, I don't think you'll ever be able to find your way.'

Felix couldn't speak but she didn't need to. D.W groomed his flank whilst Felix tried to swallow the sizeable lump which had worked its way into her throat.

'But how will we get out?' she thought to D.W. 'Fiddle has all the exits rigged with alarms if I try to leave.'

The dire wolf's eyes glowed in the orb light. 'You forget, I can read minds. And I happen to know that Fiddle has a secret hatch in the basement.'

Felix grinned.

The secret hatch was hidden deep in the bowels of the London Library.

Under the cloak of night, the girl and the wolf crept as stealthily as they could down to the basement and past the kitchen. It was eerie in the silence and so dark that Felix soon began to feel disorientated; each time she blinked she opened her eyes to blackness so that she felt like she was blind. Luckily, the dire wolf could see in the dark.

He led her down a long, winding corridor that seemed to slope downwards. Felix was certain she had never been down this far before. Left then right, then another left, now right...she would never remember this. But just when Felix thought she was going to meet some kind of monster in this underground labyrinth, the wolf stopped her and told her they had reached the door.

Felix reached out and felt the damp, cold smoothness of a wooden door but despite scrambling around, she couldn't find the handle.

'Oh this is silly!' she whispered in exasperation. With a roll of her hand, a bright white flame appeared out of the centre of her palm. Now, she could see.

The corridor disappeared into a fog of blackness but she could see doors lining each side of the narrow walkway. She shivered. This all reminded her too much of her dreams.

'Where does it open?' she asked D.W. The wolf was suspiciously quiet.

'Don't you know?' Felix hissed and saw him shake his head ruefully.

'It doesn't matter. I can lead you to Monument from anywhere.'

'What if it opens in Spain or something?' Felix asked, frowning angrily. D.W shrugged. Felix mumbled under her breath and considered going back to her room where her warm, cosy bed seemed very inviting. But then, she would never get to Monument...and she needed to. She had to.

Reaching for the metal door handle and taking a deep breath, Felix looked down at D.W who looked back up at her expectantly, golden eyes sparkling in the dim light.

'Here goes!'

She opened the door and they both stepped through into the darkness.

As Felix had never travelled by hatch before, she hadn't really known what to expect. She had thought it was a simple as walking through an open door and coming out the other side somewhere else entirely. That was not what happened.

As soon as the door shut behind them both, the blackness consumed them both and a breeze that felt like icy breath on the back of her neck blew out the tiny blue flickers of light that Felix had cast.

'Err, what now?' Felix asked. Her voice echoed in the darkness. 'Where are we?'

'We're in the Midst. The place between hatches.'

'Well how do we get out?!'

'Just find the door.'

Felix swallowed. She tried to cast some more fire, but she felt very afraid in the darkness and she struggled to ignite a fire properly.

'Stop panicking. It's only darkness. Just find the door.'

'Can't you see it?' Felix asked, trying to breathe but she felt as though the air was running out.

'No. This is a magical void. Stop trying to ignite a fire – you're in between places. Magic won't work here. Haven't you ever wondered what an empty room looks like when there's no-one there to see it? That's where we are – we're in the emptiness behind a door.'

This did nothing to sooth Felix's nerves. She stepped forward, which was very disconcerting as she couldn't feel any ground beneath her and she reached her arm out trying to find a door. After a few footsteps, her hand made a dull thud as it hit a very hard and very metal door. She ran her hands all over it, found the large handle, like a handle on a refrigerator and tugged at it.

She fell through the hatch, gasping for breath and bent forward, resting her hands on her knees. D.W came trotting happily behind her. The door slammed shut with a soft 'flumph'.

'I don't like hatches,' Felix breathed.

'You'll get used to them. I think you're supposed to walk pretty purposefully through the first door and find the exit door before it closes.'

'You might've mentioned that before,' Felix grumbled. She looked up and took at her surroundings. They were in a huge and empty stainless steel kitchen and the hatch they had come through belonged to a massive refrigerated pantry.

D.W walked to a door where a green glowing sign indicated that it was an exit. He jumped up and opened it easily with his front paw. Felix followed him, thankful that the door had not been locked.

The door led out onto a rusty old fire escape and they climbed down quickly, making a racket as they did. D.W's claws kept getting stuck in between the metal slits causing him to yelp a few times and he jumped the last six steps, growling quietly.

'So, where are we?' Felix asked. She took a deep breath of the cool night air and felt a surge of elation that she was no longer in the library and was outside for the first time in days.

'It smells like we're near the river,' D.W said, sniffing the air. 'Near a hospital.' He darted up the street a little and then stopped, sniffing the air again before nodding and confirming that they were near Guy's Hospital.

'It's across the river from the Citadel,' he told her.

'Can you get us to Monument from here?" she asked and pulled her hair back into her usual messy bun. D.W nodded.

'We'll need to cross the river but it's easy enough. We'll have to be quick. There will be COPPs around...and other things.'

Felix wanted to ask what he meant by other things but stopped herself. She didn't want to know. Her main focus now was to get to Monument.

They began to jog down the backstreets of London, keeping hidden in the shadows. The city was quiet with only a few magicians pacing through the darkness, walking with a purpose to their destinations. A few times, they saw magicians falling merrily out of the pubs and inns that they crossed, the stench of honeymead and cigars pouring out of the doors, but on the whole Felix thought they were lucky not to have crossed paths with anyone or anything more sinister. Too lucky.

Within fifteen minutes, they had reached the open crossing of London Bridge, next to the crumbling and forgotten ruins of a cathedral. In the eerie, blue light of the bridge, the cathedral loomed over them menacingly. D.W lifted his nose into the air and stopped suddenly, his ears flattened.

'What is it?' Felix asked, her heart thundering against her ribs.

'I smell something.'

'Well?' Felix asked again after a few heartbeats.

'I'm not sure. I'm getting several scents. I think we're being followed and I can smell...snotterlings.'

Felix groaned under her breath. She knew what snotterlings were. She had several snotterling cards in her growing Quest deck. They were slimy, snot coloured little goblins who were small but deceptively hard to escape from. If they latched onto their catch, they nipped and clawed at the skin, bringing their victim out in nasty little slime filled boils and a bad fever.

'Felix...you're going to have to get on.' D.W said is a strained voice whilst his throat was growling. His hackles were rising.

'Huh?'

'Climb on my back! We need to get across the bridge. Quickly!'

Felix jumped at the fierceness of his voice but then grabbed a fistful of fur on the wolf's neck and jumped up, drawing her long skirts up around her thighs and mounting his long flank. Her trainers barely skimmed the floor.

'Hold on tight,' D.W said, setting his body down low before darting forward across the bridge. Felix clung on for her life, because the wolf's shoulders rose and fell very quickly, making it hard for her to get a good grip but as she looked over her shoulder, she saw the light reflecting off the slime of seven snotterlings, all scuttling with surprising speed after them. With a gasp, she saw more spouting out of the ruined cathedral like ants out of an ant hill and she willed D.W to run faster. She turned her head and saw the end of the bridge in sight. She gasped.

'What's *that?*'

On the other side of the bridge, like a leviathan of white marble shining in the moonlight, was a building so grand that Felix couldn't help but admire it. A tower pierced the night sky with a large glass dome shimmering at its peak. Beneath it, like wide arms protecting the Tower, red brick walls with arched doorways wrapped around it. Although her view was obscured by other, smaller buildings, Felix could see it clearly. She knew what it was before the dire wolf answered her.

'The Citadel.'

Fear gripped her tightly making her clench hold of D.W's fur a little too hard with her gloved hands, making him yelp.

'We're too close,' she whispered. 'Godspell is in there.'

'Monument is just over the bridge,' D.W said to her.

He continued to bound across the bridge and when Felix looked behind her, she could see the snotterlings falling behind.

Some of them were turning and running in the opposite direction.

'Oh, they're running away,' Felix breathed in relief, but she felt D.W shake his head.

'They're going for what was following us,' he said. 'We're not safe yet.'

They crossed over the other side of the bridge, the streets seeming brighter from the glow of the Citadel. It seemed entirely too large to be allowed and dominated the North East side of the bank. D.W continued to run and lurched right into a side street, shadowed by a grey, steepled church. He stopped, his tongue hanging out of his mouth as he gasped for breath.

Felix climbed down and stroked his fur gratefully.

'Are we safe?' she asked, her eyes flitting around them anxiously.

'For now,' D.W dipped his head and rested on his haunches.

Felix looked up at the church, which seemed dirty with neglect and age, an abandoned relic that stood sad yet proud in the shadows. Stepping around the wolf, she edged her way around the corner of the building, peering around it to see if the snotterlings were still chasing them but was relieved to see that they were alone. The sign outside the faded church read "St Magnus the Martyr."

'Well, St. Magnus,' she whispered, looking up at the dirty white bell tower. 'We could use a hand.'

It was deathly quiet. She could hear nothing but the ragged breaths of D.W. Allowing her heart rate to return to normal, Felix stepped gingerly out onto the main road, looking at the bridge and then turning her head to the Citadel. Fiddle had been right. It *was* too close. This was dangerous. She swallowed, feeling a bubble of guilt in her stomach that she had not listened to him. If she was caught, her parents' death would have been for nothing and D.W...he could get hurt too.

'Don't worry about me,' he comforted her. 'Besides, we're here now.'

Felix looked down at D.W in confusion but he motioned her to look in the opposite direction, away from the bridge. She looked in the direction he had pointed and stepped further into the street. Then she saw it.

The Monument, a thin, needle like obelisk reached up behind the steeple of the church. From where she was standing, Felix couldn't see its base, nor could she properly make out the top of it so she ran, ignoring D.W calling out to her.

Despite it seeming so close, the Monument was still a few streets away from her. She meandered in and out of darkened narrow side streets, the structure never out of her view until finally, she burst into a tiny, clustered square.

The monument stood in front of her, a stone, grey column reaching higher than Felix had imagined. When she looked up to the top of it her head began to spin, and she wasn't sure if that was because the column was so high or if it was because she could see a golden urn at the top, wreathed in perfectly moulded flames and twinkling in the darkness, so that it looked like it was really on fire. Each side of the Monument's square base had huge panels with inscriptions in a language that she couldn't read carved into them, and on one panel there was a beautiful marble relief. But she wasn't looking at that; Felix stared up at the urn. She had to squint to make it out clearly, but she could see it.

'Is that where...?' but she couldn't finish the question. She felt D.W behind her and she sensed rather than heard his answer. Her parents' ashes were in the urn.

'It was built by Christopher Wren in tribute to the Flame of Magic,' D.W explained in a soft voice.

'Of course, the commoners think it's just a monument to the Great Fire of London of 1666. Wren built it sometime in the 19th century; he thought it would be funny to have a memorial to 'The Great Fire' and have commoners none the wiser. It was his little joke.'

But Felix was only half listening. She was staring up at the golden urn, ignoring the little drops of rain that were beginning to fall onto her face. She tried to feel her parents' presence, to feel some kind of comfort emanating from urn but instead she felt broken.

It was a noble thing that Fiddle had done, to give her parents such a fitting resting place but once again he'd been right. There was nothing for her here; no hope or comfort. It was just a statue and nobody knew that all that was left of her parents was up there, overlooking the city that they had once helped govern.

Slowly, she inspected the inscriptions on the panels and her eyes rested on the stone relief. It was a carving, as intricate as any that Felix had ever seen, of a young girl slumped on the ground in defeat, her sword at her side. Some kind of angel was trying to pull her up, and there was a figure of a woman over the girl, pointing a sceptre into the sky towards rolling clouds and the image of two women, watching the young girl. Around the girl, the city was in flames and the people of London were encouraging the girl to stand. The sculpture captured Felix and she looked at it closely, intrigued by the young girl who seemed to embody Felix's emotions. She wished she had an angel to help her.

'It's not an angel,' said the dire wolf gruffly. He had been respectfully quiet as Felix had inspected the Monument and his voice made her jump. 'It's Father Time. The message is that Time helps us to rise no matter how defeated we may be.'

He nudged his head under Felix's limp hand so that she rested it on top of his head. Absently, she stroked him, still looking at the sculpture.

'Who are the women?' she asked. There was something unusual about them and the way they looked down at the girl. And the woman with the sceptre was odd too, but Felix couldn't put her finger on the reason why.

'I'm not sure,' the dire wolf said uncertainly. 'Maybe goddesses? They look like warriors to me, with their headdresses and swords.' Felix nodded slowly, a nagging feeling in her stomach. She walked behind the column, her eyes drifting back up to the top.

'Are you watching me?' she said softly to the urn. 'Are you with me? Mum? Dad?' And her tears mingled with the rain.

The dire wolf started to get nervous.

Dawn was creeping ever closer and he was conscious of the Citadel lurking close by. Yet, he couldn't disturb the girl. She sat, cross legged at the base of the Monument, staring upwards with sad eyes and no matter how miserable the situation, no matter how anxious he felt that they would get caught, he felt a calm within Felix that he had never known before. Yes, he thought only to himself. She needed this. He stayed out of her thoughts respectfully, but this meant that he was at a disadvantage for he could not hear the thoughts of those who may have been drawing closer to them. He kept as careful a guard as he could but, this close to the river, the only scents he could catch were the Thames and the sewers. His instincts alone made his hackles rise. They were being watched.

'Felix, we have to go,' he murmured, hesitating to interrupt her.

A dawn breeze drifted over them. Too late, the wolf caught the scent of leather and boot polish and danger. He growled viciously.

'Well, ain't this a pretty picture, eh Mr Mortimer?' said a voice that made the hair on the back of Felix's neck stand on end. She jumped up and saw two men dressed in scarlet coats and matching gloves. The man who had spoken was tall and muscular with a hooked nose and a shaven head that faded artfully into red skin and hungry eyes.

'Oh yes, Mr Murphy; very pretty indeed. Touching, you might say,' said the other man, who was quite large and had long, lank hair. D.W growled and his ears flicked back. He leaned forward threateningly. Felix stood behind him, her heart tripping over itself. Slowly, the two men walked towards them, their hands held behind their backs casually. The badges on their jackets read Commoner's Order Police Patrol with an intricately crafted G underneath it. Felix swallowed hard.

'Yes. Of course, you're right, Mr Mortimer. Touching is what it is, to see a young Drow and her wolf so close to the Citadel; touching, to see her walking freely to her own demise.'

The dire wolf's mouth was frothing with rage as his lips curled back over his fangs. He alone was all that stood between the COPPs and Felix, who was flattened against the panel of the Monument, her thoughts drowned out by overwhelming fear.

'I think we should escort them, don't you, Mr Murphy. It's only fair; they've been so nice as to come this far on their own.'

They were only inches away from them now. They smelt sour and unwashed. Felix could see their frighteningly ruddy skin and thirsty eyes and her stomach churned. The dire wolf snapped his jaws and sprinted forward but the lank-haired man, Mr Mortimer, was ready for him. He kicked down on D.W's leg with a force that Felix had not expected from one so round. There was a sickening crunch and the wolf fell to the floor yelping in pain as he tried to stand and attack again. Mr Murphy took this chance and stepped towards Felix but the wolf dove straight for him, clamping his jaws around the man's leg. Mr Murphy grunted loudly, trying to loosen the animal, who held fast.

'Run, Felix!' D.W shouted to her with his mind as Mr Murphy began to shake his leg free. Felix backed away, faltering and not wanting to leave the wolf. Mr Murphy seemed to have grown agitated and called out to his colleague.

'Mr Mortimer, if you please?' The tall COPP stepped forwards as though this was all very boring and with a twitch of his wrist, a red baton appeared in his hand. He brought it down heavily on the back of the dire wolf's head.

'NO!' screamed Felix, as she saw D.W sink to the ground where he did not move again. Without thinking she ran at Mr Mortimer blindly, for her eyes were blurry with tears, but he grabbed Felix's hands and held them tightly behind her back so that she cried out in pain as her joints were twisted. Anger coursed through her but it was dampened by fear as Mr Mortimer breathed hard and intimately against her cheek.

'Now, don't you scream,' he cooed greasily into her ear.

Felix whimpered, her breath uneven and she struggled to free herself, trying to kick at Mr Mortimer's heels.

'Get off me! Get OFF me!' she yelled.

'Now that's not very nice is it, Mr Murphy?' Mr Mortimer asked silkily as he held her like a vice, his groin pressing into

Felix's back as he slowly licked her cheek where her spirals were.

'No, it's not,' said Mr Murphy through gritted teeth as he bent down to inspect his bitten leg. There were holes in his black leather boots and, with some satisfaction, Felix noticed blood seeping through them. She looked down at the dire wolf, willing him to move. She saw his flank rising and falling; he was breathing. Relief flooded her, and she began to kick at her captive again, though every moment tore at her shoulders.

'I think we should take them to the Tower, don't you?' said Mr Murphy breathlessly, as he lifted the dire wolf onto his shoulders.

Felix stopped struggling, her eyes widening with horror. She felt the blood drain from her face. The Tower of London.

'No! Please!' she cried out. Felix clamped her eyes shut, calling for the Furyfire to come but all she could feel was Mr Mortimer's sour breath on her neck as he breathed in her scent, his greasy hair pressing against her spirals...spirals which remained dark and powerless in her fear.

'Oh yes,' he said, a smile spreading across his crimson face. 'That's a mighty fine idea, good Sir. Though I think we could have some fun first.'

Felix pulled against Mr Mortimer with all her strength, terror numbing her to the pain of his grip upon her.

'Stay still, girly, and your family might still recognise you when we're done,' Mr Murphy sneered, holding the baton up to her face.

'I have no family,' Felix spat.

'An orphan eh?' Murphy smiled, revealing black poppyblood stained teeth. 'Oh I do love the orphaned ones. Their blood is always sweeter.'

Felix lurched away from them in disgust, but Mr Mortimer's legs pinned her against him. The rage came, hot and brutal, flooding through her and she threw her head back, smashing it into Mr Mortimer's nose. He let her go instantly and she grabbed Mr Murphy's baton and swung it hard between his legs so that he fell to the ground, creased in pain. She backed up towards the stone relief of the Monument and she felt the square shape of it, solid and strong behind her and it gave her an idea. Using all of her might, she turned and stared at the stone cuboid at the bottom of the Monument, fighting to look past Father Time and the strange warrior women. The particles of magic within it started to vibrate and it cracked away from the base, twisting and grinding as it moved. It was harder than Quest, much harder, but it was working. First, antlers erupted from the stone and then legs sprouted, as grey as the marble they had come from, and last the vicious snout came roaring out of the rock.

'It's a bloody wendigo!' Mr Murphy cried from the ground and he stumbled to stand. Felix ordered her stone wendigo to attack and it staggered forward on uneven legs, roaring a deafening howl at Mr Murphy.

Felix watched as her wendigo stood over him, four or five feet taller than the red-skinned man who was cowering beneath. She pictured her wendigo stooping to bite but before she could finish the thought, Mr Mortimer's baton came flying towards the back of her head.

As everything went black, the stone wendigo fell to rubble and was no more.

16
Private Practise

Linus Godspell was sprawled out on his bed fiddling with the Spectoccules that his father had given to him. He felt a strange concoction of emotions at the gift from his father and the words that had accompanied it.

'Practise hard, my boy!' his father had said. 'This world will be yours one day, along with the Second and the Third and the Flame. It will all pass to you so learn how to see it.'

Linus gulped inadvertently, remembering how his father's regal form had dissolved in front of him as he'd passed onto the Second Plane before his very eyes. It was like Godspell's body had dispersed into the air with his exhalation; so effortless and fluid. His father returned in the same manner, smelling faintly of sulphur and a strange, cloying scent with a whisper of a cobweb on his otherwise immaculate suit. Linus applauded and promised to practise before his father dismissed him. Since then, they had only talked twice, though to say they had talked would be a generous elaboration. Merely, Linus had breakfasted in his father's presence whilst the man read The Monacle as the boy surreptitiously observed him in frustrated awe. When Linus did speak, Godspell flinched as though he had forgotten his son was there and he replied with a tension in his jaw that made Linus feel like an obligation; a duty that his father had no choice but to fulfil.

Linus wished with every particle of his body that they could spend more time together, but he understood that the positions of Firelighter and Grand Vizier were a great responsibility and his father was very proud of these responsibilities.

Of his mother, they spoke little or not at all. She was a magician of unremarkable parentage with no living family. She had died giving birth to their son and this was a great pain to Linus. He felt his father's grief whenever he felt those cold blue eyes resting on his face; it felt like resentment. But Linus could forgive his father this transgression for he had clearly been devoted to her; it was a punishable crime to mention his mother's name, all pictures of her had been destroyed and even the history books appertaining to any knowledge of her had been burned. Godspell erased her and all of his family from history. Even Linus did not know his own mother's name nor what she looked like, though he did not find this as painful as he had done when he was a young boy. Now, he agreed with his Father's opinion that that the past was a mirror but the future was a hatch; you could walk through and find something new on the other side.

It had been an unexpected surprise that Linus had been called in to his father's study a few nights ago and it was an even bigger surprise to receive the Spectoccules.

'Practise hard, my boy!'

But that was the problem.

The thing was, Linus hated magic. It was just too difficult for him. He had always struggled to manipulate the magic around him. It exhausted him just to move a glass across a room, or to change the colour of his bedroom walls so how on earth could he possibly control the Flame? Politics was fine; he could handle the commoners and their uprisings; he could control the Magistry for he'd been trained to understand politics since he was a little boy. But being the Firelighter was a duty that Linus was terrified of inheriting. Keeping this a secret from his father had been a nightmare. He had practised his magic secretly so that his father would never suspect that his son was a magical idiot. He had given himself nosebleeds in the past because he was concentrating so much on changing something, or trying to manifest the fire that he, as the future Firelighter, was supposed to have an affinity with.

What use would he be as the Firelighter?

Linus rolled over onto his front and looked around his ridiculously large room as though it could give him an answer. He had every luxury and gadget that a young man could want. He had thirteen pairs of gloves, some with fox fur lining, some with silk. He had Grieve's and Hawkins' suits pouring out of the massive wardrobe, books resting on shelves that reached the domed ceiling of his room, an unlicensed chalkey that could create a hatch wherever he drew one, the magical staff of Merlin shoved in a corner gathering dust and amulets and charms of varying powers thrown carelessly in cramped and disorganised drawers. And his pets? Oh he had plenty of pets! There was the rare Chinese Firefox that could light fires anywhere when he beat his tail on the floor. His stables held his Frannygird, a polymorph creature that could become any animal he wanted it to be and laid sparkling eggs, and he had a real ivory dragon egg that had been given to him from a visiting dignitary who had said the egg had been waiting to hatch for thirty years. Yes, he had everything he could ever want and now he had the Spectoccules. Any other magician boy his age would have been thrilled to receive them at so young an age and yet Linus wanted to hurl them against the wall, smashing the shimmering lenses to a hundred tiny pieces.

He sighed and put the Spectoccules on. His father wanted him to practise and practise he would. He was no stranger to practise. Linus adjusted the lenses the way his father had shown him, flipping each lens over the other until he could see the swirling mists of the Second Plane. He felt a tug of curiosity as a scent of wildflowers and rain-soaked rock sifted through the mists, but the Second Plane would have to wait. His Father would let him spend time there when he felt Linus deserved it. Godspell wanted his son to see the Third Plane first though Linus felt sure that he should practice on the Second before moving to the Third. But his Father had given strict instructions; the Second Plane was out of bounds.

Sighing, Linus lowered a green lens on the Spectoccules, manoeuvring the lenses until he found the arrangement that worked for him. Once he was more adept at seeing the Third Plane, he could lift each lens up until he was only using one lens on each eye but for now he needed most of the lenses. He squinted, focusing on seeing the particles of magic in the mist. He could see the beads of blue light but seeing the magic was easy enough, actually seeing through it was more difficult.

He tried to push his vision past the beads and see the image behind them. His father had said that the Third Plane was different for everybody. He'd said that because it was so close to the Flame, it contained the most condensed magic and that you had to tear through it like one was tearing through a thick veil of cloth. Well, Linus could see the magic; he could feel the heat on his face. He pushed himself further, straining his mind to push through the magic. For a moment he thought he saw something solid. He tried not to think for a moment, desperate to hold onto the fleeting solidarity of the Plane. The mist seemed to thin and he thought he could see a brief outline of a door. *A hatch!* Linus thought. He swallowed, tasting singed air. Reaching his hand out to the hatch, he had the sensation of being underwater, like his limbs were heavy and having to work harder to move. Linus' hand found the hatch to his amazement. The wood felt warm to his shaking hand. Sweat began to pour out of him, but not because of the heat. He was doing it!

Now he had to align himself with the Plane as his father had told him. This was not easy. It felt like he was straddling two worlds and if he lifted a foot from either, he would fall and crash. Linus remembered that had to move his body and the magic within himself to the Plane, not unlike stepping onto an unsteady bridge. He tried to keep a mental grip on the door as he stepped one foot at a time in front of it. Linus paused for moment, already feeling exhausted, and looked down. Yes, his whole body was with him. He felt the magic buzzing around him and the burning feeling that usually tingled in his hands when he practised magic was now all over his body. The important thing now was not to let go, to keep holding onto the magic. The door in front of him seemed to become brighter. He could make out the patterns in the wood and, yes, he could see the shiny bronze handle of the door. Now all he had to do was walk through it and he'd be safe. He'd be on the other side and ready to explore the Third Plane. He reached for the handle and felt it burn through his gloves. He grimaced. His head was throbbing with the effort of holding the magic together. There was a faint knock on wood. Was it coming from the door in front? The knocking grew louder. The door was slipping away. Mist was beginning to swirl around him again.

'No!' he shouted as he felt himself falling back onto the First Plane with a stumble that made him fall to the floor. The knocking continued more loudly. Somebody was banging on his bedroom door. He removed the Spectoccules angrily.

'What?' he barked, feeling a frustrating urge to cry. He thumped his fist on the floor. The door opened and his father's advisor, Larkin walked in. He stopped abruptly when he saw Linus on his knees in the middle of his room.

'What do you want, idiot?' Linus snapped, briefly surprised at how much he sounded like his father. 'You just interrupted my practise!'

Larkin's face was pale. He bowed low and rubbed his hands together nervously.

'I'm so sorry, Sir,' he snivelled, 'but your father told me to come and get you. He needs you in the Tower. He says he wants you to see something.'

Linus stood up quickly, a wave of dizziness making him sway and he gripped the edge of his desk. Fear began to snake through him, chasing away his disappointment. His father would be so angry at his failure.

'Are you well, Sir? If I may say, you look exhausted.'

'I'm fine, Larkin,' Linus mumbled, rubbing his eyes. They felt dry and prickly.

'Take me to my father and tell me, what could he possibly want me to see in the Tower?'

17
Rumours and Revelations

Felix opened her eyes groggily. For a moment she thought she was blind. The darkness was a deep as the Midst and she waited for her eyes to adjust, but there was no inkling of light to lend shape or form to anything.

The stench was horrific. Worse even than the smell of Mount Mudslop; it was a fog of excrement, sweat and the metallic twang of blood. Felix sat up and found she was next to a wall. Her shoulders ached, and her head was splitting with pain that made her so dizzy she had to rest one hand on the floor and one on the wall behind her to steady herself.

She had no idea where she was. Her thoughts seemed slow as she struggled to remember what had happened and then it came to her: the COPPs, Murphy and Mortimer, had captured her and taken her to the Tower of London. She dimly remembered the looming buildings that stood like giants in the dark as her captors pulled her through gates and over bridges and now here she was, locked away in a cold, stone tower with no light.

Her heart thumped as she thought of the dire wolf and the how still he had been after Mortimer had hit him with the baton. She felt a lurch of dread in her stomach and began to shiver.

Please let him be alive, she thought. *Please let him be ok.*

Felix closed her eyes and tried to breath, gagging at the smell. She began to shake and she choked down a scream of terror.

Think, Felix! She commanded herself. *You can get out of here. You're a magician!*

Her hands groped at the wall behind her and lifted herself up to her feet and rested her cheek against the wall to stop herself from falling. It was damp and slimy. She fought down nausea. For a moment, she saw pinpricks of light and she thought she would faint but she sucked in a huge gasp of air. Putting her gloved hands against the bricks, she closed her eyes and tried to force them to change; a window, a door, even a grid would help. The heat of magic surged through her hands and into the wall. There was an almighty cracking noise and the whole room shook as she was thrown backwards, her right flank hitting the solid stone of a column. Dust and rock fell down from the ceiling.

'Ow,' she moaned, rubbing her shoulder. Her coat and blouse had torn and she had a deep gash on her arm. Clutching at the wound, she squinted in the darkness trying to see what had pushed her.

'It's an anti-magic barrier,' said a woman's voice, quietly. Felix flattened herself against the column that had injured her.

'Who said that?' Felix demanded, clenching her hands into fists ready to punch if she needed to, though it hurt her arm. She strained her eyes and thought she saw a patch of even darker blackness crouched against the wall. Felix wished she had a candle.

'I did,' said the voice coming from a part of the wall that Felix had been next to moments earlier. 'Liberty Linnyshaw.'

Felix felt anxiety and panic rising again and tried to beat it down. She had to stay calm. She had to get out of here.

'What are you doing here?' she murmured, her voice hoarse with fear.

'Same as you it seems,' said the voice. The accent was eloquent and rich. It didn't seem suited to such a place as this. 'I'm a prisoner; a traitor to the head of state or some other such nonsense. And don't try to use magic again, or you'll wake the children. You've already woken most of the others.'

'Others?' Felix breathed. She couldn't see anybody else, but then she couldn't see anything. She heard the strike of a match and the room was lit with an orange glow as Liberty lit a candle. Felix saw her pale, birdlike features and long hair which looked like it should have been white blonde but was darkened with muck and grime. The woman's thinness and gaunt, purple shadows under her large green eyes scared Felix. Her eyes seemed too big for her face.

'Yes, the others,' whispered Liberty, scanning her owl eyes across the room. Felix followed their direction and raised her hand to her mouth in horror.

The room was larger than she had first thought. It was round and completely made of large stone bricks and slabs with stagnant water trickling down the walls. Straw was scattered on the floor covering mounds of waste and vomit. Curled up and shivering against the walls were people. She could hear the chattering of their teeth and the guttural wrench of their haggard breathing and she wondered how she had not heard it before. Now it seemed to fill her ears. They looked like skeletons, like living corpses decaying in front of her very eyes. Some were sleeping, huddled together for warmth but still shaking like they were having fits.

Then she saw children. So many children. Some looked like they were only just out of nappies, bone thin and filthy. The elderly, of which there were few, were leaned against the wall together, their skin sallow and clammy. A few of them were deathly still and grey, the colour of life gone from their faces.

There was no food, no water, though there were some dented and dirty bowls next to the children. Several curious rats shuffled around the feet of the captors and those who were awake had no strength to even shoo them away. Two emaciated men scrambled desperately to reach the vermin and Felix could not look away as they punched and kicked each other out of the way, the victor's hand finally capturing a rat as he lifted it to his mouth; predator gorging on his prey.

She counted thirty-two people.

Felix slumped to the floor and wretched emptily. She was horrified and silently, furiously angry, but it was mixed with fear so that any power that her anger might have exuded was quashed. The people in front of her were dying. Some were dead. They looked as though they had been there for weeks. Many of them looked like they'd been there much longer.

She scanned her eyes around the room again quickly and she felt her heart sink even lower. Where was the dire wolf?

'Hold on D.W,' Felix whispered. 'I'll find you.'

'D.W?' Liberty asked, looking at Felix properly for the first time. Her eyes drifted over the spirals on her face and Felix lowered her head, hoping her abundance of hair would cover her.

'My friend. He's a dire wolf. Where would he have been taken? Please...'

The woman narrowed her eyes before answering.

'If he's not been killed already, he'll be in the Lion Tower. That's where the animals are kept. You're in the Bell Tower. In the Tower of London, obviously,' Liberty said. Felix tried to slow the hammering of her heart.

Please, don't let him be dead.

'What's your name?' Liberty asked. Her voice was curious and gentle.

'Felix Spark,' Felix replied before it even occurred to her to lie. Liberty showed no expression, but she lifted Felix's hair out of her face.

'Well, Sparky,' she muttered. 'Try and cover up those markings on your face before the others see. Most won't recognise a Drow but there are some older ones here who will know the markings. You'll be worth a pretty penny to Godspell I'm sure and there are some in here who would use you to bargain for their freedom.'

Felix rubbed some muck off the wall onto her face, wincing at the smell.

'You know Drow?' she asked hopefully. Liberty shook her head.

'Extinct. I haven't seen a Drow for a long time. Godspell will want to try you in the machine.'

'What?' Felix asked but Liberty fell silent. The woman was rocking gently, her head twitching as she bit at her blackened nails which were already so chewed that they were bleeding.

'How long have you been here?' Felix asked her quietly. There was a long pause.

'Since the 26th August,' Liberty said.

'6 days,' Felix calculated.

'Is that all?' Liberty whispered, her face in despair. 'It feels so much longer than that.'

'What happened? Why did you get thrown in here? What about the rest of them?'

Felix asked desperately, helping Liberty to sit on the floor.

'I'm a freedom fighter,' she said simply. 'Part of an uprising against Godspell. No need to look so shocked, Sparky. Most of us in here are rebels of some kind.'

'You're a magician?' Felix asked, her eyes flicking to Liberty's gloveless hands.

'Yes. The COPPs...they take your gloves when they...question us. Degradation, you know? Makes us see that we're no different to commoners in Godspell's eyes.' She motioned to the others around the room. Felix noted the difference in their clothing. There was a young girl wearing jeans and trainers, a man wearing work clothes that were so frequently seen in the Commoner's Quarter. The more she looked, the more she saw. Commoners and magicians held captive together. There was a very clear divide between them. The magicians huddled on one side of the room, the commoners on the other. As she looked at them, they began to notice her, their eyes cautious and hungry as they watched her. Felix lowered her head again.

'You said you're part of an uprising?' she asked quietly. 'Did you attack Godspell?'

Liberty considered Felix for a moment before nodding her head.

'I work...worked at the Citadel. I was a Magistry member in the International Relations sector. You seem surprised? You never imagined that Magistry workers would be enemies of Godspell? Well, there are plenty, Sparky.' Liberty paused and then she lowered her voice further. 'Godspell creates enemies everywhere. Enemies who work for him, even serve the food that he eats. We had insiders, but Godspell wheedled out all but one of them.'

'If he has so many enemies, why don't they do something?' Felix asked, frustrated.

'Fear,' Liberty shrugged. 'Godspell captures whole families and sends them to the machine. I don't know many people who would be brave enough to go against him instead of pretending to 'owe him their allegiance' and all that rubbish.'

'What do you mean by machine?'

Liberty flinched and closed her eyes. She shook her head vigorously and began to rock back and forth again. She seemed to flit between madness and sanity. Felix hugged her knees to her chest.

'Don't mention that infernal invention,' grunted a man in a vermillion waistcoat. He had prematurely grey hair and a handlebar moustache that was so heavily waxed that it had not been affected by the conditions he was living in.

Felix turned and looked at him. He was laying on the ground against the wall on the side of the magicians.

'And stop gossiping, Lib. She could be a spy.'

Liberty drifted back into sanity.

'I hardly think she's a spy, Sigbert. She's just a kid.'

'Godspell gets them when they're young. You know that well enough,' the man named Sigbert sighed.

'I'm not a spy,' Felix said, flitting her eyes between the two.

'That's what a spy would say,' Sigbert said, smiling a little as he sat up. He brushed off the straw from his tweed trousers in a futile attempt to tidy himself.

'Sigbert Goodnight at your service,' he said, reaching out his bare hand to Felix. She shook it gingerly, noticing several of his fingernails had been removed.

'Co-conspirator to the attempted murder of Godspell,' he continued, grinning proudly.

Felix swallowed and introduced herself. She suddenly felt very out of her depth.

'Myself, Sigbert and a team of three other rebels were to attack Godspell and kill him,' Liberty was explaining, 'but we failed. We always fail. There's only me and Sig left now.'

'What happened the others?' Felix asked. The silence that resulted was ominous.

'Do you guys know someone called Aubrey Dovepeace?' Felix changed the subject. Immediately, Sigbert and Liberty stiffened.

'I told you she was a spy!' Sigbert hissed, scrambling over to Felix and pushing her against the column. She tried to shove him away from her but her injured arm offered little strength.

'I'm – friends – with – Aubrey!' Felix cried through gasps as Sigbert's hands closed around her throat.

'Sigbert, do get off her and use your head,' Liberty pulled the man off Felix. He looked vaguely shocked at what he had just done.

'Look at her face, for goodness sake,' Liberty whispered into his ear, just loud enough that Felix could hear. Sigbert gazed at her face intently and saw the tell-tale spirals through the dirt that covered them.

'Oh I say,' he cried out, waking the remaining sleepers in the room. They all turned to look at the three of them. 'I'm frightfully sorry! I didn't know who you were...of course not. Nobody does. Ha!'

'Alright, stop making a scene!' Liberty muttered. 'And stop gawping at her. You want the others to notice?'

Sigbert backed away from Felix, his hands up in contrition. Felix stared at him, eyes wide in fright and shock.

"Ere, what's that commotion over there?' an old woman shouted from the commoner's part of the room.

'Nothing, Old Nell. Go back to sleep,' Sigbert called over to her.

'We got a new one, have we?' Old Nell asked, ignoring Sigbert. 'One o' your lot or ours?'

'It's another magician, Nell,' a little girl squeaked. Felix started. The girl, aged about seven years old, was stood behind the column that Felix leaned on. Old Nell began mumbling incoherently.

'Wotcha,' the little girl said. She sat down cross legged in front of Felix, who tried very hard not to notice that the child had a black eye so swollen that it hid the eye underneath. 'I'm Gertie.'

'Felix,' smiled Felix.

'Whatchoo in for?'

'Err. I had a disagreement with some COPPs,' Felix lied, glimpsing at Liberty who was holding a finger over her lips.

'Nasty lot, them COPPs,' Gertie nodded. 'They nabbed me at the Borderlock, try'na get into the Mire to scavenge a bit.'

'Gertie, you get away from that magician!' Old Nell shouted. One or two other commoners mumbled in agreement with Nell's command.

'Leave it out, Nell. She's alright, this one.'

'I ain't never seen a magician that's 'alright'. Get back 'ere! And you, magician; stick to you and yours and we'll stick to ours. Bad enough we've got to share a prison, let alone talk to each other!'

Felix felt as though she had been slapped. She hadn't forgotten the enmity the commoners had for magicians but she hadn't thought she would be a victim of it, not when she had grown up as a commoner. She looked down at her clothes. As dirty and as torn as they were, there was no doubt that they were the clothes of a magician. She traced a finger over her mud-covered face. She had to admit it, she was a magician now. She was no longer a commoner; she never had been. It hurt her more than all of the wounds she had suffered.

Silence began to invade the room again and it stole away the consciousness of the prisoners. After a while, Liberty blew out the candle she had lit.

Felix slept.

***

'Psst! Oi! Pssst!'

Felix stirred. She couldn't tell how long she had been asleep. It could have been minutes or hours.

'Are you awake?'

'Gertie?' Felix asked, reaching out in the dark. She flinched when she felt a bony little arm very close to her.

'Yes, it's me. Shhh!'

'What's up?' Felix rubbed her head. Everything felt very thick and foggy.

'Can't sleep. Never can in here. Old Nell can sleep anywhere.'

Felix felt the little girl shuffle closer.

'How long have you been here?' Felix whispered. She felt Gertie shrug and she was silent for a few minutes.

'You're a nice magician,' Gertie said very quietly.

'Thank you,' Felix replied, lowering her head.

'See, Old Nell thinks you're all the same, all bastards she says. She's old though. Ancient even. I seen enough magicians to know that you're all as scared of Godspell and Dr Nyxon as we are.'

'Who's Dr Nyxon?' Felix felt Gertie tense up.

'He's a monster,' Gertie mumbled.

'He's a venephysicist,' Sigbert's voice cut through the darkness, loudly. Both Felix and Gertie jumped. Even in the blackness, Felix could feel the other prisoners beginning to waken and stir again. A tremor of annoyance ran through the prison, like it was a living breathing thing.

'He created a machine,' Sigbert continued, 'many years ago. It harnesses magic and magnifies its power. Nyxon had it patented as a machine that could have been used by commoners, as a way of bringing magic into their lives in a practical way. But when Godspell came to power, he recruited Nyxon and corrupted him. Now the machine is used for...other purposes.'

'What other purposes? What does it do?' Felix climbed to her knees and turned in the direction of Sigbert's voice.

'It kills yer,' Old Nell's voice shouted. 'Sucks out yer memories.'

'Nah, that's a lamia, you nitwit. Don't you commoners know anything?' said another voice, coming from the side of the Magicians.

Voices began to rise, and insults were hurled in anger across the room. Liberty, who had been silent, lit her candle and Felix blinked in the light, horrified at the hatred etched onto the hollow faces of the prisoners as they shouted to one another.

'Common as muck...'

'Unnatural creatures...'

'Ignorant animals...'

'Terrorists!'

'Will you all shut up?!' Felix shouted over the din. The roof of the prison shook and dust fell from the cracks between bricks.

'Careful, Sparky,' Liberty warned. 'The anti-magic barrier...don't get all fired up.'

Felix looked at Liberty, who had a knowing expression on her face. Felix rose her hand to her face fleetingly and let it drop, breathing in her anger.

'Don't you think this is exactly what Godspell wants?' she said to the prisoners. 'Why else would he put commoners and magicians together? Far easier that we kill each other than he do it himself.'

They silenced for a moment before Old Nell, who seemed to be the speaker for the commoners, spoke up.

'Oh I don't think he wants us to kill each other, girl. I think he takes great pride in his machine doing that for him.'

'Will someone please tell me what this damn machine is?' Felix asked. She noticed that most people, commoner and magician alike, shuddered when she mentioned it.

'The machine is an invention that amplifies the magical properties within an object,' Liberty said. Her voice was low and her eyes were closed. All turned to look at her.

'Like Sigbert said, it was intended to be used by both magicians and commoners. But Godspell found another use for it. With Dr Nyxon's help, he began to test the machine on people. At first, Godspell said he was doing it to help commoners, to try and bring out the magic within them.'

'He was trying to turn commoners into magicians?' Felix asked. Liberty nodded.

'Yes. He had us all convinced, all of us at the Magistry. It seemed like such a noble aim. Equality for all, no more divide between us; everyone would be a magician. It didn't occur to us that commoners wouldn't want to be magicians...'

'That's cos yer all arrogant little-'

'Shut up and let her finish, Nell,' Gertie interrupted. Liberty waited a moment and then continued.

'But, the machine had no effect at all on commoners. There isn't enough magic within them to amplify, you see. It rests upon them rather than them being made of it. Dr Nyxon had an idea that using the Flame of Magic would make the machine more powerful.'

'What's the Flame of Magic?' asked Gertie.

'It's the source of all the magicians' power,' Felix explained. The magicians cried out and swore at Felix for revealing the secret of the Flame. She glared at them with fire in her eyes.

'Keeping secrets is what created this whole mess,' she motioned to both the commoners and the magicians and the prison surrounding them. 'This is their world too and they have a right to know.'

Felix looked back at Liberty who was staring at Felix with sad eyes. She shook her head ever so slightly.

'What?' Felix asked.

'Nothing,' said Liberty. 'But you sound a little like Godspell.'

Felix opened and closed her mouth in surprise. The silence in the room felt suddenly very threatening.

'Go on,' Gertie said to Liberty. 'Nyxon said that using this Flame of Magic thingy would make the machine more powerful...'

'Yes,' nodded Liberty. 'So Godspell did the unthinkable and used the very Flame he's sworn to protect. By using the machine to magnify its power, the Flame became a deadly force. When Nyxon tested the machine on the next batch of commoners, it killed them all. It's killed everyone who has ever set foot inside it. Even magicians.'

'He's testing it on magicians too?' Felix asked, eyes wide. 'His own kind?'

'Yes of course he is,' Sigbert interrupted angrily. 'He had to see how it affected magicians; maybe they held the key to changing the commoners. But no, it killed them too. So now, thanks to Dr Nyxon, Godspell has a machine that kills indiscriminately. A happy accident for Godspell, I'm sure. But he wants his machine to work; he wants it to convert commoners.'

'There's more,' Liberty said softly. 'Before Sigbert and I left the Magistry, we heard rumours. Godspell wants the machine to convert *anyone* who is put inside it. He wants to use it to drain magicians of their power. We think.... We think he wants to create his own race of magicians: convert the commoners into a magician army and then drain the magicians who oppose him.

'I said I worked in the International Relations Sector in the Magistry. Well, working there, one hears things. Europe is unhappy with the influence Godspell is having on other countries. Russia, Japan, Italy...they see what's happening in Britain as an excellent example of Magical dominance. Godspell's reign is spreading and we think he is planning to spread his power across the world.'

Felix was reeling. She imagined Godspell's terror spreading across the old atlas she had looked at in the school Book Room like a red virus.

'We've got to stop him,' she whispered.

Sigbert laughed. It sounded unhinged.

'What do you think we've been trying to do?' He spread his arms out wide. Felix remembered what Liberty had said earlier about most of them being rebels of some kind.

'Are you a rebellion too?' she asked Old Nell. She was annoyed that the commoners began to laugh.

'Wouldn't call it a rebellion,' Old Nell said. 'Not enough of us.'

'But there are some of you!' Felix cried.

'Some. Ha. Yeah there are some. Hiding in the Quarter, shuffling from house to house having secret meetings. And wanna know what we do? Eh? We write newspaper articles. We mock and joke and ridicule Godspell in writing and send it out into the Quarter. The Touch Papers we call it and tha's all we do. We ain't no fighters, no rebellion. Just a bunch of writers who fancied havin' a laugh and look where it got us! Wha's the point, eh? Ain't no point in fightin anymore!'

'That's not true,' Felix said, the frustration tightening her throat. Gertie began to cry. Felix thought that somebody should comfort her but everybody looked defeated. Not a single person in the prison could offer any hope or comfort.

'So that's it?' Felix said quietly. 'You're all just going to give up?'

'Felix...' Liberty began.

'No! No we have to fight. Look at what he's done to us! Don't you see that we have to stand together? We can't be commoner and magician anymore. We're all victims and we have to choose to fight against him.'

Old Nell rolled her eyes and Gertie began to sob harder. Felix watched from behind a veil of black anger as many of them turned away, rolled over, ignored her words. Even Liberty and Sigbert looked resigned and hopeless.

The anger boiled inside her and she didn't try to control it. Beneath her feet, the ground began to shake and more dust fell from the ceiling.

'Felix!' Liberty shouted, but it was too late.

All it took was a flicker.

18
Escape!

Several things happened at once. Just as the first flames of furyfire sprang to Felix's fingertips, the anti-magic barrier cracked loudly and the door of the prison split open, right where Nigel had whacked it with magical force to break the oak beams of the door. He stood there, damp from the rain and coughing, dragging dusty air into his lungs.

The prisoners screamed and Felix called out in surprise, feeling the gloss of the furyfire fading away. Nigel glanced around with wide eyes behind dirty glasses, spluttering in the rubble.

'Felix, hurry. We have to go, now! We knocked out these two COPPs but others will be on their way.'

Felix looked down and saw Murphy and Mortimer passed out on the floor. Murphy had a rather nasty looking bite mark on his face and Felix saw the dire wolf looking through the prison door, his mouth proudly arched and spattered a little with blood.

'D.W!' Felix cried, leaping forward and throwing her arms around the neck of the shaggy, blood-soaked wolf. The commoners in the prison looked on as though she was insane.

'I'm ok,' D.W reassured her, though he was limping badly.

'Felix, please,' Nigel pressed. 'We don't have time. We really have to go.'

'The others,' Felix said, pointing at the prisoners behind her who sat hunched and terrified in the light leaking into the prison from the corridor. Nigel peered into the room, swallowing at the conditions of the room but he shook his head.

'We can't take them,' he said, grabbing Felix's hand and tugging it but Felix pulled her arm back.

'I won't leave them, Nigel,' she said. Nigel considered her for a moment, looked at the prisoners and then sighed.

'Come on then. Quickly, all of you. Down the stairs and through the courtyard. Make for Traitor's Gate. There's a boat waiting. But be careful!'

Just as he spoke, a high-pitched shriek of an alarm sounded.

'Go!' Nigel cried. 'Now!'

Felix reached for Gertie's hand and pulled her to her feet. Then, she rounded up the commoners, Old Nell included. The magicians hesitated and many ran but a few, including Liberty and Sigbert stayed to help the commoners who were too weak to walk unaided.

They scrambled down the stairs at a slow pace and Felix tripped over steps under the weight of Old Nell, who was leaning on her shoulder. Screams from the courtyard stopped them dead in their tracks. A terrifying hissing wail broke through the wall and drove fear, like a nail, into Felix's heart. She turned to look at Nigel and D.W.

'Lamias,' Nigel breathed.

Felix let go of Old Nell and pulled herself up to a thin slit of a window in the stairwell. Outside, she saw the glistening scales of the lamias' tails and the black holes of their eyes as they extricated the memories of the prisoners who had run away first. The victims stood frozen with expressions of confusion and bewilderment on their faces. Then one by one, they fell to the ground. They were grey shells, all life gone from them. As the lamias continued to scream, the prisoners' corpses faded, leaving just the clothes their frail bodies had been wearing and the stench of sulphor.

The lamias' wails continued and Felix watched them slither over towards the doorway of the Tower door, COPPs following close behind in their crimson outfits, with bloodthirsty eyes.

'Get Nyxon!' one of them shouted and a group of COPPs ran to the Tower opposite.

'Felix, Murphy and Mortimer are waking!' snarled D.W, his eyes resting on the ceiling of the stairwell.

'We're trapped!' Felix yelled, her mind clawing for a solution.

'Not if I can help it!' D.W growled. He bounded down the stairs, ignoring his broken paw and howled so loudly that Felix had to cover her ears.

'The howl of a dire wolf,' she whispered, remembering Nigel's Quest card. 'It can kill a lamia!'

The sound of hissing and snakish screaming poured through the air as the lamias fell, banging their hands against their heads as though trying to stop the howl from reaching their ears. D.W continued to howl, darting in between the lamias like a dog teasing cats.

'Run!' Felix cried.

As quickly as they could, they raced down the stairs, following D.W's increasingly breathless howls. The beating of COPPs boots on wood told them that the enemy was rushing up to meet them, but Sigbert Goodnight thrust his hand towards the faces of the COPPs and Felix hardly had time to see their expressions crumble in pain as he magically broke their noses. The COPPs hooted, gripping their faces, tripping over each other and blocking their exit, but Liberty simply circled her hand and the stairwell widened.

'Wow," Gertie whispered in awe before being yanked further down the stairwell and into the courtyard by Felix.

They ran past the twitching bodies of the lamias and the empty clothes of the unfortunate prisoners who had run first. Felix had to fight the urge to stop but she could hear Murphy and Mortimer screaming out of the window of the Tower to the COPPs below and she could feel bursts of magic being flung towards them in attack. The alarm continued to shriek.

'Which way?' Felix called to Nigel. When he didn't answer, she turned and saw him holding up his hands as though holding a shield to protect them all from the magical attack that Murphy was throwing down at them through the window of the Tower.

'To the right!' he said through gritted teeth. His nose had begun to bleed. Before she had time to think about what she was doing, Felix handed Gertie to Liberty and ran to Nigel. She could feel the heat of the magic from behind the invisible shield that Nigel was projecting from his hands.

'Go!' he screamed at her. 'It doesn't matter about me! You're all that matters!'

Somewhere inside her a hook pulled at her stomach and her heart and, in that moment, she understood everything that Fiddle and Aubrey had been trying to tell her. She was the one to end all of this. She was the Firelighter. People needed her. But she could not leave Nigel.

Felix rested her hand on Nigel's and envisioned all of her anger and all of her fear pouring out of her into his shield. She saw a large wavering disc fan out from their joined hands, visible, but only just, like waves of heat on the horizon. The shield floated away from them, growing larger but fainter as it spread.

'Come on,' Felix said. Nigel gaped at the shield she had expanded and then they ran.

By the time they made it to the boat, D.W had already filled it with Liberty, Sigbert, Gertie, Old Nell and the few others who had joined them. The boat was an old lifeboat, only a little bigger than a rowboat and it was already dipping under their weight, but Nigel and Felix had no choice but to leap into it. They could hear the cries and shouts of the COPPs behind them but Felix and Nigel's shield was blocking their way. It wouldn't last much longer, though. Sigbert and Nigel untied the rope that had held the boat in the dock and pushed away from the stone steps, through the small black dock of Traitor's Gate.

'We needed to make the boat invisible,' Felix said through gasps of breath.

'Already done,' Liberty smiled.

'Unnatural...' mumbled Old Nell, but her complaints trailed off and she offered Felix a grimace which Felix thought was an attempt at a smile.

'Thanks,' Nigel said gruffly to Felix. 'Thanks for not leaving me.'

Felix nodded and somewhere inside her, the hook twisted and seemed to let loose a nest of butterflies. Next to her, D.W smiled toothily.

"How did you know where to find me?"

'I'll explain later,' Nigel panted. 'Right now we need to get to the Safeplace.'

'The Safeplace? Where's that?'

Nigel flashed her a lopsided smile.

'Belfast,' he said.

19
Belfast

Nigel would say no more, much to Felix's annoyance, but she felt too weak to argue. In fact, she had never felt as bone tired and world weary as she felt in that moment. The boat cut through the inky black depths of the Thames as effortlessly as a blade, though nobody was rowing it. Water slapped against the wood and lulled Felix into a doze, her matted head resting against Nigel's shoulder.

'There's a lot she doesn't know,' Felix heard Liberty's voice float through her consciousness. But she was sleepy. So sleepy.

'I know.' Nigel's voice was a rumble next to her ear. She felt a hand stroke her hair and she lifted her head towards it like a cat.

A low grumble of voices around her soothed Felix, like white noise and she let herself fall deeper into sleep but within a few moments, she was being shaken awake.

'Felix,' Nigel whispered to her softly. 'We're here.'

'Already?' Felix yawned, her head thumping heavily. *How can we be in Ireland already?* She thought to herself. D.W chortled at her thought and she opened her eyes and her mouth fell open.

They were certainly not in Ireland. In fact, they had not left London. They hadn't even left the Thames. Turning around unsteadily on the boat, she saw Tower Bridge and the ghastly goliath of the Tower staring out at her from across the river. She could just make out the shapes of COPPs running around, red ants on their hill. It made her terribly glad that their boat was invisible. But then again, she doubted that anybody would have predicted that the Safeplace of the rebellion would be so absurdly close to the Tower and the Citadel. Just across the river, in fact.

Felix looked up at the leviathan that emerged from the black abyss of the water. The shining metal looked dense and hefty with chains thicker than her arm clinking from the hawseholes in the hull of a great warship and descending into the river.

'Welcome to the HMS Belfast,' Nigel smiled at her.

HMS Belfast was a ship, but not a ship like Felix had seen in picture books. It had no sails, no wooden deck, no beams. Instead it looked like a floating tank, impossibly heavy and sturdy, so much so that Felix couldn't understand how it was managing to stay afloat.

Raised voices from the lifeboat diverted her attention away from the ship. The commoner prisoners were shouting at Sigbert and Liberty angrily.

'That's a *commoner* war ship!' a frail looking man was shouting. Wrinkles fell around his eyes but they didn't hide the anger within them. 'How dare you pollute it with your... your abominations!'

'Tha's from the war is that! Don't you 'ave no respect?' Old Nell joined in, glad of another reason to fight with the magicians. Gertie rolled her eyes.

'Look, you can either come aboard with us and let us take care of you or you can risk it in the city on your own...with COPPs and lamias on the loose,' Sigbert reasoned, struggling to keep the anger out of his voice. 'Think about what happened to other prisoners, for goodness sake! We are not your damn enemies!'

The lifeboat wobbled in silence as Old Nell, the wrinkled man and the other commoners eyed each other nervously. After a moment, Gertie exhaled loudly and stood up, struggling a little to keep her balance.

'How do we get on it?' she jutted her chin towards the Belfast. Nigel smiled at her before putting his thumb and forefinger to his tongue and whistling. Felix was impressed. She never could whistle like that. A second later, another whistle came from the unseen deck of the boat and Nigel threw up a rope attached to the lifeboat. Little Gertie fell down as the little boat lurched towards the helm of the ship as someone on the vessel pulled the lifeboat closer and held it tightly against the metal side. Felix saw rungs of a ladder jutting out from the side of the ship and figured that was how they were going to get onto the ship. D.W nodded at her and she began to climb up the rungs. It was difficult. Her feet hardly found grip on the tiny protrusions of metal but as she reached the top, she felt sturdy, coarse little hands grab her blouse in between her shoulder blades and with a tug, she was careered over the top onto the deck of the boat.

'Phew. Thanks,' she breathed but froze when she saw that the hands belonged to a man so short that he could not have reached higher than the middle of her thigh. He wasn't exactly fat, but he wasn't a slim man either. In fact, Felix thought of the word 'squat' immediately when she looked at him. The second word she thought of was leprechaun and a disbelieving giggle bubbled up out of her mouth.

'You gotta problem, have you, deary?' the man said with a strong Irish accent. He had a shock of bright red hair and matching stubble on his chin and jaw.

Felix couldn't answer; she just stared and the man went back to helping up Gertie, who tumbled onto the deck, closely followed by Old Nell.

'What on Gawd's green Earth are you?' Old Nell cried out, pulling Gertie away in horror. To be fair to Old Nell, the little man did look a bit surprising. Whilst he did look human, there was something...different about him, other than his height. Maybe it was the way his ears were just a little bit too large for his head, or the way they were just a little too pointed. Or maybe it was his hands, which were flat and wide and strong and looked far too big for his stature. Or perhaps Old Nell was shocked by the nearly luminous green of his eyes, which glittered with menace and magic.

'I'm all that's standing in the way between you and a horrible watery death, deary. You can be sure of that. Stand back.'

He continued to help those scrambling up the side of the boat and realising too late that he was doing this on his own, Felix joined him just in time to help Nigel and Sigbert onto the boat, who, between them, had D.W perched rather perilously between them, his front paws resting on Nigel's shoulders and his hind paws on Sigbert's behind him. Felix wondered if it was possible for dire wolves to look a little green but bit her lip when D.W flashed a toothy snarl at her before collapsing onto a heap on the deck.

'Thanks, Carrig,' Nigel nodded at the little man, who frowned deeply at him in return.

'You're lucky you got away,' he mumbled as he turned away, leading them all along the deck towards a door that was open a crack.

'Lucky, huh?' Nigel said, winking at Felix. She smothered a laugh.

Carrig led them down through the door and down a steep metal staircase and then onto a narrow corridor. Lights flickered on as they passed and Felix didn't have enough eyes to take in all the switches and dials and knobs of all the control panels that mounted the walls. There were no portholes and the corridor was so thin that two people would have struggled to pass each other if they were walking in different directions. Pipes travelled along the ceiling of the corridor in varying colours and Felix vaguely wondered what each of them did.

Carrig, it seemed, knew the ship well and led them down corridor after corridor, through doors and passageways before they eventually reached a closed deck with rows of tables and benches. Closed portholes with blinds over them studded the walls. It smelled faintly of old cooking.

'This is the Officers' Mess,' Carrig grunted. 'It's the main common area and where we eat. I have no doubt that you'll all be hungry. I'm not cooking! But if you're lucky, there'll be some leftovers from supper. I'll be right back.'

Felix waited for him to leave, which didn't take long. He was surprisingly light on his feet and scuttled away quickly.

'Ok, Nigel,' she said folding her arms. 'Spill.'

'Is that....a leprechaun?!' Old Nell asked and was immediately shushed by Gertie.

'Unnatural!' shouted the wrinkled old man. Liberty and Sigbert threw up their hands in frustration and went to sit down at one of the tables. Sigbert put his feet up on the polished wood, apparently quite at home.

'Nigel?' Felix asked again. Nigel looked at D. W and reluctantly began to explain.

'The HMS Belfast is a Safeplace. It's a place for magicians who are against Godspell to come and...express their views.'

'A rebellion?' Felix said excitedly, looking towards Liberty and Sigbert who smiled at her sadly.

'Don't get ahead of yourself, Sparky,' Liberty said, biting at her nails. Nigel nodded in agreement and continued.

'A rebellion implies that the magicians who meet here are fighters. They're not. They're Magistry workers, shop owners, glovemakers... everyday people. Remember what Aubrey said? They're more like a protest group. They meet in various Safeplaces across London...probably across all of Britain. Pockets of people have tried attacking Godspell or the COPPs - '

'That'll be us!' Sigbert cried out, bowing with a flourish.

'But the key word there is tried,' Nigel said, ignoring the interruption. 'Thing is, we're out numbered and underpowered. We don't have the resources to fight against Godspell, his COPPs and the Magistry members who are loyal to him.'

'Or Dr Nyxon,' Felix added quietly. Nigel studied her for a moment.

'Those rumours are true?' he asked.

'Not only are they true but they're massively inaccurate. Nyxon's machine kills,' Liberty said, blinking and beginning to rock a little in her chair. Felix watched as Sigbert rested his hand on hers, trying to calm her but it all seemed too much for Liberty. The relief of being rescued and the horrors she had endured left her in shock and she kept looking about, as though she was trying to find someone. Sigbert placed his hands gently over her eyes.

'She'll be here,' he whispered softly to her. 'Sleep now.' Immediately, Liberty crumpled against him, sleeping deeply.

'Hold on,' Felix said quietly so as not to disturb Liberty. She flopped down onto a bench. 'Let me get this straight. Across the country, there are groups of magicians who actually want to overthrow Godspell? How many are we talking?'

'Hundreds,' Nigel guessed.

'Thousands,' Sigbert said more firmly.

Felix looked towards Old Nell and the small huddle of commoners who were still standing and watching the whole exchange very curiously.

'And you, Old Nell, you say there is a group of commoners writing secret newspapers, spreading the truth about Godspell's lies?'

'Well, I... err. Yes,' Old Nell replied.

'So why hasn't anyone rallied these people together?' Felix asked, her voice louder than she meant it to be. 'Why hasn't Aubrey or Fiddle actually gone and *bloody* done something?'

'Because neither Aubrey nor myself are leaders, Felix.'

Felix turned to the door that Carrig had exited through and saw Fiddle walking through it, holding trays of food, followed by Aubrey and Carrig who were carrying similarly laden trays and jugs of cloudy looking liquid. Felix's mouth immediately began to water as she recognised Nigel's lemonade.

Fiddle laid the trays down on the nearest table and there was pandemonium as the rescued prisoners attacked the food. Felix remained where she was, looking at Fiddle squarely in his eyes and feeling a faint blush rising to her cheeks.

'I'm sorry I ran,' she mumbled but she jutted out her chin determinedly to show that she would do it all again.

'It's good to have you back, Felix,' Aubrey said but her eyes were locked on Liberty's sleeping frame, curled up on a bench with Sigbert's coat as a pillow.

'She's fine,' Sigbert said to her through a mouthful of cream cakes. 'Told you I'd keep her safe. Let her sleep.'

Aubrey chewed on her lip and her eyes were shining with tears but she nodded. Felix suddenly realised how it was for them and she smiled, seeing a different side to Aubrey who was stroking Liberty's hair tenderly. Aubrey caught Felix's eye and gave her a bashful grin.

Felix glanced at Fiddle who looked ashen and exhausted and she felt guilty for running away and frightening him. She knew she'd have to talk to him eventually but for the moment, she just wanted to speak to Nigel.

'Thank you,' she said, nudging her shoulder against his when he came and sat next to her. 'For coming for me.'

Nigel rubbed the back of his neck as his freckles disappeared into the redness that spread over his face.

'Couldn't have left you there,' he said a little gruffly.

'How did you find me in the first place?' she asked him curiously. 'Don't get me wrong. I'm so glad you did!'

'Err. Well, don't get angry, ok? I followed you.'

Felix drew back a little and nodded slowly, waiting for him to explain. It turned out Nigel had heard Felix and D.W sneaking down the stairs. He'd followed them as far as the basement hatch before doubling back to tell Fiddle, who contacted Carrig to get the Belfast ready for an attack if it came to it. When Nigel got through the hatch, he'd run around frantically trying to find them and had eventually spotted them as they were crossing the bridge. Guessing that Felix was going to Monument, Nigel had panicked, fearing for Felix's safety, especially when a nest of snotterlings had started chasing them.

'I went after you. By the time I arrived at Monument, I saw those two COPPs dragging you and the dire wolf through a hatch. I figured you'd be taken to the Tower. When I got back to the library, Alchemus already had Aubrey there and was waking up everyone he could think of to help. He was half mad with worry, Felix. I've never seen him like that.'

Felix looked down ruefully and dared not lift her eyes to look at Fiddle. She felt sure he was watching her. Then a thought occurred to her.

'Hang on, why didn't Fiddle or Aubrey come for me? Why send you?'

Nigel frowned, insulted by Felix's tone.

'Hey,' she said, squeezing his hand. 'I said I was glad you came. I just mean... if I'm as important as they say I am...why did Fiddle not help you himself. I mean surely the master is better than the apprentice?'

'I volunteered,' Nigel said, ice touching his voice. He pulled his hand away and walked off to get some food. Felix winced. That had come out all wrong and now he was mad at her. After all she'd been through with the COPPs and the Tower and the lamias, Nigel being angry at her was what made her want to cry.

'Ee-jit girl,' Carrig said as he came towards her, resting a goblet of lemonade in front of her. 'He didn't give anyone else the choice of coming for you. Just said he was going for you and wild horses couldn't stop him. I deal in luck...and you have more of it than you know to have him on your side.'

Felix exhaled loudly and gulped the lemonade down hoping the taste of sunlight would warm her sinking heart.

***

It turned out that Carrig wasn't the only leprechaun on the HMS Belfast. The ship, which was alarmingly huge and labyrinthine, was crewed by nearly fifty of the little men and women, who had blessed the ship at its completion in Belfast in 1939 and had never left. Like most magical creatures, they were largely invisible to the commoners who sailed on the vessel but to the commoner prisoners who had found refuge on the ship after Nigel had rescued them, they allowed themselves to be seen, much to the horror of Old Nell and the wrinkled old man, who Felix eventually learned was called Eugene, and was just as cantankerous as she had first thought him to be.

The leprechauns weren't exactly gracious hosts. They grudgingly allowed the Belfast to be used as a Safeplace because a: they respected and almost liked Fiddle, who had once helped them recover a stolen pot of Fortuna which Felix understood to be some kind of powdered essence of 'luck', and b: the leprechauns hated Godspell since he had banned their return to the Second Plane several years earlier and they encouraged any kind of revolt against him.

They had their own brand of magic and though Nigel had been decidedly frosty with her since their talk, he had told Felix that they were skilled mechanics and inventors and, if lucky enough to be blessed by a leprechaun, luck or 'Lady Fortuna' as they occasionally called it, would work in your favour until the blessing wore off.

On the morning after the rescue, Felix and the other freed prisoners were asked by a gruff sounding leprechaun by the name of Grunnion, to gather once again in the Officers' Mess.

In the daylight, the cabin looked far more spacious than it had done the night before, with grey light bouncing off the waters and through the portholes. Through a yawn, Felix saw that the prisoners had all been given fresh clothes and they looked clean and well rested. Wounds had been bandaged, bruises doused in arnica and hair brushed. They no longer looked like the undead, though they were in want of a few more meals. Felix made a determined pact with herself to ensure they were looked after before they parted ways. Even the commoners.

Especially the commoners.

Of the thirty-three prisoners crowded into the nightmare chamber, sixteen of them were aboard the Belfast. Some had run from the Tower and the lifeboat, chancing their escape, but most of them had been victims of the lamias' cruel scream. Just remembering the sound they had made brought goosebumps to Felix's flesh. She tried not to think of the piles of empty clothes in the courtyard, strewn haphazardly as though dropped, twitching in the night wind. Not even ashes to save and honour. The lamias had left nothing.

A cry made Felix jump out of her seat. She spun towards the sound and saw Liberty rushing to Aubrey Dovepeace, tears streaming down her face as Aubrey held her tightly. Liberty's body was shaking with sobs mixed with a strange hiccupping laughter. Felix couldn't help but grin as she watched their reunion and she caught Nigel's eye as he stood at the entrance of the Mess. His eyes held hers for a moment, magnets unable to pull away.

'Unnatural,' spat Eugene glancing at the two women.

'Oh shut up!' shouted Felix, Old Nell and Gertie in unison, making the eyebrows on Eugene's face jump so high, they got lost in his wrinkles. Felix began to giggle. Old Nell smiled and gradually, the infection of happiness spread around the room. Even Carrig and Grunnion were smiling, revealing golden tooth caps and laughing cheeks.

The mood was significantly lightened and as the leprechauns served breakfast (bacon, sausages, eggs cooked every which way, hash browns, crumpets, toast, jam and heavenly chocolate spread) even the commoners relaxed.

Felix scraped a crumpet with some jam and ate silently, taking in the faces of her fellow survivors. There were the magicians, five in total, not counting Felix, their hands now dutifully covered in gloves. There was Mrs Thwaites, a mouse-like lady in her mid-forties with delightfully silvering hair and protruding teeth who only wanted to talk about her two children, whom she was desperate to get home to. Felix hoped that her family were there waiting for her as much as she did. Mrs Thwaites had apparently been found purchasing commoner antiques by the COPPs. She said she liked to study them. All her family did.

Thaddeus was a tall, heavy built man with rippling muscles that made his black skin shine beautifully. He had a deep laugh and shining eyes, and a knack for creating illegal hatches. Sitting next to him was Imelda, a teenage magician with bright pink hair in a Mohawk and several piercings around her ears and lips. Eugene and Old Nell kept looking at her disapprovingly, but Imelda didn't seem to notice anyone apart from Thaddeus. Felix didn't know why she'd been captured, but she couldn't help but think that she just *looked* a bit rebellious and wondered if that was the only crime she'd committed.

The final two magicians were Liberty and Sigbert whom it was clear knew Aubrey and the Belfast well. That meant they would know Fiddle. Felix scanned around for him, helping herself to more crumpets, which seemed unending as well as delicious, but she couldn't see him.

Of the commoners, Felix only knew a few of their names and stories as they were distant and reluctant to talk. They were sat, clustered together on their own table and Felix frowned. Even here, on the Belfast, there seemed to be a pecking order, like a food chain in a jungle. Lifting up her tray, she climbed over the bench of her table, where she was sat next to Sigbert and Imelda and went to the commoner table.

'May I join you?' she asked. Ten commoners raised their faces to her in a range of expressions. The most prevalent was fear and suspicion. 'Please?'

'Sit next to me, Felix,' little Gertie said, shuffling down the bench right into Old Nell, who squirted a little too much ketchup onto her hash browns.

'Thanks,' Felix said loudly, jutting out her chin and pretending to ignore the stares of the commoners. The spirals on her cheek tingled under their scrutiny. Judging from the volume of conversation, the magicians were looking at her too. Everyone suddenly seemed to have run out of things to say.

'Did you all sleep well?' Felix asked, her voice higher than it usually was. Internally, she rolled her eyes at herself for asking such a dull question. Some nodded. Others continued to stare at her. Eugene had begun mumbling incoherently under his breath.

'Good,' she replied, taking a bite of crumpet. It suddenly felt like wool in her mouth. She swallowed it awkwardly.

'Can we help you, miss?' asked a man with kind, tired eyes. He had the look of a young man who had aged too quickly. He reminded her of Fiddle.

'I just wanted you to know that whatever help you may need, anything at all...I..we will help you.'

The table was quiet apart from Eugene's mumbling.

'What makes you think we need your help?' A girl not much older than Felix asked. Felix thought she'd heard her being called Evelyn. She was pretty, with hair now much blonder than it had been in the Tower. Pretty, even with the three gashes cut across her right cheek and the look of hate in her eyes.

Felix swallowed and kicked herself under the table. She was acting like she was better than them.

'You don't,' she conceded. 'But our help is yours if you want it.'

A man with very pale skin and dark eyes let out a laugh.

'Look sweetheart,' he growled, pointing a fork in her direction. 'Just cos your lot got us out of that prison don't make us pals. It was your lot who put us there in the first place.'

Several members of the table nodded and mumbled in agreement.

'Magicians are all the same,' Evelyn whispered harshly, tracing a finger over her cuts. The mumbling grew louder and Felix felt the weight of hatred in their eyes.

'Nah they aint,' Old Nell said, her mouth full of ketchuppy hash brown. All eyes turned to her but the hatred had turned to shock. Even Felix couldn't stop her mouth from forming a small round 'o'.

'I hate magicians, as you well know Janus,' she said, nodding to the man who was still pointing his fork at Felix. 'We've all suffered at their hands. But so have this lot.' At this, Old Nell motioned around to the Magicians. 'Else they wouldn't have created this place. They were prisoners too, weren't they? For no greater reasons than we were. Those two there tried to kill the old geezer from what I heard, ain't that right?'

She was asking Felix, referring to Liberty and Sigbert.

'Oh, uh. Yeah. They attacked him.'

The commoners shuffled on their benches, casting their gaze over towards Liberty and Sigbert who feigned distraction by being suddenly very interested in their scrambled eggs.

'What are those marks on your face?' Evelyn asked curiously. Felix felt the silence grow even louder. Everyone was listening now. Felix squirmed uncomfortably, wishing she'd kept her big stupid mouth shut.

'Umm,' she began and then cleared her throat. Fiddle had told her that being a Drow, even a half Drow, was dangerous. Liberty had warned her to cover the spirals in the Tower to protect her from the other prisoners who might use her as leverage for their freedom. But there was no fear of that now, was there? And yet...how many of these people could she trust? Any of them could sign her over to the COPPs for any reason and plenty of these people had reasons to make deals with the COPPs. Clearing criminal records, releasing family members... She swallowed noisily.

'They are the mark of the Drow,' Fiddle's voice rang out loudly and clearly from the entrance to the mess. There was a collective creak of benches as each person swivelled round to the door. All except Felix.

'The Drow were a race of magical beings from the magician's world whom Godspell slaughtered because of their powerful magic, which he deemed to be a threat to his policies. Felix's mother was a Drow, her father a magician.'

Fiddle walked into the mess with the stoop of an old man but with the grace of a man steady on his feet. He inspected the trays of food quite intently, as though he had not just revealed one of Felix's biggest secrets, one that he himself had told her to keep.

'Hold on,' Mrs Thwaites piped from the magicians' table. 'Are you saying that she's the daughter of...' she gasped before she could finish her sentence.

'Daughter of who?' asked Imelda impatiently.

'Yeah!' cried one of the commoners, a young man with pockmarked cheeks and a bandaged, bloodied stump where he'd lost a finger.

Felix turned around slowly. She was holding her breath and she forced herself to let it out slowly. D.W, who had come in behind Fiddle with Aubrey, limped over to her and sat beside her. Felix stroked the scruff of his neck with one hand and twiddled a lock of hair with another. She stared hard at Fiddle, wondering which of her secrets he would decide to share next.

Fiddle was examining the sausages but when he looked towards Imelda, he jumped theatrically as though surprised to have so many people paying attention to him.

What's he playing at? Felix wondered, directing her thoughts to the dire wolf. He shuffled from his good paw to his bad paw and ignored her pointedly.

'My, aren't we curious all of a sudden,' he exclaimed, resting his hand on his chest.

'Mrs Thwaites, Madam, whilst you do not look anywhere near old enough to remember the events, I know that you do. Felix is the daughter of Calantha and Everard, our beloved leaders before they were murdered by Corbin Godspell. I am Alchemus J. Fiddle. You may remember that I was accused of their murder?'

Mrs Thwaites nodded, her face paling quickly.

'Yes, well,' Fiddle carried on inspecting his nails. 'It was rather unpleasant. Sufficed to say I am innocent of their deaths. I assure you all, Corbin Godpsell murdered Felix's parents, not I.'

Felix was watching him in bewilderment. She was quite sure that only those who knew Fiddle well would be able to see that he was playing a game. A faint sheet of sweat covered his face, dampening the impressive curl of his moustache and she could see the pulse at the side of his neck throbbing quickly. Whatever he was doing, he was nervous. She leaned down to D.W to ask again what he was doing but she noticed the wolf was also tensing, watching the enraptured crowd carefully; he was listening to their thoughts.

'But then-' Mrs Thwaites began but D.W let out a high-pitched whine, alerting Fiddle to him.

'Madam, I beg you,' Fiddle cried out, somewhat melodramatically. He even held out his hand to stop her. 'This is a very distressing subject for Felix and I refuse to talk more of this. I tell you only so that you know that she has every reason to loathe that damnable man more than any of us and that if we all, commoner or magician, are united in hatred for Corbin Godspell, then she will be the one to lead us against him.'

Silence dripped into the room again. Felix took a deep breath; she'd been forgetting to breathe. Fiddle was avoiding her gaze. It was obvious to her. He was hiding something...something he was afraid that the others would reveal. Which meant there were more secrets. She shook her head and bit down hard on her lip, clenching her fists so hard she could feel her nails digging into her flesh. It wouldn't help to start a furyfire right now.

'Please just trust him, Felix,' D.W's gentle voice spread through her mind.

'He's making that very hard,' Felix said. D.W whimpered.

It was like Fiddle had cast some kind of spell. If Felix hadn't known a little more about magic now, she would have guessed that's what he'd done. Nobody said anything else; people just seemed dazed. Nigel especially looked distracted and this comforted Felix; maybe *he* wasn't keeping secrets from her.

Slowly, as Fiddle helped himself to a plate of sausages and bacon, the sounds of knives and forks on plates resumed and the dull hum of conversation started again.

20
Best Laid Plans

Corbin Godspell did not eat his breakfast that morning. His plate of almond croissants rested on his breakfast table unaware of the festering anger that was flushing away Corbin Godspell's appetite.

Sunlight poured through the paned glass of the morning room and glinted off Godspell's oiled hair. Like a statue he sat, still and austere as he glared with icy eyes at his food. Moving only to cross his silk pyjama covered legs, hidden under the red Persian robe he wore, he contemplated the catastrophes of the last couple of days. How had things gone so utterly wrong? How had he allowed this to happen? He who prided himself on his ability to foresee all circumstances and read people's actions as though their bodies were maps; how had he not seen this coming?

And the Drow girl?

Godspell was not a stubborn man. On the contrary, he believed that flexibility and change were vital not only in the government of a country but for one's own sanity. He could appreciate that the commoners were unhappy with their lot and sought change. Had he not also done the same when he seized power? He could, too, understand the magician sympathisers though he felt disgust at their ignorance at failing to comprehend the greater vision of the Magistry: a united, powerful people, superior to all others. It was the noblest of causes and the commoners were, what was the term they themselves used in war time? Ah yes: collateral damage.

He could see every angle, every perspective connected like axons in a nervous system and he knew, the way that fire knows to burn, that the people he governed were fragile. They needed to be told what to think, what was dangerous, what was good and pure. It was the reason why the Magistry controlled the press, why his image shimmered in the windows and glass of London with his charge: Godspell's London: You Owe Him Your Allegiance, why the Tower loomed large and threatening over all, for fear was a vital tool in governance. It was brutal and it was ruthless. It was chess.

And the Drow girl? She was a new player on the board and she was winning.

When Mr Mortimer and Mr Murphy, the two imbeciles that headed the Commoner's Order Police Patrol had told him that they had captured a Drow, he had started to doubt the accuracy of his actions all those years before.

A young girl, they had said. About sixteen, they had said. Yes, Godspell's nerves were rightly justified. If she was the girl that he thought she was then he had to dispose of her quickly and quietly. Dr Nyxon could take care of her easily enough, making sure she was no longer a threat to him. Godspell had run his fingers through his oily hair. Of course, it was impossible that she was *that* girl, he'd thought. He'd been promised the girl was dead all those annums ago and he'd never had any doubt that it was true. Why would he? The proof had been delivered to him one week after her death. Drowned in the river and then found and presented to him. Definitely dead. No, he'd assured himself, it's not her. But just to be sure I'll send the girl to Nyxon. One less Drow in the world can't hurt.

In fact, it provided an ample opportunity to further Linus' training. It would be the making of him to see the light leave a person's eyes as they died. And if it broke him instead? Well, then it would prove once and for all what Godspell had suspected all along; that Linus was a weak, incompetent failure. And besides, there was a beauty in these events; a poetry that rather satisfied him. He wanted Linus to see the Drow killed in the Tower.

And so he had sent Larkin for his son.

But the best laid plans of magicians and men often went awry.

When Godspell and Linus had entered the Tower courtyard, they found chaos. And Godspell loathed chaos.

'What do you mean the prisoners have escaped?' Godspell's voice had bellowed, echoing in the Bell Tower. He had stood rigid, his lip twitching and foot tapping, with Linus at the bottom of the Bell Tower whilst Murphy and Mortimer stuttered their way through an explanation.

They were dishevelled and bleeding and Murphy's stained red cheek was half hanging away from his face. Behind them, a tangle of COPPs tried to contain the lamias who reached towards them with scaled hands their innocent façade forgotten now that they had tasted the memories of their victims.

Evidence of the dead was all around them. Torn and tattered clothing that looked strangely empty, like shells littered the ground. The odour rising from them was atrocious.

Behind them, an oak door had been blown apart. Blood was spattered across the ground.

'Sir,' Mortimer had started in a tremulous voice. 'It was an ambush. We were completely outnumbered.' Murphy nodded emphatically. Godspell had grimaced as he saw the flap of skin from the bite mark, still covered in blood, wobble as he nodded.

'Outnumbered?' Godspell's voice had been terrifyingly quiet. 'By one boy and a dog?'

'It was a dire wolf, Sir,' Murphy declared. 'Their howls kill lamias. It gave the prisoners time to escape.'

'I KNOW WHAT DIRE WOLVES CAN DO, YOU SNIVELLING LITTLE SLUG!'

Linus, Murphy and Mortimer had jumped back in alarm. The two COPPs sank to their knees, trembling, their breath coming in short little bursts. Godspell had felt the fear pulsing from Linus and it had angered him even more.

'Tell me about the Drow girl,' he said very quietly.

'An orphan, Sire! She's just an orphan. Probably she escaped the Drow slaughter.'

'Possibly,' Godspell frowned. It was the most likely scenario...but still. He could not take that risk. And an orphan didn't necessarily mean her past was a dead end. He had plenty of COPPs to search the orphanages... But first he had more pressing matters at hand.

'You, gentlemen,' he barked, 'are entrusted with the security of this prison and those traitors who reside inside these walls. For over nine hundred years it has been a fortress. Commoners have guarded this place far better than you and yet you, two magicians of noble parentage and acute magical strength could not detain a group of starved, half dead prisoners.'

Hatred had engulfed Godspell's body. His son's breathing was almost as haggard as the two fools quivering in front of him. He almost dared them to speak, just to give him an excuse...any excuse... to inflict pain. To see them scream and writhe.

'Linus, my boy,' he'd whispered, his eyes clamped closed and his neck tilted at an awkward angle. 'Weakness is not tolerable. The stronger must dominate. Only those born weak will look upon this principle as being cruel and horrible. But look at what you see before you. You see weakness, two worms wriggling in the eyes of death.'

He'd looked to his son and saw his pale face nodding slowly, his eyes darting down to the two insects in front of him.

'Good Sirs,' Godspell had proclaimed, 'I promised that I would show my son the mighty work of Dr Nyxon tonight. I will not disappoint him. Now, considering that you two fools have denied him the chance to see a prisoner punished, you shall take their place and accept punishment as I see fit.'

The two men had cowered further and bowed their heads.

'Noble Sir. Please. Please, we beg you, let us find the prisoners! Let us prove ourselves worthy to you. We'll do anything!'

'If you'll do anything, then you won't mind marching up those steps to the laboratory. Follow me, Linus.'

A knock interrupted Godspell's memory of the night before. The door to the morning room opened just a little.

'Yes, what is it?' Godspell asked, without turning his head. He knew exactly what Larkin was here for though it gave him pleasure to see the man struggle.

'Sir,' Larkin's voice simpered. 'Sir, might I have a moment?'

Godspell's advisor waddled into the room with surprising quietness. There was a faint sheen of sweat over his thick eyebrows. Godspell noted this and smirked, crossing his legs in his silken pyjamas.

'What is it, Larkin?'

'Master Linus, Sir.'

'Yes?'

'Is it....is it wise, Sir?'

Godspell flicked his eyes towards Larkin and narrowed his gaze, recognising the bravery in the man's question.

'You doubt me?' Godspell asked, picking up his tea cup filled with cold cinnamon tea and taking a sip absently.

'Oh, no Sir. Of course not,' Larkin replied quickly, bowing his head. 'I only wish for you to consider an alternative punishment. He's just a boy...'

Godspell took another sip of the tepid tea and pursed his lips. Then he stood, straightening his robe for a moment, before walking towards Larkin and striking him across the face with a force so hard that the man fell against the polished mahogany door.

'I admire your loyalty to this family, Larkin,' he said to the man, who clutched his cheek with green velvet gloves that shook slightly. 'But never question me again.'

Larkin's jaw clenched and he drew his feet underneath his knees. Godspell thought he saw a flash of defiance and he could not help but smile at this, especially when he saw it fade as Larkin uttered the words, 'Yes, Sir.'

'I don't tolerate failure, Larkin,' Godspell purred, leaning down over the trembling man. He reached out a hand towards Larkin, who flinched, but Godspell simply stroked the man's cheek where he had struck him.

'Nor do I tolerate weakness.' He pressed his finger into Larkin's face gently. Within seconds, his advisor was shrieking in pain as Godspell's burning hand blistered his skin, like a cigar extinguished on flesh.

'Linus is weak, and he failed me. He is a coward. That is why I sent him to the Tower, Larkin. Do I need to send you to join him?' The malice dripped from Godspell's voice.

Larkin shook his head as much as he was able. 'No, Sir. I'm sorry, Sir,' he begged.

Godspell lifted away from him and wrinkled his nose. The morning room smelled of burning flesh. Larkin scrambled to his feet, his hand clamped over his wound.

'What shall I tell your son, Sire?' he whispered. Godspell could not help but admire the man's bravery...yet he was like a terrier yapping for favour after his master had kicked him.

Godspell sat down in his chair and poured a fresh cup of cinnamon tea and reached for an almond croissant. He took a bite, chewed and swallowed. Then he smiled, almost maniacally and his shoulders began to shake.

'Tell him,' he said in between laughter. 'Tell him he's no son of mine.'

21
The Protest Group

Felix felt a firm hand gripping her shoulder and she woke with a gasp. She found Fiddle standing over the hammock that Carrig had assigned her. Felix rubbed the sleep from her eyes and groaned, but Fiddle put his finger over his mouth and motioned her to be quiet.

Silently, he conjured a small, dim flame in his hand and by its light, Felix saw the cabin was filled with people sleeping in their own hammocks, telling Felix it was not yet morning.

Moaning internally, she rolled out of her hammock, which was surprisingly comfy, and followed him out and up, climbing the tiny rungs of a ladder to the main deck.

'I don't need a lecture, Alchemus,' she said petulantly, but he didn't answer her and instead, led her down a galley and out of an oval door onto the outer deck of the ship.

The cool river air welcomed her in the pink light of the early dawn. Overhead, birds were starting to chirp, though she had no idea where they could possibly nest in such a built-up place as London.

'It's so peaceful,' she whispered, not wanting to break the calm. Fiddle nodded.

'Isn't it?' he said. 'I like to come here before the sun rises. The air feels cleaner here...easier to breath. Did you know you can't see the sky anywhere else in the city but by the river? Isn't that sad?'

Felix raised her eyes and sure enough, behind the haze of the steam and smoke and smog, the sky flashed its colours of azure and purple and orange.

'The sky in the quarter is always grey,' she mumbled. 'As though the clouds are perpetually waiting to burst.'

Fiddle took a deep breath for a long time, like he was taking the air right down to his boots.

'Viruses will always lurk in the shadows ready to pounce when neglect, poverty, famine or war lets down the defences,' he said, reeling off the words like he had memorised them from a book.

'Sorry?' Felix asked, confused. Fiddle was acting strangely, far more than normal.

'Forgive my maudlin attitude this morning, Felix. I rather thought I had lost you.'

Felix didn't know what to say so she said nothing. Fiddle leaned against the rail of the great warship, his eyes never leaving the view of the Tower across the river.

'I ought to have told you about your parents' ashes at the Monument but ashes is all they are. Comfort cannot be found in the dead, only in the life and the love they leave behind. Your parents were good and honest people, flawed in many ways, as we all are, but loyal and strong and true. They would have loved you and they would never want their deaths to be in vain by having you murdered in the blasted Tower of London! You must understand this, Felix; you are no longer just *you*. Perhaps I was foolish and Aubrey was right and I should have made it clearer to you from the start. People, magicians and commoners alike, are relying on *you*, Felix. You have to -'

'To what?' she interrupted him. 'to kill him? That's it, isn't it? Kill Corbin Godspell and take my rightful place as Firelighter. What then? Rule the Magistry? Alchemus, I have no idea how to do any of that.'

Felix paced back and forth, running her hands over her hair in frustration.

'You think you'd be alone? People will follow you, Felix. Those people sleeping below, magicians and commoners sharing a cabin – do you think they would be sharing a room had it not been for you bringing them together?'

'They hate us,' she said, shaking her head. 'The commoners. They sleep on their side of the room. There are still divisions.'

'Change doesn't just happen overnight, darling girl,' Fiddle said softly, resting his hands on her shoulders. 'But it starts with a single voice in a crowd.'

'And I'm supposed to be that voice?' Felix asked, frowning. Fiddle nodded slowly.

'You knew that,' he said.

'Yes, I did, but I thought there would be more people to back me up and support me. I've been practicing magic for less than a month, Alchemus, how am I supposed to defeat the Firelighter, for goodness sake? He has more power than I do and more people at his command. I couldn't even free myself from those COPPs who attacked me, and you still haven't told me how I'm supposed to use magic to defeat him!'

Fiddle took a step back and gave her a moment to compose herself. Felix closed her eyes and grounded her feet to the ship, feeling the solid metal beneath her, keeping her strong and steady. Getting angry at Fiddle was pointless but he was so infuriating.

'I never said you'd need magic to beat Godspell,' he said when she was calmer. 'You have something in you that he doesn't. You're a Drow, Felix. I still don't think you realise how much power that enables you to possess. Your power stems from your emotions. Anybody can duel with magic, anybody can kill with magic. It's simply a matter of concentration and working with the magic inside your enemy.'

'So, I have to use my anger to overpower him? That sounds an awful lot like evil to me. Anger is a flaw-'

'No, anger is a useful energy if used for the right reasons. I'm not asking you to kill hundreds of people. I'm asking you to help us kill a man who has oppressed the commoners, people you grew up with, a man who is killing magicians and commoners alike. A man who killed your parents.'

Felix looked up at Fiddle and shook her head. He had taken her in and sheltered her, given her information about her past and had given her a purpose, but Fiddle was still using her for his own gain.

'Why are you so determined to kill him?' she challenged him, coldly.

'Why are you not?' he deflected.

'Alchemus, Godspell killed my parents. I know what he did and I want revenge more than anyone here could possibly understand, but I can't imagine myself killing him. I can't imagine myself killing anybody. This anger, this Drow power that comes from my mother feels dark and ugly. It fills my skin with a burning that I don't like and I feel like I might lose control when it happens and it frightens me. Anything that makes me feel like that isn't a good thing, even when used for a good cause.'

The two magicians looked at one another, each of them disappointed and frustrated with the other. They were at an impasse and they both knew it.

'I'm sorry, Alchemus,' Felix said quietly. 'I'm sorry I ran away and scared you and I'm sorry I can't be the cure to Godspell's virus that you want me to be.'

'I want you to be all that you are,' Fiddle responded with a voice drained of all energy.

Together, they watched the sun rise through a steam veil and they said nothing more.

***

The dire wolf's paw was healing well. Imelda was a trainee healer and she had managed fix the broken bone, though it was still weak and needed support.

'I'm not much good at splints,' Imelda had said but she'd put together a wonderful clockwork contraption that supported his weight and bent at his joint, helping him move more easily. D.W had spent a full afternoon with the girl, repaying her by telling her what Thaddeus was thinking. Her giggles could be heard from the other side of the deck.

Felix liked Imelda, and Thaddeus and Liberty and Sigbert. She still had reservations about Aubrey but each time she saw her with Liberty, she liked her a little more.

From them, she learned that the 'protest group' as Aubrey had called it back in the library, was a network of hundreds of magicians, some actively attempting to overthrow Godspell and his Magistry, some merely supporting the cause.

'They're scared to do anything more than offer support,' Thaddeus said one night over dinner. It was the first night Old Nell and Gertie had abandoned the commoner table in favour for the magicians'. After that, the rest followed...even Eugene.

'What have magicians got to be scared of though?' Evelyn asked. She'd warmed considerably to the magicians, especially Imelda who had healed the cuts on her face and now the two were becoming fast friends.

'Godspell thinks nothing of bribery and blackmail, though he would call it persuasion,' Sigbert explained. 'He can find something, anything at all that you've done wrong and hold it over your head. Trace words are one thing but the COPPs have eyes everywhere, even on our kind. You've seen what he did to us and we're magicians. He'll stop at nothing until he gets his pure race or whatever diabolical idea he has.'

Felix listened to their flow of conversation. They talked of Godspell of course, but mainly they spoke of life, shared stories and became friends. Surviving a dungeon and torture chamber had that effect.

By the fourth day on the Belfast, there was no divide in the cabin anymore.

'It's luck,' Carrig said to Felix and she smiled, knowing that it was something more but accepting whatever luck that he was sending their way.

On the fifth day, it was time to leave and there was a cloud of sadness aboard the Belfast and a sense of an opportunity missed. Nobody really wanted to go and as they sat eating their final meal of bacon and eggs and sausage together, unspoken words hovered above them.

Felix could hardly stand it. She was sick of Fiddle flashing his meaningful glances at her and of Aubrey failing to hide her exasperated stares.

Nigel had hardly spoken to her and whilst Fiddle and Aubrey were looking at Felix, Felix was looking at Nigel who was doing an excellent job of ignoring her.

'I'd just go over there and apologise if I was you,' Imelda said sympathetically. 'No point falling out just because you were a plonker and said the wrong thing.'

The dire wolf nodded emphatically.

'He'll forgive you, you know,' he assured her.

Felix grimaced and straightened her blouse under the leather corset Imelda had said she looked 'hot' in and took a seat next to Nigel, who was turning his beans over with his fork. He didn't acknowledge her at all.

'I'msorryImadeyouthinkIwasn'tgratefulthatyousavedmewhenIwas,' Felix blurted in one breath. Nigel looked up at her confused.

'What?'

'I'm sorry,' Felix repeated, feeling her spirals burn with embarrassment. 'For what I said. You're more than apprentice and I'll never be able to repay you for coming for me.'

'You think that's why I'm mad?' Nigel asked, turning to her and shaking his head in bemusement.

'It's not?'

'No,' he laughed. 'Felix...you're as bad as my aunt!'

'Oh,' Felix grinned. 'Well then...why are you mad at me? What did I do?'

Nigel's smile faded and was replaced by sternness.

'It's more of what you've not done,' he said slowly.

'What did I not do?' Felix asked, growing uneasy. She had a feeling of where this was going.

'Felix,' Nigel said, clasping her hands and holding them between them. 'I don't care what Fiddle and Aubrey want you to do. I don't care what Liberty or Sigbert or Old Nell or any of us want you to do. I don't know what it's like to walk in your skin and be subject to so many expectations, but the only expectations that matter are the ones you have of yourself.'

Felix swallowed hard and dragged her eyes away from Nigel's. The room was silent as all eyes were on them as they talked.

'A leader listens to advice, Felix,' the dire wolf said, just to her. 'But they decide what to do on their own.'

'I don't know what I want to do,' Felix whispered. 'I only know what I don't want to do.'

'That's a good start,' D.W said.

'Go on...' Nigel encouraged her, nudging her so that she was standing up in front of everyone.

'Um...hello, everyone,' she mumbled, giving a half wave, half salute. 'I'm here because I've been told that I have to help you kill Godspell. I'm really sorry but I don't think I can do that.'

A murmur of surprise rippled through the room. Felix met Fiddle's eyes with her own.

'Listen to me,' she continued. 'Godspell is an evil man. He destroys hope and joy. He rules your lives and your freedom. I know that he has to be stopped. But you're not the only ones that hate him. The magicians support our cause and I know for sure that the commoners can't stand him, right Old Nell?

'I know that you think that a surprise attack from me is your greatest strategy but I disagree. Godspell is in power because people are scared of him. Take that fear away and you are left with anger.'

'So what do you propose we do, Felix?' asked Liberty, 'It's all very well and good saying take away the fear but the Tower is the Tower no matter how brave you are.'

'Yes. Secrecy is our weapon,' Old Nell agreed.

'No, secrecy is what you hide behind,' Felix retorted, 'I say we don't hide anymore. We tell the people, commoner, magician and creature alike about our cause. Godspell relies on his subjects. How many times a day do you hear his voice or see a sign ordering you to 'owe him your allegiance'? You owe nothing, to nobody. Godspell can't kill thousands of his own people without a global uprising. It'd be his downfall.'

'I wouldn't want to put that to the test,' Eugene croaked. 'I've seen too many wars end in too much bloodshed. I don't want to see another.'

'We're already fighting a war, Eugene. Every time we look away from a COPP beating up another kid, we're letting him win. Each time we refuse to help one another because of some stupid divide between us, he wins. If we want to punish Godspell, if we want to beat him, then we need to work together and do what people are scared of attempting: reveal ourselves, tell people our message and give them strength to fight.'

Felix's heart was pounding hard. She could feel it in her ears. Looking to Fiddle, she found him expressionless, his face old and blank. Felix felt panicked. She had failed. She couldn't talk them into doing this. What had she been thinking? It was impossible.

'This isn't what we expected, Felix,' Imelda said, shaking her head.

'I thought you were supposed to be a secret weapon?' Eugene taunted her.

'What if people don't fight with us, Felix?' Sigbert asked, his face, at least, was kind and patient.

Felix looked down at Nigel and the dire wolf. Nigel was looking up at her but she couldn't see his eyes through the reflection of the light on his glasses. D.W's head was turning to each magician in the room, reading their thoughts. His expression was hard to read but then Nigel stood up slowly. He reached for her hand and gripped it tight.

'Then we fight anyway,' he said to the audience. Felix looked at him gratefully. Old Nell snorted.

'You're just kids! What do you know of fighting?'

Felix frowned as she watched her friends begin to mumble amongst themselves, their faces marred by concern. Felix hung her head, feeling like she had let everyone down. But then the voice of Fiddle broke through the din, sounding stronger than he looked.

'They know that they'll be fighting their entire lives if we don't attempt to overthrow Godspell now.'

Felix straightened as he walked over to her side so that she was flanked by Nigel and Fiddle with the dire wolf sitting in front of her. She had to suppress a coy smile.

'We are old,' Fiddle said, smiling at Old Nell and Eugene, and Felix doubted they knew that Fiddle wasn't nearly as old as he looked. 'We have been fighting this man for fifteen years and we are in a worse position now than when we started.' He glanced at both Felix and Nigel.

'This is their future,' he shrugged. 'When we're gone, they're the ones who will have to battle against Godspell. So, I think they know a great deal about fighting. And, ultimately, I think Felix is right. She has come into our world only to discover loss and pain and yet here she stands, prepared to fight with us. Our secret attacks aren't working. I think it is high time we try something different. What difference does it make if Felix's plan fails? We will be found eventually anyway and sooner or later we will have to face Godspell. Let's make it sooner. Godspell won't expect it.'

Felix scanned the faces of her friends with Nigel's hand still firmly gripping hers.

'He's right,' said Aubrey nodding as she looked carefully at Liberty. 'They're both right.'

Felix smiled. They were coming around. There would be questions, of course, and they would still need to devise a plan of action, but they were agreeing with her.

She turned to Fiddle and hugged him tightly, slightly alarmed by his thinning frame.

'Thank you,' she whispered.

'I think your thanks is deserved elsewhere,' Fiddle smiled down at her and nodding his head towards Nigel.

Felix grinned and spun around to Nigel, hugging him so tightly that he fell back against the table.

'I guess this means we're friends again,' he said in a pained voice.

Felix laughed, and it was a laugh that healed all ills.

22
Corpses In The Glass

Linus Godspell, son of Corbin Godspell, heir apparent to the Magistry of London and Sacred Flame of Magic woke with a gasp and clutched at his chest where his heart was squeezing and burning.

For a moment, he thought that the scalding grip of death was upon him and he screamed, stopping only when his voice resounded around him, making him jump.

The sound of his cry, drenched in dread, bounced off the cobbled walls where cobwebs spread like ivy.

He was still in the Tower.

The heart in his breast contracted painfully as though it were sobbing at the betrayal of his beloved father, the father he had spent so many years trying desperately to impress. And it was all for nought.

In some secret part of him, Linus knew his father had never loved him. It stung to acknowledge it, finally. No father would treat his son this way, imprisoning him, starving him and sending the COPPs to beat him whilst he slept.

Linus shifted painfully, his bruised ribs from the last beating complaining at him. He rested his head against the damp stone of the wall and closed his eyes, but quickly opened them again when he saw, in a flash, the dead, cold eyes of Murphy and Mortimer in that damnable machine, looking to him for help even in their moment of death. Would he be forever tortured with that vision? Linus knew he would be for the rest of his days...though he did not know how many days he had left. The stark, hard truth that his father had left him here to die hurt him more than his cracked ribs.

He thought about how excited and nervous he'd been when Larkin had told him his father wanted to meet with him and how intrigued he'd been about what was in the Tower that he wanted Linus to see.

The excitement had turned to terror very quickly as soon as he'd reached Tower Hill.

Scorch marks on grass. Blood sprayed on the walls. And the piles of clothes, limp and lifeless and horrifying.

But for all the horror of the Tower courtyard, Dr Nyxon's laboratory had been far, far worse.

Linus had been unable to do anything but watch as Mortimer and Murphy had cringed and cowered up the staircase to the lab, which was on the highest storey on the west side of the White Tower.

As soon as he'd entered the chamber, Linus's palms began to sweat inside his gloves. He felt his father glaring at him and he tried, he tried so hard, to look as though he was bored by everything that was happening.

But Linus was not a good actor nor was he a liar. His pounding heart betrayed him, pumping hard as adrenalin coursed through his system, sending a sheen of perspiration to his upper lip and excess saliva into his mouth. He could feel his pulse in his neck banging against the skin and he knew his father could see it too.

Though small, the laboratory was crammed to the very nooks and crannies of the walls with books, parchments and scrolls, jars and Bunsen burners, chalkboards with alchemical equations taking up every available space, some even carved into the glass of the windows. With all of the chaos, Linus, his father and the two quivering COPPs struggled to fit into the room.

The reason for the clutter around the perimeter of the chamber was hard to miss. At the centre, taking up an intimidating amount of space, stood a glass box, tall and wide enough to fit a large man and give him room to step in a circle quite comfortably. It was framed with a dark metal that Linus recognised as titanium and a cylindrical glass pipe was screwed into a hole at the top of the box. The pipe ran towards a crate, sealed and transparent and glowing with blue light. It was so bright that Linus had to shield his eyes from it, but he didn't need to see it to know what it was. He could feel the power in the air; that strangely sensual warmth and the sharp static touch of it on his skin.

The room was filled with magic. Strong magic.

Linus was so distracted by the contraption in front of him that it was a few moments before he realized that there was a man scribbling away at a half-hidden desk in the corner of the room.

His father cleared his throat and the man visibly started. Looking up, his drawn face broke into a smile that revealed too many teeth. He rushed over to Godspell and shook his hand, bowing his head in adulation.

The man was clearly a venephysicist; his eyes were magnified by spectoccules, so that he resembled a fly and he wore a long blue coat with white gloves. Wrinkles around his eyes betrayed his tiredness but the pure blue passion in his gaze revealed his dedication. He looked like he had not eaten a proper meal in days, such was his rakish frame. His lab coat hung off him like a curtain on a rail.

'Dear Sir,' he'd said in a voice that was subtly accented, 'and Master Godspell too, I see. What an honour!' He reached out and took Linus' hand between his own. Linus thought he felt cold and clammy, even through his gloves. His pulse quickened.

In times of peril, our bodies have adapted to warn us. Perhaps on some unconscious level, we are always searching for danger, plotting escape in some remote and coy part of our brains. Maybe we can detect danger through smell, through taste, through minute sounds and visual clues that reveal the intentions of our enemy. Whatever, nature has given us this defence, this everyday piece of magic that we call 'instinct' that lives somewhere in our guts. It induces 'fight or flight' and, as an intelligent species, our survival has been dependent on making wise choices. Fight only when you feel you can win. Flee when you know you can't.

Linus knew this. He was quietly weighing up his options, recognising that this room was a trap, as much for him as for Mortimer and Murphy. How he knew this he could not have told you, but he felt it; the danger. Every instinct he had, every last drop of the meagre amount of magic he had been born with told him to run.

He scanned the room but there was only one exit; the way that they had entered, blocked now by his father. Godspell's eyes, hooded and cruel, laughed when they found his son's.

Why are you doing this to me? His eyes implored. The question was ignored.

'Good evening, Dr Nyxon,' Godspell said smoothly, his attention now on the venephysicist.

Mortimer and Murphy were huddled together in the corner, scrambling at the wall as though trying to claw themselves out; rats in a cage. Their squinting eyes were fixed in terror upon the machine at the centre of the room, at the blinding blue light in the adjoining crate.

'Two new test subjects, I see?' Dr Nyxon asked, looking hungrily at Mortimer and Murphy.

Linus' father had nodded nonchalantly.

'Magicians of course,' Nyxon said, more to himself than Godspell, but Godspell nodded and smirked.

'They are undeserving of magic,' he spat in the direction of the COPPs. 'My son will be observing tonight, Doctor.'

Linus was beginning to tremble. His father would not put him in danger, surely. His father was trying to educate him that was all. Surely that was all.

Yet he remembered the scurry girls and the floo workers and the brass waxers at the Citadel before they had been banished. He remembered their fear filled whispers in corridors and empty rooms. He thought of Larkin and the newspapers he sometimes read, illegal commoner ones that Larkin obtained for Godspell but read himself first, scraps of revolution that Linus stole glances of when Larkin wasn't looking. They spoke of his father as a dictator, as a megalomaniac; as a murderer.

Linus shivered.

But he was a magician. He was Linus Godspell. He was heir apparent to the Sacred Flame. His father would not hurt him.

And yet....

Nyxon had grabbed the two men who were shaking in the corner. The smell of urine filled the room. Mortimer appeared to be sobbing whilst Murphy's wide eyes had flitting around the room in terror, his cheek bleeding and torn away to reveal his teeth under it.

It struck Linus then that they knew what this machine did when he did not. His throat went dry.

The doctor threw them, one by one into the box. Linus almost wondered why they didn't attempt to use magic, why they didn't fight. He almost wished that they would.

Murphy and Mortimer pressed their hands against the glass and began to plead with Godspell. Their appeals were lost upon Linus' father, who could not hear what they were saying from inside the glass. Linus couldn't hear them either, but he'd imagined what they'd been screaming. He watched in disgust as Mortimer vomited.

Nausea drifted up from Linus' stomach into his throat. He had never seen a magician treated in this manner. He had heard of commoners being punished and abused, but they were simply commoners. Magicians had a right to justice and a fair trial by law. He was certain of this. It was a direct contravention of the Magistry legislation on Magician Rights. He may not have been the best magician, but Linus knew politics.

No magician should be treated with such cruelty. Nobody should.

Maybe not even the commoners.

Dictator. Megalomaniac. Murderer.

Linus felt himself backing away from the glass chamber. Mortimer and Murphy had turned to him now, sinking to their knees and banging on the glass. Their eyes were filled with terror and desperation. It was horrifying.

'I've made some new alterations to the machine,' Nyxon explained. He seemed totally oblivious to the two men and there was something so frightening about the way he showed no concern for them.

Godspell nodded. He had taken the red handkerchief from his pocket and was wiping at a speck of mud on his shoe.

Linus was frozen. He couldn't make himself move. He watched the events unfolding like he was watching a performance at the theatre. He saw Nyxon pressing some buttons and pulling some levers on the machine. He was like Frankenstein animating Adam. It was not really real. He saw the dazzling blue fire swell and dance in the crate.

Nyxon explained what he was doing and Godspell nodded in understanding, but all Linus could hear were words like, 'electro-magical currents' and 'micro-kinetic flames' and he couldn't follow.

The blue flame was beginning to rise into the pipe that ran towards the glass chamber. It was crackling and hissing and the laboratory was filled with electricity making their hair stand on end.

Dread crept over his body like an icy fog.

The fire in that machine was pure magic. Pure magic was dangerous.

In fact, it was so dangerous that it could not be obtained anymore. Only once had pure magic been distilled from the Third and that....

At that moment, he had understood.

He looked at his father in horror.

The flickering fire that was powering the machine was part of the Sacred Flame.

He could do nothing but watch, aghast as the source of magic reached down the transparent pipe, spreading like ink in water when it blazed into the glass cage that held Murphy and Mortimer.

They screamed. They shrieked. They fought for their lives as every cell in their bodies was incinerated.

When they died, their bodies were not charred and their clothing was not reduced to ashes. The Sacred Flame did not burn in that way. Had a commoner observed, they would have seen two men wailing and howling in a glass box. No flames. No smoke.

But Linus had seen.

He knew the reason why the Sacred Flame made them scream so much. It was the same reason the magicians wore gloves. Magic *burned.* It burned the way a fever burns, the way sunburnt skin feels like it has been scalded, the way your face scorches when you're embarrassed. It crept into your skin and found the magic within you, set it alight until you were ablaze from the inside out. Nobody was exempt from this. Even commoners had resting upon them.

This machine would kill all who fell victim to it.

Some minutes later, Nyxon stopped the machine and the blue fire reduced itself to the glass box at the centre of the machine. He stared at the chamber hungrily before punching his fist onto his desk. The wood splintered under the force. Linus stared at the crack. Better to look at that than the corpses in the glass.

'Another failure?' Godspell asked with a menacing arch of his brow.

'On the contrary,' replied Nyxon. 'I have succeeded in learning what not to do. Failure is only failure if you give up.'

The doctor stared into the machine and pulled down the lenses on his spectoccules in different combinations.

'They have been successfully converted, Sire. That is progress.'

'Yes,' said Godspell, standing up and walking around the chamber as though it was something dirty. 'The problem is keeping them alive. Dispose of them.'

He rested his hand on Linus' shoulder, squeezed it hard and did not let go of his grip. Linus' throat was dry. He allowed himself to be steered out of the room as his father led him out of the laboratory, but all Linus could see were the pale, dead faces of Mortimer and Murphy.

'Better luck next time, Doctor,' Godspell said, tipping an imaginary hat in the direction of Nyxon.

Linus shifted his eyes to his father slowly, knowing the words were going to come out no matter how hard he tried to stop them.

'Next time?' he choked.

Godspell looked at Linus and a sneer spread across his mouth.

'The machine is not yet perfected, Linus,' he said slowly, each word a drip of malice. 'It will need more tests, more... subjects to experiment on if this machine is to convert commoners to magicians. We are performing a service to them. Bettering them, if you will.'

Dr Nyxon nodded. 'A noble cause!' he said slimily.

'Noble?' repeated Linus. 'But it *kills* people. How is that noble?'

The smile faded from Dr Nyxon's face. Godspell considered his son for a moment before speaking. His face was stern, but there was victory in his eyes, as though he had won an argument with himself.

'Those men had failed me, Linus. I do not tolerate failure. From anyone.'

Linus swallowed hard and shook his head.

'No,' he stammered, 'no, I won't be part of this. I won't let you murder people. No goal is worth that.'

It took all his remaining strength to utter those words, knowing he was sealing his fate.

Linus was spoiled, entitled, blind to those in need....he'd heard what others said about him. But he was not an evil person and he would not grow up to be so.

He would not grow up to be like his father.

'I knew you were weak,' Godspell whispered, his voice darker than shadow. But his grin was the worst of it. It was maniacal.

Now, in the cold tower, Linus wrapped his arms around his ribs. He was helpless.

I'll go mad here if I don't keep my focus, he thought. *I can escape.*

He had to cling onto that belief. He would escape or somebody would come and find him. Perhaps Larkin, his father's servant? He had always been kind to Linus... maybe he would come and find him?

But then again Larkin was a dedicated servant, always loyal to Godspell. No, he couldn't pin his hopes on Larkin.

He reached for the flask of water. There were only a few drops left. He drank them, wrinkling his nose at the stagnant taste.

'Help me,' he whispered as he rocked against the wall, his head in his hands. 'Please, somebody help me.'

23
Spies and Lies

The sunny weather of August was long gone. Days were damper and dimmer as September embraced them, bringing with it the back to school sensation of a task to be completed.

Felix had set their small rebellion in motion. Liberty, who would not be parted from Aubrey again, Sigbert and a hesitant Imelda, who had not wanted to be parted from Thaddeus, made up a small unit who had a special mission; to rally supporters and spread the word of a rebellion rising.

Thaddeus was to parley with the Houdinis and the sewer pirates, some of whom he'd had dealings with whilst trading fake hatch licences and unregistered chalkeys. He had been excited, and the stained teeth of his grin told Felix that Thaddeus might have other agendas for visiting the Houdinis. She hoped he would not hurt Imelda, who seemed one heartbreak away from bitter.

Other magicians had volunteered to create small units of spies for the rebellion. So many of them worked close to the Citadel; they would listen a little harder and question a little more. Whatever they learned was to be delivered to the London Library each evening by the Touch Papers.

It was a simple plan but as with all simplicity, the devil was in the detail.

Old Nell, upon discovering that Fiddle was a loyal and dedicated reader of the Touch Papers, agreed to let the magicians use it to pass their information to one another. It was an unlisted newspaper, difficult to trace. It was there to be read, added to and passed on so that each copy was unique.

Both commoners and magicians would keep their ears to the ground and report their news in the Touch Papers. It would be passed, person to person, by hand or by hatch (secret ones, thanks to Thaddeus) before being delivered to the Library via the hospital hatch in the basement.

Old Nell and Gertie had left the magicians on good terms. Felix was not optimistic enough to use the word 'friends', as she understood all too well the deeply ingrained hatred that commoners had for the magicians. But they had agreed to rally what commoners they could to join with the magicians in a united rebellion.

'Don't count on it, petal,' Old Nell had said, patting Felix's hand and frowning a little at the gloves. 'But we'll try.'

That was all Felix could ask of anyone. That they try. She would try too; try to lead, to reunite the commoners and the magicians. And she would try to force down the anger and frustration that seemed to fill her body, like a sticky tar swallowing all thoughts of happiness.

***

The day Felix returned to the Library after her stay on the Belfast saw rain lashing down from the heavens. She stood with Fiddle in St James's Square, outside in the rain, the collar on her blue coat up against the wind and proving fruitless. In the wet, the library shone like a lighthouse.

'I don't need to read minds like the dire wolf to know when there's something wrong, Felix.' Fiddle's voice was a low grumble.

Felix ran a hand over her hair, plastered against her face so that any passer-by could not have distinguished her black curls from her black spirals. She hated the way she could no longer feel anything with her hands anymore. The world now seemed to be permanently made of silk.

'Darling girl. What is it?'

Felix shook her head and looked to her feet.

'Something is coming, Alchemus,' she whispered. 'I can feel it. Something dark and dreadful. And I think it's coming from me.'

She jumped as Fiddle grabbed her shoulders and shook her slightly.

'Now you listen to me,' Fiddle said, his blue eyes beseeching. 'You listen. Do you hear me? Your heart is fire. It burns for us all. I have asked so much of you…so much. And yet you stand here, ready to fight, ready to burn like a firebird hatched in a sparrow's nest. You have power, yes, Felix you do. But it is only dark if you will it to be.'

Felix pressed her lips together firmly and took a deep breath. It steadied her.

'Let's go home,' she said, and held the old man's hand the way she had always imagined holding her father's.

***

Nigel and the dire wolf had returned to the library some days earlier and so it was with some surprise that Fiddle pushed at the door and found it locked. He furrowed his brows and looked at Felix who suggested that Nigel had forgotten to open the door that morning. Neither of them believed it. For all of his complaining, Nigel was a proficient assistant and librarian.

Fiddle knocked loudly on the doors. Still no answer.

Anxiously, Felix looked through the windows and saw nothing but the dusty books and shelves, obscured by condensation on the glass.

The two magicians looked at each other apprehensively, their necks stiffening as they braced themselves. Then, mumbling under his breath, Fiddle placed his hand on the wooden door and made the faintest flick of movement with his glove-covered fingers. The latch clicked out of place and the door opened.

Stepping through the doors quietly, Fiddle reached his arm out in front of Felix.

'Careful,' he murmured. 'The library is protected against forced entry. Expect it to protect itself.'

Felix couldn't help but smile at the idea of the library defending those who lived within it and felt a surge of affection for the old place. But stepping inside, she felt a tightness prickling the air around her. The library was holding its breath, watching them and waiting.

'It thinks we're intruders,' she whispered and hugged herself as she shivered. She was soaked through and the library felt icy. It was completely different to the warm and welcoming sanctuary she had found when she first entered.

'Nigel?' Fiddle shouted, breaking the silence. His voice echoed in the rooms of the library. He walked with trepidation over to the empty reception desk, as though each step would trigger some kind of booby trap, and rang the bell three times. They heard an annoyed groan on the floor above them.

'Three times is just cruel!'

Felix breathed a sigh of relief as she saw Nigel stumbling down the stairs, grimacing and rubbing his head.

'Why is the library closed? And where have you been?' Fiddle asked angrily. Nigel held up his hands to calm his master.

'I'm sorry, Alchemus, but there was an emergency.'

'An emergency?' Felix asked.

'You'd better follow me,' Nigel said still rubbing his head and climbing the stairs two at a time.

'Oh, and if ye mean no harm ye may enter freely into this place,' he said quickly, waving his hand in a dismissive way. Felix looked at him confused but felt the library unfurl around her, like it was relaxing after clenching its fists for a long time.

Felix bounded up the stairs after Nigel, hardly noticing Fiddle was keeping up with her in spite of his usual hobbled pace. There was a knot tightening in Felix's stomach. They couldn't handle more complications, not now, not after the small victory she'd had convincing the rebellion to give her a chance. Gritting her teeth, she tried to keep up with what Nigel was telling Fiddle.

'He was waiting when D.W and I arrived,' he was panting, 'he was quite distraught. It took us some time to calm him down.'

'He has been discovered, then?' Fiddle asked, a grave look on his face. Nigel shook his head as they reached the landing of the fourth floor and stopped outside a solid oak door.

'No, but he has news. I was about to use the hatchway to come and find you but then you rang that bell and...well. Here you are.'

'Wait, who has news?' Felix asked Nigel, her eyes darting between him and Fiddle.

'Our inside man,' Fiddle said. His voice betrayed the nerves that they all felt and for a moment, the three of them were a tripod of exchanging glances. Then, with a small nod, Felix pushed open the doors to the reading room.

'Shylock, my old friend!' Fiddle said warmly, holding out his arms in welcome. A squat man with a balding head and quite a big belly stepped forward, a look of relief on his round face.

'Alchemus, thank heavens you're here.'

The large man and Fiddle embraced fondly. Felix shuffled nervously into a corner with Nigel and smiled down at the dire wolf who was lay on the floor, with his head between his paws, and a book on North American Mythology at his side. As soon as he saw Felix, he sat up, wagged his tail and trotted over to her side.

Shylock followed the movements of the wolf until his eyes rested on Felix. His eyes widened noticeably, and his intense gaze sent a flush of embarrassment to Felix's cheeks. She stroked at her hair again, pushing it out of her face.

'Hi,' she said holding up a hand in a half-wave, 'I'm Felix.'

'Lady, I know who you are,' Shylock said breathlessly and bowed deeply in front of her. 'Alchemus told me that you were here, of course, but I could scarce believe in such a hope until I see you now.'

He stood up in front of her, his eyes flicking over her spiralled cheek. Felix swallowed nervously. She could not get used to the distinction the spirals gave her.

'So like your mother,' Shylock whispered, his eyes puckering in remembrance. 'It will be an honour to serve you, lady, as I served your mother and father before you.'

'Err. Thanks?' Felix said, in what she hoped sounded like a grateful voice though really, she was confused. Fiddle seemed to notice her emotion because he stepped forward.

'Felix, this is Shylock Larkin,' he offered gently, 'He serves the Firelighter and has been our inside man for a long time now. He works for Godspell, or rather Godspell thinks he works for him. Shylock has been our main source of information since Godspell took power and has been invaluable to the Rebellion.'

Shylock squirmed uncomfortably, unused to praise but he nodded bashfully anyway.

'It has been an honour to know that I would one day aid you to your rightful position as Firelighter.'

Felix frowned but tried to smile at the same time. The result was something of a grimace.

'Felix?' Fiddle said. He was fussing with the teapot and the strainer. The smell of cinnamon tea permeated the air.

'Felix...Shylock is the man who rescued you when you were a baby. He brought you to me.'

Felix looked at the man. He was entirely unremarkable and yet he had saved her life. He seemed now, the stuff of legend, a knight and the bravest man she could imagine. She stepped towards Shylock and looked into his eyes. If eyes could blush, his would have been neon. It struck Felix that he was as innocent as a child's teddy bear; not an ounce of evil in him. She felt a great chasm between them and, as if in a bid to close it, she threw her arms around him and hugged him.

'Thank you,' she whispered to him. 'I owe you my life.'

Shylock was caught off guard by such affection, but he shook his head and pulled away, holding onto her hands reverently.

'Lady...you owe nobody anything. To see you here, alive and glowing with magic...to see your beautiful spirals...it is what has kept me strong.'

Felix smiled gently and squeezed his hand, knowing she would never be able to repay such loyalty. It saddened her.

'So what's this news?' she asked, pulling away and standing by Nigel who appeared to be a little misty-eyed. Shylock immediately locked eyes with Fiddle.

'The boy?' Fiddle asked. Shylock nodded.

'Locked in a tower. He witnessed the work of Nyxon,' he spat the name out in disgust, 'He couldn't handle it, the poor wretch. I understand of course. He's a good boy, Alchemus. Had a gentler wind blown on him, he would have grown as strong and true as Felix here.'

'Are you talking about Linus Godspell?' Felix asked, tasting the familiar bitterness of blood at the memory of his nose breaking slap so many annums ago.

'He's a prisoner now, Felix,' D.W said. 'He's a victim of Godspell too.'

'Hmf,' Felix snorted. She found that very hard to believe. Her knowledge of him was steeped in pain and fear.

'Linus is just a boy,' Shylock said softly. 'I have tried my best to protect him, as I protected you. He is my responsibility. I cannot abandon him to the Tower. Linus is no-one to fear, Lady. But Godspell can twist even the strongest root and Linus...well. Linus is not strong. Godspell could use him. Please. We need to save him before - '

'Before he becomes a threat,' Felix finished, more harshly than she had intended. Shylock bowed a little.

'Alchemus...there's something else too,' Shylock said carefully, his eyes drifting to Felix.

'Felix, I think you should go and rest or get something to eat,' Fiddle said after watching their exchange.

'Nigel, D.W; go with Felix.'

The girl stared stonily at Fiddle and folded her arms. The wet leather of her coat squeaked pathetically and she sighed.

'Fine,' she said sullenly, turning on her heel. If they wanted to waste precious time rescuing some stuck-up brat of a magician then that was up to them. Linus Godspell was nothing to her.

She followed Nigel and D.W out of the reading room, conscious of Fiddle and Shylock's eyes on her back. As soon as she closed the door, she heard the lock snap into place and the dull murmur of voices as they began to talk.

Nigel was leaning against the bannister waiting for her when she turned around. His auburn hair was messy, falling into his eyes behind his glasses. Felix fought the urge to push it back. He gave her his familiar lopsided smile.

'Hungry?' he asked. Felix felt her stomach squirm and shook her head.

'I could do with some of your lemonade though. I'm not feeling quite myself right now,' Felix admitted.

Nigel looked at her. Slowly, he pulled off one of his gloves. Felix had never seen the bare skin of his hands before. They were pale, his fingers long and lean. He pressed his hand, gently, to her forehead. The fire in her spirals set alight.

'Hmm,' he mumbled 'you feel very hot. And your face is flush.'

His brow creased in concern, but Felix didn't notice. She was keenly aware of her skin where he had touched it.

They drank their lemonade in the StoryRoom. Felix felt restless sitting next to Nigel, who had his nose stuck into the pages of a book that was reading the words lazily to him. She got up and began to wonder in and out of the corridors, and into the different alcoves that housed hundreds of books that lay scattered and unorganised. The dire wolf followed her. He often felt restless himself if he stayed indoors for too long.

'He likes you too, you know,' he announced in his secret voice. Felix tripped over a stray stack of books.

'Who does?' she asked in a voice an octave higher than it normally was. She looked around making sure they were out of Nigel's earshot they were now in the Genealogy room, ages away from Nigel and his stories.

'Nigel, of course,' dire wolf replied as though it was blatantly obvious. 'You don't have to be a genius to work that out.'

Felix bent down and picked up one of the books that she had toppled over. It was small, leather bound and covered in dust. She leafed through the pages and pretended to be interested.

'Why should I care about that?' she asked in what she hoped was a bored voice.

The dire wolf sat down in front of her and for a second he looked like he was raising an eyebrow, if in fact dire wolves had eyebrows. Either way, Felix thought the expression was one of mild amusement. She coughed and turned another page of the book.

The chapter read "Firelighters: from 1750 to present day".

She squinted to try and read the small words aware of the dire wolf's unblinking glare.

The dire wolf's ears flattened as he watched the girl in front of him change slowly. Her eyes travelled over the page of the book in her hands and he could hear each word she read.

Instinctively, he bowed his head, smelling the danger emanating from her like smoke from a fire.

'No,' she said, flipping the page back and forth. 'No! Where's the rest? WHERE IS THE REST?'

The dire wolf yelped and clambered away, but he was cornered against book shelves.

'Did you know?' Felix asked him. She looked at him desperately, begging him. The dire wolf could feel her anguish; it twisted like a cramp inside him. How he longed to ease her suffering, but he had no words to comfort her.

'Dire wolf, please. Did you know?'

Such loss. Such deep, deep pain. Such betrayal.

'Yes,' he answered.

Her face contorted. First there was hurt. It clouded her pretty face like a raincloud on a summer's day. Tears brimmed in her eyes and dripped down her face.

Then the rage came.

It shimmered in her skin as the spirals on her tearstained face glowed like embers. Sparks flitted at her fingers but the furyfire did not catch. She held it, contained it within her.

Felix spoke, and her words were like ashes.

'You have been a friend to me and I do not wish you harm. But if you...if any of you ever come near me again,' she paused and looked in the dire wolf's eyes. 'I'll kill you myself.'

24
The Torn Page

Firelighters: from 1750 to present day
Regarding The Firelighter and the Genealogy of the Firelighter Families

The Firelighter, as all magicians will know, is a powerful and highly respected figure of authority, leading a government of magicians known as the Magistry and guarding the Sacred Flame of Magic. The honour of the title is usually passed through generations of magicians within one bloodline, allowing for the wealth and power of the Firelighter to be inherited. However, a Firelighter can be chosen outside of the bloodline. A recent example is Arthur Godspell who was appointed Firelighter by Deacon Lovelock in 1954 after Lovelock's only child, Paris, decided he wanted to abdicate the role when he was but ten annums old. Arthur Godspell took up Deacon Lovelock's reign when he died in 1954 and the Firelighter honour has stayed within the Godspell bloodline, passing to the current Firelighter, Everard Godspell in 1990. Should he never have any children it is assumed his younger brother, Corbin Godspell, as heir apparent, will take up the role of Firelighter.

The nomination of an heir apparent is made when the Firelighter first assumes his role. This is to protect against any circumstance where magicians are without a ruler and is a requirement due to the unfortunately short lifespans of the Firelighters. Whilst there has been frequent musings of a curse upon them, this is simply conjecture based on misfortune.

The Godspell Clan

Our current Firelighter, Everard Godspell will forever be famed for mastering the Great Revelation and mediating a truce between the mortals on the First Plane and the magicians of the Second. His love for Calantha of the Drow Sisterhood residing in the Glade on the Second was his motivation for ensuring all races, magical or not, be treated equally and without fear. This agreement, known as the London Treaty, has held strong under his guidance.

Everard Godspell married Calantha in 1995. His younger brother, Corbin, was his best man and bond bearer.

Corbin is the heir apparent to the Sacred Flame and will inherit his elder brother's titles and responsibilities, an honour, it is said, that Corbin is anticipating. He has been described as 'a genius' by his tutor, Minister for Education, Alchemus James Fiddle.

'Quite simply, he is the most brilliant magician I have taught. He is ambitious, perhaps to a fault, but he is passionate. And that is his greatest attribute.'

At the time of going to press, Corbin Godspell will inherit The Sacred Flame Of Magic and become the third Godspell Firelighter.

However, in a recent interview, Everard and Calantha talked of their longing for a child.

"A baby would bring such fulfilment to our lives," Everard said. "We have so much love to give to a child."

25
Sulphur and Salt

The streets were empty. Rain rinsed the people from the streets, sending them indoors save for an unlucky few who ran for cover through the downpour, copies of The Monocle above their heads to shield them.

The clouds were as heavy as Felix's heart.

She wandered through the rain, lost again, in London but this time feeling more adrift than she had ever been before. There was no dire wolf to save her this time. No Fiddle to welcome her. No Nigel.

The anger she had felt in the library had diminished, leaving only an aching sense of betrayal that permeated her whole body. If she thought too hard about the dire wolf's yelping and quaking as she threatened him, she felt sick to her stomach. It had been an empty threat, spoken only in anger and betrayal but in that flashing moment of rage, she had thought she meant it. Now, she only felt hurt.

In her gloved hand, she still held the page that had changed everything. It was nothing but mulch in her soggy grip, but it didn't matter. She had read it so many times that the words were seared into her memory. Each time her eyes had drifted over the words, she'd hoped she would find a different meaning, something that would tell her that she had misunderstood, that she had it completely wrong, that she had not been betrayed by all who had claimed to care for her.

That she had not been betrayed by her own blood.

What was it the Catchoo had said at the Circus?

'The biggest test will be your own blood... You are on your way to your destiny, but there are things waiting for you that you will wish you had not found. You must ask yourself this: will the good things you find outweigh the bad?'

Everything she'd said had been true. Every word of it. D. W had said to ignore her and Felix had done that, thinking less and less of the prophesy. Now, the importance of the Catchoo's words seemed vital and she felt foolish for ignoring them. Nanny Maude was right; she never did heed good advice.

Did the good things outweigh the bad? She wasn't sure.

She was a magician and she had learned magic. She still had much to learn, but the joy magic gave her was not to be dismissed. Felix remembered the peace she had felt when Fiddle took her to the Second Plane. And of course, she had met magicians whom she cared for and friendships were budding as she forged an alliance with them. Aubrey and Liberty, a couple who loved each other dearly, Sigbert, Imelda, Thaddeus, even Mrs Thwaites...all magicians who had started to show Felix how good and kind and true magicians could be. Then, of course, D.W, her friend. Was he still her friend? And Fiddle, whom for all of his lies really did care about her. And Nigel.

Her breath hitched in her throat when she thought of him and the ache in her body suddenly seemed to centre in her heart.

But all of them had lied to her.

It seemed so very obvious now. Each time Fiddle had paused, choosing his words carefully; on the Belfast when he had explained Felix's parentage to the passengers, he had stopped the questions, D.W scanning the crowd's thoughts to warn him. Felix had wondered why. She understood now.

Everyone knew that Corbin Godspell was the brother of Everard. Everyone knew that he was her uncle. Fiddle had been afraid someone would reveal this to her.

Well his fear had been wasted. It had been a book, a dusty, battered, forgotten book that had spoken the truth.

Corbin Godspell was her uncle.

Alchemus J. Fiddle had been his tutor.

The man she had trusted had taught the man who had killed her parents.

As she cried, the rain fell harder. She welcomed it.

Felix could feel the eyes of the passengers on her as she rode the locomotron to the Borderlock. Whispers surrounded her and she tried to ignore them, keeping her vision trained on her feet.

She couldn't blame them for staring. It was rare for a magician to travel to the Commoner's Quarter. Rarer still for one with spirals on her face.

The dim carriage swayed and rocked as it travelled through the underground tunnel. Whenever a commoner bumped against her, they pulled away instantly, fear animating their faces. Felix ignored them. She knew all too well the fear they felt, but she had never imagined that one day she would become the one whom they feared.

I have become the enemy, she thought, and she couldn't suppress the little bubble of laughter that rose up from her belly. *Me, who hated the magicians so much...I have become one of them. Maybe I am my own enemy.*

The thought was not comforting and too familiar. Felix drew back her thoughts to the locomotron. Nanny Maude would have a shock to see her again, especially looking as she did, but she thought...she hoped that Nanny Maude would show pity and take her in, if only for a few nights to help her get on her feet somewhere.

Felix bit her lip and tossed her hair over her shoulder, remembering how Nanny Maude had always brushed it so gently when it got all tangled. A small smile, the first since she had read the torn page, played on her lips.

Nanny Maude had said: *'You know, you and my Lily was nearly the same age? If she'd have lived, I reckon she would have turned out a bit like you.'* There had been real love in her eyes. Felix had no parents. She knew that now. They were dead and gone and they would have loved her, she understood that. But they'd been robbed of that chance. Those whom they had trusted most had betrayed them and the same thing had happened to Felix. Nanny Maude was the only one who had been there for her, even if she did have a sharp slap and a stinging bite to her words. She was harsh and sometimes cruel, but she cared for her orphans and Felix would be safe with her, as she had been safe all through her childhood. Nanny Maude was the only mother she would ever know.

Stepping out of the carriage and into the Borderlock, Felix had to cover her nose and mouth with her hand. The air that once seemed mildly offensive was now unbearable. Knowing that her behaviour was rude, she sucked in a deep gulp of air through her mouth and let her hand fall to her side, though she understood now the magicians disgust at the stench of the commoners. Had she reeked as badly as this? She thought of how Nigel had looked at her in distaste when she first arrived at the library and she flushed. But it was pointless to think of Nigel now…though her heart stuttered when she pushed the memory of him aside.

It was easier to leave the Borderlock than to enter it. She had a privileged exit, saved only for magicians, and the COPPs automatically waived her through, tipping their red hats to her and offering her a polite 'ma'am,' as she passed. For a moment, she thought about walking with the commoners but from the looks of hate they were throwing her, she thought it best to avoid them. It made her wonder how often magicians had felt afraid of the commoners' resentment. The commoners had a habit of intimidating them and any overtures of friendship with venomous eyes and heated words. She had never considered the magicians perspective.

Felix walked through the quarter and saw it with new eyes. The boarded-up windows where glass had been broken; the litter and mess that blew in from the Mire; everything had a sense of hope lost.

Her feet knew the route to the orphanage well and took her there almost unconsciously until she was stood in front of the grey brick house.

She stared at it blankly.

The building waited there, dirty and broken, weeds growing in the cracks of the pavement that led to the front door, which was ajar, yellowing net curtains twitching in the breeze at a smashed window.

There was no life. No vitality that children often bring to a home.

It was empty. Everyone had gone.

A dirty draft of air blew at Felix's face and her dark hair stuck to the wet tracks on her cheeks. With leaden feet, she stepped up the path to the front door and pushed it open.

Inside was a mausoleum.

Tattered teddy bears face down on the hallway carpet. Threadbare clothes, so tiny, scattered around, empty and hollow, collected in pools as though the little people wearing them had just disintegrated. She saw a smashed pair of small spectacles at the bottom of the stairs, blood splashed on the shards of glass in the frames. Lingering smell of Sulphur; it was the scent of death.

Felix somehow found herself in Nanny Maude's office. The door was always kept closed and it hurt her that it had been left open. She shut it, carefully and quietly, the way Nanny Maude would have told her to do it.

The office was a shambles. All of Nanny Maude's small, insignificant treasures had been smashed and broken; her books, the ones Felix had always looked at longingly, were spread open on the floor. Everything had been violated in some way. Sheaves of paper covered nearly every inch of the worn carpets and Felix bent to pick one document up. It was the record of one of the orphans, written in Nanny Maude's hand: little Raji, a five-year-old girl who couldn't speak after she'd seen her parents killed in front of her by the COPPs. Felix's eyes scanned over Nanny Maude's familiar writing.

Raji, aged five. No known date of birth. Parents were killed. Next of kin unknown.

A delightful, beautiful little girl. So affectionate and loving. Just needs care and attention. Hoping for a quick adoption for this special little one.

Felix remembered her arriving. She'd been so small and dirty, all big, stern eyes that had seen too much horror. She never got adopted. None of them did.

Felix slowly gazed around the room at the records Nanny Maude had written for each orphan. Then, she dropped to her knees and began to collect them, piling them against her chest carefully, keeping them safe until her hand found a small glossy, creased photograph. She looked down at it and saw Nanny Maude's happy, joyful eyes and the laughing faces of her children, Lily and George, her husband Bill stood proudly next to them.

The wail that escaped from Felix seemed to come from her deep inside her. She clutched the photo and the orphans' files to her chest and rocked back and forth, wondering if the wail of grief would ever stop. The salt from her tears was bitter and it mixed with the sulphur the lamias had left behind.

She didn't even flinch when she felt a gentle hand on her shoulder. It was gloved and she knew instantly who it was. No thoughts of anger or vengeance filled her now, only the deep blackness of pain and she spun around and let Fiddle hold her. He wrapped his arms around her tightly, like he was holding her together, and he absorbed each rattling sob that seemed capable of breaking her apart into a million tiny pieces.

He said nothing. There was nothing he could say. Grief knows no comforting words, no hope of laughter and cheer. Grief is the darkness that we all fear, no matter how old we are.

After a long while, Felix's sobs started to run dry. It felt to her that she had cried all the tears she possibly could and yet she still felt full of them, like she would never be able to cry enough to expel the feeling inside her. Forever, her soul would hold a tear for Nanny Maude, for Raji, for every orphan who had died here.

'How did this happen?' she asked with a cracked and painful voice. She felt Fiddle take a deep breath against her cheek but she didn't lift her head. When he spoke, it was a comforting grumble.

'Shylock came to tell me that Godspell was hunting a Drow girl who escaped from the Tower. He sent COPPs and lamias to every orphanage…even in the Magistry.'

'He knows I grew up in an orphanage?' Felix asked, pulling away and looking up at Fiddle. Gently, he wiped her cheek dry and in horror Felix remembered what she had said to Murphy and Mortimer at the Monument.

'*I have no family.*'

'No,' she whispered. 'It's all my fault.'

Fiddle shook his head emphatically.

'It is *not* your fault. It was an act of terror to scare anyone who may be harbouring and aiding you.'

'Has it worked?' Felix whispered. Again Fiddle shook his head, more firmly this time.

'No, Felix,' he said pulling her to him again. 'On the contrary, it had shown the magicians what he is truly capable of. This was an act of weakness. Liberty and Aubrey will be able to recruit more easily now. Not that it's a consolation. Felix...I'm so truly sorry. Maudie...she was my friend. I..'

Felix looked up at Fiddle and saw his eyes brimming with tears. He looked as devastated and she felt.

Fiddle looked down at her. He positioned himself against Nanny Maude's desk, his legs stretched out in front of him in his brown corduroy trousers. The silver tip of his beard rested against his lean middle. Felix thought he looked out of place, sitting so casually amongst the chaos, but she sat next to him and joined him.

'You know I used to work in the Magistry,' Fiddle said. 'I was Minister for Education. Well, I knew Maudie through that. She was a wonderful Nanny, highly sought after by magicians and commoners alike, back when it didn't make a difference what you were. She always had such a love for children. That's why I brought you here. I didn't want to endanger her so I left you on her doorstep. I thought she and William would raise you as their own, that you'd be safe here. I had no idea...what happened to her family.' Fiddle sniffed roughly before continuing.

'I only found out later, when I'd gone into hiding. By then it was too late. I had no choice but to wait for you to come and find me. And I'm so glad you did. Maudie raised you well, I think. I see so much of her in you. Your stubbornness, your feistiness and your honesty. She said to me once, "*Alchemus, children see the world for what it is. They are honest because they have not yet learned how to lie. We should always strive to remain childlike in our honesty.*" I didn't agree of course. We had some lively debates here before William, her husband, banned me from the house. He was becoming fearful of magicians...me included, I'm afraid.' Fiddle looked around the office though he was really seeing something else, a memory perhaps.

'I understand what Maudie meant now, Felix. About honesty. Lies, no matter how well intentioned, will always hurt. I should have been truthful with you from the start.'

Felix watched the old man as he talked. With each word, his age slipped away revealing the true Alchemus J. Fiddle underneath; a man with too many cares, too many mistakes and too many regrets. He was a lesson to her of what not to become and for the first time, Felix pitied him.

'I'm not as fragile as you think I am, Alchemus,' she whispered. 'I need to hear the truth. I can't keep finding out the truth about myself second hand.'

'This isn't the truth about *you*. You are so much more than your family and their past. You are your own person. It may not seem like it now, but I was trying to protect you by keeping so much from you.'

'But Alchemus, you're wrong. The past can teach us so much. If only we looked to the past a little more, we'd all learn to stop making the same mistakes again and again.'

Fiddle thought for a moment and nodded slowly. Felix stared down at the photograph she was still holding. Her heart hurt.

'Nigel and the dire wolf...don't hold my betrayal against them,' Fiddle said softly. Felix tensed at the mention of Nigel and, despite the grief, butterflies stirred. 'They were acting on my orders and I can be quite forceful when I want to be. One of my many flaws.' Fiddle gave a half smile and shrugged a shoulder.

For a moment, the two magicians were silent. Had the clock from the library been present, it would have been ticking in a quick, heavy, even rhythm.

'What else do you need to tell me?' Felix asked. Fiddle smiled a little and looked down at Felix.

'You know me too well,' he mumbled. He stood and pulled Felix up and motioned to her to sit though she chose to stand.

The chair still held the indentation of Nanny Maude like a memory. Fiddle sat in the chair opposite, the very chair Felix had sat in when she had been presented with the library card.

He took a deep breath and closed his eyes. When he opened them, all traces of his age had faded. Fiddle was stripped of his lies and secrets and was as honest as he could ever be. When he began to speak, his voice was clear and deep.

'I have sacrificed years of my youth to wear age like a mask. My name is dangerous to all who dare speak it. I am the StoryKeeper of the London Library. I should have a thousand tales to tell. In the end, I have only one. Yours, Felix.

Sit for a spell. It's time to tell you everything.'

26
Fiddle's Final Story

As he spoke, Felix began to notice that she was no longer hearing the words. Instead, she saw the story he told in her head, events unfolding as though she was watching them. She wasn't there; it wasn't as simple as that. She was omniscient, part of the story and at the same time not. It struck her that this is what a movie must have been like. And as his calm voice washed over her, she saw, rather than heard what had happened to her, sixteen years ago.

Night was hanging thickly over London. The storm clouds above descended to a mist throughout the streets. The man, Shylock Larkin, walked quickly, peering over his shoulder every few steps to be certain that he wasn't being followed. A red London bus passed by him slowly, grumbling into the night. Larkin pressed himself against the wall, hiding in the shadows and sucking in his large belly. His eyes darted back and forth frantically. The man waited for the bus to turn a corner before sighing, visibly relieved.

He gripped tightly at a bundle in his arms and looked down the narrow street. It was empty save for a cat running across the cobbles but even that was enough to unnerve him. Wrapping his long coat around him and the bundle in his arm, he opened a rickety wooden door and stepped through it into the darkness.

The street was deserted.

He did not appear on the other side of the door.

Silently, Larkin stepped through a battered back door in an alleyway on the other side of London. The cobblestones beneath him were damp and shining in the lamplight. He felt cold and scared, wondering if he had made the right decision. Carefully he pulled out the bundle and folded down the newspaper it was wrapped in. Yes, he thought, the right decision. The events of the last two hours weighed down on him and terror seized him. If I'm caught... But he could not let himself finish the thought. He slid down the brick wall he was leaning against and rested on his knees, not caring that his immaculately pressed trousers would be dirtied. He felt a guttural sob rising inside him as he thought about what he had nearly done.

Murder.

The word resounded inside his head and he immediately jumped to his feet and started to jog deeper into the alleyway, away from the lamplight. A sudden flurry of wings panicked him as he disturbed a flock of pigeons.

'Fenton House!' The man cried suddenly, opening a large black door with a strange marking upon the front of it. He stepped through it, slamming it behind him and once again he disappeared.

He burst through a garden shed door landing on the grass in front of a beautiful house in the middle of a walled garden. There was no sign of the alleyway he had left behind. The bundle he held in his arm wriggled and the man ran up the long gravel path to the front door and knocked several times. His breath was strained and beads of sweat were building on his forehead. Again he knocked desperately until at last the door opened revealing a tall, angry looking gentleman in his nightgown and cap.

'You,' Alchemus Fiddle sneered, looking at the sweaty, squat man who still glanced around the garden anxiously.

'Let me in, man,' he whispered, his eyes wide. Fiddle seemed to be judging the situation until his own eyes began to widen in understanding and he opened the door and ushered him in.

Larkin abandoned his manners and slumped down into an arm chair in front of a dying fire in the parlour, but the gentleman he had disturbed was not ready to let him rest.

'Do you mind telling me why you're here?' Fiddle demanded, taking off his nightcap and running his hands through his brown hair. The guest did not pay any attention to the gloves the gentleman was wearing, despite it being the middle of the night and a cosy temperature in the room. In fact, he did not even remove his own gloves, though he removed his long coat and carefully laid down the newspaper wrapped bundle on his knee.

'It's happened,' he finally said to the Fiddle. He tried to keep his voice steady but his nerves betrayed him. 'They're dead, both of them.'

Fiddle's mouth fell open as he too slumped into a chair. He seemed to struggle with this piece of information.

'When?' he asked though his voice was unsteady.

'Not two hours ago. I had orders myself...'

Fiddle looked up sharply at his guest and noticed for the first time the bundle resting on his lap. He stood quickly and picked up the package from his Shylock's knee and pulled back the newspaper revealing a blanket embroidered with spirals. He gasped as he saw the curing black hair of a baby girl, her face squashed in sleep, wrapped in the blanket. She squirmed in his arms, quite comfortable and oblivious to the newspaper clinging to her face and arms which were still sticky from her birth.

'I had orders to kill her,' Larkin said resting his head in hands and shaking. 'But I couldn't do that. I took her and I ran. I've been all across London trying to lose anybody who might be following me.'

'Following you?' said Fiddle, fear creeping into his voice for the first time. 'You think he knows you've taken her?'

Larkin shook his head.

'No. Not yet. She's not even two hours old. He told me to take the girl and kill her, then dispose of her. Nobody was to know of her existence. I didn't know what to do. I didn't know where to go! But then I remembered that her parents had already chosen you to be her Magister. I thought if I could just get her to you... she'd be safe.'

'You think she'll be safe here? With me?' Fiddle angrily. 'I was their friend, their ally against Corbin! Do you think he will let me go about my life as if nothing has happened? Do you really underestimate him enough to think that he wouldn't anticipate retaliation, an act of revenge? We can't underestimate him. We have already done that, and Everard and Calantha are now dead!'

'What was I meant to have done? I didn't know where else to go. I thought you would know what to do,' sobbed Larkin in the armchair. Fiddle gazed down at the baby and nodded slowly. Gently, he patted his guest's shoulder.

'You did the right thing, I suppose. In your shoes I would have done the same thing. But she can't stay here with me. We must send her away. Somewhere where she will be safe from him.'

'But how could she possibly be safe from him? When he finds out that she's alive...'

'Then he will not find out,' said Fiddle firmly. He sat down in his chair and rocked the baby in his arms. 'You will go back to Corbin tonight. You will tell him that you followed your orders. Tell him that she is dead. You must have courage, Shylock. He must not suspect.'

Larkin sobbed silently but nodded.

'Where will you send her?' he asked.

'Away,' said Fiddle. 'Away from him and the magicians. She should be raised away from magic. She will come of age at sixteen. Until then, she will have another name...another history.

The gentleman absently pointed towards a polished writing desk in the corner of the room. As if by magic, a fountain pen stood to attention over a blank sheet of paper, poised to write as though an invisible hand was holding it.

'My old friend,' began Fiddle and as he said the words, the pen began to write them. 'The time that we have all feared has arrived. I place my trust in you, and the trust of those recently departed, with a package of extraordinary worth.'

He paused, his eyes dark with emotion as he looked down sadly at the baby in his arms. 'Her name is Felix. Felix Spark.'

Fiddle stroked the little girl's cheek, spiralling his finger gently over her soft skin.

'I never thought I would be naming you, little one,' he whispered to her. 'But I hope the name grants you protection and, in time, hope.'

Fiddle sighed as the letter folded and placed itself inside an envelope, along with a small white card with gold letters that said The London Library upon it. He motioned towards it with his gloved hand and the envelope glided across the room to him.

His guest, who had regained some composure, looked at him.

'Times of trial lend to us friends we would not otherwise have known. I trust that you and I will no longer be enemies and so I must ask you to listen a while longer. There is more to tell...'

'Nanny Maude knew I was a magician then?' Felix interrupted. The spell of the story lifted for a moment and she was back in Nanny Maude's office. Fiddle smiled.

'Yes. She knew. She didn't know for certain exactly who you were but I'm sure she had a pretty good idea,' he said.

Felix thought about this for a moment, added it to her list of things to think about later and motioned for Fiddle to carry on.

'What is it?' Fiddle asked Larkin, his eyes lifting away with difficulty from the baby girl.

'Calantha gave birth to two babies tonight,' Larkin said. 'The little girl you hold in your hands...and a boy.'

'Twins?' Fiddle gasped. 'But for a Drow to birth a boy...that's so rare!'

'I know,' Larkin nodded. 'He will be special. Just like this little one.'

'Where is he, Shylock?'

Larkin closed his eyes and shook his head.

'Not dead?' gasped Fiddle.

'No...Corbin took him. Calantha...my god I shall never forget. Calantha was in the bed, bleeding and screaming for her babies. Everard was already dead. She was so weak...it had been a difficult birth. She was trying to summon her power, those beautiful spirals on her skin were glowing but Corbin picked up the boy, and said 'a boy to carry the powerful Godspell name'. He told me to kill the girl...and then he killed her. He just snapped his fingers and she...she bled. She wouldn't stop bleeding. She looked at me...as she died. Alchemus...I failed her.'

'No,' Fiddle said gruffly. 'No, you only fail her if we let her children fall victim to that monster. We have to protect them.'

'But how will we protect the boy? Corbin has him. By morning, everything will be different. You won't be able to save the boy. He plans to blame you, to call you murderer.'

Fiddle's shoulders slumped and his face went slack. He looked down at baby Felix, who was waking and gurgling, her blue eyes locking with his for a moment.

'Then I must have a new name too,' he said quietly. A single tear rolled down his cheek and landed on the spiral blanket. He took a deep sniff and looked at Larkin, a man who had betrayed his best friend to save the child of the woman who had always seen the good in him; good that nobody else had seen. Calantha had been right about Shylock Larkin. There was strength and light within him that could shine if he was given a chance.

'Look after the boy, Shylock,' Fiddle said. 'Never leave him. Be there to guide him, when you can and protect him always. Calantha would want you to do this for the child...for her.'

When Fiddle and Larkin stepped out of the Fenton House, the sky was already turning blue, as though it, too, was weeping.

Fiddle held the baby in his arms and Larkin looked like he held the weight of the world. They looked at one another sadly.

'Where will you go?' Larkin asked.

'Somewhere I can always find solace and wisdom,' Fiddle smiled. 'The library.'

Larkin smiled.

'Ah, that old heap of bricks. It's about time it opened again.'

'Yes. Old things are just new things with more memories and stories to tell.'

Larkin chuckled.

'Good luck, Alchemus,' he said, stretching out his hand.

Fiddle took it in his.

'Good luck, Shylock.'

And two enemies became friends.

27
Godspell's Grievance

It was turning out to be a very bad day for Corbin Godspell.

He had locked himself in his office on the top floor of the Citadel and was pacing backwards and forwards with his hands firmly clamped behind his back.

It was turning out to be a very bad day indeed.

The meeting with Larkin earlier in the day had proven to be most illuminating. 72% of magicians, in a random trace poll, were talking about the orphanages and the deaths of magicians, and, surprisingly, commoner children. Even the magicians took offence to dead commoner children, it seemed. When he'd cast the trace on his name himself, disbelieving of such disloyalty, he'd heard phrases like, "Godspell is insane", "Can't believe Godspell would do something like this..." He'd even heard Paris Lovelock, one of his own Magistry elects saying, "Corbin's gone too far this time. How are we supposed to clean up this mess?"

How indeed.

It was probably the lack of faith he'd seen in Paris that meant Godspell was so unperturbed when word came to him that Paris was missing.

No. Not missing.

Kidnapped.

What a deliciously dramatic word that was, though far too inconvenient to be enjoyed at this moment in time.

Godspell had travelled to the Magician's Shield, the meeting room where he and members of his Magistry would meet each day to discuss issues of the day and when he'd arrived into the glass domed room, he'd found the room agog with confusion and the bizarre excitement that comes with a mystery and bad news.

'Gone?'

'Just like that...'

'Not in his rooms,'

'...belongings everywhere'

'And a note!'

'A note?' Godspell had interrupted, pleased to see them jump and recoil as he stepped towards them, a fox amongst hens.

'Yes, Sire,' Maleficent Howl nodded whilst trying to curtsey, so that the result was some kind of bobbing goose. She handed him the note, a scrap of paper with a hole at the top that looked suspiciously like it had been pinned to something with a knife. The writing was a mere scrawl that read:

Who's next?

'It was, err, stuck to his desk here, Sire.' Maleficent motioned to Paris' desk in the third row of the circle. As he had thought, a knife rested on the polished mahogany, a deep wound at the head of the desk where it had been stabbed.

This had not worried Godspell as much as one might think. Paris Lovelock, as Master of the Guild for Commoner Care (a pretentious name that Paris himself had chosen, despite the 'guild' consisting of only himself) was unimportant. It was likely that the commoners had taken him.

Well, if that was the case, then they could keep him. He'd sent a specialist team of COPPs to search for him of course and he'd released a statement to the press, though they had more important work to do. The COPPs had additional orders to clamp down on Commoner freedoms. If they were going to break into the Citadel's heart, the Magician's Shield itself, and make threats and take a member of the Magistry from his own home, then their homes would be raided and searched. Threats would be made to them. The press were to release a story that showed the strength of the magicians, the unity of their power in the face of the loss of Paris Lovelock, a brave magician who only ever fought for the welfare of the very people who kidnapped him. Paint the Magicians as fair, wise peacekeepers and the commoners as ignorant terrorists...like an older brother sighing at an errant sibling's mistakes.

An eye for an eye...and more.

But the day only got worse.

The afternoon saw the newly appointed Chief of Commoner's Order Police Patrol, Jonathan Wicklow, go missing too. At first, Godspell had thought he was late for their meeting. Godspell, angered by this of course, had opened his drawer to ring his summoning bell to call for Larkin, had found a COPPs top hat, crushed and dirty, its scarlet silk plush scuffed and torn. Lifting it out, a slip of paper had fallen from the bowl of the hat. Godspell was annoyed that he could not stop his fingers from trembling slightly as he reached for it.

Worried yet?

Godspell had ignited the hat and note immediately in a rage. He watched them incinerate in seconds, as the nervous realisation that the commoners had broken into his office and placed this within his locked drawer sank in.

His eyes scanned the room as though it would hold clues; over his carved clubfoot chaise longue, over the vibrant Afghani rug, at the decanter of ashwater and gin. Nothing. The room gave no obvious clues, but what about magical ones?

Godspell's long gloved fingers found his golden spectoccules and he put them on quickly, squaring his shoulders and pulling down three lenses. The room shimmered around him as he searched for the magical footprints of the immediate past. He saw the shadow of himself entering the room, and walking to the decanter, pouring himself a drink. Before that, a faint echo of Larkin entering, waddling over to the decanter and topping it up, leaving in a scurry. But before that...nothing. The imprints of the past were too hard to read any further back. Which meant that the hat had been placed there whilst he'd been at the Magicians Shield, briefing the COPPs and the press team.

But how on earth had commoners broken in? He'd had additional security placed around the Citadel, stronger shields. After he'd been lynched from his own bed, he'd only heightened it.

Corbin Godspell was frustrated. He could not see the answer...and this made him very, very angry. It reminded him of being a small boy, his perfect brother getting every answer right on tests, every decision applauded and he failing in some way, at least in their father's eyes. Arthur Godspell had always favoured Everard. Godspell had been glad when he'd died. He used to feel guilty about that. Not anymore.

Godspell took the spectoccules off and placed them down carefully. His tutor, that fool of a magician whom Everard had adored, used to say: *"when you don't know what to do, do nothing. The answer will present itself in time."*

Well, perhaps Godspell would follow his advice on this occasion. He locked his drawer, wiped the ashes of the hat and note from his desk and went about his daily business.

Next on his agenda had been a visit to Dr Nyxon, to check the progress of the machine. This was always a dull task though he enjoyed the walk to the Tower. The remnants of the Common Time were still so clear here, with their boarded up public houses and their tarmacked roads. There was a beauty to their simplicity; an ingenious quality to their imaginations. How boring their lives were, how pathetic their existence without magic, doomed as they were to die of illness without magical aid, to never see the Second Plane that existed beyond them. To never see the Nebula.

They had their faiths and their religions, their pitiful gods who were promised to come again and bring a rapture of fire and judgement. That had already happened at The Great Spark. Gods had been born into the First Plane at the Great Fire of London. How did the commoners fail to see that all they had prayed for had been delivered to them?

"We are never satisfied Corbin. When we get what we want, we always want more. It is the human condition."

My, my, Alchemus you really are in my mind today, Godspell thought, walking past the Hung, Drawn and Quartered pub. His tutor's limited wisdom often invaded his mind when he was melancholy.

Godspell's blue mood turned to darkest doubt as he arrived at Dr Nyxon's laboratory in the Tower. The door at the top of the staircase was locked shut. When Godspell unlocked the door with a twitch of his fingers, he found the laboratory undisturbed, dark and cold. The wicks of the candles had not been lit, the wax was not wet. In the machine, the blue flame floated and glowed as though it slumbered and the crackle of magic it exuded was quieter; it had not been used today.

Stepping out of the laboratory, Godspell went down a floor to Dr Nyxon's private rooms. He found himself hoping he would find the good doctor to be ill. He would forgive him his neglect if he was ill on this occasion, such was the anxiety of Godspell in that moment.

But he could forgive nothing. For upon the door of Dr Nyxon's chamber, was a small, creased oddment of paper. Godspell could hardly dare to look at it but his eyes read the same handwriting he'd seen twice already today.

I'd be nervous if I was you.

A very bad day.

A day of trials, of grievances. *But they are mere trifles,* thought Godspell, pacing in his office. A lock of hair fell into his eyes and he did not push it back into place. He staggered a little, a tumbler of ashwater in his hand. He emptied the glass and poured himself another drink.

What to do, what to do? He thought. He had expected treason of course. One did not take power by treason and then not expect it in return. A tooth for a tooth. He was a fair man...a realist. The commoners had lost hope and were rebelling, that was all. All dying animals lash out one last time before death comes.

Time. Time was all he needed.

"Time has a habit of getting lost if one doesn't keep an eye on it."

'Shut up, Alchemus!' he shouted and flung his glass against the decanter. Godspell ran his hands through his hair, flinching a little when he heard the sharp patter of a knock on his door.

'What is it?' he snapped, relaxing a little when he saw Larkin enter with a large sealed envelope resting on a silver tray.

'Tomorrow's papers, Sir,' Larkin bowed. Godspell nodded and motioned for him to put the tray on his desk. Larkin's eyes flicked to the tumbler laying on its side, un-smashed on the rug.

'Is everything alright, Sir?'

Godspell walked around his desk and stood in front of Larkin. He was almost twice as tall as him with Larkin slumped over as he was, cowering.

The sharp thwack of Godspell's leather-gloved hand on Larkin's cheek resounded throughout the room.

'Get out,' Godspell spat down at the man who was laying on the floor, clutching his face.

Larkin scrambled to the door but before he left, he turned.

'Goodnight Corbin,' he said very quietly.

Godspell pushed his hand in the direction of the door and it slammed shut, pushing Larkin out and into the hallway.

The proofing of the papers was another dull job that came with being Grand Vizier. Of late, he'd tasked it to Linus who, he must admit, had been rather good at it. Now, the responsibility fell back to him.

He beckoned for the lone tumbler on the floor and it floated towards him, filling with golden, smoking liquid as it did. Taking a long pull on the ashwater, he unsealed the envelope and let the proofs fall out onto his desk. Sitting down, Godspell pulled them towards him and looked at the headlines.

The first, was The Monocle, the only decent and respectable newspaper amongst the three that were printed and the only one he read himself though, of course they all served their purpose.

For a moment, Godspell read the headline with confusion, thinking there must have been a printing error, then he looked at The Town Cryer and the wretched tabloid The Daily Moon underneath it.

As he lifted the last of three newspapers, a fragment of paper floated down and landed, blank side up on the silver platter to the side of him.

Godspell's heart began to skip. He had not felt it beat in years.

Each headline read the same with a menacing identical typeface that he'd only ever seen on The Touch Papers, that forbidden rag that the commoners kept publishing.

Magistry Mayhem As Godspell Goes MISSING!

He flicked through the proofs, hoping what he was seeing was the result of too much to drink. But he could not deny the headline, glaring and loud, leaping off the page at him three times as he looked down at his Magistry controlled newspapers. How had the commoners infiltrated the press? It was impossible. Unless...

Unless it wasn't just the commoners.

Swallowing hard, Godspell turned over the note on the platter. That same, sickening scrawl read the words:

You're next

Godspell remained still and calm. It would not do to lose control now. He had to think.

Once more, he began to pace back and forth, listing the events of the day over and over again.

Fiddle had always said *"retrace your footsteps until a new path opens up to you."*

Well, that's what he would do...that's what he did in times of crisis. Despite everything, Godspell smiled, wondering if his old tutor knew he still had so much influence of his pupil's decisions. For a moment, Godspell paused, thinking that perhaps Alchemus was behind all of this. But the old man had been dead years. Larkin had found his dead body at Fenton House.

Godspell furrowed his brows. Something...something was tugging at his brain.

Larkin?

Larkin!

He had the access... he had the means.

No.

No, no, no. Larkin is loyal. He doesn't have it in him, Godspell thought. He had grown up with Larkin. They were best friends...or they had been once.

"Goodnight Corbin." Now Godspell remembered all those flashes of defiance.

Dear God, it couldn't be?

Godspell slumped down onto his chaise longue and thought hard. Shylock Larkin had always been by his side, running after him like a pet dog. When Godspell took power, he'd made Larkin his secretary, his personal assistant, his man servant. He'd kept Larkin close; an honour, surely. Larkin was his right hand.

But then...a Drow girl escaping the Tower. Could it really be *her*?

And the kidnapped magicians, taken right from under his nose.

Stolen news.

Larkin had assured him the girl was dead. Drowned, he'd said, in the river. A week later, Larkin had brought him the bloated corpse, so ugly and sickening that Godspell had not thought to inspect it. But in hindsight, it could have been so easy for Larkin to falsify it; to magically manipulate some piece of trash from the river. He thought of the commoner story, Snow White. The Huntsman had brought the evil queen a pig's heart instead of Snow White's.

Had Larkin brought him a pig's heart?

But Larkin had come back wet and trembling the night he'd taken the girl away, had carried baby Linus to the nursery. He'd helped cover up the deaths of Calantha and Everard, blamed Alchemus, a man he'd always hated as much as Corbin had...

But Calantha...yes. He's always held a spark for her. She had captured him with her barbaric Drow magic.

Was it possible? The Drow in the Tower...had it really been *her*?

Godspell's anxiety filled the room. He felt, as he had felt so many years ago, afraid. Wary of those more powerful, of those who made him feel so inferior.

'My God...it's been Larkin all along,' Godspell whispered, feeling a sharp sting, a sluicing stab of betrayal.

'Larkin!' he called out, rushing over to his drawer and opening it, ringing the summoning bell.

'LARKIN!'

But nobody came.

As night fell, in the silence of the Citadel, Godspell felt fear for the first time.

28
Through A Flame, Burning.

Felix waited outside the doors to the Reading Room, arms folded and shuffling her feet in her old battered trainers. She gnawed on her lip, occasionally twiddling with a stray strand of hair. The thought occurred to her that she would like to cut it, but she knew she would keep it long...for Nanny Maude.

Inside the Reading Room, Fiddle was speaking with Nigel, the dire wolf, Aubrey and Liberty. He was telling them everything that they had talked about, revealing that finally, Felix knew everything there was to know. Corbin Godspell was her uncle and his son, Linus, the boy who had broken her nose all those years ago, was her brother. Her twin brother.

This was not yet sinking in. It felt so unreal, like a story in a book. She remembered at the orphanage (and the memory brought a fresh twinge of grief, as all memories of the orphanage would from now on) wondering who her parents had been. She had felt like a storybook princess, locked away and hidden. The truth was not so far removed from that.

The great doors of the Reading Room opened and Fiddle, in his true form, stepped out with a reassuring smile. Felix visibly relaxed and entered the room, trying not to let her eyes drift to Nigel immediately, but it was pointless. Her gaze was like a searchlight that found him instantly. He looked back at her, but his face was unreadable.

She scanned around the room. Aubrey and Liberty were stood together by the staircase, a striking couple of white hair and red, gazing at her warily. The dire wolf was the only one to come near. He stopped a few paces in front of her, sat on his haunches and tilted his head. Felix knew he was listening to her thoughts and she opened her mind freely. It was the only way he would know how sorry she was. After a moment, he trotted over to her and Felix fell to her knees and buried her face into his fur. It was warm, a little spiky against her spirals, but soft and welcoming. He smelled of life and cinder toffee.

'I didn't mean what I said,' she cried into his neck, shaking her head. Her arms wrapped around him. 'I didn't mean it.'

D.W pulled away and pushed his wet nose against her cheek, his toothy grin spread on his face.

'I know,' he said, only to her. 'I know who you are, Felix. Who you really are.'

Felix nodded. She was beginning to see. She was starting to understand.

'Please don't be scared of me,' she whispered. 'All of you. Please. You don't have to be afraid of me.'

The ice melted in the room. Aubrey and Liberty hugged Felix at the same time and D.W stayed close to her legs. Only Nigel didn't come near her.

'You gotta keep it together, Sparky,' Liberty said. 'For those we love. That's how we get through. We stay strong and everything will work out.'

Liberty's eyes spoke of fear and Felix wondered what horrors she had suffered at the hands of the COPPs in the Tower. For her and for everyone, it had to end.

'I just...how do you know that?' Felix asked, pushing her hair out of her eyes. Liberty smiled and reached for Aubrey's hand.

'I have the love of a good woman and faith that fate knows what she's doing. I don't need anything more than that, Sparky.'

Felix smiled at the pair and her eyes drifted once again to Nigel. He was sat on the arm of Fiddle's armchair, staring into the fireplace, the flames reflected on his glasses so that Felix couldn't tell what he was thinking or feeling.

'Come on folks,' Fiddle said softly. 'Let's leave the young people here. It's been a long day and my bed is calling to me.'

He smiled gently at Felix and she returned it warmly. She understood him now. Alchemus J. Fiddle was the kind of man to fight fiercely for those he loved, and he loved fiercely too. But he had been fighting and loving so angrily, for so long, that he had forgotten how to do both. Besides, Fiddle wasn't a fighter or a rebel, not really; he was a StoryKeeper. She was the one to fight, the one to seek vengeance...a vengeance he had kept safe for her until now.

From behind her, D.W nudged her legs.

'Talk to him,' he said to her. 'Be honest with him.'

Felix swallowed, the nerves in her body alight with fear.

'Love is the only pure thing in this world, Felix,' D.W said. 'Don't pollute it with lies and secrets before it even has chance to blossom.'

And with that, he pushed her towards the armchair so that she stumbled, and he followed Fiddle, Aubrey and Liberty out of the room.

The clock on the wall stopped ticking. She had come to realise that it didn't measure magic, as she had originally thought. It measured feelings. It had stopped now because she didn't know what to feel. Nor did it seem, did Nigel.

'Nigel...I..'

'You left again,' he interrupted her, not moving his eyes away from the flames in the fireplace.

Felix nodded, knowing he could see her in his periphery.

'You left me.' His voice was quiet and sad.

'Yes,' she whispered.

He turned to her now, his face flush from the fire.

'Why didn't you come to me, Felix? I could have helped you. I could have explained!'

'It wasn't up to you to explain, Nigel,' she said simply.

'You can't keep running away from everyone, you know. That's not how this works.'

He motioned his finger back and forth between them.

'And what is this?' Felix asked. Her heart was at the back of her throat, pounding in her ears. She could barely say the words. Nigel looked at her deeply for a moment and rubbed the back of his neck.

'Friendship and trust...and love. You have to trust those that you love and care for. I...I trust you.'

Felix stepped towards him.

'I trust you too,' she whispered.

She saw Nigel swallow.

'What will you do now?' he asked her, closing the distance between them a little.

Felix inhaled.

'I want to go and find Linus,' she breathed in one big gush. 'He's my brother and by all accounts he's as much a victim of Godspell as any of us are. And he's the only family I have left. Aside from Godspell himself, of course.'

Nigel nodded and his brow creased. He stepped forward and took one of her hands in his. Felix let him take it and she watched with wide eyes as she removed his glove slowly and then removed hers. He gave her all the time in the world to stop him. But she didn't.

'We are your family, Felix,' he whispered, his breath warm on her cheek. She felt her spirals glow.

'We are with you, through whatever you choose. You're the Firelighter, right? Isn't that what all this mess is about?'

Felix laughed a little. His hand felt solid and smooth and warm, and his fingers laced through hers. She could feel his pulse, racing. The flames of the fire reflected on the lens of his glasses and through a flame, burning, Felix could see his green eyes gazing down at her. Felix sucked in some air for she had been forgetting to breathe.

'I can't ask you to come with me,' she said.

'You don't have to,' he replied softly and he stepped closer to her, so that his body was against hers. 'Some things burn brighter than fire, Felix.'

And then he kissed her.

The clock on the mantelpiece began to chime.

She woke with a start. Wincing, Felix bent her neck, trying to stretch out the sore stiffness from sleeping on the rug in front of the fireplace. In the grate, embers still flickered and warmed her, and she smiled shyly as she saw Nigel crunched up in sleep on the armchair.

They had talked late into the night. It had been the best night of her life and she stored each second of it away in her memory and she would revisit it, again and again. It occurred to her that memories were the only true form of time travel. She'd hoped, when she found out that she was a magician, that time travel was possible. If it was, she could go back to the night of her birth and change everything. But Fiddle had assured her that it was beyond the scope of magic. *'A blessing,'* he'd said. *'For the past is only a mirror for our memories. We must live in the present and look to the future. Time travel would rather muck it all up.'*

Well, if time travel had existed, she would have gone back to last night forever.

Nigel stirred. He yawned, big and loud before noticing Felix and blushing, his freckles fading into the red of his cheeks in that way that Felix had come to love.

'Morning,' he said sleepily.

'Morning,' Felix replied.

'Good morning!' Fiddle called, pushing the Reading Room doors open and casting them an exaggerated look of surprise.

'My, my,' he said, pressing his hand against his tweed waistcoat. 'The flurries and flesh of young love!'

Now it was Felix's turn to blush. But Fiddle laughed, winked at the pair of them and left them, stopping only to shout that there was to be a meeting in the kitchen in ten minutes.

Felix and Nigel glanced at each other fleetingly and burst into laughter.

Down in the kitchen, Aubrey and Liberty were eating breakfast. Sigbert Goodnight had joined them, along with Shylock Larkin, who seemed more at ease than he'd been when Felix had first met him; unbound somehow, despite a large bruise forming on his cheek. The dire wolf was laying down in a corner, looking annoyed, which Felix noted immediately when she and Nigel walked in together.

They nodded their good mornings at everyone and took their seats, coyly reaching for bacon and rounds of toast. Nigel poured Felix a cup of sweet cinnamon tea, her favourite in the morning. She glowed.

'What is it?' she asked D.W in her thoughts. He rolled his eyes and shook his head.

'Aubrey,' he said secretly. 'Taking charge as usual. Doubt you'll like her plan.'

'Oh.'

Well, Felix would hear her out. But she had her own plan and one she would be sticking to.

'Nice to see you again, Felix,' Sigbert said, nodding his head to her after he'd swallowed a mouthful of toast and jam. His handlebar moustache twitched as he smiled warmly at her.

'A pleasure, lady,' Shylock nodded.

'How's it gone then?' Felix blurted out. Everyone looked at her. 'Might as well get to the point.' It embarrassed her when people spoke to her like she was somebody special.

'Exactly,' Fiddle nodded. 'Reports, everyone please.'

One by one, Sigbert, Aubrey and Liberty told their progress. Magicians had been recruited to the rebellion. Sigbert said that the Sewer Pirates were ready to help in any way they could. They longed to break free from their barges and take to the air in their glorious skyships once again.

'They'll fight if we need them,' Sigbert said in certainty.

After the orphanages, it had been easier for magicians to agree to strike back, like Fiddle had promise it would be. It didn't matter who you were, killing children was something everyone agreed was heartbreakingly immoral.

Liberty explained that many were striking. Marches were being held today, Magistry workers were refusing to go to work, shops were closing...people were ready to stand up to Godspell. Many magicians simply agreed with them and sat at home...waiting.

'Waiting for what?' Felix asked, chewing nervously on a lump of toast.

'You,' Aubrey shrugged.

Felix swallowed the lump with difficulty and coughed. Nigel patted her on the back, his hand lingering between her shoulder blades.

'Felix the Firelighter,' he whispered to her and she smiled, thankful for him.

'It only takes a spark of fire to set a blaze burning,' Fiddle said gently, patting her hand.

Larkin told his tale last, of how he had executed Felix and Fiddle's plan well. Paris Lovelock, Jonathan Wicklow and Dr Morell Nyxon had been taken, directly from under Godspell's nose. He spoke of how Nigel had been a great help and Felix looked to him, struggling to hide her smile and the pride in her face as he squeezed her hand under the kitchen table.

'They're in the basement,' Larkin said of the three prisoners and at this, Felix's happiness turned sour.

'What? Here?' she asked, looking to Fiddle.

'Yes,' Aubrey said, leaning back in her seat, arms crossed. Her back was straight and stiff, and she looked as though she was dressed in invisible armour.

'Why are they here?' Felix directed her question to Fiddle. This had not been part of the plan. They were to be taken to the Belfast. Carrig and his crew were supposed to guard them. It annoyed Felix when Aubrey answered and she felt her anger flicker, though she quelled it.

'Here we go,' D.W said, placing one paw over his eyes.

'They should be killed,' Aubrey said simply.

Felix didn't try to contain her shock. Her mouth fell open and then her eyes squinted, as though she couldn't figure out what Aubrey had just said. To gather herself, she ran her gloved hands over her scalp and down her hair.

'What?' was all she said, shaking her head. She looked to Fiddle but his face was blank and expressionless, his younger features harder to read.

'Aubrey thinks no mercy should be shown when Godspell has shown none himself,' he said evenly.

Looking around the room, all eyes were trained on her. Nigel's hand rested again on her back and rubbed it a little. It helped to ground and sooth her and the anger she knew was fighting to get out.

'If we kill them,' she said quietly. It felt like trying to talk when you were about to cry, only the lump in her throat was anger. 'How are we any better than him?'

She felt Nigel let go of a breath he had been holding and she felt rather than saw him smile at her. The dire wolf peeped put from behind his paw and nodded at her, his tongue hanging happily from his mouth.

'I agree,' Liberty whispered. Aubrey whipped her head to look at her so quickly, Felix wondered how it hadn't gone spinning off.

'I'm sorry, my love,' Liberty continued. 'When all around you is pain and suffering and death, you learn very quickly that it is never ever the answer.'

Sigbert sniffed loudly and exclaimed his agreement and Larkin said he would follow whatever orders Lady Felix gave.

Aubrey stared hard at Liberty, at the dark secrets her eyes held that she would have to relive forever. And she nodded.

'Ok,' she said tightly, her arms unfolding and wrapping around her wife. 'Ok.'

'Felix,' said Nigel. 'Why don't you tell them what you want to do next.'

His eyes encouraged her and again she looked to Fiddle, who took the seat opposite her and beckoned for her to begin.

'I know you all want me to be a version of what you think is good and true,' she said, her voice clear and crisp as a bell. 'But if I try to please everyone of you, then I'll fail before I've even started. The only way we can win is if I am true to myself and if I'm allowed to do that. No more hiding things from me, no more protecting me like I'm some sort of fragile flower that will be crushed by a cruel wind. If I am to be the Firelighter and unite the magicians and the commoners again, like my father before me, then I'll need advisors, and I'll need all of your help. Bu, understand, this is my battle to fight. Linus is my brother; Godspell is my uncle. I need to find them both.'

'Godspell will kill you!' Larkin shouted out.

Felix let the fire spring to her fingers, let the lava flow through her skin where her spirals burned red and she smiled.

'Maybe he won't,' she said.

The Drow power that she had been so afraid of would aid her. It was what made her different and what made her the only one who could defeat her uncle. He had overlooked her, sought a male heir. It was perhaps her ego that would help her prove to him that she would never be overlooked, downtrodden, treated like muck ever again. And neither would anybody else.

29
Shadows In The Smoke

Night fell like ink on paper, stretching its darkness slowly until the light had been blotted out.

Felix stood on the open deck of the Belfast, listening to the water beneath her in its choppy rhythm beating against the boat.

London looked so beautiful at night. Dots of lights popped up like fireflies in tar as the magicians of the Magistry lit their lamps for the evening, oblivious to the girl with the spirals on her face who stood watching and waiting.

In the distance across the river, Tower Hill stood strong as it had stood for hundreds of years before, guarding the Thames with its many turrets; Medusa guarding her cave. Behind it, the Citadel squatted over the abandoned remains of St. Pauls, lit with beams of lights from floating orbs circling the top of the shard like vultures circling carrion.

A sharp wind blew up from the water and pulled Felix's hair this way and that until she grabbed it, twisted it and secured it in a messy pony tail.

'That's better,' The dire wolf smiled, sitting beside her and looking up at her.

'I should really cut it,' she murmured.

'But you won't.'

Felix smiled and shook her head.

'But I won't.'

'It all looks so calm from here,' D.W said, his secret voice quiet in her mind. She reached down and stroked his ears.

'The calm before the storm, they say. Can you hear anything?'

The dire wolf twitched his ears and his head, straining to hear any errant thoughts that might aid them.

'I can hear children's dreams and lovers' whispers, and I can feel the lost adrift,' he said. 'But all is quiet at the Tower.'

'No lamias?' Felix asked, relief in her voice. D.W shook his shaggy head.

'No. I'm still coming with you, though.'

Felix bent to her knees so that her face was level with the dire wolf's.

'No,' she said firmly, taking hold of his fur fondly. 'You're not.'

She stood again and looked towards the Tower and the Citadel, knowing what was left of her family was waiting in those buildings, just a short way away from her.

'I need to do this alone, D.W.'

The wolf listened deeply to her thoughts and nodded, a yelp coming from him in sadness.

'I can't feel you anymore,' he murmured. "You don't feel lost."

'No,' Felix agreed and stroked him again. 'That's because you found me and brought me home.'

Rubbing his nose against the old, dirty denim jeans she had put back on, the dire wolf felt his lost girl, now found, grow strong against him and she knelt down once more and hugged him.

'Ready to go?' Nigel interrupted softly. He was followed by Fiddle who leaned against the rigging like a man too tired to hold himself up. Felix nodded and took a deep breath.

'Thaddeus made a hatch,' Nigel said, his voice cracking. 'It'll take you to Traitor's Gate. It's how I was able to get close to the Citadel to help Shylock. It will close at dawn so you have to get back through by then'

Felix nodded and Nigel wrapped his arms around her, burying his head into her neck. She breathed in his scent. Lemons and books and Nigel.

'I'll make it back,' she promised, and she stepped to Fiddle.

'Any advice?' she asked, her voice beginning to tremble.

'Remember you can beat him,' Fiddle said, taking her shoulders. 'You are and always have been stronger than him.'

Felix nodded and swallowed.

'The Drow power...yes.'

Fiddle shook his head.

'It's not all about anger, you know,' Fiddle said softly. He lifted his hand and placed it gently over her heart. 'It is more powerful when it comes from love.'

Felix smiled slowly, tears blurring her eyes. And then she was ready to go.

Fiddle led her to a door, sketched roughly in uneven angles onto the side of the deck in chalk. He opened it. Inside was the black of the midst.

With one last glance at her family, Felix stepped into the darkness.

She stumbled out of very old cobbled wall with moss growing in the cracks. There was no need to open the door because it was already spread wide, the salty snap of the Thames flowing through it as foamy little waves washed up against the stone staircase where she had landed. She saw she had come through a door drawn onto the wall of the Thames, next to the entrance to Traitor's Gate. Across the murky waters, she could see the silhouette of the Belfast, staunchly swaying on the tide.

The hatch being open unnerved her, but Felix took a deep steady breath, knowing that across the river, Fiddle and Nigel and D.W were watching her, and she took the steps down to the water of Traitor's Gate.

She had expected to wade or swim through the water, maybe even swimming under the gates, but she found the gate open and a little wooden row boat bobbing up and down on the black waves.

It became clear to her then. Godspell expected her.

This did not scare her very much. In fact, she realised she had been anticipating this. Godspell, she had been assured, was an intelligent man; a genius by all accounts. It would not have taken him long to figure out that she had survived once he'd learned of Shylock's abandonment.

Felix made sure the boat was sturdy and finding that it was, she clambered aboard it. It immediately began to travel through the dark depths as though it was being pulled and it took her through the open gates and underneath the surrounding walls of the Tower.

It was a short journey and the boat docked at the stone stairs that led up to the Tower courtyard. Taking the same steps so many people before her in history had taken on their way to their deaths, Felix braced herself for the attack of COPPs or lamias or both.

But D.W had been right. The courtyard was empty. Eerily empty.

She heard only the squawking of the ravens overheard, standing on the turrets and walls, watching her with their black and beady eyes.

Where is everyone? Felix asked herself and she hated to admit that the emptiness made her more afraid than if a whole barrage of COPPs and lamias had come for her.

Felix squared her shoulders and tried to navigate her way to the Bloody Tower, where Shylock had said Linus was being imprisoned. In her mind she saw the Tower of London map, like an upside down horseshow. The Bloody Tower was directly in front of Traitor's Gate and she started to walk, slipping into the shadows and grateful for her foresight to wear her old trainers.

She had taken only a few steps when she stopped abruptly, feeling herself being pulled in a North Easterly direction. Felix cried out in surprise and dug her heels into the gravel, her eyes darting around her to see what was pulling her.

'Tut, tut little niece,' came a voice inside her mind. It was not the soft, gentle nudge of a dire wolf's secret voice, which was no more unfamiliar that a thought in your mind. This felt like an invasion and Felix scrunched her eyes up, holding her head and shaking the foreign voice out of her mind.

'You're going the wrong way,' the voice said again. It was silky and deep and sounded completely calm.

Felix felt herself tugged again, like a rope was coming from her belly button and being pulled; a magical umbilical cord. She was powerless to stop it and it dragged her, her feet scraping across the stones and the grass to the entrance of the square castle to the right of the courtyard. It was the White Tower, the fortress of Tower Hill.

'This way. Take your time. We can wait,' purred the voice in her mind. Felix shook her head. It was the sensation of nails on chalk board, or ice in your brain. The voice left her and she was stood, breathless and afraid at the bottom of a makeshift wooden staircase that led to an oval door.

Godspell waited for her inside. And he had said 'we'. Did that mean he had Linus?

Felix tried to slow her heart. She wondered if she would find her brother dead before she had even got to speak to him. Did he know? Shylock had said he didn't. He was innocent. He would believe Felix. He was a good person. Felix had doubted at first, but she was learning to trust and she trusted Shylock, the man who had saved her. If Linus was alive, she would save him.

As she approached the door, it opened with a creak and the great hall that she stepped into suddenly illuminated with firelight as the lamps lit a pathway to a stairwell. She followed it, knowing Godspell was guiding her.

Each step she took up the spiralling staircase made her feet feel more leaden and her mind feel dizzier. The walls seemed to close in upon her and she struggled to breath for the air felt close and dense. She wondered if this was Godspell's magic or if it was just the simple, pure fear she had dreaded. It made no difference. She had to push through it.

Eventually, with her thighs burning and her heart on fire, she reached the top of the staircase and found herself staring at a door. Surprise was not was she was expecting when she reached the top, but surprise is what she felt.

It was an old wooden door, cracked and splintered in places. Age worn and hinged in place with rusting iron claws that gripped the old oak. Felix knew what sound this door would make if someone was to bang upon it. She knew how the dust would fall from the old doorframe and she knew how the wood would splinter if it was burst open with force.

It was the door from her dreams, from the room of ways out. Only now, it was an entrance.

The door frightened her. She could not deny it. The fear crept over her like fog and it blurred her vision and her purpose. She wanted to turn and run away, back to the past where Nanny Maude was waiting at the orphanage with the children...the children whose lives had been robbed from them, both in life and death.

I have to do this, Felix thought, the terror of what lay behind the door making her shake. *For them I have to do this.*

Her arm stretched out to the handle but as it did, the door opened itself, groaning on its hinges. Felix took a staggered breath and entered the room.

It was a laboratory, that was clear from the moment she entered, and she realised that this was where Dr Nyxon worked. Her eyes found the machine she had heard tell of when she had been captured. It dominated the room; a glass and metal construction with connecting pipe leading to a smaller box that glowed with a pulsing light. It made Felix think of the old phone boxes scattered around the Commoner's Quarter, the ones most people used as public lavatories. The laboratory shared the same smell as those phone boxes. The whole room reeked of fear and death.

As she entered, the door behind her closed and the light in the smaller glass box grew brighter, as though it recognised her. It was only by this light that she saw the boy inside the glass chamber. He was slumped on his side, tall and skinny with a shock of black hair that fell over his face as he lay, unconscious. A deep red gash on his forehead bled dark scarlet blood slowly, collecting into a pool on the bottom on the glass.

Felix lurched towards him, pressing her hands against the glass, pulling away when she felt the heat even through her gloves.

'Linus,' she whispered, raising her voice then to shout again. 'Linus!' She banged her fists against the glass, in spite of the searing heat.

'Now, now,' came the silky voice of Godspell from behind her, so close that Felix could feel the breath on her hair. It made her skin prickle.

'He's not quite dead yet.'

Felix turned slowly until she was looking directly into the eyes of her uncle, Corbin Godspell.

Time stopped, just for a moment as the two observed each other. There were similarities between them. The dark hair, the high cheekbones and the striking blue eyes. Had her brother not broken it when she was younger, Felix's nose would have been straight and long like Godspell's. But his chin was more prominent, his eyes more hooded, eyes which traced over the spirals on her cheek hungrily.

'It really is you,' he murmured. 'What did they call you?'

'Felix,' she answered, her voice a mere croak.

'Ah...Felixia Solis,' he said, a faint sliver of a smile on his face.

Felix looked confused and Godspell chuckled, fastening his hands behind his back.

'You don't know everything, then,' he said.

'I know enough,' she spat in return. 'You killed my parents.'

Godspell nodded. 'I did.'

He walked around Felix, looked momentarily into the machine and then took a seat, crossing his legs in his pinstriped trousers. Felix swallowed. This had not been what she had expected. Fire tickled at her fingers but curiosity was winning over her anger.

He's stalling, Felix. He wants your curiosity, she told herself. But she kept the sparks at bay, just for now.

'Why?' she asked, walking around the machine to sit opposite him. She sounded wounded, like a child. Godspell shrugged.

'They were in my way.'

'Like the orphans?'

Godspell chuckled and shook his head. When he looked at her, his eyes were scheming.

'Do you really think I would kill orphaned magicians? Commoners, yes. But I value every drop of magical blood. Those orphans were future COPPs, future Magistarians. I am not reckless, Felix. And it's rather convenient, don't you think, that the infanticide of so many innocents should come just as your pitiful rebellion needed support?'

'What are you saying?' Felix asked, trembling. Godspell examined his fingernails and let the question linger before answering.

'I suggest you ask Alchemus. J. Fiddle. I'm assuming he's behind all of this? I ran a trace on his name and found it to be quite active. I must admit, it surprised me. I believed him to be dead as I thought you were. Larkin has much to answer for. He has surprised me more than anything.'

There was a flash of disappointment on his smooth features before it disappeared behind his cool, calm expression.

'Alchemus would not do that,' Felix shook her head. 'And Shylock Larkin is a brave man.'

Godspell arched his eyebrow and smiled slowly, showing his straight white teeth. He was shark-like in his composure. Felix thought on his words. Alchemus would not kill orphaned children. She knew him. For all of his faults, for all of his lies and secrets and betrayals...she knew him.

'*Trust him,*' came the dire wolf's gentle voice from her memory.

She did. She trusted Fiddle. Not this shark of a man in front of her. The power rolled off him and she could feel the static of magic. At the edge of her vision, she saw the fire in the machine blazing brightly. When she was aware of it, the flame grew bigger. Felix's lips parted as she realised what the fire was.

'Yes, little niece,' Godspell smiled. 'The Sacred Flame. You're powerful...I can see that. It recognises you.'

He stood swiftly and looked into the Flame of Magic. In the glass chamber, Linus began to stir and Godspell looked down at him in disgust.

'I can admit when I have made an error,' he said, gazing again at the fire.

'After I killed your mother, I took the boy, believing him to be the stronger of you. I had thought you an abomination. A half creature, not full magician and not full Drow, could never be as powerful as a boy magician with the blood of a mighty clan. But you are both with and without...and I can see the magic all over you like you are made of fire itself. I chose badly.'

Linus sat up in the machine, his hand held against his bleeding head.

'Father...?' he moaned but his eyes met Felix's and he paused, his bloodied face a question. Then he saw the machine surrounding him.

'Who...? What am I doing in here? Father no! No! Please! Please Father!'

Felix pressed her hands against the glass, horrified by the wretched boy inside, begging evil for mercy.

'So weak,' sneered Godspell, his lip curled at the boy he had called son for sixteen years.

'Please let him go,' Felix whispered. 'He isn't a threat to you.'

Felix could see the magic in the boy but it was faint and fleeting.

'But I have brought you here to show you, Felix,' Godspell said, turning to a control board of switches and dials and levers.

'I know what you're doing here,' Felix growled at him. The anger was coming now and she welcomed it. Her spirals heated with rage.

'If you knew then you would understand,' Godspell said, turning to her. 'One race. One united world. Isn't that what you want too? Isn't that what you, with your little rebellion, have been working towards? Unity and peace? That's what I can bring, Felix. That's what we can do together. I was wrong to take your brother. With you at my side, with your power, this machine can work. It just needs more power...power only you can give!'

As he spoke, Linus looked at Felix, his eyes wide and face pale from blood loss and shock.

'Brother?' he whispered. Felix pressed herself against the glass.

'I'll get you out, Linus, I promise,' she cried.

Godspell watched her and the light from his ambition fell away from his face, leaving it shadowed with menace.

'You are just as bad as him,' he spat, and he flicked his hand at her. Felix felt the tug from her stomach again and then felt the tight grip of Godspell's hand around her wrist. She called for the furyfire, reached deep within her for it but found only fear. The fire of her anger was gone.

Godspell opened the glass chamber and pushed her inside so that she fell against Linus. He pulled away from her quickly but then helped her to stand, his whole body shaking and his face awash with confusion.

'You can't do this,' Felix screamed at Godspell. Inside the chamber it was sweltering. She remembered Alchemus telling her that heat amplified magic and she shut her eyes, focusing on his face, on Nigel and the dire wolf, on Nanny Maude and little Raji and the countless orphans who would never grow up, and Liberty and Gertie... and then she felt it, the fire rising through her, filling her with the warmth of love, hotter than any furyfire she had felt. But the anger came too; rage at what Godspell was doing, rage at all he had done, at all he could do if she didn't stop him. Smoke began to billow out of her. As she breathed, smoke poured out of her lungs. The heat in her hands was unbearable. She disintegrated the gloves instantly.

'I am the Firelighter,' Godspell's voice broke through her eruption. 'I can do anything I like!' He began to pull at the levers and turned the dials on the control board and above them, the Flame of Magic surged through the glass pipe.

Linus shook in the corner of the glass, and Felix pulled her to him.

'Hold on to me!' she called to him and he obeyed.

The glass chamber was filling with thick, dense smoke and the Flame fanned down over them. With her bare hands, Felix reach up towards it.

'What are you doing?' cried Linus. 'It will kill us!'

'It's magic,' Felix chanted to herself. 'It's magic. We're made of this.'

She thought of Fiddle.

'It's magic.'

She thought of the dire wolf.

It's magic.

She thought of Nigel.

We're made of this.

She thought of her parents.

The spark of fire from her fingers engulfed her body, surrounding her and Linus with furyfire just as the Flame of Magic surged over them. She shrieked as it burned into the flesh of her hands and her spirals. Flame met flame and it consumed her. Linus clung to her, her furyfire protecting him as she absorbed it, every blistering lick of fire that came from the Sacred Flame.

There was a clatter of wood and cries and shouts. She saw shadows in the smoke as the shape of Fiddle burst into the room. Nigel and dire wolf too. Flashes of light. Larkin's voice. Cracking thuds against walls. She held on tighter and screamed through the pain.

It could have been a century or it could have been minutes, but when the flames finally died down, Felix would have welcomed death. She dropped to her knees, every inch of her skin scalded though no mark had been made upon her. The Sacred Flame was nowhere to be seen, and the furyfire and its smoke sank back into her. Linus was unconscious next to her, he too unmarked by the fires.

Outside of the glass, Fiddle lay against a wall, blood pooling underneath him though his chest moved slightly as he breathed. The dire wolf had a torn ear and he was growling at Godspell, his fur spattered with blood, and she could not tell if it came from him or from Larkin, who lay dead, his throat slit and his arms stretched to the machine, desperate, even in death, to save them.

She took in the scene before her as though she was looking at a painting. It was when she saw Godspell holding Nigel by his head, his hands ready to twist his neck that the fear returned.

'No!' she screamed. 'No, I beg you! Kill me! Kill me instead!' She scrambled to the glass and found that it was no longer hot. Next to her, Linus woke. He saw Larkin's body and he immediately began to bang against the glass, calling out Larkin's name.

Godspell froze in an instant, pushing away Nigel who slumped to the floor on a broken leg. He stared with disbelieving eyes at Felix.

'You survived,' Godspell whispered, walking slowly towards the machine. He gazed inside, reached for a pair of spectoccules on the control panel and scrambled to pull down the lenses.

'It worked,' he said, his voice hoarse. He was looking at Linus who was pulling himself up to a standing position, but he kept stumbling as his body was rattled by sobs. 'He has been drained of magic.'

Godspell's voice was victorious. Felix looked at her brother. She could see that it was true. Godspell may have had spectoccules to detect it for certain, but Felix could feel no magic coming from Linus. She could not see the minute flames that make up a magician and every magical creature. It had gone. He was a commoner.

'How?' Godspell asked, incredulously. 'Come now, you must tell me.'

As he looked to Felix through the spectoccules, he drew back and gasped, glancing quickly to the smaller glass crate where the Flame of Magic had once glowed but that now sat empty and cold.

Godspell removed the spectoccules and behind them, his eyes were wide. He shook his head.

'It's not possible,' he muttered.

Felix watched him step away from the machine and her eyes flicked to Nigel, who was looking at her with as much shock as Godspell. But when he met her eyes, he smiled, his eyes green and glowing. Nigel glanced at the dire wolf, who was hobbling protectively near him whilst growling viciously at Godspell, his mouth foaming. But suddenly, he stopped and looked to Felix in the glass machine.

Godspell was stepping closer to the door, his eyes glued to the girl in the glass. He tripped over Fiddle's feet and fell to the floor.

'Felix,' the dire wolf called to her in her mind. When she looked at him, he was grinning. 'You've got the Flame inside you.'

She knew what to do, then. Rubbing her thumb against her fingers, she felt the crackle of the Sacred Flame beneath her skin and the furyfire behind it. Gently, she rested her gloveless hands on the glass. Instantly, it fell to sand at her feet, freeing them from the chamber.

'How?' Godspell asked, his face wide with wonder as he stared up at her. Felix walked towards him, stepping over Shylock Larkin's blood and swallowing down the tears. She didn't need to stretch out her hands, or find the magic within him and wield it with her hands. The magic was all around her and part of her at the same time. As she looked at the man who had murdered her parents, her eyes blazed with the Sacred Flame and her spirals lit up, revealing the fire within her.

Godspell clambered to his feet, rushing away from her. She could see his fear, see the tiny little flames of magic within his heart pumping manically. It would be so easy to make it stop.

'How?' He asked again, his back pressed against the glass of the window.

'I'm the Firelighter,' Felix said simply. 'Like my father before me. This Flame is my birthright...and Linus' too. A birthright you stole from us, just like you stole our parents and just like you stole us from one another.'

Felix felt Linus standing next to her. He was weak. She could sense it, but his mind was strong. Godspell had underestimated him.

'Brother and sister...' Godspell mumbled to himself. 'I needed you both. I should have taken you both!'

And those words were his death sentence. Linus lunged forward. With the last of his strength, with the annums of mistreatment and the blood of Shylock Larkin at his back, Linus Godspell pushed his father out of the White Tower onto the stones below.

30
Parting Gifts

She was back in the library. She knew it before she even opened her eyes. The smell of lemonade, cinder toffee and old, dusty books felt like home now and she basked in the comfort of it for just a few moments longer. When she opened her eyes, she wasn't sure what she would find outside of her bedroom door.

Her whole body ached and burned; a reminder of the events in the White Tower. If she thought about it all too much, it seemed dreamlike and unreal, like she could not quite believe she had lived through something so horrible.

But she could not hide in her room forever. She was the Firelighter now.

Opening her eyes, the daylight dust motes danced on a shaft of light, spreading over her bed. As she sat up, her head thick and thudding, the dire wolf lifted his snout from her rug at her bedside.

'You're awake,' he smiled gently but it did not reach his eyes. She noted his bandaged paws and ear and the pink stain on his fur where the blood had been rinsed away.

'Nigel-' she began but D.W stopped her with a nod of his head.

'- is fine,' he finished. 'A broken bone in his leg that Immelda is trying to fuse together...but he's not sitting still long enough to let her. He's desperate to see you.'

Felix grinned, biting her lip and she hurried to get dressed.

The dire wolf limped down the hallway with her, taking her to the kitchen. Aubrey, Liberty and Sigbert were sat, cupping steaming mugs of tea in their hands. As soon as Felix entered, Sigbert bowed with a flourish.

'M'lady!' he grinned and swamped her with a hug. Aubrey and Liberty followed, embracing her tenderly. Felix thanked them but her eyes searched for Nigel.

'He's with Fiddle,' Liberty said, smiling at her. 'He'll be so mad that he wasn't here to welcome you.'

'Come on,' Aubrey said, resting her hand on Felix's shoulder. 'I'll take you to him.'

'How is Alchemus?' Felix asked quietly, as Aubrey led her down a corridor she had once come down to find the secret hatch in the basement. She dreaded the answer as soon as Aubrey's face crumpled. Felix had never thought Aubrey would be one to cry and yet the tears fell freely down her face.

'He survived,' she said in a shaky voice that sounded girlish. 'But...'Aubrey could not finish. Felix felt the spike of tears behind her own eyes. But she could not cry...not yet. She had to keep it together whilst she had questions.

'Why did they follow me there?' she asked, trying with difficulty not to let her irritation show. She had told them specifically not to follow her.

'I believe Alchemus had the dire wolf eavesdrop on what was happening in the Tower,' Aubrey explained. 'Once D.W told them of your distress in the machine, Shylock ran straight into the hatch. The others followed him.'

Felix looked down at the dire wolf who glanced at her sheepishly.

'Shylock is dead,' Felix mumbled, fighting the lump in her throat.

Aubrey nodded sadly.

'He died trying to protect you both, Felix. He knew what he was up against; he would have gladly given his life ten times over if he knew you and Linus would be safe.'

Felix wiped her nose on the back of her hand. Her skin crackled as her tears fell.

'What happened to the Sacred Flame I took into me?' she asked, looking down at her hands. She had not put her gloves back on. It felt right to be without them. It always had done.

'I have no doubt it's still inside you, where it should be,' Aubrey said, smiling. 'The Firelighter and the Sacred Flame belong to each other, Felix. The Flame will work for you and you will work for the Flame. Godspell was a fool to keep it stored in a flimsy glass box. The Flame is safest inside its guard.

Your father always kept the Flame close to his heart and wielded it with his bare hands the same way you did. It's instinctive and the mark of the true Firelighter to know how to wield the Sacred Flame.' Aubrey stopped and smiled down at Felix with something that appeared to be respect. Felix felt herself blush.

'And Linus? How did I save him?'

Aubrey tilted her head and shrugged a little.

'We can't be sure...but we think that your furyfire shielded him from the Sacred Flame's destruction. He is not the Firelighter, Felix. You are. The Flame chooses its guard. Your own special magic, the power of the Drow, meant you could shield him with it whilst taking the Flame into yourself.'

'But I thought you said furyfire was dangerous to others...that it could hurt them?'

'It can,' Aubrey nodded. 'When it comes from anger. But the fire that you conjured around you and your brother didn't come from fury, but from love and a desire to protect him and all those whom you love, so furiously. It is deep, deep magic, Felix.'

Aubrey stopped and held Felix's hands.

'I won't ever lie to you, Felix,' she said. 'You've known enough of lies. And so I must tell you that your brother is gone.'

'Gone?' Felix asked, alarmed, jerking her hands away. 'Gone where?'

Aubrey sighed.

'I don't know for certain. But this morning, we found he'd disappeared from the room he'd been in. We though perhaps he'd gone back to the Citadel, but then we found that Paris Lovelock had been broken out of his room with a wrench.'

'Paris Lovelock? From the Guild of Commoner Care?'

His name tickled at the back of her mind, but everything felt a little foggy. But she knew there was another reason why his name was important.

'Yes. I think Linus broke him out, though heaven knows why.'

Felix nodded slowly, disappointment filling her and rendering her heavy and sad. Next to her, the dire wolf rubbed his nose against her leg.

'We'll find him,' he reassured her and Felix nodded, though she wondered how. If he was a commoner now, even D.W couldn't find him. If he heard her, he said nothing.

'We're here,' Aubrey said, nodding to the door behind Felix. 'I'll leave you with him.'

Felix thanked Aubrey and pushed open the door, which was open a little, and walked inside, holding it open for the dire wolf.

As soon as Nigel saw her enter, he jumped to his feet, one of his legs in one of Immelda's clockwork splints and he half ran and half hopped to her. Scooping her up in his arms, he kissed her hair, her ears, her cheeks and finally, blessedly, her mouth.

'I thought you were dead,' he said, his hands clinging to the side of her face. 'I thought he had killed you in that machine.' He kissed her mouth again before she could speak, and she poured all of her emotion into that kiss. All the pain, the loss, the hurt, the anger and the love she had, she gifted to him. She would spend her whole life giving everything she was to him, if he let her.

When he pulled away, she felt bereft, but over his shoulder, Felix saw the frail shape of Fiddle, swallowed by the blankets of a bed. He was watching them happily, his face white, as though all the life had been drained from him.

'I think he's been waiting for you,' Nigel whispered. Felix swallowed and she went to the bed, resting on the side of it softly. Fiddle looked as though he could be broken very easily. For the first time, he looked old. Not the magical façade of a hobbled, wise old StoryKeeper, but old like he had spent a lifetime at war.

'Hi,' Felix mumbled. 'How are you?'

Eugh! Stupid question! She thought and mentally kicked herself.

'Better for seeing you,' Fiddle replied, kindly. He pushed himself up, with difficulty, and Felix could see the wound at his head.

'Can it not be healed?' she asked, looking at Nigel. He shook his head, his own eyes glassy with tears.

'Not all wounds can be healed,' Fiddle said gently.

'He won't let us,' Nigel said, bitterness in his voice.

'What?' Felix looked from Nigel to Fiddle. 'But that's silly – here.'

Felix reached out her hand to Fiddle's head but he grabbed her hand and held it tightly. He shook his head.

'No, Felix.'

'But...why?'

Felix couldn't hold back the sluice of tears. They fell from her blue eyes and dripped onto their joined hands.

'Look inside,' Fiddle told her. 'I know you can, now.' He motioned to his chest and Felix looked, glazing her eyes to see the particles of magic, the little blue flames that Fiddle himself had taught her to see. And there inside, she saw it. The knot of rotting life; the mutated cells. Cancer. Not even magic could stop it. Suddenly the hatch in the basement, the one that led to the hospital, made sense.

'Why did you not tell me?' Felix asked, anger flashing and fading, replaced only by sadness.

'What difference would it have made?' Fiddle shrugged. 'I wanted you to trust me because you trusted me. A dying man wants nobody's pity.'

Felix sobbed and lay her head down into Fiddle's hand in hers. With his other, he stroked her hair.

'Learn to let go, Felix,' he said. 'That's all I have left to teach you. The pupil becomes the master...or mistress in your case.'

He smiled, and Felix could feel his joy as she rested her tearstained face against his hand.

'Please, darling girl. Don't look to the past when you have such a beautiful future.'

Felix looked up at him and wiped her eyes. Behind her, Nigel was sniffing loudly and she could hear the dire wolf's whimpers in her mind.

'What will I do without you?' She asked shaking her head fearfully.

'Go to the Glade,' Fiddle whispered. Felix blinked away tears.

'Another secret?' she frowned.

'Think of it as a gift,' Fiddle smiled.

And like fireflies flickering in the dusk, Felix watched the lights in his eyes fade, as the magician named Alchemus J. Fiddle slipped away.

The air left Felix in a loud sob. She knew Nigel's arms wrapped around her, holding her up but she could feel nothing...nothing but the pain that seemed to be echoed in the dire wolf's mournful howl.

Epilogue

It was the dream again. Hatches everywhere. The room of ways out. But Felix did not panic this time. Instead, she looked at each door and examined them carefully. She sat in the centre of the room, crossed her legs and let it all spin around her. It had been a mistake to give it that name. *Sometimes*, she thought to herself, *we just need to change our perspectives.*

These were not ways out...but ways in. Felix knew that now.

The spiral door was ajar, tempting as ever. It led to the Glade, the ancestral home of the Drow on the Second Plane. But if she stood to go to it, she would be stuck in place. No. She was not ready for that door. But one day...soon.

Two new doors had arrived.

The first was door to the orphanage. She knew that if she went to that door, it would be open. It was not a magic hatch, but it was special in its own way. It was a type of door that even commoners could dream of, if they wanted to. She would go through that hatch when she needed the comfort of Nanny Maude. She would tell her about Nigel. Nanny Maude would have liked him, Felix thought. It made her smile.

The old, cracked door was gone, the one that had banged and boomed its way through her nightmares, hiding the truth of her past behind it. Felix wondered if, on some level, she had known the violence of her entry into this world. If she had remembered the doors Shylock Larkin had opened for her to keep her safe; if she had kept the brief and newborn memory of her uncle locked away in the darkest corners of her dreams. There was magic in the mind and what it could achieve, and it didn't need a Flame to work miracles.

In the place of old door, stood the second new hatch. It was painted an emerald green with a bronze door knocker and held up by two beautiful Doric columns. Above the wood, on its lintel, a handmade sign, painted in a familiar swirling hand, read 'Fenton House'. She had seen this door twice before, once in a painting and the second time in a story.

Felix grinned and stood up, marching to the door and knocking on it twice, the wood hard and solid beneath her bare knuckles.

'Enter,' he said.

And knowing that she would wake soon; knowing that the next day would bring new trials and tests that she would have to weather, Felix opened the hatch and stepped into the midst.

GLOSSARY

Ardere Academy: from the Latin *ardeo* meaning 'to burn'. A university that trains magicians in areas of adept magic on the Second Plane and home to the Privy Council.

Ashwater: a potent golden drink resembling whiskey that is always warm and smoking due to the particles of golden ash from the Ashfjord on the Second Plane, where it is brewed.

Chalkey: a banned magical tool made of chalk. It can be used to create unlicensed hatches or to unlock locked doors.

Citadel: the ostentatious home of the Firelighter and home of the Magistry. It is occasionally referred to as the Magicians' Shield.

Commoner's Quarter: a slum on the outskirts of the Mire where the commoners, people of no magical ability, have been herded and kept.

COPPs: Commoners' Order Police Patrol. A police force made up of magicians and controlled by Corbin Godspell to keep the commoners in order. Easily recognisable by their red outfits and red skin.

DCC: Department Of Commoner Care. An advice and benefits centre in the middle of The Commoner's Quarter which is severely understaffed and underfunded.

Drow: the singular and collective term for a sisterhood of witch elves who live in the Glade on the Second Plane. There are rare male Drow but they have limited magical ability. The Drow have distinguishing spirals that appear on their sixteenth birthday when they come of age. Spirals can be of any colour and can appear anywhere on the body. Much of the magic of the Drow comes from their emotions.

Firelighter: the name given to the leader of magicians. The firelighter can wield the Sacred Flame of magic and keeps all three Planes in balance.

First Plane: see *Planes*

Furyfire: a type of magic summoned by the Drow.

Gloves: the mark of a magician. All magicians wear gloves as the magic they wield can burn their skin.

Hatch: a hatch is a magical doorway that allows a magician to enter it and travel to another location. Some hatches lead only to one place, others are open hatches that lead to the *hatchway*, a network of magical pathways to other doors. To use the hatchway, one must simply say the name of the place they wish to go before stepping into the hatch. If your location of choice has a registered hatch, you will open the door to your chosen location.

Houdinis: magicians who have limited power or addled brains due to overconsumption of poppyblood. Houdinis are often simple tricksters and illusionists whose magic cannot last very long. Houdinis are rather unpleasant to encounter but are usually pacified with either custom or money. They are often found in the Magistry's circuses at Piccadilly and Oxford Street and in the underground sewers.

Locomotron: a magic and steam powered contraption resembling a train that takes commoners from the Commoner's Quarter into the Magistry using old drainage pipes underground.

Magical Creature Charter: a list of magical creatures ranked between level one (not dangerous) to level five (highly dangerous). Dire wolves and Catchoos are level one animals, but lamias and wendigos are level five creatures.

Magicians' money: *vims, tans, pyres:* one vim is the equivalent of £2. Thirteen vims makes a tan (£26) Ten tans make a pyre (£260)

Magicians' Shield: see *Citadel*

Magister: when a child is born into the magical world, parents nominate a Magister; a person who is sworn to protect and guide the child, much like a Godparent. In some cases, a child will become their Magister's apprentice and will learn magic under their tutelage.

Magistry: a city that is ruled by magicians. Also the collective noun for the magicians' parliament.

Midst: a magical void in between hatches.

Mire: a wasteland of dead earth surrounding the Magistry. The mire was once the suburban towns and villages of London until Corbin Godspell took power and attacked these areas, pushing commoners into a slum now known as the Commoner's Quarter. The Mire is home to dangerous magical creatures and the area is feared by both magicians and commoners alike. It is also a dumping ground for the waste and excrement from the Magistry.

Mount Mudslop: a mountain of waste on the edge of the Commoner's Quarter which is what makes the Quarter smell so bad, earning the residents their epithet of 'commoners' due to them smelling 'as common as muck.'

Planes: *First, Second and Third.* Worlds behind worlds. The First Plane is our world, where magic does not naturally exist. The Second Plane is the natural home of the magicians and magical creatures. They are able to practise magic as the veil between the Second and Third is thin. The Third Plane is a mysterious and powerful Plane where magic originates. Nobody can live on the Third Plane. Venephysicists at the Ardere Academy were once able to distil magic from the Third Plane, creating the Sacred Flame of Magic. Magicians have the ability to drift between Planes though it is difficult for many to do so and they need the aid of spectoccules to see the veils between Planes. It is forbidden for any magician to enter the Third Plane without a licence for it is an incredibly dangerous place due to the concentration of magic found there.

Quest: a type of card game and a popular magician pastime.

Sacred Flame, the: also known as *Flamma Di Magica*. Whilst this flame is often called the 'Source Of Magic' it is in fact a very small part of the Flame that is found on the Third Plane. Only the Firelighter can wield it.

Sewer Pirates: magicians who once flew great airships but who refused to hand over their ships when Corbin Godspell took power and so adapted them to sail in the sewers. Rarely seen above ground and tend to keep themselves to themselves.

Spectoccules: a magical tool that enables magicians to see the other Planes in order to gain access to them. They are made of many different coloured lenses that can be flipped up and down. Each magician will need a different combination of lenses to see the Planes. All spectoccules require a licensed practitioner.

Venephysics: from the Latin *vena* meaning 'vein' and *physica* meaning 'natural sciences'. Venephysics is the study of magical particles. The inscription *'magia corre nelle loro vene'* meaning 'Magic flows within their veins' is found at the Ardere Academy.

ABOUT THE AUTHOR

Jennifer L. Rothwell always wanted to call herself an author.

She dreamt of saying it one day, back when she was scribbling stories in her endless piles of notebooks and back when she would sneakily read whatever novel she was immersed in by hiding it inside the dust jacket of To Kill A Mockingbird at school.

(Don't worry, she'd already read it. To Kill A Mockingbird remains one of her favourite novels.)

She is also a teacher, a coffee drinker, a cat enthusiast, a keen foodie and most importantly, a mother to Sebastian.

Jennifer writes Young Adult fantasy because she never really grew up and she still can't believe that she's an adult. But at least now she can call herself an author.

P.S: She's sorry for being so sneaky in your English classes Mr Kerr!

ACKNOWLEDGEMENTS

Many people think that writing is a solitary activity. The writer sits with a notebook and a laptop and copious amounts of coffee and they venture off into their imaginary worlds which they somehow try to convey through words.

That's part of it (especially the coffee) but writing is far from solitary. So many people helped to make this book a reality and I am indebted to each and every one of them.

Firstly, to Lisa, intrepid publisher and editor supreme who has the eyes of an eagle and the patience of a saint. Thank you for answering all of my endless questions and for taking a risk on me. I hope you're as proud as I am.

Thanks to Anthony Kelly for the book cover of my dreams. You're an artist, Sir.

Thank you to all of my students at All Saints RC High School. You were my first readers and harshest critics. I may have been your teacher but you taught me to toughen up to criticism and I became a better writer because of your honesty. You told me I was 'on to something' and your encouragement has resulted in this book. I cannot thank you enough.

To my dearest friends, old and new. Thanks for the cocktails, the coffees, the shoulders to cry on and the joy you've given me over the years. Rachel, you were the best beta reader I could have had. I hope you like the ending that you finally get to read! Tori, thanks for the advice and words of wisdom. Your reasoning keeps me steady. And Emma: if I'm able to write anything of friendship, it's because of you. Love you, sister.

Thank you to my family; the Riley's, the McFarland's, the McArt's, the Bryan's and the Rothwell's. You gave me strong roots so that I could grow tall enough to reach my dreams. Where would I be without you?

To Nan: you knew I had it in me. Thanks for being my guardian angel.

To Dad. I know this was your dream too. Thank you for passing it down. It's the greatest gift you've ever given me. I love you.

To Mum. There are no words I can say or write that will ever express my gratitude. Simply put: I love you. I am who I am because of you and all you've done for me. You make me want to be better.

To my wonderful step-parents, Linda and Shaun. Not only did you make my folks happy but you took me on as well! Linda you've always made me feel like one of your own. Your kindness never ceases to amaze me. Thanks for never giving up on me, even when I made it hard. Shaun, you never tried to be my father. Instead you became my friend. Thank you. Over time you have become the voice in my head that guides me. You're my D.W.

To my sisters, Beth and Mollie. Magic exists; you just have to find it inside yourself. Dream big, both of you. We can rule the world.

To Sebastian. Before you, Nanny Maude was very different because I never knew a love like this existed. I am so lucky to be your mother.

To my husband, who has put up with my wittering on about 'my story' for fifteen years. My darling Dean; thank you for your honest feedback even when I didn't like it and your ideas and visions even when they were better than mine. But mostly, thank you for your unwavering faith in me. You never had any doubt that I could do it. This book that you hold is as much yours as it is mine. I love you, always.

And finally, to you. YOU. The person reading this. Thank you for picking up this book, for reading it and forming an opinion about it. Whether you liked it or not, you shared your time with me. My dream was always to tell stories. You're making it come true. Thank you.

Other Authors With Green Cat Books

Lisa J Rivers –

Why I have So Many Cats

Winding Down

Searching

Luna Felis –

Life Well Lived

Gabriel Eziorobo –

Words Of My Mouth

The Brain Behind Freelance Writing

Mike Herring –

Nature Boy

Glyn Roberts & David Smith –

Prince Porrig And The Calamitous Carbuncle

Prince Porrig And The Perillous Pet

Peach Berry –

A Bag Of Souls

Michelle DuVal -

The Coach

Sean Gaughan –

And God For His Own

Elijah Barns –

The Witch and Jet Splinters:

Part 1. A Bustle In The Hedgerow

Part 2: The Shadow Cutters

David Rollins –

Haiku From The Asylum

Horsey

The Monster In The Fridge

Brian N Sigauke –

The Power Of Collectivity

Bridgette Hamilton –

The Break The Crave System...7 Steps to Effortless Lifelong Weight Loss

Michael Keene –

For The Love Of Tom

The Other Life

Richard Tyndall

The Aldwark Tales

Steve P Lee

The Oblivion Trilogy:

        Oblivion

        The Department 44 Files

        Assault On Charlestown

Truth C Matters

I Rest My Case

Deborah Carnelley

Milo

Dinky The Mermaid

Tianna

Zapher Iqbal

Lucy At The Snake Sanctuary

Jon Carvell

Chaos In Camelot

Amber Purnell

The Plug Monster

Daddy, Daddy, What's That Sound?

Shirley Cawte

Fine Wine From Chipped Cups

Daniel J Hainey

The Adventures Of Maddie And Liv

Betty Valentine

A Twist Of Starlight

Diana Hardy

A Dog Is For Life

Victoria McDonald

Billy's Red Ball Saves Christmas

Timea Ashraf

Bibi And The Butterfly King

James McCann

Fairy Unfairly

ARE YOU A WRITER?

We are looking for writers to send in their manuscripts.

If you would like to submit your work, please send a small sample to

books@green-cat.co

GREEN CAT BOOKS

www.green-cat.co/books

Printed in Great Britain
by Amazon